SPILT MILK MURDERS

A Novel

Joan Hoyt & Gare Thompson

ISBN-10: 979-8-88955-1 eBook
ISBN-13: 979-8-88955-583-4 Paperback

Cover design by Vaughan Thompson

Printed in the United States of America

Chapter 1

Rita jerked upright in bed. *What was that?* Something had woken her. It wasn't her dream; that had been pleasant and peaceful. No, it was a noise, an odd noise.

There had been several break-ins in town recently, and she wondered if the noise was a window breaking or a door slamming. Rita quickly scanned the room but saw nothing unusual. Still, she pulled her covers tighter.

Dewey, her precious Samoyed, might have barked a warning if an intruder had entered the house, except Rita knew that was just wishful thinking. Dewey was so friendly she would probably just wag her tail at a robber, then put her head down and go back to sleep. Rita decided to check out the house.

Creeping down the stairs, she could practically hear her sister Ronnie's voice, "Good watch dog you've got." Rita tuned out Ronnie's imagined sarcasm. Once downstairs, she held her breath and listened.

The house was silent, so Rita went back to bed and tried to relax. *Must have been my imagination,* she thought. Though unlike her sister, an actress "on hiatus," Rita was not prone to imaginings. *Maybe it was Ronnie getting a drink of water,* she wondered. *I'll just have to get used to having Ronnie back in the house.*

Since Ronnie was still asleep, the noise wasn't her. It also wasn't someone breaking in. *So, what was the noise?* Rita knew she wouldn't solve the mystery of the noise, and so her mind wandered back to her sister. Close in age, the two had been inseparable until Ronnie entered high school, when she became the "older" sister. From that time on, Rita had taken a backseat to Ronnie, but remained in awe of her.

Ronnie had recently come to live with Rita, and they were still not used to living together. Lying in bed, Rita remembered their talks as girls in Ronnie's room, and no matter the topic--boys in Ronnie's case or the latest science experiment in Rita's--Ronnie always fell into a dead sleep as soon as she laid her head on the pillow. She closed her eyes and that was it. Whereas Rita had always loved solving problems, her mind remained active until sleep finally overtook her.

A widow for the last ten years, Rita had grown to love the solitude of her home, even though she deeply missed her husband, Adam. Of course, Ronnie's arrival had upended her solitude.

Sometimes Rita was amazed that two sisters could be as different as she and Ronnie were. Rita was quiet and thoughtful, and seemed always to be thinking. Ronnie was boisterous and dramatic, living in the moment and jumping to conclusions rather than thinking things through. If a noise had woken Ronnie, she'd probably fly out of bed and frantically search the house, armed with a broom. Rita laughed at the image. Ronnie's solution was to act, whereas Rita was methodical and logical, thinking through each part of any puzzle.

Rita could never resist the urge to solve a mystery. Even as children, she and Ronnie had loved playing detective. First, they played Nancy Drew. Ronnie had been Nancy and wished she had Nancy's roadster and cool clothes. Rita played the sidekick. Then they moved on to the Hardy boys, turning those mysteries into the Hardy sisters. Rita then devoured Encyclopedia Brown, loving his "scientific and logical" mind. As teens, they became Sherlock and Watson, though Rita always thought she was more Sherlock than Watson, but Ronnie always insisted on the lead. As adults, they became Agatha Christie fans, Rita using her "grey matter," and Ronnie using Miss Marple's keen observation of people. And so they solved life's mysteries.

Rita's thoughts returned to the mystery of the noise. She had already eliminated two solutions--not a burglar, and not Ronnie. She'd keep going until she solved it. Then she could sleep. She started listing possible reasons for the noise.

But before she could finish her list, a white beacon suddenly streaked across the room and landed on the bed next to her. She smiled, knowing she could easily solve the mystery of the white beacon. It was Dewey, whose white guard hairs sparkled, reflecting the early morning sun. Dewey lay on the bed, panting and patiently waiting for their morning routine to begin.

"Did you wake me?" Rita asked. Dewey rolled over as if to say, 'It wasn't me.'

"Fine, it wasn't you, but it wasn't Ronnie either. So I guess that leaves the wind. Mystery solved." Rita smiled at her dog, gently stroking her side as they lay next to each other.

Instead of getting up, Rita sank back into the pillows and pulled Dewey closer. "Let's just cuddle for a bit and enjoy the silence. We both know as soon as Ronnie is up, silence is history." Dewey barked, as if in agreement.

Dewey and Ronnie were still feeling their way around each other. Ronnie was not a dog person, and progress was slow. Rita amended that thought. *She's not an animal person. Period.* "I wonder if Ronnie will ever fit in here. After all, life in Castleton is very different from her old life. What do you think, Dew Drop?"

Rita didn't have to be a dog whisperer to know Dewey's answer: *It will take time. Be patient.*

Alone and recovering from breast cancer, Ronnie had felt she had no choice but to move home. She hated to admit it, but she needed help. If not physically, she needed emotional support. Her husband, Simon, had left her, leaving her feeling fragile. She needed Rita.

There had been big difference between the sisters' lives. Rita had stayed in their hometown, teaching, happily married, and making lifelong friends, whereas Ronnie had been like a nomad, going between plays, and movies, and TV. Her fellow actors became her family, but only while they worked together. Once work finished, her "family" moved on, and they lost touch. Thus, Rita had been the only constant in Ronnie's life. And as the younger, adoring sister, she had made sure the two remained in touch and were there for each other.

Rita remembered writing her sister long letters about everything that was happening in Castleton, and even though nothing exciting ever happened, the letters formed a bond between them. Ronnie, in turn, wrote chatty, gossipy letters about her life in the theater. Still, neither sister had been prepared for Ronnie's husband deserting her and taking a good chunk of her money with him. Her pride prevented her from prosecuting Simon, and instead, she quietly divorced him.

Rita hadn't given her sister any other option: the solution was to come home to Castleton and live with her in their old family home. Ronnie had protested, not vehemently--it was more an acting exercise--but Rita had been firm. There was no way she was going to let her sister recuperate alone, no matter how difficult she could be. Besides, she knew Ronnie really wanted to come home. And given their many letters over the years, Ronnie knew enough about Castleton to feel it would be a safe haven for her. Besides, she missed her sister.

Rita had looked forward to forging a new and stronger bond with Ronnie. And if she were honest, which Rita invariably was, she was glad Simon was out of the picture. (Rita couldn't remember if he had been husband number three or four, but she hoped he was the last.) He had always been much more interested in her money than he was in Ronnie. Rita had tried to warn her, but it had fallen on deaf ears.

With Rita lost in her thoughts, Dewey became restless and began whimpering, hinting it was time to go outside. "Okay, you need to go out. But let's keep the noise level down. We don't want to wake Auntie Ronnie. She needs her rest." Rita swung her legs over the edge of the bed and sat up, adding, "Besides, there'll be hell to pay if we wake her! We both know what it's like when *Madame*'s beauty sleep is interrupted: 'Aging Star Gone Wild'." She giggled, reached for her fleece robe, and pulled it on. The two were off to start their day.

Rita padded down the hall, stopping briefly to listen at Ronnie's door. She heard nothing and gave Dewey a thumbs-up. "Silence is golden," she whispered to Dewey as the two companions continued to the kitchen. *Well, I guess my hypothesis was correct. Clearly, Ronnie was not the source of the noise. It must have been the wind after all.*

Dewey raced across the hardwood floor, her nails clattering as she danced back and forth, waiting expectantly by the door. *So much for silence.* "Okay, I get the hint," Rita replied, quickly opening the door. Dewey made a beeline to the grass.

She watched her dog for a few minutes, then softly called her back inside and set down her breakfast bowl. "Time to eat, girl," Rita said. Then she stifled a laugh. She realized she was becoming one of those old women who talked to their pets and expected a reply. *If I'm not careful, Ronnie will have me committed*, she thought, chuckling to herself.

But shrugging her shoulders, she continued the conversation anyway. Even though she was a retired biology teacher and believed in the scientific method, it didn't mean her dog couldn't have empathy. There were several studies that proved her point. *Let it go. No one is committing you. Yet.* Rita laughed. *A month with Ronnie, and I'm a drama queen.*

Rita poured some grapefruit juice and remembered a time Dewey had held the local vet's office enthralled as she methodically visited each person in the waiting room and seemed to be holding a conversation with each in turn. By the time the vet called her name for her appointment, Dewey had everyone in the waiting room chuckling and talking to her. Of course, Ronnie would have simply raised one of her well-manicured eyebrows and said animals can't talk unless it's in the movies.

Thinking of Ronnie and her situation made Rita think about her own life. Looking around her sunny but silent kitchen, she was glad she had moved on with her life after Adam had died. However, until Ronnie arrived, she hadn't realized how empty her life was. Oh, she had plenty of interests that kept her occupied, but it was the quiet moments like this when she missed Adam the most. Although nobody could replace him, she knew that having a human connection, even an irritating older sister who was most definitely not a morning person, had made her life more joyful. "Time to get moving, Dew Drop!" She finished her juice and began to plan her day. Rita loved having a schedule.

"Time for gardening. Let's go," she said as the two stepped outside. Gardening was one thing that kept her grounded. She loved the feel of the earth, and pulling out weeds gave her a sense of accomplishment and satisfaction. Gardening also let her mind wander, which she cherished. Working in her yard, she wondered if life could ever be as simple and organized as a well-maintained garden. She doubted it. Even small-town Castleton had deep-rooted secrets, hidden from daily life and waiting to be discovered. She laughed, thinking *Pull more weeds, girl. You are turning into your sister. Castleton is not a film noir movie set.* Though Rita was sure there were some dark secrets lurking in Castleton.

Ronnie continued to flit in and out of Rita's mind, as she did many mornings. Pulling weeds, as physically satisfying as it was, did not stop her from worrying about Ronnie. She knew that no matter how much time the two spent together, Ronnie would never completely let down the walls she had erected for protection and self-preservation. Rita realized she'd just have to keep chipping away and get as close to her sister as possible. She knew she was up to the task. *Ronnie may be older, but not necessarily stronger or smarter,* she thought.

After a while, Dewey, covered with dirt, meandered over and leaned into her side. Rita brushed off the dirt and smiled, then sat back on her heels next to her dog, and the two observed the cows in the distant fields. If she listened carefully, she could hear them mooing. "You hear their sweet songs, don't you, Dewey?" Dewey ignored her and instead, chased a butterfly. *I might as well be talking with Ronnie,* Rita sighed.

Slowly a dark cloud settled over her. Life in Castleton was not as lovely and postcard perfect as it might appear. It was not like the Cotswold villages in her favorite mysteries, full of town fetes, social gatherings at the church, and delightful tea parties. Castleton was fast becoming a commuters' paradise. Though countryside itself, it was close enough to the city and had convenient highways and an express train. Consequently, developers were buying up farms and green space, building enormous houses and luxury apartments. Castleton's peaceful country life was dying. Rita ripped out more weeds, wishing she could as easily get rid of the developers.

Yanking at the weeds, she thought about who and what had made Castleton developer heaven. *Was it the local government officials who seemed to be encouraging the developers? Or maybe no one wanted to farm when they could sell their land at a good price? Or maybe it was just progress?* Whatever the reason, Rita hated it.

"You know, Dewey, the sad thing is the developers will be gone once the checks have cleared, and then those of us who live here will be left in a Castleton we no longer recognize or love. "Money does make the world go round, Dewey," Rita said in a disgusted tone.

She despised the mini mansions and "luxury condominiums" that were popping up all over the village. Luckily, Rita and a few vocal others worked to stop them. But though she and many of her long-time neighbors had protested the latest developments, signed petitions to stop them, and wrote fierce, biased letters to the local paper, their work so far had been in vain.

Suddenly, Rita stood up and defiantly shook her hands free of the weeds and dirt. "Tomorrow is another day," she proclaimed. Then looking down, seeing Dewey staring up at her, she burst out laughing. "Oh dear, Dewey, I've become Ronnie!" She brushed the last of the dirt off her hands, and still chuckling, headed back inside. "Time for a nice cup of tea. I'm not Scarlett O'Hara, so we'll leave the drama to Ronnie." Though she had to admit, it was kind of fun and liberating. *Maybe Ronnie knows something I don't?*

As she sipped her tea, she remembered the happy times she and Ronnie had had playing in their neighbor's many fields. Winter days were filled with sledding and hot chocolate. Rita remembered her older sister pulling her on her Flexible Flyer up the hill, and then the two would careen back down. In summer, they had captured fireflies in peanut butter jars with holes poked in the lids, and had played hide and seek until their parents called them home. But if the current rate of development continued, today's kids would never have those wonderful memories. She shook her head and hoped the town would wake up to what it was allowing to happen. *There has to be a way to stop it, but how?* She sighed and decided to stop thinking about it.

"Let's just enjoy the peace and quiet, Dew Drop, before the queen makes her entrance. Brooding won't help."

While she waited, Rita decided to make some healthy flax bran muffins. She knew Ronnie didn't like to eat in the morning, but the flax and bran would be good for her. Besides, she needed something to do.

Dwelling on the developers and lack of foresight from the local officials depressed her. She knew the officials had good intentions, but none of them had any foresight whatsoever. Baking muffins, even healthy muffins, would make her feel better.

She gathered up the ingredients, including some fresh herbs from her garden, and got to work, humming a show tune. Humming the tune made her feel better. *Thanks, Ronnie.*

Chapter 2

The morning sun streamed into Ronnie's room, and she covered her eyes, trying to wish away the bright light. Unless it was a spotlight, Ronnie preferred soft lights.

And pink lighting was the best. It took years off your appearance. And she had to admit, these days being bathed in soft, rose-colored lights was about the only thing that made her look better. Chemotherapy had done a number on her looks. Plus, her eyes were still sensitive to sunlight, even though she claimed she was now in perfect health.

Although Rita disagreed with her, Ronnie refused to acknowledge she needed more time to gain back her strength that the chemo and radiation had zapped. So instead of admitting how weak she was, she did what she always did in bad situations she couldn't control: she lied to herself. Having done theater for so many years, her body was used to staying up late and sleeping into the mid-morning hours. Now, whenever Rita gave her that familiar look of pity, she simply said she was not a morning person, and she relied on that for justification for being out of sorts. Finally, she had trained Rita to nod brightly at such statements and accept her white lies. It made their lives much easier and more comfortable.

Ronnie heard Rita downstairs, chatting away to her fluffy white dog, whose name she tried to recall, but she gave up after a few seconds. All she could remember was not to call it a fur muff. That comment had really aggravated Rita, who for once had actually yelled at her. But it did look like one, and Ronnie was not a dog person. Hence, she couldn't even remember its name; though she seemed to think it was something Drop. *Lemon Drop? No, that wasn't right. It had something to do with water.*

While she luxuriated in her room a while longer, Ronnie did one of her favorite things. She eavesdropped. She listened to Rita and the fur ball in the kitchen as their movements and conversations floated up to her room. The dog's feet tapped on the hardwood floor, and Rita was humming a show tune.

Ronnie smiled. Rita was tone deaf and couldn't remember the lyrics to any songs, but her attempt at singing always made Ronnie smile. Leave it to Rita to make her feel better. Her little sister always looked on the sunny side of the street, not blindly, but Rita's cup was always half full. An attitude Ronnie knew she should take to heart.

Deciding to savor a few more minutes of quiet time, she snuggled back under her down comforter, her fingers tracing its lovely rose pattern. However, Ronnie kept her movements to a minimum, because if Rita heard that she was awake, she would immediately be at her door, demanding that she come down to the kitchen and eat a healthy breakfast. Ronnie laughed quietly, her idea of breakfast was strong black coffee and a cigarette. Well, the cigarettes were gone, but she still hadn't given up coffee, no matter how hard Rita tried to push her herbal teas.

Ronnie shuddered. Those teas tasted horrible. To please her sister, she had tried one, once. And as far as she was concerned, once was enough. She had gagged on the sip and quickly poured it into a close-by plant. Luckily, the plant hadn't died instantly. Now, each time Rita tried to push the tea on her, Ronnie complained it made her ill, clutching her chest and acting as if she were dying. Naturally, Rita gave up on the tea and decided they could compromise on decaffeinated coffee.

Ronnie heard the back door open and shut. She breathed a sigh of relief. *Thank God, I've escaped Nurse Rita and her trusty sidekick, Cotton Ball!* Ronnie knew her sister was outside in her garden, working diligently away. Rita was dependable if nothing else, and she kept to schedules and routines. *Must be from her years of teaching,* Ronnie thought.

It still felt odd to Ronnie waking up each morning in her old room. Rita had not changed it at all. The wallpaper was girly pink and covered with roses, like something out of *Alice in Wonderland.* Ronnie had probably chosen it when she was twelve. *You should have changed it, Rita. We're not children anymore.* She arched an eyebrow and shook her head gently from side to side. *Or maybe at the very least have painted the walls-- something more mature and subdued, such as peach, or soft blue* as she had done in her apartment in Paris. Ronnie sighed. Being back in Castleton was like living in the past. *Ah, but those years in France were magnifique!*

Ronnie had gone there for a small part in a movie in the early sixties, and when the movie was done, she had stayed. She'd married a count. Well, Jacques claimed he was a count, and while Ronnie had her doubts about his lineage, she had no doubts about his charm. He had even won over Rita. The three of them had had a wonderful time in Paris when Rita visited.

As far as Ronnie knew, it was the only time Rita had ever left the country. Once she had married, her husband Adam had only wanted to explore the United States. *Why? Did foreign places scare him?* Adam and Ronnie had never been close, but she had to admit, he had loved and adored Rita. In fact, Ronnie had envied her sister's loving marriage. Adam may not have been worldly, but he was the perfect husband for her little sister.

While Adam and Rita had had enduring love, Ronnie and Jacques had had passion. Ronnie still quivered when she thought of those gorgeous blue eyes and that aristocratic, hooked nose that only certain French men can carry off. Jacques acted like a true French aristocrat: snotty, sarcastic, and for Ronnie, wonderful. But the marriage had not lasted long. Jacques loved to race his Fiat and had died in a car crash. Ronnie thought her world had ended, but it hadn't. She packed up and returned to New York and the stage.

Her New York years were what Ronnie referred to as the "supporting star" years. She smiled at the memory. She was nominated several times for a Tony, finally winning in a rather barren year. It was for "featured" actress, which meant not the star. The play had had a short run, and Ronnie had never been able to capitalize on the win, but she had worked steadily.

The roles were often second banana to her friends such as Angela Lansbury, and then playing the mother to Barbra Streisand. *Now there was a star!* Ronnie kept at her craft, and she fully believed one day her name would be in lights above the play title. But it never was. "Not quite right, dear," was the phrase she often heard after auditions. *Not quite right my ass,* she thought. She had never played any casting couch games, and she was convinced that was why she hadn't achieved the stardom some lesser talents had.

But finally, came THE role. She remembered the day as if it were yesterday. She was sitting in a coffee shop on Seventh Avenue, watching the men wheeling clothes racks up and down the sidewalk, when her agent burst through the door. She had just gotten out of an affair with a married star who kept promising to leave his wife. Ronnie had stopped the affair. Rita had been right; he would never end his marriage. Hedda Hopper had given her a full paragraph, and she was thrilled. (Even if her name was not in print, everyone knew it was Ronnie. Rita had said everyone in Castleton had even guessed it was her!)

"Ronnie, darling, you are not going to believe it!" cried Joshua Lambert, her agent, good friend, and staunch admirer.

"Believe what? Do sit down and stop flapping!" Today Ronnie would have wondered if Josh had had ADHD or Asperger's, but back then it was just called "affectations," his arms flying and his hands clapping, all punctuated with outrageous facial expressions.

Ronnie leaned in closer and hissed, "What am I not going to believe? Spit it out."

"I've got you an audition with Spelling Productions. It's for the lead in a new television series. Now the word is that Angela turned it down as she wants to do Broadway, and Jean Stapleton said no. So now they want YOU," he explained breathily.

"Television?" Ronnie rolled her eyes. Sure, she had done some live TV, such as the Alcoa Hour and Playhouse 90, but a series? Then she remembered how famous and rich Lucille Ball and June Allyson became by doing their own shows. Even Loretta Young and her stupid staircase made tons of money and won an Emmy.

"What is it?" Ronnie waited. Joshua was the only person she knew who was more dramatic than she was. He really should have been born during Shakespeare's time; he would have been a fabulous Lady Macbeth.

"The series is called 'The Big Ranch.' It's about a matriarch who is widowed and runs this huge ranch. It's set in Texas. You can do a Texas accent, right?"

"For the right price and the lead, I sure can, pardner," Ronnie drawled. Accents were one of her specialties. She liked the idea from the start. And so, she had gone to Hollywood to read for the role, and the rest, as they say, is history. The series lasted five years, and it still popped up on TV Land. Ronnie was nominated for an Emmy each year the show was on the air, but she never won. Instead, she got to repeat that hated phrase, "It's such an honor to be nominated...." That role defined her career and gave her enough cachet that when she returned to New York, the roles were larger and paid better.

However, as she aged, she competed with Jessica Tandy, Helen Hayes, and dear Angela. And with few roles, she often lost out or was the understudy for them. Her star kept dimming. She slowly moved into the "grandmother" roles and commercials, which she hated, but work was work.

Then came the cancer. *And here I am in Castleton, stuck in my old room. How had this happened?* Ronnie knew it wasn't only the cancer. Nor the money loss. She was still comfortable after all. She could even have stayed in New York, but depression and loneliness had settled over her, and Rita had convinced her to come home. Temporarily, of course, but still, here she was, in the old family home, dependent on her younger sister. *Stuck in the pink room.*

Ronnie refused to admit she needed her sister, and that her last husband, Simon, had been a thief and a cad. Rita had wanted her to press charges against him, but she had refused. There was no way she was going to let the world know she had been that foolish. So instead, Ronnie had divorced him, sold her apartment, and come home.

Ronnie shook her head. There were worse things in life than losing money and pride. She knew that first-hand. She never spoke of the loss of her only child. Emma had died when she was three. Ronnie still couldn't think of her without her heart breaking. She had had Emma right after her television show was cancelled. It was one of those unexpected pregnancies late in life, so Ronnie had assumed she was in early menopause. She was ambiguous about the pregnancy, but once Emma was in her arms, she had loved the child more than anything. She ended up being a single mother, but was so happy with Emma that it didn't matter.

Rita and Adam had given her unwavering support. The two frequently came to New York, and they adored their niece. Ronnie felt bad at first, as she knew how much the two wanted children of their own, but her little June bug won them over--as she did everyone. Then too soon, Emma was gone. No one was sure how, but Emma had caught meningitis and was gone before her symptoms could even be diagnosed. Ronnie was in Los Angeles when Emma had died. She wiped away the tears running down her cheek.

Suddenly, a loud voice outside distracted her. Glad for the distraction, she got up to peer out the window. *Georgia!* Ronnie grimaced. That woman had been her worst enemy since high school, and Ronnie still despised her.

Each time they encountered each other, it was as if they were back in high school, vying for the role of lead mean girl. *What on earth does she want? Well, there's only one way to find out.* She pulled on her silk robe and prepared to make an entrance and put Georgia in her place.

Ronnie knew insulting that stupid woman would cheer her up no end. *On with the show*, she thought as she made her way down the stairs and to the front door. She'd wait inside for just the right cue to open the door and step onto the porch. After all, timing is everything. And Ronnie was positive that Georgia, the silly, obtuse woman that she is, would provide the perfect cue.

Chapter 3

Rita set the muffins out to cool and went back out to the garden to water her plants. The sun was getting hot, so once she was outside, she put on her well-worn Panama hat. It was her mother's, and Rita wore it for sentimental reasons. However, Ronnie claimed she was trying to make a fashion statement. *Ridiculous*, thought Rita. *We are so different.*

Ronnie thought Rita should throw out the hat; its time had passed, so why keep it? But unlike her sister, Rita loved having things from their past. The memories the items evoked comforted her. However, now that Ronnie had been back in Castleton, she noticed Ronnie seemed to appreciate the past and was more open to renewing past relationships. Rita smiled as she toyed with the idea of Ronnie and her high school admirer, Wendell, getting together.

Wendell, the Police Chief, had carried a blazing torch for Ronnie in high school, and even though he was a star athlete and popular, she would have nothing to do with him. After all, Wendell was two years younger than Ronnie. Wendell had been a boy, while Ronnie had always been mature and sophisticated.

Rita thought, *how times have changed. Now a younger man is in vogue!* She knew Ronnie had always dreamed of leaving Castleton and becoming a star, but she sometimes wondered what Ronnie's life would have been like if she and Wendell had gone out. *Oh, well, it is what it is.* Still, who knows what the future might hold?

Rita finished watering and admired her well-tended garden. A slight breeze carried the smell of her freshly baked muffins, and her stomach grumbled. No matter what Ronnie thought, they smelled good. "Come on, Dewey, time to see if the muffins have cooled. We'd better get to them before Auntie Ronnie throws them out."

Regardless of whether Ronnie liked the muffins, Rita knew they would take their tea out to the porch to start their day with a good chat in their rocking chairs. They would hash over the town's goings on and solve any number of problems—at least in their minds. Ronnie had decided that if they oversaw the town, the troubles of Castleton would "exit stage left"! Rita was not so sure about that, but she did agree they were excellent problem solvers. Both considered themselves competent Miss Marples. Though in Ronnie's vision, she was much more glamorous.

Sweat trickled down Rita's neck. "It's getting hot; time to go inside, Dewey." Making their way to the kitchen, Rita heard someone stomp up the front stairs and onto the porch. She checked her watch; it had been Adam's, and she loved it even if Ronnie thought it was too masculine. *Who is here this early, and what could they want?* she wondered. And please don't let them wake up Ronnie, she prayed silently.

Fortunately for today, Ronnie was not a morning person. "Come on Dewey, let's go investigate," Rita said as she and her dog changed course and went through the gate toward the front of the house.

A loud, abrasive "Good morning!" assaulted her; she recognized the voice immediately. It was Georgia Thorndike. Georgia rarely visited the sisters, so Rita wondered why she was here before 10 AM.

Rita waved and headed up the stairs to join Georgia. Facing her, Rita sighed. Georgia had a habit of creating messes in town through gossip and outright lies, and then claiming ignorance and letting her poor husband, George, clean them up. Neither Rita nor Ronnie had had any patience for Georgia and her antics. In high school, Georgia had once told a blatant lie about Ronnie being "loose," and the sisters had never forgotten nor forgiven her. Besides if anyone had been "loose," it had been Georgia. *Come to think of it, rumors have even been swirling now about her and her next-door neighbor.*

"Hello, Georgia! How are you?" Rita hoped that sounded as if she actually cared.

"I'm fine. Thanks. Here's your morning paper," Georgia said and thrust the paper directly in Rita's face. "Of course, my poor George is not fine." She let her statement hang in the air. Rita had a flash of Georgia lacing poor George's coffee with arsenic, but quickly put the thought out of her head and waited for Georgia to tell her what was wrong with George. Obviously, she was going to play this scene for all it was worth. *Where is Ronnie when I need her?*

"What's wrong with George?" Rita asked bluntly.

"Actually, it's your sister, Ronnie, that I came to discuss," Georgia replied, then struck and held a dramatic pause.

Wanting to get this scene over with before Ronnie had a chance to join them, Rita simply asked, "So what has my sister done? I'm sure she didn't make George ill."

"She most certainly did. You know George has an ulcer and weak stomach." Rita didn't, but she remained silent. Georgia took a deep breath and kept going.

Realizing she had to respond if she wanted to keep the tale going, Rita nodded.

"I thought you should know about your sister's performance last night at the Cultural Council meeting. She outdid herself, and I wanted to tell you about it privately, out of her earshot." She glared at Rita and added, "You have to tell her to stop it."

Rita bristled, and replied, "Oh? Stop what?"

Georgia continued full speed ahead. "Don't play innocent with me. You know exactly what I mean. Your sister was so demanding and arrogant about what the town should do with empty buildings and land last night that she upset my poor George and made him sick. He wasn't feeling good at all last night, and he still isn't this morning. In fact, I'm out to get him some more medicine now. We ran out in the middle of the night. The new 24-hour CVS is not 24 hours!"

Rita raised an eyebrow. The mention of the mega-pharmacy reminded her of her battle with the town over selling open spaces, but this was not the time for that argument. Instead, she simply said, "Well, it's too bad George is ill." Though she didn't think Ronnie had anything to do with it. Still, now was not the time to argue with Georgia. She wanted her gone.

"It is. So please try to control your sister. I won't have her making George sick." Georgia grumbled. "All he could eat last night when he came home was cereal with milk. He hasn't been able to keep anything down. And he's been sick all night." Again, Georgia paused.

"I hope it's nothing serious," Rita replied sincerely. *Please just go before Ronnie makes an appearance and all hell breaks loose.*

"You'll speak to your sister," Georgia demanded.

"Yes, I will speak to Ronnie." Though Rita knew it wouldn't do any good, and besides, she was sure Ronnie was not the cause of George's illness. The cause was standing right in front of her on the porch.

However, like a dog with a bone, Georgia continued without missing a beat. "Your sister was over the top last night, and judging from the effect it had on my poor George, she should learn to control herself. She kept pushing her ideas as if she were giving a monologue on stage. I don't know how you stand it with her back in town. Castleton is not her private stage."

Rita bristled visibly and couldn't help but respond. "I would think people would be glad someone just recently returned to town would take the initiative to attend meetings and make suggestions. Many who have been here their whole lives don't make that effort." She refrained from pointing her finger at Georgia, as the only thing Georgia had ever done for the town was complain. Rita had also heard Georgia had convinced George to sell land to the latest developer. If it was true, Rita was livid, as George had promised to sell it to the town for green space. *One way to find out.* "Are you and George selling your land to the developer?"

Georgia ignored the question and continued. "She kept talking about converting the unused primary school building into an arts center. Hah, the only people that would benefit would be Ronnie and those useless artist friends of hers. Does she think this is New York?"

Rita tried to say she thought that was a good idea and would invigorate the town center, but Georgia was on a roll.

"Developments are the future and we need to keep up in order for Castleton to prosper." Georgia stomped her foot for emphasis.

Rita bit her tongue. Enough was enough. Still hoping to see Georgia on her way before Ronnie came down, she moved closer to the porch door and said over her shoulder, "I'll talk to Ronnie. I hope that medicine helps George feel better!"

"What will really make everybody feel better is if Ronnie keeps her hair-brained ideas to herself. I hold Ronnie responsible for George being sick, and I hold you responsible for Ronnie," Georgia bellowed, pointing her finger directly at Rita.

As if on cue, Ronnie burst through the front door and onto the porch. "I'm responsible for George being ill? I doubt that, Georgia," Ronnie said. She sounded as if sugar wouldn't melt in mouth, which Rita knew meant Ronnie was livid. It was obvious she had been listening for a while.

Oh Lord, here we go, thought Rita. In high school, Ronnie and Georgia had engaged in competition after competition with each other. It seemed to matter little to Georgia that Ronnie always won. Nothing had changed since then, either. Once Ronnie was gone from Castleton, Georgia had considered herself the queen bee, but with Ronnie back, their absurd competition was on again. Plus, Georgia's lie hovered between them. It should have been forgotten long ago, but Ronnie nursed her grudges. And it could take her years, but she believed in getting even with her enemies. Rita wondered how much of an act Ronnie had put on at the meeting.

"Well, well, well," said Georgia. Her hands punctuated the air, creating commas as she drew out each word longer than the last. "Look what the cat dragged out."

Ronnie didn't say a thing, which made Rita shudder. Instead, Ronnie simply smiled at Georgia and leaned back against the door, striking a pose. Rita knew that look, and it didn't bode well. She knew Ronnie was about to humiliate Georgia, so she tried to intervene.

"Take care, Georgia. So nice of you to stop by," Rita said, trying very hard to send Georgia on her way.

"Now, Georgia, dear, what on earth makes you think I made George ill? I spent time with him at the meeting and he certainly was riled up, but not because of me. In fact, he thought my idea for the art center was a good one. No, the truth of the matter is there's trouble in paradise." Ronnie lobbed that bomb directly at her enemy.

"He's sick, and I'm positive it's because of YOU!" Georgia said acidly. "I was just telling Rita she needs to stop you from running rough-shod over everybody in town. You need to play a silent role around here. And that should be easy for you. Most of your parts were just walk-ons."

Georgia smiled benevolently at Ronnie. Ronnie smiled back, having decided silence was a better weapon. When no response came, Georgia shook her head. Not one hair moved. She focused her beady eyes on Ronnie as she directed one last comment to Rita. "Well, I'm off. I have a sick husband to care for. My sympathy to you, Rita dear, as you have an ill person to care for, too. Mental as well as physical."

"Oh, Lord," Rita muttered to herself. "Here it comes." Rita steeled herself and prepared to stop Ronnie from strangling Georgia. Everyone knew Ronnie did not discuss her illness. Ever.

Ronnie straightened her posture and clenched her fists by her side. Not a good sign. "What do you mean by that?" Ronnie hissed as she moved to the center of the porch.

"Well, everybody knows you came home because you were ill. And people in town are wondering if it was physical or mental."

Rita figured she had fewer than five minutes to get Georgia off their property before Ronnie exploded, and the conversation descended from Noel Coward banter to David Mamet screaming.

"You never think of anybody but yourself, but making my George sick is the last straw. I won't put up with you acting like the queen bee. We're not in high school anymore. Stay away from George. He's in no condition to cope with you."

"Did it ever occur to you that if you spent half as much time and attention on your husband as you do on your next-door neighbor, poor George might be much happier and healthier?" Ronnie asked in a perfect stage whisper.

"Why I never! That's a lie."

"You should know. You're the queen of lies."

"I would watch my back if I were you, Ronnie. This isn't a silly television show, and you are NOT the star here," Georgia spat back. "I'm not the only person you're making angry. I'd be careful if I were you." And with that, she marched to her car, got in, and then screeched off down the street.

Ronnie called smugly after the disappearing car, "That silly show is still on TV," then strutted into the house, letting the porch door slam behind her.

Rita sighed and opened the porch door. As she and Dewey stepped into the house, she said, "Come along, Dew Drop. We need to see how Sarah Bernhardt is doing." Who knew what Act 2 would bring?

Chapter 4

Rita went down the hall and into the kitchen, where Ronnie was sitting at the counter, wrapped in her robe. She had a faraway look on her face and seemed drawn. It was as if all her energy had been spent on arguing with Georgia. Rita was appalled at how the silly fight had drained Ronnie's energy. *Maybe I do need to coax Ronnie into being less dramatic*, she thought. In a calm voice, she asked her sister, "Was that necessary?"

"Georgia started it," snapped Ronnie. "Besides, didn't you hear? I'm a single-minded, self-centered…you know, a … shrew!"

Rita shook her head. Ronnie sounded like a spoiled child. "If you were one of my students, you'd be in the principal's office now."

"Well, I'm not, so there," and Ronnie stuck out her tongue. Both sisters laughed. "It's good to laugh," Ronnie said in a quiet voice.

"It's the best medicine." Rita reached out and patted her sister's hand. "Let's have some muffins and tea. It will pick you right up."

"Since you don't have butter croissants and espresso on the menu, it will do. Thanks." Ronnie looked at Rita; her smile wavered, then disappeared.

Still, a comfortable silence settled over the kitchen as Ronnie watched Rita brewing the tea. "So, what did you discuss last night? And what set you off?" Rita inquired gently.

"Well, you know we have the empty primary school building in the center of town?" Ronnie replied.

Rita nodded as she set out dishes, cups, and jam. Ronnie was on a roll.

"Well, the old fools decided we should tear down the building or sell it. So, I said that tearing it down was probably not a good use of town money, and given the current real estate market, it also didn't make sense to sell it. We would get almost nothing for it. Then I suggested we turn it into an arts center.

The town is full of local artists." Ronnie paused. "They need a place to show and sell their work. Besides, many towns have revitalized their downtowns with art centers. And it's a boon for small businesses."

"Actually, that suggestion sounds as if it has merit. What was the reaction?"

"You'd think I had suggested we open a swingers' club. And of course, those fools thought they had a better idea." Ronnie shuddered just thinking about it.

"And what was their idea?" Rita knew, of course, Ronnie probably dismissed it outright, as it was not as brilliant as what she had proposed. On the other hand, knowing the players involved, Rita knew their idea was probably worthless.

"Can you believe it? They thought the building should be a senior center or assisted living. But anybody with any sense at all knows neither of those will draw tourists to the center of town. Unless we plan on selling Depends and wheelchairs, it's stupid. And I told them what I thought of that idea."

Rita shook her head and sighed. "I'm sure you did." Whenever Ronnie believed in something, there was no stopping her. Rita felt quite sure she had steamrolled everyone at the meeting, as Ronnie did not believe in using honey to solve problems or win people over to her side.

"Yes, well, maybe I could have been a little more politically correct in my remarks, but their short-sightedness drives me around the bend. It's not just about bringing culture to the town; it's a practical solution. We have lots of artists. They could give classes and rent studio space. It's a solid, financially sound use of the building."

"But did they listen? Oh, no! Half the old coots ended up screaming at me. The gist of their argument being I am a woman, and what did I know about what made a town vital? After all, this is not Paris, they muttered. So, I screamed right back at them."

"Poor Trudy. You know--the town clerk? She tried to calm us all down, but her attempt failed miserably. No one listens to her unless she's gossiping. So, she was useless. Everyone kept arguing. Then poor George jumped in and tried to defend me. It was quite sweet. I think he still has a crush on me." Ronnie batted her eyes.

Just as she often had as a child, Rita remained silent. Ronnie was convinced every man or boy in town loved her. The sad thing is, she was right. Most did have a crush on her.

"He really is a dear and should leave Georgia. Anyway, the meeting turned into total mayhem. Finally, I just stormed out." Ronnie smirked at the memory.

"Ah, another grand exit!" Rita chuckled.

"I didn't plan on it. No, I can't even lie, you're right. I do tend to do the grand exits when I can. Remember the time I got mad when we were sledding down by where the ice cream stand is now? I can't even remember why I was so mad, but I clearly remember marching home with my sled bumping along behind me. Lord, I was silly. Missed a whole day of sledding just because I was mad. And there was no one to see my grand exit. What a waste of time."

"It was a waste of a perfect day for sledding. I had to come home, too, because there was no one there to watch me. One of the many days I had to follow you home."

"I wasn't that bad a big sister, was I?"

"No, there were plenty of good times. Remember you and your dates would take me to the movies? I was the envy of all my friends. Plus, you let me buy whatever candy I wanted. Most of the time, I didn't like the movie, but I loved being there with you."

"And we used to fly kites and go swimming afterwards." Ronnie's voice trailed off, and the sisters enjoyed their precious memories for a moment.

"You know, we did have a good life," Ronnie added. "I feel bad for the kids today. The town has little space for them to explore. It's so sad. They rarely get to use their imaginations and really play. Again, the arts center and classes would be such a boon, and a good use of space. Oh, this town is so aggravating."

"Don't get me started on the how this town is going to you know where in a hand basket." Rita frowned and shook her head as she poured the tea into the cups and passed Ronnie the muffins.

"You can say 'hell.' You're a grown woman."

"I say 'hell,' but that's not the point. We need to take a stand. We must do something about the developers taking over our town. Soon there won't be any green space left."

"I agree, but first, let's eat. These muffins smell almost good."

"Almost? They are; trust me." Rita opened the jam and spread it over her warm muffin. "Let's take our tea and muffins and eat them on the porch."

Dewey began jumping up and down in anticipation. When Rita turned her back to gather up her plate and tea, Ronnie fed Dewey a piece of muffin.

"I saw that. My dog will end up fat," Rita said, smiling. "But they're very *healthy* muffins," Ronnie added, and the sisters chuckled. Then they made their way to the porch and settled into the rockers.

"This is nice," said Rita as she sipped her tea. "It is," agreed Ronnie.

But just as they were enjoying the tranquility, a siren pierced the air. At almost the same moment they cried, "What's going on?"

Both sisters sat up ramrod straight, looking over the railing at the scene. An ambulance raced past the porch, and following it was a blue Buick. And hot on the trail, following the car, was Trent Fowler on his bike, looking like Ichabod Crane on his horse.

"I think that was Georgia," murmured Ronnie. Both women rose and hurried to the porch railing, watching the caravan disappear over the hill.

"It was. It must be George in the ambulance. I wonder why she didn't ride with him. I hope he'll be all right. It's odd that he got that sick so fast," commented Rita. "It sounded like he just had a stomach flu. I know he has a weak heart and his immune system is compromised, but still, it's odd."

"You're right. It's almost like an Agatha Christie novel." Ronnie answered. "But even stranger, why is Trent following them? There must be story brewing. Otherwise, our intrepid reporter would not be racing to the scene."

"That's not funny, Ronnie," Rita said. The sisters stared at each other and wondered *What is happening in our town*?

Chapter 5

The two sisters turned toward each other. There was no need to talk, as they had a lifetime of picking up each other's silent cues. Rita knew Ronnie's furrowed brow meant she did not like what she had just seen, and things seemed odd. Ronnie, meanwhile, saw Rita purse her lips and pull at her left ear lobe, meaning she had some significant questions, and was forming a hypothesis of what was happening. Once they sorted their thoughts, they'd share their ideas.

Almost as one, they dropped back into their rockers. Ronnie started rocking immediately, her mind racing. Rita sat still, gazing off into the distance, past the gazebo, slowly filling in her working theory.

Rita spoke first. "Well, this is an odd development. I wonder what exactly is wrong with George. I doubt it's the flu. It's not flu season, and I haven't heard of anyone else being ill. Plus, I know George got his flu shot. He was there when we got ours."

"That's right, he was. So, if it were not a bad case of the flu, why would Georgia lie about his illness? And why would she make me the cause?"

"Those are good questions. She must have an ulterior motive, but what is it?" Rita asked.

"Well, on the one hand, it seems as if she's setting up an alibi. Giving us the timeline of his illness and putting blame on me. We know it's out of character for her to be so concerned about George's health. After all, the world revolves around Georgia, not George." Ronnie frowned. "I don't like her, but I must admit, I wouldn't think she'd intentionally hurt George. And if she did, she's not a good enough actress to fool anyone."

Rita agreed. It did seem as if Georgia were setting up an alibi. But why would she need one? That was the important question.

"You know, Ronnie, I don't like to gossip, but" Rita started . . .

"But my foot!" Ronnie interrupted. "Spit it out. I'm sure it's based on fact coming from you. Besides, you know where there's smoke, there's fire." Ronnie leaned toward her sister. She didn't want to miss one word of Rita's theory.

"Well, as you know, Georgia's neighbors have been commenting that Georgia seems to be spending much too much time with her neighbor, who happens to be an eligible bachelor." Rita looked at her sister and waited, surprised Ronnie wasn't leaping on that comment.

Instead, Ronnie replied slowly. "It would explain why she wanted us to know what a good wife she is. Though I don't believe her for a minute. She married George because she had no other offers. In fact, I remember she claimed to be pregnant. And by the time George found out she wasn't, or had lost the alleged baby, she'd married the poor man. She'd trapped him, plain and simple.

And the fact that George would inherit his father's business was her motivation. Poor George never had a chance once she set her cap for him."

Rita watched her sister carefully, as she knew Ronnie had always had a soft spot for George. Oh, she would never have dated him or even had a fling with him, but he had always been sweet on Ronnie, and Ronnie loved being admired. So, Rita took her sister's comments with a grain of salt. Though she did think they might hold more truth than fiction.

"But that's more of a reason for George to get rid of her, than the other way around," Rita said. "Not that I think George would ever do anything like that."

"No, think about it. George was the type who always said, 'I've made my bed, and so I lie in it.' George doesn't believe in divorce or running from his obligations, and he sold his father's business at a profit, and with his investments, he has built up a good nest egg. And don't forget they own some land that that developer–what's his name? King-Young? –is interested in buying." Ronnie's disdain for the developer was apparent, as Rita was certain Ronnie knew his name perfectly well. Both sisters had disliked the man immediately upon meeting him. "It's too bad King-Young wasn't in the ambulance. His demise would do the town good," Ronnie snorted.

Rita ignored Ronnie's last comment. She was more interested in Georgia's reaction to George being ill. "That's true. I heard Georgia really wants to sell it, but George doesn't. He's thinking of donating it for tax purposes."

"I think you're right about George," Ronnie added. At last night's meeting, he gave the distinct impression he would not sell. I think I convinced him about the importance of green space. And if I did, that goes a long way to explain Georgia's anger towards me."

Rita hated to give her sister credit for saving the land, but this time she felt that Ronnie was right. She nodded. "Yes, that could explain why Georgia was so angry with you."

Ronnie continued, "Furthermore, if Georgia is in love with her neighbor, George could donate the land rather than let her get it in a divorce. George dead works much better for Georgia than George alive."

"What? You actually think Georgia could kill George?" Rita sputtered.

"No, I don't. It's just a thought." Ronnie looked away, almost embarrassed by the idea. Still, there was a logic to it. "But I would think that King-Young is capable of almost anything, including murder. He thinks and acts like he's the town kingpin."

"I can't argue with you about him. He's like the villain from central casting." Ronnie smiled at Rita's attempt at a movie analogy.

"But you know, there's something odd about him. To me, he seems more like an actor playing a role than a real person. Also, there's something oddly familiar about him. For a newcomer, he knows too much about everyone in town and how to play them."

"You're right. I can't put my finger on it, either, but we need to watch King-Young." Ronnie cleared her throat. "However, let's get back to Georgia. I'm still having trouble believing that she is so greedy that she would purposely hurt George." Then she paused for a moment. "Now that said, what if she delayed his care on purpose?" Ronnie smiled. She liked that idea.

"You think Georgia would let George die? Really, Ronnie, isn't that a bit much?" Rita asked. But as she thought more about it, it did make sense. The thought made her shiver. "You know that would be murder. And one that could never be proved," she added.

"I know, but it would also explain Trent Fowler furiously peddling his fancy Italian racing bike after the ambulance. To see him, you would think he expected to break the story of a lifetime! Maybe he knows something," Ronnie proposed. "And if he does, we'll soon see it in print. After all, you know Trent's dream is write a Pulitzer prize-winning story."

Rita pondered what her sister said. It made sense, but still seemed rather far-fetched to her. She thought carefully before replying. "I must admit it's all very intriguing and mysterious. It makes me think we're right that it's more than a simple illness like the flu. I agree that Trent wouldn't believe it was a great story if George died from a flu-like illness, but if there were suspicious circumstances around his death, it would be a hot story. And Trent is quite the snoop, so he might know more about George and Georgia than we do. Still, it's hard to picture Georgia poisoning George."

Ronnie nodded her head, but then added, "Remember all the Miss Marple mysteries? A lot of deaths by poison."

Rita agreed. "True. And we could make a case for it. If there's something suspicious about George's illness, Trent will ferret it out. He won't miss the chance to break a headline story and create a big splash for himself and his career."

"So, as I said, where there's smoke, there's fire. Besides, there's money at stake, and we know greed is a great motivator," Ronnie stated.

"My Lord, this is getting to sound more like a mystery novel than real life," Rita mused. "I know the new development is creating all kinds of issues and tensions, but do you honestly think there's 'foul play' afoot?"

"I hope not," Ronnie replied, then added, "It's probably just a reaction to all the acid that's built up in his stomach after being married to Georgia for so many years. That seems like a natural reaction to me after living with that shrew and having to look at her first thing every morning." Both sisters chuckled.

"I do hope it's nothing serious," Rita answered. "I would hate to see anything bad happen to George. Besides, you know Georgia would sell their land in a second if she had the chance. And then, there go our open spaces."

"That's true, and that would be a sad day for the town. We need to prevent that from happening," Ronnie replied firmly. Rita was glad Ronnie was on her side about the open spaces and trying to stop the development. They made a good team.

"As for Trent," Rita continued, "There's no telling what story line is swirling around in his head. It wouldn't be the first time he invented a news flash! I swear he wants a Pulitzer so badly he would do anything. He just hasn't realized Castleton doesn't have Pulitzer Prize-worthy stories."

"You can say that again!" Ronnie laughed back. "Though I always wanted to be the star of some dramatic story growing up here."

"Well, it was not for your lack of trying! Remember the time you were convinced you were about to be kidnapped?"

"Well, it was the 25th anniversary of the Lindberg kidnapping. The world was ready for another one. I was young and beautiful. Why wouldn't I have been kidnapped?" Ronnie stared at her sister, daring her to deny she had been a beauty. "Besides, we did have some German immigrants move to town."

Rita shook her head. She knew how to dodge that bullet. "First of all, we didn't have any money. And second, we weren't famous. And third, those 'immigrants' were a family from the Midwest, not Germany."

"Well, that's *your* opinion." As usual, Ronnie was dismissing Rita since she didn't agree with her.

However, before Rita delivered a retort, a voice startled them. They immediately looked to see who was calling to them. It was Lana.

"Oh, hi, Lana," Rita called out. "You're looking well this morning," gesturing for the young woman to come over to the porch.

Ronnie muttered, "I swear, she acts as if she were Lana Turner, not Lana Newton," as the visitor came to the porch. Ronnie did not approve of Lana's clingy top. "But you have to admit she is quite attractive in the old Hollywood *femme fatale* way. I'm sure she has her claws into some man in town." Ronnie did not believe Lana was as innocent as she seemed. *Maybe it's the name Lana. I never did like Lana Turner.*

"Quiet," Rita hissed. She found Lana an enigma. Her stories seemed to vary, depending on whom she was talking to, and so Rita was never sure who Lana really was. With Rita and Ronnie, she acted innocent and naive. But, like Ronnie, Rita didn't really buy her act.

Lana leaned on the railing, her hand lying across her stomach, and asked how the sisters were doing.

"We were talking about this morning's goings-on. It's been quite a busy start to the day." Rita filled Lana in on the visit from Georgia, the ambulance, and Trent's hot pursuit.

"Oh, how awful," Lana replied. She looked stunned. "I don't really know George or Georgia. I have seen them at the dairy when I've been buying my milk from John, but only to say hello. John is just so nice when I'm there. He's a real gentleman." Lana abruptly stopped talking and looked away. But then she added, "You know, I grew up on a dairy farm. It's hard work. I really respect John."

Ronnie smiled at Lana. Rita knew it was a fake smile and wondered what her sister was up to. "Lana, you look wonderful this morning, so full of life you are practically blossoming along with the buds on the trees." A blush crept up Lana's long, ivory neck.

"I guess the spring weather agrees with me. This year we certainly were reminded just how long a New England winter can be, weren't we? I'm glad it's over," Lana stammered, turning redder by the minute. "Besides, it's nice to be living out in the country and working here instead of Boston. I had really missed the countryside. Plus, I enjoy my job in Town Hall. The work is interesting, and the people are really friendly. They all seem to want to know what I'm doing."

The sisters looked at each other and smiled sweetly. Each was thinking about the rumors circulating about Lana. Yes, the townspeople, especially the wives, were extremely interested in what exactly Lana was doing. *She can't be as innocent as she acts*, thought Ronnie. *She seems like the type of woman who has a plan and will quietly achieve her goal. And I think I know what her goal is.*

Lana glanced at her watch. "Sorry, but I have to run. Lana moved abruptly away from the railing, smiled broadly, and waved as she headed back toward Town Hall. "Everyone will be abuzz if I don't show up for work soon. Enjoy your day, ladies. And I hope George is fine."

The sisters continued rocking, watching Lana sashay up the street. Once Lana was out of earshot, Rita curtly said, "Well, you certainly made that awkward. You know the rumors about Lana that are circulating, and I have to say, I am beginning to wonder if they are true."

Ronnie interrupted, "Did you notice she seemed to be protecting her stomach? Plus look at her walk. She's got to be pregnant with a walk like that. It's the same walk I used when I played a pregnant woman. And did you notice her blush when I mentioned her blossoming?"

"I caught that."

"I knew you wouldn't miss it," Ronnie said.

"Well, let's not jump to conclusions" Rita replied, chewing her lip as she thought. "Though that is the first time I've heard her mention she grew up on a dairy farm."

"Interesting tidbit, isn't it? Gives her an excuse for spending time at the dairy with John," Ronnie said. "I wonder if it's true. She seems more *femme fatale* than farmer's daughter."

Ever since Lana had moved from Boston to Castleton and found the job as an Administrative Assistant at Town Hall, the rumors had flown about her. She was single, attractive, and seemed competent. Why move to town from the city? So, every time Lana was seen alone with a man, any man, the rumors began. And those weren't the only rumors.

People passed along many rumors about why she moved to town. Most were absurd. She had come to escape her past. She was on the run, having left behind a string of broken hearts (and families), and been forced to leave the city. Those about Lana being a black widow were Rita's favorite. If nothing else, she was too young to have left behind a string of dead husbands. Besides, black widows have money; where is hers if she is a black widow? If anybody were a black widow, it would be LaMerle.

Ronnie loved hearing the rumors, but neither sister believed them. And Lana's latest comment about growing up on a dairy farm gave some credence to the rumor about her and John. And nobody could argue they didn't spend a lot of time together.

Of course, similar rumors had circulated about John's wife, LaMerle. She had arrived in Castleton claiming she was doing research on her family history--the unknown part of the family that was rumored to have roots in New England, unlike the rest of the family tree that had been planted firmly below the Mason-Dixon line for generations. It turned out she was really looking for a husband. She had hooked herself John, the local widower, whose family had helped found Castleton. Quite a feat for LaMerle as an outsider.

And it earned her the disdain of most of the women in town. Now there were rumors that their marriage was in trouble, much to the delight of those same women. Both Rita and Ronnie felt LaMerle and John were mismatched.

So Rita did wonder about John and Lana. Physically, Lana was a younger version of LaMerle, and Rita was sure that fact was not lost on either LaMerle or John. Rita had noticed over time, Lana had even adapted some of LaMerle's mannerisms, such as throwing her head back when she laughed, and dressing to show off her figure. It also didn't help that Lana did nothing to dispel the rumor. Rita was beginning to believe the rumors were more true than false. So who knows what Lana would do to win John over?

At one time, Rita had thought maybe John's daughter, Caroline, and Lana would become friends. They were nearly the same age, and Caroline was an open, friendly young woman.

But they never did. Rita now realized it was because Lana was too interested in Caroline's father. And Caroline was over-protective of her father. She had never taken to LaMerle, and it made sense she would like Lana even less.

Rita wondered what Ronnie knew. She glanced at her sister and asked, "You have heard, haven't you, the latest rumor about Lana and John?"

"I'd have had to be in a coma to miss that!" Ronnie replied.

"I must say, if anyone were to ask me, and fortunately they don't, although I certainly don't condone infidelity, I think Lana and John are a good match, much better than John and LaMerle. Especially if Lana growing up on a dairy farm is true," Rita confessed.

"One of the cows would be a better match for John than his current wife, if you ask me!" Ronnie replied, in typical fashion. This time, both sisters laughed out loud.

"Well, I don't know about you, but I'm still hungry. Shall we go inside and have another muffin and another cup of tea? Then we can decide on our day. OK?" Rita rose from her rocker and called to Dewey. "Inside, girl!"

When the three reached the kitchen, Ronnie said, "I think I'll skip the muffin and just have some Cheerios. They're healthy. All this talk of upset stomachs makes me crave some nice milk to soothe my own this morning," Ronnie said, as she poured it on her cereal, carried the bowl to the table, sat down, and took a large spoonful. "Oh, NO! This milk is spoiled!"

She spit the cereal back into the bowl, rushed to the sink, and threw the contents of her bowl into the disposal, grumbling the whole time. "Well, so far, this entire day has been a dress rehearsal for disaster, hasn't it?" she said to no one in particular. She continued grumbling as she retrieved the milk from the refrigerator and dumped the rest down the drain. She said, "I guess I was saved by the first bite. Bad milk can make you sick." Both women thought of George, but neither said anything. "I guess I'll have another one of your muffins after all."

Rita, smiling, held out a small plate toward her, and said, "Let's each have one, and then go to the dairy for some more milk."

Ignoring Rita's look of disapproval, she slathered the muffin with butter, hoping to make it tastier. Rita took the butter away, but Ronnie wasn't done. "More butter, please."

Rita passed back the butter. "You sound like an orphan from *Oliver Twist*. If all that butter makes you sick, I'm not taking care of you," Rita laughed.

"I'll call Nurse Georgia." Ronnie licked her fingers, then said, "Let's go."

Chapter 6

The sisters finished their tea and headed up to their rooms to get ready for their trip to the dairy. Rita decided she didn't need to change. She felt comfortable in her regular outfit: a man's shirt from L.L. Bean, khakis, and her everyday Birkenstocks. However, Ronnie, ever the fashion plate, had changed. Dramatic as ever, she now wore a bright purple over-blouse, white pants, and yellow espadrilles. She had even added a Hermes scarf to complete her ensemble.

"Well?" Ronnie didn't expect an answer; nevertheless, she gave Rita a smile worthy of a curtain call as she held her arms out to her sides and twirled. She tilted her head and arched one eyebrow, signaling Rita could show her admiration at any time. The silence that greeted Ronnie told her what her sister thought of her outfit, but it didn't bother Ronnie. Her over-the-top outfit was payback for the healthy muffin. *It's so easy to embarrass Rita.*

Rita shook her head. "You do realize we're just going to the dairy, right?"

Mission accomplished. "One must always dress as if one is going to some special place. And you never know who you'll bump into. Besides, it makes me happy." Ronnie flounced out to the car.

"Ah, life with a diva. You stay here and guard the house, Dewey. We'll be back in a few." Rita locked the door and went out to the car.

"Did you lock the door?" Ronnie asked. Rita nodded. With the recent spate of burglaries, everyone now locked their doors. One more change in Castleton that Rita despised.

They settled into the car and were off. Minutes later, they arrived at the dairy, which was just down the street from their home. As kids, when John's father ran the dairy, they used to walk there for their milk; now both were a little too old for that. Besides, the road carried much more traffic now, and would not be the safest place for anybody to walk.

The pair emerged from their Volvo, slamming their doors at the exact same moment, and walked together across the parking lot toward the store.

Ronnie adjusted her scarf and muttered, "Let's hope this is the first thing that goes right today, and that LaMerle is not working this morning. It would be a refreshing change not to have to listen to her southern accent wishing us a good morning. She's about as sincere as Georgia."

"Oh hush, y'all," Rita said in probably the worst attempt at a Southern accent Ronnie had ever heard. Rita reached for the door and practically shoved Ronnie through, preventing her from making her typical entrance. Rita was not in the mood for drama. Once inside, she exclaimed, "Why, Trent, hello! We didn't expect to see you here."

"Yes, we saw you racing after the ambulance in hot pursuit," Ronnie commented. "You looked like you were competing in the Tour de France." She raised her eyebrow. The signal was clear to Rita. *Let's find out as much as we can.*

Rita followed her sister's lead, but decided to do it in a friendlier, more easy-going manner. She calmly said, "It's nice to see you, Trent! You too, John! Nice morning, isn't it?"

John hesitated, then shrugged and decided to say what was on his mind. "I'm not so sure it's a good morning, considering Scoop, I mean Trent, here has been grilling me since he came through the door." John glared at Trent, who stood there positively beaming, with his pen poised over his notebook. Clearly, he had some story going. *But what was it?*

"Grilling you?" Rita asked.

John answered before Trent could get a word in. "It seems that George Thorndike was admitted to the hospital, and they think he may have listeria poisoning. So, Trent is here, trying to put the blame on me. I run a dairy, so of course my milk is the source of the listeria." John shook his head in dismay, and then looked at Rita, imploring her for help. "Rita, you're a biologist; maybe you can tell him something about listeria. Milk is not the only thing that can transmit listeria, right?" Beads of sweat were forming on John's forehead even though the dairy was cool.

Rita tried to gather her thoughts. "Listeria?" Trent's accusation shocked her. She knew John was fastidious about his dairy, and inspectors had always commented that you could practically eat off his barn floors. Even as children, John had been the neatest, cleanest, and most proper of their group. There were no plaid shirts and overalls for John. He wore crisp white shirts, his khaki pants were always sharply creased, even on gym days, and he always went to the boys' room to wash his hands before they ate their lunches in the classroom. No one would ever guess John lived on a farm, as the farm odor stayed on the farm, not on John. In fact, their group had called John "Mr. Clean." Rita now realized John probably was a little OCD. Still, his rigidity about cleanliness shot large holes through Trent's theory. *No, the possibility of John's dairy as a source of listeria was not likely. As Ronnie would say, "Something's not right in the state of Castleton."*

Meanwhile, Ronnie pretended to be looking for milk while she tried to read Trent's notes. However, Trent kept waving his notebook back and forth in excited gestures, making Ronnie want to rip it from his fluttering hands. Ronnie glanced at Rita and shook her head. She couldn't read the notes.

Oblivious to the storm of emotions he was causing, Trent practically jumped down Rita's throat. "Yes, Rita, tell me all you know about listeria." He put away his pad and pen and pulled out a small tape recorder. He was serious. And like a pit bull with prey in his jaws, he was not letting go. He stared intensely at Rita, thinking he could force her into saying what he wanted to hear.

Ronnie coughed, trying to hide her amusement at Trent's actions. It was clear Trent had never been Rita's student or he would have known that no one could intimidate Rita. Least of all with a stare. Everyone knew Rita was the queen of stares who could control her classroom with one look.

Rita knew her reply was important. She felt like an expert giving testimony at a murder trial. She spoke slowly, carefully weighing each word. She knew if she made the wrong statement, she could harm John's business. "I don't really know all that much about listeria, Trent." Trent shoved his mini-tape recorder into Rita's face. She slapped it away. "But here's what

I do know. It's a bacterium that can contaminate food. It makes people quite ill, especially babies, the elderly, and those with compromised health. Symptoms can appear any time within 24 hours."

"So that's why George suddenly became so ill," Ronnie said.

Rita held up a hand and stopped her sister's flow of information. She turned back to face John and Trent. "Most people do recover from listeriosis. It's usually not fatal, although it can become invasive and prove fatal. It's most often spread through contaminated food."

"Doesn't listeria spread from dairies and tainted milk?" Trent pressed on. Reluctantly, Rita nodded. Trent exclaimed gleefully, "Well, since we know George buys his milk here, then that makes John the lead suspect for the source of the outbreak." He snapped his recorder off with a great flourish and looked triumphantly at John.

John's look once again pleaded with Rita to help him. Trent was known to run with a story before verifying all his facts, and this story could ruin John. Even Ronnie nodded toward Rita. *Help him.*

Rita took a deep breath and tried. "It's true that milk can transmit listeria very easily, but that doesn't mean the milk is the source." Rita carefully enunciated each word. She noticed that Trent had not turned his recorder back on, nor was he taking notes. "And it certainly doesn't mean the listeria came from John's dairy. The state health agency will have to run tests to locate the source. The most common test is called pulse-field Gel Electrophoresis. It determines the source. It's like DNA or fingerprints."

Everyone was silent for a moment, and then Ronnie walked over to Trent, put a hand on each side of his face, and forced him to focus on her, not John. "Nobody--do you hear me? Nobody--said a word about a listeria outbreak." Trent nodded. "And if you print anything that remotely resembles the word 'source,' I will personally pay for John's lawyer to sue you! DO YOU HEAR ME?"

Ronnie let go of Trent. He wiped his nose.

Rita smiled. *Ronnie's listening after all*. And she was surprised and relieved that Ronnie had not ripped off Trent's head.

John blurted out, "Rita and Ronnie are right. You can't accuse my dairy of being the source of listeria." He ran his fingers through his hair. "I'm having enough trouble trying to keep my business going, competing with the large commercial dairies. Not to mention fighting off the developers who want to buy me out. And you know my kids. They look at the dairy and all they see is dollar signs. My son locks himself in a biology lab, hoping to discover something that will make him rich. And Caroline thinks about the cash she needs to start her own business."

Rita vigorously shook her head from side to side, but John was lost in his thoughts and didn't even realize he was digging his own grave. A listeria outbreak would give John reason to sell. It might even force him to sell. Ronnie wanted to stop John, but for once in her life, couldn't think of anything to say.

John rambled on. "And LaMerle is the last person on earth to be content living on a farm up here. She wants to return down South and would love me to sell the farm. Shall I go on?"

Trent smiled, his yellow teeth glistening with saliva. "Please, do. You've given me plenty of suspects who'd want to see the dairy sold. And listeria is the perfect solution." Trent turned his recorder back on. "Note to self: find out which developers are buying land in town." Trent was so happy that it turned Ronnie's stomach.

Rita cut in, "John, there's no need to upset yourself with this. Let's get the facts first."

John quickly added, "Facts are fine, Rita, but you know as well as I do that in a small town like Castleton, rumors count for more than facts or the truth. People would stop buying my milk before the facts would clear me." He hung his head, looking defeated. Then he looked up, and Ronnie could swear she saw him smile. *Did I just imagine that?*

"Still, the most logical source of the listeria is the milk, right?" Trent asked, yet again.

Ronnie really did want to rip off the idiot's head, or at least smack him. "Did you not hear us?" She reached over and snapped off his recorder. "There's no need to continue this discussion. Trent, maybe you should run, I mean pedal, along. Surely there's a real story out there somewhere with your name on it. But it's not one about listeria."

Trent put his recorder back in his pocket, looking totally chastised. *But not remorseful,* thought Rita. *Trouble is definitely brewing.*

"Remember, there are laws for slander and libel, so be careful what you print." Ronnie smiled through her teeth at the reporter, then strode to the cooler and pulled out two glass bottles of milk. She was putting on quite a show of buying milk, all for Trent's benefit.

"Didn't you ladies buy milk just yesterday?" asked John. He appreciated what they were trying to do, but he knew they didn't drink that much milk.

Rita leaned in and whispered, "Actually, we don't want to upset you, John, but the milk we bought yesterday was spoiled. Ronnie put it on her cereal. It was sour, and we had to throw it out." Ronnie distracted Trent so he didn't hear what Rita had said, but as Trent glanced over, he saw the stricken look on John's face. That clearly told him Rita had not delivered good news. Trent moved towards Rita.

"Come on. Spill it, Rita. What are you two whispering about? It's better you tell me than let me guess." *It wouldn't be the first time,* Rita thought. Trent thrust the tape recorder once again into Rita's face.

"I said our milk was sour. Not a big deal," replied Rita, aggravated she had to explain herself to Trent. And just as she feared, Trent leapt on that information as if it gave credence to his theory. Rita could see the headline now: *Local Dairy Closed Due to Listeria Poisoning*, with the name of John's dairy displayed prominently below Trent's byline. This was not good.

"You should have taken the spoiled milk to the hospital and had it tested," Trent blurted out. "It might have been tainted by listeria."

The three glared at him, as Ronnie said, "I mean what I said, Trent. Go along. Now." She took a step toward him.

Trent backed up, then whirled around, and snapped, "Alright, alright. I'm leaving. But I'll be back. This story is not going away. You'd better think about how much your dairy is worth, John. I think a sale is imminent." Then with a flourish that even Ronnie had to admit was wildly dramatic, Trent turned and marched to his bicycle, leaving the door wide open. He could almost feel six eyes drilling into his back as he fled the scene.

The three fully expected Trent to fly down the road on his bike, but instead of leaving, he stooped down and began fiddling with his hubs, clearly stalling for time. Ronnie stepped forward and slammed the door shut. "There. I don't think he can hear us now."

Rita turned to reassure John, "Please don't worry about this. You have enough on your mind with developers constantly on your case trying to get you to sell. You've got a business to run. Focus on that. Let the police and officials handle this."

Ronnie wanted to tell John that she and Rita would solve the mystery of the listeria, but instead said, "That's right. There's more than enough right here to occupy your time and your mind. You have cows to tend, your greedy children, not to mention your wife."

"Ronnie!" Rita blurted out.

Ronnie smiled at her sister and held up her hand. "I was just going to say, you are trying to keep your wife happy here in Castleton, and everybody knows that's hard," Ronnie finished, as Rita glared at her.

But John hardly heard any of their reassurances. Trent had really gotten under his skin. "I run a clean dairy; I pass inspections. Just last week the state inspectors were here, and the dairy passed with flying colors. There's no way my dairy is the source of an outbreak of listeria. But if it is, I don't know what I'll do." John cleared his throat and swallowed hard. "Well, back to business. Please take the milk, no charge. I hope it is fresh and you enjoy it."

The sisters thanked him, and Rita stepped behind the counter and gave John a reassuring hug. Then they walked out the door.

In the parking lot, Ronnie dramatically opened one of the bottles of milk and gulped some down. Wiping her mouth with her hand, she turned and glared at Trent. "See. I'm fine. Put that in your story." Then she took Rita's arm, and the two walked toward their car. They spoke in whispers, hoping Trent would just leave.

"Poor John," Rita sighed as she got in and slammed the door. She adjusted her mirror and saw Trent was finally moving. "I hope Trent realizes for once in his life he should not report a story until he has all the facts."

"I agree, but I seriously doubt he will. Clearly, he is deluded enough to think he might win a Pulitzer with this story." Ronnie frowned and added, "For once, Trent could be right." She hated admitting such a thing.

Rita agreed with her sister. "This is definitely one big mess that could ruin lives."

"You can say that again. Even I know John runs a clean operation. But he has so much on his plate. Maybe he forgot to do something? I mean, how else would listeria get in the milk?" Ronnie was grasping at straws, forging ahead, and trying to solve the mystery before they were even sure what was happening.

Typical Ronnie, Rita thought. "Let's not get ahead of ourselves, Ronnie. Nobody has even said the bacteria came from the milk; so let's not convict John of anything before all the facts are in. Remember logic."

Ronnie groaned. She much preferred leaping to conclusions and acting than solving things using Rita's logic. They rolled down the car windows, as the car had gotten quite hot while they sat in the lot, focusing on their thoughts and conversation. Neither saw Trent move closer to their car. Close enough to hear them clearly.

"Fine, we'll do logic," Ronnie acquiesced. Suddenly she stared at Rita and blurted out, "Would it be possible to introduce listeria on purpose?"

The question startled Rita. "It would, but why on earth would someone want to do that?"

"Simple, really," Ronnie replied. "To force John to sell the dairy."

"You may be right. I think we should investigate this. I know science, and you read people so well." Rita paused and broke into a grin. "You can be Sherlock Holmes and I'll be Watson."

"As it should be. After all, I am the star," Ronnie smiled broadly.

Rita, for once, would have liked to be the star, but she knew that would never work. Ronnie was the star, and that was that. Always had been and always would be. *Some things never change no matter how much time passes.* The sisters had been so intent on their conversation and theories that when they drove off, neither noticed that Trent was still in the parking lot and had been listening to every word.

Chapter 7

Watching the sisters drive off, Trent thought about what he had overheard. *I get my best information eavesdropping,* he thought, smirking. They had given him a lot ponder.

Ronnie had asked some very good questions, and Rita had also given him some ideas to explore. And their conclusions? Right on. There definitely was something strange going on in town, and John's dairy seemed to be the center of it all. Trent's mind raced. The whole listeria thing was one big, wonderful mystery he knew he could solve. But even more important than the solution would be what the story would do for his career. At last, he'd be able to leave Castleton for good.

Trent had worked his way through college. It had taken him seven years to finally get his degree. All the while, he had watched fellow students breeze through in four years. He resented those lucky students who didn't need loans or jobs waiting tables or flipping hamburgers while they were in school. They also had internships on larger papers, while Trent had to settle for the lowly Castleton Gazette. And if truth be told, he'd been lucky to get an internship even there. When he finally finished his degree, the only job he could find was in Castleton. The larger papers had rejected him.

Trent considered most of his fellow students clueless about what it meant to be a good reporter. Half simply wanted to be newscasters or see their name in print. Oh sure, he wanted his name in print, too, but only because of the power it would give him. Still, it hurt to see his former classmates succeed when he believed himself much more talented and worthy of the success they were achieving. Sadly, that need for success drove him to be reckless in his reporting. He often neglected to fact check his stories, and sometimes added elements to make his stories that much more compelling. Even if they were not completely true.

His dreams of a Pulitzer Prize and working for the *New York Times* could come true with this story. The listeria story would be his golden ticket out of Castleton and into the big leagues. Nothing would stop him. *New York, here I come! I just need to put it all together.*

Trent stood in the parking lot, reviewing what he had learned. Although he felt the story was almost writing itself, he knew it had to stick to the facts. Oh, he could twist them, but that's where he had to start – the facts. So, *what do I know? A listeria outbreak coming from the dairy just might, no would, force John to sell. But was there more to it than that?* Taking a more sinister approach, Trent decided someone could plant listeria to commit murder. *I'll have to check and see if that is even possible, but I think it is. If so, that gives me plenty of suspects.*

But murder in Castleton? Trent laughed at the idea. Murders simply didn't happen here. Probably people thought about committing murder, but no one ever actually did. There had been no murders in town during the years since he started reporting.

Then he thought of the mysteries his grandmother had devoured. Her favorite sleuth had been Agatha Christie's Miss Marple. The two had read the Miss Marple books aloud when he'd spent summers with her.

In those books, murders happened in small towns all the time. Often the police simply concluded the murders were "accidental" deaths. However, Miss Marple had seen past the "accidents," investigated what the police thought were "coincidences," established that they were murders, and discovered the identity of the killers. *It's what I'm doing here in Castleton*, Trent thought. However, he saw himself more as a dashing reporter, such as Robert Redford in *All the President's Men*. Certainly more than Miss Marple. He'd leave the Miss Marple investigation to Ronnie and Rita.

Trent remembered there had been deaths in Castleton classified as accidents but were somewhat suspicious. There was one where a spouse had fallen down the stairs after a fight, and another, a car accident the police concluded was an accidental hit and run. As he thought of these cases and how they might be similar to the current situation, Trent smiled and continued reviewing what he knew and suspected so far. A death by listeria could logically be classified as accidental, but Trent, channeling Miss Marple, decided it could also be murder. After all, he'd often heard people say they wanted to kill someone. Maybe someone meant it.

Trent smiled, practically salivating at the thought of murder. *Wouldn't it be something if a murderer were at work!* He could see the headline: *Killer Exposed* and there below it-- Trent's byline, big and bold. Yes, a killer loose in Castleton would be his ticket into the big time. He'd probably even land a book contract. He could become the next Anne Rule. *Maybe the murderer was a serial killer.* Trent let out a deep breath. *Calm down. First, focus on the listeria mystery. There isn't even a victim yet.* But Trent remembered Rita saying that listeria could kill the elderly, especially if they were weak. That profile fit George. *What if he died? Focus, Trent!*

First, he had to ferret out the story. So, pulling his mini-tape recorder from his jacket pocket once again, Trent strode with determination back into the dairy store. *Time to really grill John Camden, dairy owner, and possible killer. Ronnie is not scaring off this intrepid reporter*!

"Hey, John, can I ask you a few more questions?" Trent placed the recorder on the counter. "And I'm taping our talk." Trent needed to appear in charge. John was clearly feeling vulnerable, and this was Trent's best opportunity to nail him.

Seeing the tape recorder for the second time that morning, John turned pale. He stared at it as if it were a bomb about to detonate. But then he shrugged and tried to sound convincing. "Fine. Let's just get it over with. You're going to write the story whether I cooperate or not." He bent down and spoke directly into the mic, "I've got nothing to hide."

"So how would your milk become tainted with listeria?" Trent slid the tape recorder closer to John's side of the counter. "I mean, what did you do--or not do--that might contaminate the milk?"

John narrowed his eyes, and his face reddened. He swallowed hard and replied, "First off, NO one knows if it's our milk. Once the hospital reports George's illness to the state, the inspectors will probably be right over here to test our milk and other dairies in the area." John emphasized the fact the inspectors would be investigating all local dairies, not just John's.

"That's only the first phase. They'll get samples of my milk, but also of the food that George ate most recently. They'll be checking the stores where he bought it. Don't forget, listeria can be in food as well as milk." John was clearly warming up to the subject. He would point the finger at as many sources as he could in order to keep Trent from claiming his dairy was the only source. "I'm not the only place in town that sells milk. They'll have to check every place George and Georgia might have bought milk. They don't get all their milk from me. And if they ate out, and he ordered milk, they'll have to check the restaurant where they ate. And I happen to know Georgia hates to cook, so they eat out a lot, and George's favorite lunch drink is milk."

John was determined Trent was not going to pin this on his dairy. Business was shaky enough without an outbreak of listeria stopping people from buying his milk. Plus, soon the local ice cream stands would be buying milk to make their ice cream. And to stay afloat, he needed every one of those sales. With a local developer nipping at his heels to buy his land, John had to prove the dairy was making money, not losing it. If he defaulted on his loan payments, the bank would have no choice but to force a sale. Plus, he didn't need his children and wife producing any more reasons he should sell. And listeria would be the perfect excuse for them to push the sale. Maybe a listeria outbreak was a sign that he should take the money and run. He could divorce LaMerle and pay off her and the kids. Still, if he did sell, he wanted to do it on his own terms and not be forced to do it.

"Don't you go pinning this on me, Trent," John stated. "You don't even know if there is an outbreak. It could be one isolated case, and who knows what would cause that? Remember, only George is sick. Georgia is fine. Maybe she gave George some milk she knew had a problem. Did you think of that? There's a LOT of possibilities here, Trent. You'd get more play and coverage if the story is bigger than my dairy." John knew his last remark would get to Trent, who was desperate for a story the nationals would pick up.

"You're right. This story is bigger than your dairy. But I still think your dairy is a big part of it." Trent envisioned the story growing and growing. *Was George the first victim? Who would want him dead? Were there any problems between George and Georgia?*

An idea suddenly popped into Trent's head. "Why don't you give me a tour of the dairy? Then I can write how clean and efficient it is." Taking a favorable view of the dairy would be an interesting angle, and it would make a murder scarier and more frightening.

"Sounds good," John replied. He didn't think he could trust Trent's motives, but he also didn't feel he had a choice. Besides, he knew the dairy was spotless. "Why don't you take a few photos? Photos always enhance a story." Trent pulled out his digital camera as John strode confidently into the barn and showed Trent the sparkling clean milking machinery. "See how clean everything is? And we've got 150 cows we milk twice a day," John bragged.

Trent had to admit the place was shiny clean. *So, if it's not from the dairy itself, where did it come from? Was it planted? And more important: who planted it to make John sell?*

"With so many cows, aren't there are a lot of opportunities for the bacteria to slip in?" Trent asked softly. He didn't want to scare off John before he got some good information. Besides, he'd better get as many details as he could now, because once the story ran, this might be his last chance to talk to him. Besides, John's side of the story was important for balance.

"No. Look at our milking machines. They're spotless. And here, look at our cows." John strode right up to a cow and thumped her on the rump. Trent held back for a moment, then tentatively joined him, carefully staying as far away as possible while still examining the animal. Large animals scared him. John continued, "I clean them each time before we hook them up to be milked. There's no way bacteria could grow. So, there's no way listeria is coming from my dairy." John watched Trent closely as he inspected the cows and machinery. "Make sure you write that down."

Trent examined the milking machine. John certainly was not lying about how clean all the machinery was. Trent took more notes and snapped a few pictures for his records. But even though the machinery appeared spotless, Trent thought that with one slip-up, you could be doomed. But he wasn't going to say that to John. He didn't want to get his head bitten off.

Trent had almost talked himself into thinking the dairy may have been "ground zero," but it might very well have been an accident. Then the thought that something more deadly was at play slipped back into his mind. He was slowly becoming convinced this was more than a simple case of listeria. After all, if the machines, cows, and barn were this clean, then how did the listeria get into the milk?

Wait, Rita had said listeria could be cultured. So, had someone introduced it into John's milk? And if so, how much milk had been contaminated? Is listeria like a virus, which could spread throughout the community?

John coughed and brought Trent back to reality.

"It does look clean," Trent said and patted John on the shoulder, thinking it would be better if John thought he was on his side. Wandering over to some other equipment hanging on the barn wall, Trent could see it was not quite as sparkling clean as what John had already shown him. Still, it wasn't exactly dirty either. But it seemed unlikely the listeria had appeared due to John's actions or their milking process. So, what had really happened?

Trent was trying to figure out how to frame his story. It was clear he couldn't write that the listeria was from John's dairy, since he couldn't prove that yet. Then he thought of another angle. He could imply that it was listeria in the milk that George drank. Yes, that way he wouldn't mention the dairy. However, since most people knew George bought his milk from John's dairy, it would be implied. *Yes, that will work! Genius, Trent!*

John piped up again, "Follow me to my office. I've got one more thing to show you. It will prove it couldn't have happened here." Trent followed John into the back of the barn, where a computer system hummed. "The computer is my way of keeping everything under control. Caroline helped me set up the whole thing." He waited only a moment for Trent to take it all in before he explained, "I run preliminary tests on random samples of each milking I do. So that's two tests a day, Trent. I record it all right here on the computer," he said, patting the top of the monitor. "My records go back more than a year before I close them out. Anybody can look at the spreadsheets and see there have been no problems at all. So, you see, like I said before, it's probably just one isolated case and has nothing at all to do with my dairy."

It was a good argument, but Trent was not so easily won over. A new thought occurred to him. "Do you do all the milking yourself?" Trent asked, trying to sound nonchalant.

"Most of it. Why?" John stared at Trent. "Are you saying you think someone deliberately contaminated my milk?" John scowled as he thought about what Trent was implying.

"I don't know, but if the listeria is from your dairy, you keep everything spotless, and your tests are negative, then someone must have introduced it on purpose. Who hates you, John?"

"Oh, give it up, Trent. You sound like you're writing a crime novel. No one hates me. I'm sure there are people in town who don't like me, but I've lived here all my life, so that's natural." John stared at Trent and smiled a grin a little too wide to be sincere, clenching his fists behind his back. "Probably more people hate you, Trent, than me. After all, you do tend to piss people off with your 'news' stories," he said, making air quotes. "A lot of those stories are more gossip than news."

"Hey, that's not true. I'm careful and research all my stories," Trent replied.

John noticed Trent's voice quiver. *Was it from anger or fear?* He decided to take a few shots at Trent. *Two can play this game.* "Just calling a spade a spade, Trent. No need to get your hackles up." John refrained from adding, "unless it's true." He didn't want to antagonize Trent.

The two left the barn and made their way back to the store. Trent first, and John right behind him, making sure they kept moving right along.

"Well, I'm going to the hospital and talk some more to the people there." Trent put his recorder back in his jacket pocket. "I'm sure I'll have more questions for you later."

"You know where to find me. I'm here all the time." John watched Trent leave the store and head to his bike. Suddenly John bolted out the door and into the parking lot. "Hey, Trent, you might want to interview the developer, King-Young. He wants my land." John smiled half-heartedly.

"Why? You've told the whole town you won't sell. Besides, you already said it couldn't be from your dairy. So how would King-Young fit into this?"

"True, but if the dairy had to be closed, he might think I have no choice and be forced to sell. And I'd have to sell at his price, not mine. Food for thought, Mr. Reporter."

He watched Trent absorb the idea. John would love to the developer blamed for the listeria. At the least, it would drive the man out of town. Then the dairy would be safe. And it would be better for the town. King-Young had polarized the town. He had pitted family members and neighbors against each other. His development was proving to be the scourge of Castleton. *Yes, we'd all be better off with him gone. He's a sneak trying to worm his way into the town.*

John suddenly flashed to a kid, Kevin from high school, who had been a worm, just like King-Young. He'd desperately wanted to be part of the popular crowd and was constantly devising all kinds of schemes to make it into the group. John remembered he'd had a limp, so he couldn't participate in any sports, and he had really resented the athletes. Rumor had it that he had staged several accidents to injure them. Luckily, nothing serious had happened to anybody.

Kevin was a sad, angry teen, who particularly hated John because of his athletic success and popularity. He recalled Kevin had spread some truly vicious rumors about him, and about Ronnie and Rita as well, before he disappeared after graduation. It had taken years for the rumors to die down.

Now John realized King-Young is much like Kevin, and he wished the developer would disappear, too. He shook his head. It was the first time he had thought of Kevin in years.

Leave it to King-Young to bring back bad memories. Just as he had felt about Kevin, John didn't trust King-Young at all.

John had seen LaMerle and King-Young having coffee, and he knew that King-Young had approached both his kids. It had unnerved him, but he wasn't going to share that with Trent. Besides, John didn't believe anyone in his family would hurt him.

Then John remembered King-Young had also gotten cozy with Lana. In fact, King-Young always seemed to be right in the thick of everything, and his name came up in people's conversations more times than not. He always seemed to know just what to say and how to act around people in town. Occasionally he had mentioned something from the past that had happened to John, Ronnie, Rita, or someone else from their clique. *How did he know those things? Who was telling him?*

John watched Trent disappear down the road, then let out a deep sigh. When Trent came back, John would share his latest thoughts on King-Young. Yes, making King-Young a likely suspect was a good idea. Hopefully, it would keep Trent away from his family. They wanted to sell, and that would not help his case.

Then he suddenly thought of using the listeria as a rallying point. The townspeople could work to "save" the dairy. John smiled for the first time that day. There were many who wanted the dairy to be a success, especially Rita and Ronnie. They were adamant about keeping as many green spaces as possible in town.

Trent pedaled furiously towards King-Young's office. He began to form the story in his head. He knew there was quite a list of people who would gain if it were proved the listeria came from Camden Dairy. Trent chuckled. John had carefully avoided mentioning his family, but like everyone else in town, Trent knew very well that John's children and wife were dying for John to sell. Caroline had outright told him so when they had gone for beers during a concert. Trent smiled at the memory of that night and thought maybe he should see Caroline again.

Trent also knew King-Young had been sniffing around, trying to discover the weakest link in the Camden family. In fact, every time Trent turned around, he saw King-Young talking with a new person in Castleton, or he heard King-Young's name in others' conversations.

Yes, King-Young certainly bore looking into, as he sure was smack in the middle of things. Trent wondered, and not for the first time, just what King-Young's agenda was. Then he deliberately stopped this train of thought. No, I'll investigate King-Young later. Now is the time to focus on the listeria.

It was the heart of the story. Get the listeria facts first, and then everything else would fall into place. Besides, Trent had a theory about who the weak link was in John's family. If he were a betting man, he'd put his money on John's wife, LaMerle. She hated living in Castleton, and everyone knew she wanted to return to her family down South. Caroline had backed up this theory. Trent's list of suspects was growing. He grinned as he thought of the number of articles he could wring out of this investigation.

Yes, this story could make Trent a star reporter. And if he had to bend the truth a little, he would. He wasn't out to hurt anyone on purpose, but he was determined to make a name for himself. If he took some "innocent" people down in the process, so be it.

Pedaling to the hospital, Trent decided he should listen to his recording once more before he met with King-Young. Lost in his thoughts of winning a Pulitzer Prize, which in his dream was then quickly followed by a six-figure book deal, Trent didn't hear the car bearing down on him. But at the last minute, he heard the loud engine and pulled over as the car whizzed past. *Huh, that was a close call*, thought Trent. But he was so shaken by the near miss that he didn't manage to note any details about the car.

Chapter 8

As Trent pedaled to the hospital intent on finding out more about the listeria, the sisters rode most of the way home in silence. Each was thinking about their conversations at the dairy and what they might mean. Luckily, Rita was so familiar with the roads she could drive on autopilot. Driving along, in her head she kept turning over many of conversations she'd had and heard. She glanced at Ronnie and knew her sister was doing the same thing.

"So, Watson."

"Yes, Sherlock? Let's hear your thoughts."

"I thought I saw something odd when we were talking to John. He seemed truly upset as he rambled on about the listeria and what it would do to his dairy if the rumor spread. Which, as you know in this town, is probably happening already. Trent is clearly ready to write his article, regardless of whether he researches it and reports just the facts."

"Your point?" *For once it would be so nice if Ronnie just told a story from start to finish without all her little asides.*

"No need to get snippy, Watson." Ronnie rebuked her little sister and then continued, "Well, suddenly, I thought I saw the weirdest thing." Ronnie paused for dramatic effect.

"You saw John smile?" Rita butted in. Ronnie glared at her sister. *How dare Rita spoil her moment!* But she quickly got over it. In fact, she was relieved Rita was confirming what she had thought was imaginary.

"So, you saw it, too? I wondered if I had imagined it."

"You definitely didn't imagine it, but I'm not sure what it means," Rita added thoughtfully. "What do you think it means?"

"Well, it certainly gives us something to think about, Watson. It could mean any number of things."

Ronnie and Rita slowly got out of the car, thinking about what John's smile could mean.

Ronnie shared her thoughts first. "I think it means John was acting. The question is, what was the act, and what is he hiding?"

Ronnie hoped Rita was about to offer a solution. Glancing down at her empty hands, Ronnie turned to her sister and pointed at the car. "Silly us. We left the milk in the car." Rita went back to retrieve it.

"Think it's safe?" Ronnie called out only half in jest. She was actually beginning to think that John's dairy was the source of the listeria. The act she had put on at the dairy, taking a big gulp of milk in the parking lot, was for Trent's benefit, and Ronnie honestly hoped it stopped Trent from running a story based on rumors. But as she saw her sister holding the milk, her hands automatically flew to her throat. Ronnie wondered if she'd pay dearly for that gesture. *Hopefully not.*

Rita noticed how quiet Ronnie had become. She immediately made the connection as Ronnie glanced down at the milk and then looked away.

"You'll be fine. There's nothing wrong with the milk. Trust me," Rita reassured her.

Ronnie smiled. "Well, you've never steered me wrong before."

"That's right, Sherlock, I haven't." *And I hope I'm right. Listeria could be deadly for Ronnie in her weakened condition.* "Remember we don't know John's dairy is the source. Let's stay focused and work through the listeria mystery logically."

Rita unlocked the house, and the two went inside. Dewey bounded down the hall to greet them, obviously hoping to go for a walk, or at least get some serious attention. Rita immediately bent down and exclaimed, "Oh, Dew Drop, it's good to see your happy smile right now. Isn't it, Auntie Ronnie?"

"Right," laughed Ronnie. "Now give me the milk before you and fur ball break the bottles."

While Rita hugged her dog, Ronnie quickly took the cap off the cold bottle and sniffed the milk. *Well, it smells like milk to me,* she thought. Of course, she didn't know if milk tainted with listeria would have a strange smell. She'd have to ask Rita. Still, her instincts told her that if it were tainted with listeria, she'd be feeling ill by now. Even though she hated to admit it, Ronnie knew the drugs she was taking compromised her immune system and thus made her the perfect target for death by listeria. Luckily, except for Georgia, Ronnie couldn't think of anyone who wanted her dead!

Ronnie put the milk away and returned to the hall. She silently watched her sister sitting on the floor, hugging her dog. Ronnie could use a hug, too. However, fur ball was not the hugger she had in mind, although the dog was the only one available. Ronnie still wasn't a dog person, but she did pet her from time to time, which made her feel better. But instead of wasting time thinking about that, she sarcastically commented, "Are you going to sit there and tell Lemon Drop the whole lurid story?"

Rita looked up at her sister and chuckled. "It's Dew Drop, and no, I'm not."

"Well, take fur ball for a walk. I may take a short nap."

Ronnie hated to admit it, but she felt tired. Today had already taken a toll on her, and she thought maybe a nap would clear her head, and while sleeping, she'd dream of the solution to the puzzle. Before she could stop herself, she yawned.

Rita took her cue. She might not be as talented an actress as her sister, but Rita still knew when to exit. "Come on, Dewey; let's go for a walk. I need to clear my head, and I'm sure you need the exercise. Ready to go, girl?" Rita patted Dewey. Responding immediately, Dewey leapt up and down, loving the attention, ready to go.

Ronnie watched the two of them and said, in a voice so sweet it could have earned her raves from the critics, "Well, you and Snow Drop run along. I'm sure she has a lot to say. And while you're out, maybe you'll get some ideas about what's going on here in Castleton. I plan to do some thinking myself."

"Of course you do." Rita knew perfectly well that Ronnie was going to take a nap, and she would probably dream about their "case." *Here's hoping an answer comes to her in a dream.* Rita and Dewey bounded out the door.

"Aren't you forgetting something?" Ronnie called out. Rita turned back as Ronnie picked up the leash from the hall table and handed it to her. "Let's not add your arrest for failing to obey the leash law to this morning's excitement! That would be more than Castleton could take. Or certainly more than I could take, although our least favorite reporter might enjoy writing it up," she laughed. "See, you do need your big sister!"

Rita smiled as she leashed Dewey and the two walked off. "We won't be gone long," she told Ronnie, calling over her shoulder.

Rita and Dewey sauntered down the street. Watching her sister happily chatting away to her dog brought back pleasant memories. Rita had always had a dog growing up. Back then the dogs had often been mutts she had rescued from the local shelter, but Rita had treated them as if they were award winning show dogs. Pets had never appealed to Ronnie, even when she was young, but watching her sister's pleasure with her pets had warmed her heart then, and it still did. As she had long ago, Ronnie waited to make sure her sister had safely crossed the street before she closed the door. Then she leaned back against it and enjoyed the silence.

Ronnie was surprised by how tired she felt. The tension and upsetting confrontations at the dairy had unnerved her more than she wanted to admit. She felt as if she were acting in a BBC English mystery in which everyone was in a snowbound house with a murderer on the loose. *Snap out of it, Ronnie, it's Castleton, and Rita and I know the players. Too bad we don't also know their secrets.*

Her room and bed were calling her, so she headed up the stairs. She really could use some quiet time. *Maybe I'll escape with my book.* Ronnie lay down and started to read, but even the latest Scandinavian thriller couldn't hold her attention, so she soon gave up and simply went to sleep. She dreamed that huge milk bottles chased her through John's fields, but Wendell and his men were there to save her.

Meanwhile, Rita and Dewey were heading toward Town Hall and the schools. Their pace was steady and deliberate. On a beautiful spring day like this, Rita thought she just might let Dewey run off-leash a little. *Regardless of the leash laws,* Rita thought, chuckling to herself.

So, they headed toward the running track behind the school's athletic fields. Rita doubted there would be many people on the track this late on a Saturday morning. The school track team would already be done with their practice runs, and the older runners probably would skip running in favor of some yard work. It was the perfect time for her and Dewey to be there, and it would give Rita time to sort out her thoughts.

But as they passed Town Hall, Rita noticed more cars than usual parked in the center of town. So many, in fact that the Senior Center lot across the street was also full. "There must be a meeting of some kind," she observed. Dewey had no comment except a quick bark at a butterfly that flew by. "I bet very little is going on at the meeting other than plenty of rumors about George," Rita speculated to her dog. However, Dewey, who remained oblivious to Rita's nattering, simply sniffed every blade of nearby grass. Rita shook her head and added, "Why get involved, right, Dewey?"

Nevertheless, Rita paused. She suddenly remembered what the meeting was about. Kevin King-Young was to present his "vision" of the developments he expected to build. He'd be trying to encourage people to sell him land and invest in his development plan. Rita hated to admit it, but he was a smooth talker, and she was sure there would be enough people lining up with open checkbooks, while others would have already sold their land.

Neither Rita nor Ronnie trusted him and refused to invest or sell him the parcel of land they owned, and he wanted to develop. However, unlike John's land, theirs was not crucial to his development, so King-Young had given up on trying to convince them to sell. However, Rita had noticed that he seemed to be keeping tabs on them because people in town did listen to her, and they all knew that the sisters were against the proposed development.

Rita shook her head and said to Dewey, "I can just picture the meeting. There will be two distinct sides: those who want the town to stay just as it is, claiming developments will ruin its rural character; and those who will preach that now is the time to improve the town with expansion to foster new businesses and bring new revenue into the town coffers. Personally, Dewey, I think the only coffers about to be lined are

King-Young's and maybe one or two of the greedy fools who sell him their land. I do really despise King-Young, Dewey."

As Rita thought about the developer, for the life of her, she was amazed that someone from out of town could breeze into Castleton and have as much influence on people as he seemed to have–and so quickly. *For heaven's sake, he acts as if he's from here, and usually it doesn't sit well with the townspeople when newcomers do that.* But apparently, that was lost on King-Young. However, whether it was positive or negative, there was no getting around the attention and strong feelings the man generated. He was narcissistic and self-centered, a bad combination.

These thoughts brought Ronnie to mind. Rita knew her sister was self-centered, too, but Ronnie was more of a drama queen and truly has a good heart. Rita was positive King-Young did not have a good heart. Suddenly the idea of revenge popped into her head. *Now why would I think about revenge? That makes no sense. It's all about the money. Must be connecting him with Ronnie and her love of Shakespeare. Yes, with the fight about land, it does have themes of King Lear.*

Though as Rita kept walking, she had to admit there did seem something oddly familiar about King-Young. *But what was it?* Rita couldn't quite put her finger on it, but it was more than just the fact that he shared some personality traits with Ronnie. *Oh well, I'll figure it out.*

I really do dislike that man, thought Rita. She had no patience for users. And King-Young continually tried to cast everything in a light so that it looked very beneficial to all the local people. However, Rita strongly believed he was just using the townspeople, and was only working to line his own pockets. "Oh, Dewey, he's a slippery character and way too smooth to be real. Besides, his numbers don't make sense to me. It reminds me of the old movie *The Producers*. Like Ronnie has said, it is a Ponzi scheme."

As Rita mused, she didn't even realize they had increased their pace, but the two were already at the park. "Well, we got here faster than I thought," she said as she opened the gate. And just as she had hoped, the track team was gone. There was just one runner on the track, so it was safe to unleash

Dewey. Rita stooped down to unclip Dewey's leash, and as she stood back up, she noticed the runner was female. She was pacing herself, seeming to calculate each lap she took on the track.

Dewey immediately bounded along the track, reveling in her freedom. Rita smiled at her dog's exuberance, then started to walk around the field, knowing she and the runner would meet up in a few minutes. Rita wondered who the runner was, knowing she might have to re-leash Dewey quickly if the runner complained. She wanted to be careful, because as Ronnie had so gleefully pointed out, Castleton did have a strict leash law. Rita could just imagine Wendell chuckling as he served her with a ticket.

Rita reached the far corner of the track and relaxed. She finally recognized the runner. It was Caroline Camden, John's daughter. But seeing her reminded Rita of John and the trouble at the dairy.

Rita wondered if Caroline knew about the listeria. If she did, Rita believed that as a staunch supporter of her father, she would probably be very upset. John and Caroline had always been close, especially after Caroline's mother had died. Rita also knew that Caroline and LaMerle did not get along. In fact, they had engaged in several loud, public battles. Not only that, but John had mentioned that Caroline needed cash to start her own business. Maybe she wouldn't be so upset about the listeria if it made John sell the dairy. The odd thing was it might even pull LaMerle and Caroline together. *I need to find out what Caroline knows*, Rita thought. *Get on it, Watson.*

Just as Rita decided to interrogate Caroline, Dewey cut across the field and made a beeline toward her. When they met, Rita saw Caroline reach down and start patting Dewey, who immediately rolled over to get her belly scratched. Dewey shamelessly wagged her tail, pounding it on the grass, enjoying every stroke on her fur. Rita had forgotten how much Caroline loved animals. But she remembered how Caroline had driven her father crazy when she named every animal on the farm. Rita had advised him to let it go. And he had, finally, laughing and commenting, "Well, at least I have dairy cows and not beef cattle. We'll just hope all the chickens look alike and she won't notice when one or two go missing." If she noticed, Caroline had never commented.

The pleasant scene continued for the couple of minutes it took Rita to reach the pair. "Hi, Caroline! I hope Dewey hasn't ruined your morning run! Dewey, come." She clapped her hands and moved toward her dog, preparing to clip the leash back onto Dewey's collar.

But Caroline looked up and simply said, "Don't worry about it, Mrs. Tisdale. She's not bothering me at all." Caroline smiled briefly, then a serious look spread across her face. "Running is usually a nice distraction, a way of getting away from things bothering me, but I can't say it's done that this morning. I haven't been able to put my mind at ease," she admitted. Caroline stopped patting Dewey as Rita clipped on the leash, and the two women stood looking at each other.

Rita had known Caroline all her life, including having her in classes in school, and she had warm feelings for her. She had always liked and respected Caroline, and the two had grown especially close when Caroline's mother was dying of cancer.

Rita had an idea why Caroline was so upset, but waited for the young woman to tell her. She didn't have to wait long. The words burst out of Caroline. "It's Dad, Mrs. Tisdale. I'm worried about him. And right now, it's more than the usual. You know, I worry about him and LaMerle all the time. That's no secret. They're not exactly a match made in heaven." Caroline grimaced.

Rita knew there was plenty of gossip about John and LaMerle, and recently it had gotten worse. It seemed everyone in town knew LaMerle was determined to return south, with or without John. And John, according to the gossips, did not seem to care if she did. He was supposedly in love with someone else. Rita was pretty sure she knew who that was, but refrained from mentioning it to Caroline. Now was not the time. However, Ronnie had no such qualms, and was determined to find out if Lana was John's new love interest. *I'm glad Ronnie is home napping now*, Rita thought.

Rita wanted to put Caroline at ease and keep her talking. So, in a gentle voice, she said, "You know, Caroline, you and I have known each other for a long time. Isn't it time you started calling me Rita?"

"Gosh, I guess I could try, but it's going to seem funny, Mrs. Tisda...I mean, Rita," Caroline blushed a little as she replied. However, the diversion worked. Caroline seemed to calm down. Rita hoped that she would now be open about what was troubling her.

Rita wondered if listeria was the trouble she was referring to. "What has you so worried, dear?" Rita wondered how many times she had said that to her students. However, it wasn't just idle curiosity; Rita really did want to know what was wrong.

"It's my father." Rita looked concerned, and Caroline immediately reversed roles and tried to console Rita. "Don't worry, he's not sick. Nothing like that. It's just that disgusting Trent Fowler. He's driving my father crazy."

Rita decided to play dumb. *Please let me pull this off. Where is Ronnie when I need her?* "What has Trent got to do with your father?"

"Oh, it's a mess at the dairy, and Trent Fowler is at the heart of it. I was sitting on the bench under the tree in front of the dairy store, having my morning coffee, as Trent came out of the store and rode off on his stupid Italian racing bike, looking like he was in hot pursuit of some story." She paused. "You and Ronnie had just left, too. In fact, I noticed Trent had tried to sneak near your car to listen to your conversation. He's such a weasel."

Rita kept silent and just nodded her head, signaling Caroline to continue.

"Still, that got me curious, because I don't remember Trent being a customer, so I wondered why he was even there. And once he tried to eavesdrop on you and Ronnie, I knew he was up to no good, so I decided to talk with Dad before coming out for my run."

"At first, Dad just seemed distracted, and I assumed he'd had a fight with LaMerle, and maybe Trent was going to write some story about the two of them. But I know Trent considers himself a reporter of note, and he wouldn't be interested in a rumor about a couple breaking up." Caroline let out a breath, looked away, and gathered her thoughts. "I persisted, and then Dad just blurted it out. There is an outbreak of listeria, and Trent is convinced it's from our dairy. Dad is sure Trent is going to ruin him with a story before all the facts are known. Then Dad would have to sell the farm. Oh, Mrs. Tisdale, Rita, what am I going to do?"

Caroline looked ready to burst into tears. *Or was it anger?* Rita wasn't sure. She just knew she had to calm Caroline down. She reached out and took Caroline's hand. "Do nothing, dear. Trent won't publish gossip, and right now, that's all it is. I can tell you there might be one case of listeria, but it seems isolated. There is no outbreak."

"Oh, I'm so glad to hear that." Caroline sounded relieved. Then an odd look passed across her face. "But even one case might force my father to sell the dairy." It was clear Caroline was waiting for confirmation, so Rita quietly agreed. "And you know how gossip spreads in Castleton. It's like a wildfire; it flames out of control within minutes. Remember how people said LaMerle had already seduced my father before they had even started dating?" She smiled for the first time. "It turned out it was true, but even so, it almost stopped Dad from marrying her. Too bad it didn't."

Rita had forgotten that rumor. John had been painted as not caring about his dead wife, as LaMerle and he were an item only a month after her death. No one bothered to note John's wife had been dying for the last three years and was in hospice when he met LaMerle. LaMerle had worked in the hospice, which many townspeople thought was a little too convenient.

Didn't some even think John's wife's death was suspicious? Rita couldn't remember, but she thought that was the case. She had always wondered who had started the nasty rumor. When she was talking to Ronnie about it, Ronnie had commented it sounded more like a rumor Caroline would start, as she didn't want her father to remarry. Evidently it reminded Ronnie of a play she was doing at the time. But, as Ronnie not been in Castleton at the time, Rita had forgotten about Ronnie's comment.

Now was not the time for Rita to grill Caroline, so she kept silent. But she knew she had to keep going. She had to find out what Caroline really knew.

"Maybe Dad should take out an ad, denying the listeria. We could do our own 'drink milk' campaign." Caroline laughed. Since she worked in public relations, naturally she immediately thought in terms of a campaign.

"I think that might just call attention to it, dear." Rita patted Caroline's arm. She thought her laugh seemed forced, but she was glad to see her at least attempting to make light of the situation. "Your father runs a spotless operation. I doubt the listeria is from his dairy." *At least I hope it's not*, thought Rita.

"I know he does, but let's face it, he's one of the last local dairymen left, so who else could it be?" Caroline stared hard at Rita. "What can I do?"

Again, Rita thought there was more behind her words than just concern for her father, but she wasn't sure what it was. So, she decided to placate Caroline for now.

"Caroline, it's your job to be there for your father. He needs you now as much as ever," Rita said, playing the role of the comforting teacher. *Ronnie would be proud.*

"Oh, I'm looking out for him." Caroline said harshly. "I must look out for all of us. Trust me, no one else will."

Rita noticed her tone had turned almost bitter. *Why would Caroline be bitter toward her father? Did she secretly want him to sell the farm?* Rita quickly dismissed the thought. She couldn't believe Caroline would not be completely in John's corner, and they both knew how much John wanted to keep the dairy going. Or did he? Was Rita missing something? What was it Ronnie always said about playing devil's advocate? Rita certainly had a lot to chat with Ronnie about when she and Dewey got home.

They stood there letting the silence envelope them for a few moments.

Then they noticed Trent racing on his bike to Town Hall. Behind him was John, following him in his truck.

"Oh great. There goes Trent. And there's my father." Caroline practically shook with anger. "I've got to stop this nonsense. It's gone too far. I've got to set it right. It wasn't supposed to work this way." And without even a goodbye wave, she dashed toward Town Hall.

Rita watched her race away. "Something is definitely rotten in Castleton, Dewey." She had a feeling this was just the beginning of bad things. "Come on Dewey; it's time to look at the facts. We'll leave the emotions to Ronnie."

The two set off for the meeting at Town Hall.

Chapter 9

Reaching the hall in record time with Dewey, Rita stopped to catch her breath. "We gave Speedy Gonzalez a run for his money, that's for sure, didn't we, girl?" Dewey sat down and panted. "No, Dew Drop, no time to rest, we're going into the meeting. Time to hear what the Town Fathers have to say," Rita explained to her dog as she threw open the doors. "This should be interesting to say the least. Hopefully also enlightening."

The two stepped into the lobby and saw a group congregating in the Selectmen's Room across the hall. There were a couple of dozen people. Rita could tell that the meeting would be heated, as she waved to several of her neighbors who had worked to try to halt the building of a huge new pharmacy, but had lost. Obviously, they hoped to succeed in stopping the proposed new development. Rita doubted they would be able to stop it.

Another group stood near the windows. Rita recognized several of the "Just Say No" contingent. That group was against new taxes, new buildings, and anything that cost the town a penny. However, if a development lined their pockets, they were in favor of it. *That was a little harsh.* Most of them are on fixed incomes or wanted to keep the town just like it was in the past. Still, many of them stood a good chance of making money with King-Young's upcoming development. And he had certainly won them over to his side, putting dollar signs in their eyes.

Rita noticed John and Caroline huddled in a corner. Caroline had her hand on John's arm and was leaning into him, trying to keep him calm. Rita remembered his earlier smile. She still wasn't sure what was an act and what was sincere. Her conversation with Caroline hadn't clarified anything. *Did they secretly want to sell the dairy?*

Rita poked her head into the town clerk's office just as Trudy burst through the door, nearly running head-on into Rita and Dewey. As usual, Trudy displayed her air of Important Town Official. Rita chuckled to herself and asked, "What's going on, Trudy?" Trudy could be a pain in the neck, but she did know what was happening in town. The only problem was that her information and opinion changed whenever she spoke to someone new. Rita and Trudy had grown up together, and she'd always been like that, even as a child. She always wanted to be part of the popular group, and therefore said what she thought people wanted to hear. However, she never quite got it right.

"Oh, hi Rita," Trudy acknowledged, marching along next to Rita and Dewey, looking like the Important Purveyor of Information she fancied herself to be. A little information gave Trudy power, and if there was one thing Trudy liked to imagine, it was that she had power. Rita hoped she had caught Trudy in one of her magnanimous moods where information would cascade off her tongue. She had.

"It's a meeting of the Planning Board to talk about Kevin King-Young's plans to develop different parcels of land. He owns several and wants to buy more. He has big plans for the town!" Trudy explained with a wide smile her face, since she was relaying official town business, which in her mind put her in the driver's seat. Then she added, "It's an Open Meeting, so I'm sure there'll be lots of discussion."

"So, it's an important meeting?" Rita asked. She knew it was, but she hoped her question would elicit more detailed information from the clerk. It worked. Rita's silence encouraged Trudy, who looked around and saw they were alone, so she continued sharing information. Rita almost laughed, as Trudy was acting like a spy divulging top secrets.

"You bet," whispered Trudy. Clearly, she was enjoying the thought she was "in the know" and was wielding power in her job as Town Clerk. *Too bad the power is only in her head,* Rita thought. Trudy was practically salivating. "There will be arguments, or should I say strong discussions? I can't wait to see what happens."

"I'm sure you can't," replied Rita, but the sarcasm was lost on Trudy.

Trudy suddenly stopped and stared directly at Rita. Rita flinched, thinking Trudy had understood the insult. But Trudy giving Rita the eye had nothing to do with the meeting or Rita's comments and questions. Trudy drew herself up to her full height of five feet and smugly announced, "NO animals in here, Rita. You know the rules. Only assistance dogs."

Dewey ignored Trudy and simply sat at Rita's feet, her tongue hanging from her mouth in a happy smile, and thinking she had every right to be there. "Oh, I know, Trudy, and thank you for reminding me, but we're here for just a moment. Besides, I think Dewey has something to say about what's happening," Rita replied with a straight face, and with that, she and her dog pushed through the people in the doorway and stepped into the room, leaving Trudy behind with her mouth hanging open and a confused look on her face. *Ronnie's rubbing off on me*, Rita thought as she leaned against the back wall.

The meeting was already heating up, so Rita had arrived at the right time. King-Young had just finished his Power Point presentation on the development he was hoping to build, and the crowd murmured as he shut down his computer. Rita could tell the reaction to his presentation was not completely positive, since she caught snippets of phrases, such as "Who does he think he is?" and "Completely eliminates green space."

However, others were commenting that they hoped he would buy their land, while some were saying that the development seemed like a sound and profitable investment. King-Young was encouraging local investments in the development. His slogan was "Your Town, Our Investment."

Even though Rita and Ronnie wouldn't sell him their land, he had approached them several times to invest, but neither had. Ronnie, money-smart, had believed there was something off about the project. "It seems like a Ponzi scheme to me," Ronnie had commented. Finally, he'd given up on them. However, Rita knew some people in town were prepared to invest with him. And she was pretty sure George and Georgia were among those investing.

As she envisioned the development, Rita shuddered. She believed the character of the town would change dramatically, definitely not for the better, if King-Young prevailed. It was not a welcome thought. But as she was trying to decide whether to speak out, a chair scraped across the floor, and a flurry of movement grabbed her attention.

John Camden headed toward the dais, bellowing to the Planning Board, "What do you think you're doing? I heard you might be having a 'preliminary' meeting. Nice of you folks to tell me you were going to be planning how to dispose of **my** farm and build condos in **my** fields. A customer—who just so happens to appreciate fresh, local milk—came into my store and mentioned this meeting a few minutes ago. Do you hold secret meetings these days? Have any of you heard about the Open Meeting **law**?" A member of the board tried to tell John that the meeting had been posted for all to see, but John was not about to be quieted, so he steamrolled on, making his points louder and louder.

Rita glanced over at Caroline who was shrinking into her seat, clearly upset with her father, and knowing she couldn't stop him though she had tried.

"Well, I'm not an abutter; I'm the **owner** of the land in question. The law requires you to notify the owner (ME) of any meetings like this." John paused for a moment to let the words reverberate in their minds; then he continued. "Do you think you can get away with putting in the fix so King-Young can steal my land using eminent domain or something? And don't you dare tell me his project doesn't include my land!" He didn't wait for an answer, but instead yelled a little louder, "What do I have to do to convince you vultures my land is not for sale? The only way King-Young will ever get my land is over my dead body."

At that statement, Caroline looked as if she wanted to crawl under the table, but all she could do was shake her head. She had utterly failed in calming her father. He'd basically declared war on King-Young. A war Rita was not sure he could win.

Rita's heart went out to Caroline and John. However, she thought John's outburst was out of character for him. He knew the members of the Planning Board, so why didn't he meet with them quietly? *Is this public outburst part of a larger plan?* She wondered. It certainly showed the town that John did not want to sell his dairy.

Rita looked over at King-Young, who just stood there quietly, almost as if he had expected John's outburst. And as

Rita replayed the outburst in her head, she thought it did sound a little rehearsed. In fact, it had built, gaining in intensity as it went along, making him sound like Ronnie when she delivered her monologues.

Rita certainly couldn't picture John working with King-Young. But maybe someone else close to John was? LaMerle was a good candidate, but not Caroline, Rita decided.

When John stopped yelling, the silence was pronounced, but quickly changed to a buzz throughout the room. The Chairman of the Planning Board actually banged his gavel, and said, "See here. Quiet, please." Caroline went to her father and put her arm around his shoulder, trying to draw him away. But John refused to move, and his face got redder and redder as he stood before the dais, even more agitated than when he was yelling. Caroline stared at King-Young, who simply shrugged.

It was clear King-Young had no intention of antagonizing John further, but he wasn't about to help him either. Rita reassessed her earlier thought. She didn't think John and King-Young were in on it together. They couldn't be that good at acting.

Rita's eyes met Caroline's, and she pushed through the crowd toward her and John. It turned out to be a good thing Dewey was with her, because several people unconsciously moved aside when they felt a dog rub against their legs. Rita finally reached Caroline and John, and whispered in John's ear, "Let's just sit down, John. You won't gain anything by yelling at people here." In a reassuring tone, she added, "No one can take your land without your consent." Slowly Caroline and Rita got John back to his chair. He looked worn out as he sat down.

King-Young was now sitting beside the Board members at the dais, looking more like a big game hunter zeroing in on his prey than a developer showing his building plans. He stood and smiled at the crowd, holding out his hands in a calming gesture. All Rita could think of was "oily cult leader" or "smarmy preacher," but she couldn't wait to hear what he had to say. She was positive of two things: he talks in perfect sound bites to win the crowd over to his side, and John had overreacted. She noticed Wendell had appeared in the back and was quietly observing what was happening.

King-Young moved awkwardly toward the podium and began his presentation. "No one is stealing land from anyone. I will only buy land from those who want to sell. I'm offering fair prices, so it's up to landowners whether or not they sell." King-Young stared at John. "Nobody needs to die in order for me to buy their land." His smile made Rita shudder. A few people in the room laughed nervously.

Rita had to admit the man was slick. But she had also noticed his awkward gait, almost like a limp, actually, as he had stepped up to the lectern. *Did I imagine that, or could he have fought with John or someone else earlier today?* she wondered, but decided to dismiss that concern and instead, paid close attention to his comments and John's reaction to them.

King-Young's comments only seemed to stir up John even more. "Well, I'm not selling. That's final." And with that, John turned and grabbed Caroline's arm roughly. "Come along, Caroline. We've got a dairy to run."

Rita watched as John stomped off, dragging Caroline along with him. Before she was pulled through the outside door, Caroline glanced over her shoulder at Rita and shook her head. Rita nodded back.

Once the two left the meeting, Rita decided to leave, too. "Come along, Dewey, I think we've seen enough." The two moved toward the exit as the room began to buzz with comments and reactions.

Rita also noticed Lana in the hall. She had hugged John before he and Caroline left. *I think the rumors about the two of them are true*, Rita thought. Lana turned and spotted Rita. She frowned, but then smiled and waved. But before Rita could speak to her, she ducked back into the clerk's office and closed the door. *Ronnie will have a lot to say about that scene.*

As Rita and Dewey exited the room, she heard Selectman Moore's high-pitched voice calling for order. No one listened, and the people continued their arguments. The town was definitely divided.

Out on the sidewalk, John fumed, and Caroline looked as if she might faint. Rita tried to reassure them both. Wendell had come out to check on John, too. "Remember, John, nobody can force you to sell, so you need not get so upset." She was going to continue, but John interrupted.

"Rita, please don't tell me what to do." John held up his hand to stress his point. "You have no idea how much pressure there has been for me to sell the farm and leave town. Between King-Young, LaMerle, and even my children, I feel like I'm being backed into a corner." Rita noticed Caroline didn't deny wanting her father to sell the dairy. As if reading Rita's mind, John added, "Yes, even my loving daughter here has gone over to the dark side. Your sister would say, *King Lear.*"

"Dad, I just said you're getting older and maybe you should think about your future," Caroline replied, calmly. "You do what you want, but it may be time for you to sell."

John ignored Caroline. "And now with George getting sick, it's like I'm living my worst nightmare. I swear it feels like a conspiracy."

"I thought John, Jr. wanted to help you?" Rita asked, hoping to lead him in a more positive direction. She had heard John Jr. was into biotech in a big way and had thought he would use his knowledge to help his father run the dairy more efficiently. *And was it true that Caroline had switched sides?* She'd have to talk to Caroline privately about that later.

"Oh, he did at first, but now he's all about green, green, green. I keep telling him the dairy is as green as you can get, but he just laughs. He wants me to sell and invest in some plan he's concocted to develop thermal energy." John shook his head.

Rita sighed. She knew that John had mortgaged the farm to pay for his children's education, so for John Jr. to use it against his father must feel like being stabbed in the back. Rita shook her head, genuinely sad about what was happening, but glad she was here alone. Ronnie would be quoting *Julius Caesar* or *King Lear* at this point. Rita was relieved her sister was home, napping.

"I'm sure it's not that bad, John," Rita said in a soothing voice. She wanted to calm him down before King-Young or Trent came outside and found them.

"Oh, but it is that bad, Rita. How can my own children turn against me?" John railed.

"Really, Dad, we're not against you. You're jumping to

conclusions," Caroline muttered. She signaled Rita to keep quiet, as she wanted to get her father home before any more damage was done. "It's hard, Dad, I know, but it will be fine. I'll talk to Johnny and get him to change his mind. You just wait. Johnny and I will support your decision." Caroline pulled her father toward his truck.

Rita didn't like the way Caroline placed the blame and lack of support on her absent brother. It made Rita wonder how Johnny really felt. And what Caroline's plan was as well.

John suddenly stopped in the middle of the street and turned to Rita. "Remember when we read *King Lear* in high school?" Rita nodded. "I feel like I'm King Lear. Maybe I should reread the play. I don't remember it having a happy ending."

"You're not Lear, John," Rita replied, though she did see the connections. "Let's not get ahead of things," she added. "Hopefully, we'll hear that George is fine and everyone will forget about listeria. Go home and put this out of your mind." John nodded.

"Caroline, why don't you drive your dad's truck for him?" Rita suggested as she put her hand on John's elbow and steered him toward the passenger side of his truck.

"I am fully capable of driving my own truck, Rita," John muttered. "But you're right, I do need to get away from these vultures and get back to my girls in the barn. I think my cows are the only ones on my side." He yanked open the driver's door and jumped inside. "Coming, Caroline?"

Caroline squeezed Rita's arm, and then quickly hopped into the passenger seat. John pulled out and sped off before Caroline had even closed her door.

Rita waved goodbye to Wendell and turned toward home. "Come along, Dewey, it's time to report back to Aunt Ronnie. She's going to be sorry she missed this show."

Rita and Dewey walked home slowly. Rita wondered what Wendell had made of it all. She couldn't shake the feeling the worst of times were yet to come. It certainly was not the best of times.

Chapter 10

As Rita and Dewey made their way home, Ronnie began to wake up from her nap. She stretched her arms over her head, realizing with relief that her arms were getting stronger. The surgery, and then the chemo, had taken a toll, but things were improving. Ronnie smiled as she thought *Rita's healthy cooking, though I hate it, and hate to admit it, helps my recovery. Though it's her spirit that lifts me up the most.*

But as much as she loved Rita, Ronnie enjoyed her peace and quiet, and curling up in her room and shutting out the rest of the world had always been one of Ronnie's favorite things. Even when she was married or living with someone, time she spent alone, simply staring out a window, thinking about nothing was a perfect antidote for her hectic life. She had often felt as if she were running a marathon. There were the theater performances, the auditions, and readings for new roles, followed by filming the occasional part. All of it made Ronnie feel like she was on a never-ending treadmill, so she really appreciated little oases of calm. Still, the listeria mystery did excite her. And she was confident that she and Rita would easily solve the mystery before Wendell and his department did. Yes, she was ready to take on the role of town detective with Rita serving as her trusty sidekick.

Time to get up and get ready to talk with Rita about what was going on. She was just pulling back her comforter when a blaring horn jettisoned her back to reality. She jumped up and flew right to the window. *Had someone almost hit Rita? Had Snow Drop escaped?* Thankfully, she could see neither was the case, but sputtered, "Who blares his horn and scares someone to death just to say hello? Only an idiot, and Castleton has its fair share of those."

As she scanned the street scene, Ronnie noticed lots of cars parked by town hall. Ronnie wondered if Rita would stop in to see what was happening. If she did, there would probably be a good story when Rita got home. Truthfully, Ronnie might not have minded being a fly on the wall at the meeting herself. She assumed the meeting had to do with King-Young's development plans, and she knew there was tough opposition to them. Unfortunately, the greedier folks in town who hoped to profit from his plans were probably in favor of the development. *Whatever happened to caring about what is best for everybody? My God, I'm starting to sound like Rita!*

And the development was only the tip of the iceberg as far as changes in Castleton went. Rita was part of a group that vehemently opposed any new developments. They had conducted a strong campaign against King-Young, including telephone calls (Ronnie had helped write the script), letters to the editor, and other basic grassroots strategies. None had been successful enough to stop King-Young, though.

Ronnie frowned at the thought of King-Young's development project. It was the biggest controversy in town, and it seemed to be turning the town into the set for *King Lear*, with half the town in favor, and the other half against. A huge battle was brewing over land. Mostly those in favor had land to sell or were small businesses that would benefit from an upscale clientele that might purchase fancy new condos and frequent their businesses. She thought she had left the theater behind, but it felt as if scenes from Shakespeare's comedies and tragedies were playing out all over town. Ronnie chuckled; *I need to find a major role to play.*

Ronnie's mind shifted to George and the listeria outbreak. She wondered how much the listeria had to do with King-Young and John. The two were obviously major players. King-Young needed John's land, and if the listeria came from his dairy, John would be forced to sell. Then all that wonderful open space would become cookie-cutter condos, full of new players with no relationship to Castleton or interest in its history. Yes, it was a tragedy playing out, not a comedy, and John's dairy was center stage.

While the listeria and John's dairy were the current play in town, Ronnie suddenly remembered a backstory about John and his dairy. Rita had written her detailed letters about John, his children, and the dairy--the "situation" that was developing in Castleton. When John's wife was dying, rumors flew around town about John and LaMerle. John had a thing for young, buxom women, and LaMerle had fit the description perfectly.

Slowly the details came back to Ronnie. She remembered Rita telling her about the arrival of the southern belle, LaMerle. Needless to say, LaMerle had created quite a stir, much the same as Bette Davis in *Jezebel*. LaMerle had quickly obtained a job working for the local hospice organization, and her first assignment was to provide palliative care for John's wife. Soon the rumors about John and LaMerle started. LaMerle was impressed he came from an old town family and assumed he was wealthy. As for the dairy, well it could be sold, and then John would be even richer. LaMerle was sure she could convince John to sell. So she had set her cap for John and won him. But she had never been able to convince John to sell the dairy, though people said she had kept trying for years before finally giving up.

Rita had also mentioned how Caroline had reacted when her mother died, and John officially started dating LaMerle. Caroline had made it her mission to make sure the dairy was never sold and she had succeeded. Thus she and LaMerle had never gotten along.

Rita had counseled Caroline, and the two had grown close. And when Caroline moved away, the two remained tight with a mother/daughter type of relationship.

Ronnie raised an eyebrow as she wondered how the backstory affected what was going on at the dairy now. She was anxious to ask Rita about it when she got home. The more they knew about the players, the better. And even though Rita would defend Caroline to the ends of the earth, Ronnie suspected she was not quite as pure as she pretended to be. A favorite movie of Ronnie's was *All About Eve,* and Anne Baxter was certainly not innocent in that film! Ronnie remembered how much she had wanted a role in it. *Focus, Ronnie!*

Slowly the puzzle pieces began to form a pattern in her mind. She was a regular Sherlock Holmes after all! She got out her diary and wrote down a series of questions she and Rita would need to answer. Who could isolate and cultivate listeria, and how difficult was the process? Was the listeria planted? If so, why? And, of course, most important: who would plant it, and who stood to gain the most? Ronnie turned over the questions in her mind and wondered how the pieces all fit together.

John would obviously be hurt, or would he? Caroline seemed to be on John's side, wanting to keep the dairy. At least Rita had assumed that was true, but Ronnie was not so sure. Why would she want the dairy? She didn't live in Castleton, and as far as Ronnie knew, she had no plans to return. In fact, there were rumors she needed money to start her own business. Yet, she came home most weekends to work at the dairy. Why? To meet with King-Young? She certainly had opportunities to plant the listeria. And needing money, she had motive. Besides, Rita had even said that Caroline seemed distracted and different than usual. What was causing her change in character?

Ronnie wrote Caroline's name in her diary. She realized that if John sold the dairy, Caroline and her brother, John Jr., would profit, since they had a share of the enterprise. Plus, she had heard John Jr. and his father did not get along. It had something to do with John Jr.'s mother's death. As a result, forcing the sale of the dairy, which John loved, was a good motive for John Jr. Besides, being a scientist, maybe he could cultivate the listeria. Ronnie wrote Caroline's brother on the same page. And under their names, she wrote: Motive/Money. She continued jotting down notes.

Rita had said that Caroline was working on a business plan to develop new product lines for the dairy and start her own business. So, on the surface, it seemed as if she was trying to help her father. However, Ronnie knew that for her to license products and build a brand, they did not need to own the dairy itself. They just needed to own the product concept and brand. Licensing fees were a very lucrative way to earn money, making Caroline a prime suspect in whatever was going on at the dairy. As she looked at the two names on the page, Ronnie suddenly wondered if John Jr. and Caroline could be working together. She'd have to talk with Rita about this possibility.

Ronnie then turned her attention to LaMerle. Everybody in town knew she wanted John to sell the dairy. She'd been at him to sell ever since they had married. And King-Young had offered John a good deal. If Ronnie remembered correctly, it was something about a small amount of cash up front, but a big percentage of the sales of the homes developed.

Next, she turned her attention to John and Lana, writing their names on her list. *Now, those rumors are true.* And if LaMerle found out about these two, Ronnie imagined she'd force John's hand and make him sell the dairy. And she thought *LaMerle is just the type to make him pay through the nose.* Ronnie was sure that having cold hard cash to start a new life would be much more appealing to LaMerle than continuing to help run a nearly bankrupt dairy. *But where does that leave Lana?* She wondered.

The sale of the dairy would certainly be good for Lana. LaMerle would leave, and John would have cash to start a new life. Ronnie added Lana to her growing list. *It's almost as if history is repeating itself with Lana,* she thought.

Ronnie circled back to LaMerle. *Maybe being the simple Southern belle is just LaMerle putting on an act. And if so, is she actually conniving?* Ronnie wondered. After all, the whole town was convinced she swept John off his feet while he was still mourning his first wife, Emily's, death. That took careful planning and follow-through. Ronnie remembered that some people had even hinted LaMerle might have had a hand in Emily's death, but that didn't seem true. The poor woman had had cancer. Still, LaMerle had since had plenty of time to figure out how to force John to sell the dairy.

Then there's Georgia. Amazingly, Ronnie realized that no matter how much she'd like to believe Georgia would poison her husband, she really couldn't. Ronnie believed Georgia was many things, none of them good, but a murderer was not one of them. No, George having listeriosis had to be an accident. *Wasn't it?*

But as she thought more, she decided to keep Georgia's name on the list. *Somehow, she's involved,* thought Ronnie. Georgia was getting awfully cozy with her neighbor, who was available and seemed interested in her. Ronnie doubted Georgia's pride would ever let her divorce George. *But kill him?* She had trouble wrapping her head around that idea, so she moved Georgia to the bottom of her list. As she did, Ronnie had an ominous thought. *If George had been an accidental poisoning, did that mean there were more to come? Who would be next? And how would that person's death or illness affect what was happening in the town?* Ronnie kept developing her list, increasingly confident that she and Rita could solve the mystery.

Trent was next on her list. *Oh, Lord, what a player he is!* He was like a stick of dynamite, just waiting to explode. Everyone knew if Trent had his way, the listeria outbreak would become a full-blown epidemic, leading to the Pulitzer-prize winning story that Trent so coveted. Ronnie had known many reporters who would kill for stories, and she suspected Trent was another one of them. He just needed one more victim, and he'd have his epidemic. Who knew what he would do to get his story, not to mention who the story would hurt?

She started to move Trent to the top of her list of suspects, but then changed her mind. If Ronnie had to bet on the next victim, she'd put her money on Trent. She chuckled out loud as she thought about how long that list of suspects would be if he were killed. *But would someone really kill him to stop him?*

Hearing Rita talking to Gum Drop in the hall, she called down, "Rita, is that you?" *Time to chat with Watson.*

"Who else would it be? Come down. We need to talk. You won't believe what's going on in the center of town."

Oh, I just might, Ronnie thought. "Coming!" she called out as she dashed downstairs. She couldn't wait to compare notes.

Chapter 11

Rita sighed, then said "Ronnie, I hardly know where to start." She motioned for Ronnie to sit down at the kitchen table.

"Well, don't go all the way back to the beginning or I'll die of suspense," Ronnie replied, then continued, "Cut to the chase, and then you can fill me in on the details as we go." Ronnie sat down and signaled Rita to begin.

"In a nutshell, Kevin King-Young and John had a shouting match in Town Hall, Caroline did everything she could to calm down her father, but I think she actually may not be completely supportive of him. There is certainly something odd going on between father and daughter."

Ronnie nodded. Rita's observation gave credence to her own ideas.

Rita continued. "Eventually Caroline and John left and went back to the dairy. I've never seen John so upset. His exit was more dramatic than any of yours."

"I doubt it," Ronnie smiled. "But do go on."

"Well, of course, there were two sides. Those opposing development, and those who are in favor of it. You know the players. King- Young is courting those who have land to sell, and he's also looking for investors."

"How did King-Young react to John's outburst?" Ronnie wanted to know because it could influence her thinking.

"Now that I think about it, he was very calm. It was almost as if he knew what John would do." Rita looked at Ronnie. Her sister was deep in thought. Rita knew she was "making a film" of the story Rita had just told.

Of course, Ronnie was also probably adding details and connecting the story to her own thoughts. But once Ronnie was ready to share her own thoughts she'd be on a roll, and Rita would have to sit back and listen carefully. And with Ronnie, she'd have to separate the facts from the movie she had created in her head.

After what seemed like an eternity, but was actually just a few minutes, Ronnie turned to Rita, ready to hear the details.

"I saw Caroline when she was out for her morning run," Rita began.

"Really? Tell me what happened."

Rita wondered why her sister was so interested in Caroline, and wondered what Ronnie thought she was up to. As far as Rita knew, there was no evidence to prove she had participated in anything connected to the listeria. She definitely hoped that was true, and she wanted so much to believe Caroline was more than uninvolved; she was innocent. However, the more she thought about it, she was beginning to doubt that the young woman was as innocent as she had first thought.

Rita resumed, "Well, normally Caroline is quite focused on her run. However, I had let Dewey off her leash, and she headed right over, easily distracting Caroline, who stopped running as soon as Dewey reached her. She looked over at me and seemed eager to talk."

"And what happened?" Ronnie asked.

"She bent down to pat Dewey..." Rita began.

Ronnie interrupted. "Skip the dog parts and get to the important stuff. I'm curious as to what you think is going on between John and Caroline. Tell me why you think Caroline may not be totally supportive of her father." Ronnie settled back on her chair again, ready to hear more.

"Well, when Caroline and I were discussing John, she said that Trent's insinuations about listeria wouldn't be the end of the world, and if her father had to sell the dairy, he'd just have to accept it. Then she quickly changed the subject and told me she thinks something is wrong between her father and LaMerle. Almost as if she wanted to avoid talking about the listeria."

"You didn't say anything about Lana, did you?" Ronnie asked. She hoped Rita hadn't, as that was a piece of the puzzle she preferred they keep to themselves at the moment. Ronnie believed that soon there would be a perfect time to reveal that nugget of information. But she didn't want to expose their hand too soon. Besides, they had to figure out what Lana's game plan was, and how she fit into the puzzle.

"No, of course not. But let's face it, Caroline is smart, so she must know. And it must infuriate her, especially since Lana is very close to her own age." Rita wondered why Ronnie was so adamant they keep to themselves what they knew about Lana, but she trusted Ronnie had a good reason for keeping quiet about it for now.

"I think you're right about that." Ronnie knew firsthand that a May/ December affair like John and Lana's could really upset the family. Suddenly another thought came to her. *Revenge. Could Caroline be seeking revenge? Revenge has always been a good motive.*

Rita continued, "But the listeria trumps everything. Apparently, John can't get his mind off George and how he was stricken with listeria. John would like to think the bacteria didn't come from his milk, but he's worried it may have. In fact, Caroline said he's obsessed with it. I know one part of that would be because he'd hate to have his milk make any of his neighbors sick, but I think part of his obsession is related to the fact that if his dairy is found to be the source of the listeria, it would force his hand to sell."

Ronnie cut in, "I agree on both points." She decided to share her theory on George and Georgia later when they were discussing the list of suspects.

"But what I found the oddest," Rita continued, "is that Caroline didn't seem upset about selling the dairy. She almost seemed resigned to the sale."

"And the odd part?" Ronnie prompted. Ronnie would have led with the oddest part, but Rita had always needed to tell her stories chronologically.

"What seemed to bother her most was John's insistence that they prove the dairy was not the source of the listeria. I find that very curious."

"I agree, it is curious" Ronnie tapped her nails on the counter. "There has to be a good reason why she doesn't want her father finding the source of the listeria."

"One would think so. Well, the whole thing is a mess. Between Trent and King-Young, poor John doesn't seem to stand a chance." Rita paused. "I hate to think he'll have to sell."

"Well, Watson, if we can solve the listeria mystery, maybe we can save the day." Ronnie smiled at her sister. "Two heads are better than one."

"There's more, Sherlock." Rita interjected, "Caroline seemed to have forgotten about the Planning Board meeting until she saw Trent pedaling toward Town Hall. Then we saw John's truck screech to a halt in front of the building, and he jumped out and bounded up the steps. His feet barely touched the ground as he dashed inside. Even when he played football in high school, he never moved that fast."

"Finally, the meeting!" Ronnie muttered almost to herself. "So, what happened?" Ronnie leaned into the counter, anxious to hear details.

"Well, when Caroline saw John enter the building, she raced off to join him. King-Young was presenting his development plans, and it was clear John was there to stop him."

"We knew that was the point of the meeting, but what else happened?" Ronnie asked again, hoping Rita would tell her more about the atmosphere and people's reactions to what was going on.

"Well, as I'm sure you can imagine, King-Young had a slick PowerPoint presentation, but it didn't convince everyone. I heard several comments like "the nerve..." and "no way," but that didn't stop him. But some of the people there were in favor of his proposal. Mostly those fools who thought they'd profit in some way if this thing goes through."

"That figures. Idiots!" Ronnie chimed in, but Rita ignored her and kept going.

"But then John almost threatened him, yelling that King-Young would only get his land over his dead body. Of course, King-Young replied he wouldn't need John to die to get his land, and he actually had the nerve to say nobody was trying to force a sale of–or steal–anybody's land."

"Oh, SURE," Ronnie interjected. "He's such a slippery character. Trust me, he'd be cast as a swindler, like Burt Lancaster in *Elmer Gantry,* or Robert Preston in *The Music Man.*"

"I think he's more like Michael Douglas in *Wall Street,* but you definitely have the right idea." Thinking about King-Young's slick performance at Town Hall disgusted Rita.

"Keep going. What happened next?" Ronnie pressed. She needed to hear more about the interactions between the key players.

"Caroline kept trying to calm down John, but she wasn't very successful. And John's behavior really turned people off. I don't think he helped his cause."

Rita shuddered as she remembered the threats flying back and forth. "And I'm afraid King-Young's presentation will sway enough of the people in town who see it as a get rich quick proposal. I'm worried that he may succeed, and all of our beautiful open space will soon disappear," Rita said as she stared off into space. *There must be a way to stop him. Too bad he wouldn't die. Oh, don't go there, Rita.*

Both sisters remained silent as visions of ticky-tacky condos filled their heads. They realized their town was changing, and there might not be much they could do about it. Except of course, try. And neither of them was a quitter. But first, they had to solve the listeria mystery.

Rita started up again, "King-Young has been absolutely relentless trying to get that land any way he can. He's definitely working on John's kids, always reminding LaMerle the dairy is a 'gold mine,' and that if John sells it, she would be able to move back down south with a pile of cash." Rita became more and more upset as she continued. "And let's face it, if there is one thing LaMerle wants, it's money, and lots of it!"

"That's the only green she seems to appreciate." Ronnie added in disgust.

Rita nodded. "Plus, knowing how underhanded King-Young is, he's sure to have planted seeds in Lana's ear, too. Telling her that if John sells, he'd have time for a new family and money for her. We must do something."

"We do. I hate to throw a wrench in your line of thought, but I don't think we can eliminate either John or Caroline from our investigation."

"I hope it's not either of them, but I think you're right, Sherlock."

Ronnie smiled. If Rita was calling her Sherlock, she wasn't upset with her adding John and Caroline to the list of suspects. "Both would benefit from the sale. John, because he'd be able to get rid of LaMerle and marry Lana, and Caroline would get the cash she needs to start a new business. I must say that I'm surprised you agree with me," Ronnie said quietly.

"Oh, I didn't say I agreed. I just said they should be on our list of suspects." Rita smiled at her sister. "I never said if they were at the top or the bottom."

"Fine. So, we do agree we need to get to the bottom of the listeria, Watson?"

"On that, I'm in full agreement." Rita sighed.

"Well, back to the meeting. As you can imagine, Trent was scribbling away the whole time. I'm sure he'll have his own version of the events. So, our learning the truth makes a lot of sense. And the sooner, the better." Rita smiled at her sister.

"Yes, the sooner, the better. While you were out, I started to draw up a list of possible suspects." Ronnie began.

But before Ronnie could present her list, Rita reported, "Wendell was there, too. He was observing everything." Rita waited a moment before adding, "Shall we make some tea and take it out to the porch? Then you can tell me what you've been thinking while I was out."

"Sounds like a plan," Ronnie said simply. They went to the kitchen to make the tea. Ronnie filled the kettle and put it on the stove, as she gathered her thoughts. Rita got the cups and saucers. We need to play this carefully so we don't antagonize Wendell, thought Ronnie. We don't need the Chief frustrated with us; that could hamper our investigation.

After all the excitement of the morning, it would be good to have a few peaceful minutes in the sanctity of their rockers. Rita realized she was quite tired from everything that had happened, and she figured if she felt tired, Ronnie must be exhausted. Nevertheless, Rita was also curious to hear what her sister had to say, and she didn't want to wait too long.

Ronnie and Rita sat quietly at the kitchen table, lost in their thoughts, while they waited for the kettle. After a few peaceful moments, the water began boiling furiously and the kettle started to screech. Rita jumped up to silence it. She turned off the kettle, then filled their teacups.

Just as she sat back down, the ringing telephone shattered the silence once again. Rita scowled as she rose to answer it.

Ronnie muttered, "What now?"

Rita shrugged and picked up the phone, "Hello?" Ronnie noticed her sister's face go from content to frustrated. "Oh, Georgia… hello." Ronnie immediately sliced her index finger like a blade across her throat and then gagged, a not very subtle signal for Rita to end the conversation. However, Rita, ever polite, simply turned away with her back to Ronnie.

"George is dead? I'm so sorry." Rita turned back toward Ronnie and then said, "Ronnie and I will be right there." She hung up the phone quickly, as if it had burned her hand.

Staring wide-eyed at her sister, Rita announced, "George just died. Georgia is at the hospital. We must go. NOW."

They abandoned their teacups and rushed for the door. Their mystery had turned deadly.

Chapter 12

In situations like this, people in town turned to Rita, looking for comfort and guidance, so Ronnie expected Rita to race to the hospital. However, she deliberately took the long route. Ronnie turned to her sister and was ready to ask sarcastically if Rita knew the way, but the expression on Rita's face stopped her dead. *She's really upset, and I know it's more than George dying, though that's bad enough.* Ronnie decided her best course of action was simply to let her sister work out her thoughts.

As the silence and Rita's brooding lengthened, Ronnie took a deep breath and tried to prepare herself for whatever they might face once they arrived at the hospital. Undoubtedly, Georgia would be a mess, playing the part of the grieving widow for all it was worth. And given George's suspicious death, it was worth quite a bit. *But was it an accident?* Ronnie wondered.

George's death caused Ronnie's memories to flow. She found herself back in her high school production of *Oklahoma.* Georgia, George, and she were juniors. Somehow Georgia had managed to finagle a major role. *Her father being Chairman of the School Committee* **had** *to have been a big deciding factor,* Ronnie still thought. Ronnie had actually wanted the showier role of Ado Annie, but was cast as the lead, Laurie. It was the only time she hadn't coveted the lead role. Georgia won the role of Ado Annie. She sang what Ronnie thought was the best song in the musical: *I Cain't Say No!* Georgia screeched the song, not getting one laugh out of the hilarious lyrics. Ronnie also remembered that Wendell had played the evil Judd. *He should have played the hero, Curly; after all, he ended up the Chief of Police,* Ronnie chuckled to herself. *Funny how people hadn't changed much since high school*, she mused. Old feelings still linger, coloring and affecting our actions today.

Poor George had been a lowly stagehand, and at the cast party as everyone ignored Georgia after her disastrous performance, George had paid attention to her. So, Georgia had sunk her claws into him. The poor man had never had a chance.

I hope he's at peace now, Ronnie thought as she saw they were getting close to the hospital.

Suddenly Rita spoke. "I suppose we should plan how we'll handle this?" She looked out the corner of her eye at her sister, who shrugged, still lost in her memories. Rita waited a few moments, and then added, "Well, you must have some thought about what we should do in this situation, and how we should handle things." *Come on, Ronnie, I need you now*, Rita urged.

"The finest of kid gloves come to mind," Ronnie replied. Rita laughed, and Ronnie joined in as they drove on.

"That felt good," said Rita. She brushed away a tear when their laughter stopped.

"It did, but we'd better prepare ourselves for the scene ahead. I don't think laughter is the appropriate reaction." Ronnie said and became more thoughtful and serious. "I'll admit I've never liked Georgia. She was a pain in high school. Lord, remember her in Oklahoma? I thought we'd all kill her. And she's still a pain today. But no one deserves to lose someone they love. And regardless of how badly she treated George, or whether she even loved him for that matter, they were married, and she has lost him."

Rita nodded. She was in total agreement with her sister. Ronnie's insight and kindness surprised Rita, but she was not going to comment or make light of it. They had to work as a team now.

Sooner than they liked, Rita pulled into the parking lot. As they exited the car, Rita pointed out Georgia's blue Buick parked in Emergency Parking. She turned to Ronnie and asked, "Do you feel up to driving today? We might need to help get her car home."

"Sure. It's been a while since I drove, but I could take hers. I'll try not to drive it into a tree, though I'm sure the temptation will be there." Ronnie replied.

"Ronnie!" Rita tried to sound horrified, but just like when they were children, and Ronnie said or did something outrageous, Rita smiled. And Ronnie pretended not to notice.

They took each other's elbow, unified, and stepped onto the mat. The entry door swung open, revealing a perfect view of the lobby. Georgia, in a bright green tracksuit, sat on an old leather couch, leaning her head on the shoulder of Trevor Regan, her bachelor neighbor. Ronnie raised an eyebrow and whispered, "It seems she really cain't say no."

Rita cut Ronnie off and moved quickly towards Georgia. "Oh, Georgia, dear! We're so sorry," Rita patted Georgia's arm, attempting to comfort the grieving widow. Ronnie followed. Sarcastic comments flew through her mind, but she managed to bite her tongue and simply observed the grieving widow.

Georgia seemed to be trying to summon tears, and replied in a quivering, falsetto voice, "Oh, thank you." She batted her eyes at Trevor and looked up. When she noticed Ronnie, her demeanor changed. She sat up straighter and hissed, "Oh, you're both here!" She glared at Ronnie, who mouthed words of sympathy. At least that's what Rita hoped the words were. However, it was clear Georgia's plan was to ignore Ronnie. She leaned into Trevor and looked at Rita, pretending Ronnie was not there.

"I just don't know what to do. I'm so glad you're here to help me, Rita. I can use a friend." Georgia had turned back into the simpering widow.

"Use" is certainly the right word and my, how your acting skills have improved, Ronnie thought, but continued to hold her tongue.

"That's why we're here," Rita replied. "I told you on the phone Ronnie and I would be right over." Not wanting to give Georgia a chance to say anything nasty to or about Ronnie, she quickly continued. "And it's so sweet that Trevor is here, too." Rita hoped her last remark sounded sincere.

Hearing his name, Trevor suddenly sat up straighter and put his arm around Georgia and held her tightly. Georgia sighed. She was content.

Ronnie noticed Georgia's eyes were dry, yet she held a lacy, flowered handkerchief and kept patting her eyes. Her face was perfectly made up. *Who takes the time to do their makeup when your husband is dying?* Ronnie thought as she stood behind Rita.

"She's certainly milking this for all she can," Ronnie whispered in Rita's right ear. "Do you think Trevor is part of this staged performance?"

Rita ignored her sister, but she did wonder about Trevor's role, too. *Only one way to find out.* "Oh, Trevor, how fortunate you're here with Georgia at a time like this. Did you happen to be in the hospital and hear the news about poor George?" Rita asked. Her voice sounded almost genuine, but she really wanted to know how involved Trevor and Georgia were.

"No. Georgia called me, so naturally I raced right over." Trevor paused. "To comfort her, you know," he added. He removed his arm but held Georgia's hand.

"How neighborly. And I bet you will help plan the next steps, too?" Ronnie offered. It was clear Trevor was going to play the role of the helpful neighbor until both he and Georgia felt it was proper for him to assume the role of Georgia's new beau. Both sisters were anxious to hear his reply. What were the two up to?

"Well, yes, that's right." Trevor answered brightly. "Oh, you mean about the funeral. Yes, of course," he added, almost as if he were rehearsed. "The funeral. I'll do whatever Georgia needs." Georgia whimpered something Ronnie and Rita couldn't hear.

Ronnie refused to look at Rita. Even with all her acting experience, Ronnie knew there was no way the two would be able to keep a straight face if they made eye contact. Instead, she focused on Trevor. He was like a bad character actor from one of her old B movie romances. The sad thing was he thought he was so debonair. He wasn't. Ronnie wondered what role Trevor and Georgia had played in George's sudden demise. *Had they delayed getting him care? Well, there was no way to prove that, so it was a dead end.*

Rita sat down next to Georgia on the opposite end of the couch from Trevor. She gently pulled Georgia's hands into her lap. She asked, "Do you need to talk?"

"Well, what can I say? George died. And now I'm alone." Georgia gasped dramatically.

Ronnie almost admired the simplicity of the speech and Georgia's delivery, but then, this was such an act that Ronnie's disdain for the woman quickly resurfaced. "You're not alone at the moment," Ronnie commented. But seeing her sister's "not now" look, added, in a much more sympathetic sounding voice, "And of course you have many friends who will help you through this tragic time." *That should work to get her on our side so we can ferret out information.*

"Rita, you are so right. It is tragic. Poor George. I never thought he'd die," Georgia wailed, her voice trailing off. The handkerchief fluttered, covering Georgia's mouth. Ronnie refrained from ripping it out of Georgia's hand and let Rita lead the way. Rita murmured condolences softly.

Georgia looked at Rita and continued her act, hoping to gain Rita's sympathy and favor. "I know we all die, but to die so unexpectedly. He was taken from me in his prime." Georgia's arm swept the lobby.

Dear Lord, she's gone Sarah Bernhardt, Ronnie critiqued to herself. *Really, way over the top. And "prime"? She'd just spent time confirming how weak and ill George was. He was hardly in his prime. According to Georgia, he'd been on death's doorstop.* Still, Ronnie remained silent.

Caught up in her new monologue, Georgia continued, "I didn't think something like this could ever happen to me--and in Castleton." Georgia wiped at her dry eyes.

"What do you mean?" Ronnie couldn't resist probing. "You think there's something suspicious about George's death?"

Georgia answered carefully, "Well, yes. I mean I knew he was sick after the meeting. Remember, I even went out for more medicine that morning I saw you both. But I had no idea it was this serious. He shouldn't have died."

Rita and Ronnie wondered exactly what Georgia meant. It was an odd way to phrase things. But Georgia had never been the best communicator in normal times, and these times were far from normal. Still, even for Georgia, she was putting on quite the act.

Questions floated through both sisters' heads. Was she feeling guilty? Did she purposely not go for medicine as soon as

George needed it? Did she, in fact, play a role in George's death? The sisters' eyes locked. They needed answers to their questions.

"Well, Georgia, don't blame yourself. It's very sad, but you couldn't have known George would die," Rita offered. She noticed Trevor staring off into the distance. *He's trying to avoid the conversation. What does he know?* Rita wondered.

"Is there anything you need to do here now, or can you go home? You'd be more comfortable at home, and we can come by to talk with you about arrangements if you like. I saw your car outside. Would you like me to drive you home? Ronnie can take my car."

"Oh, no!" Trevor blurted out. "I'll take Georgia home. I drove her here. She was so upset she couldn't drive herself." Ronnie almost blurted out, "How convenient," but surprisingly, she didn't. Trevor turned bright red, but continued, "She and I need to talk and make plans."

Trevor didn't wait for Georgia to respond, but again, spoke right up. "Come on Georgia, let's get going." Without another word, Trevor pulled Georgia up from the couch, and playing the helpless widow, Georgia melted into his arms.

As Ronnie and Rita watched them march toward the door, they couldn't help but notice Trevor's hand sliding nearly all the way down Georgia's back. Trevor was clearly in command as the two hurried to Georgia's car.

"Let's go home," Ronnie said. Channeling Trevor, Ronnie turned to her sister and asked in a sickly-sweet voice, "Shall I escort you toward the door?" Rita shot Ronnie a look that clearly said now is not the time for jokes. The two crossed the lobby and exited.

Once outside, they saw Trevor gunning Georgia's car, careening around the entrance, and nearly hitting a bicyclist. "Oh no! Trent!" they uttered in unison. *Here comes scene two,* thought Ronnie.

Trent was so intent on what he was doing that once again he didn't even notice he'd almost been run down. The oblivious reporter blithely pedaled toward the bike rack at the main door, jumped off, and secured his bike. He reached into his saddlebag for a notebook, and then straightened back up, not even noticing Ronnie and Rita staring at him. His mind was clearly on his story.

Another woman quickly grabbed Trent's focus. It was Caroline. Emerging from her car, Caroline stood up straight, smiled at Ronnie and Rita, and headed toward them.

"My goodness, I didn't expect us all to be here at the same time," Caroline said, but added, "I'm glad you're here." Both sisters assumed Caroline must have come to the hospital to find out about George. It was clear they all thought he had died due to the listeria.

"Hello, Caroline, dear. Are you alright?" Rita was sincerely concerned now that George had died.

"Yes. I'll be OK, although I'm not too sure about Dad. He's very upset his good friend has passed away."

Trent, with his usual bad timing and worse manners, headed toward Caroline. "But that's all I'm going to say for now," Caroline angled her head toward Trent.

Rita and Ronnie knew they wouldn't get any information from Caroline in front of Trent, and as much as they wanted to question Caroline, they didn't blame her.

Everyone knew not to talk freely in front of Trent unless you wanted to see yourself quoted in the newspaper the next day. *Misquoted, actually,* Ronnie thought.

"Caroline, ladies. I assume George's death has affected you all. How are you all doing?"

"That's a rather loaded question, Trent," Rita replied, neatly avoiding giving Trent any tidbits for his story. Caroline stood rigid and silent. Ronnie also was uncharacteristically silent.

"We were just about to leave. And we have nothing to say. Goodbye." Ronnie forcibly interjected, and then she grabbed Rita's elbow and began to steer her away. Rita went along with it, and the sisters moved together toward the parking lot. "Come, Rita, there's nothing we can do here. Nothing at all."

"Good-by, Caroline. Please give your father our best. Tell him not to worry," Rita called out. The sisters picked up their pace on the way to their car.

As they drove away, they were dismayed to see Caroline and Trent still standing there. Neither looked happy, and Caroline's straight back and hand motions signaled anger. But suddenly Caroline relaxed as Trent reached her. *Poor Caroline. I hope she'll be alright*, Rita thought. Ronnie, on the other hand, worried far less about Caroline's feelings and how she was. Ronnie wanted to know what story Caroline was about to spin, what Trent would do with it, and how much he would print. *What do they both know that we don't?* she wondered.

Chapter 13

Trent watched Rita and Ronnie drive away. The sisters had a reputation for creatively solving problems, and Trent knew he could use their help. There was a major story in what was happening in Castleton, but Trent was not sure he had the all the parts of the story. Plus, he was light on facts. Mostly he was building a story on rumors and intuition. He needed facts.

Trent knew Caroline would be a good source. He was sure she knew much more than she was sharing, and as a dogged reporter, it was his job to ferret out what she knew. Recorder turned on and notebook ready, Trent focused on Caroline, and closed in on her for an interview.

Determined to throw him off his game, Caroline threw Trent a winning smile. She knew Trent had a secret crush on her, and she planned to use that to her advantage. Trent's heart skipped a beat. He remembered the first time he met Caroline. He was covering a Newcomers meeting at Town Hall. Longtime residents and businesspeople were there to meet newcomers and tell them about the town. The goal was to make newcomers feel welcome and part of the community. However, everyone knew no one was considered a "townie" unless his or her family had lived in Castleton for at least 100 years. Rita, Ronnie, and John Camden were townies. In fact, the Camden family might be "land rich, dollar poor," but their ancestors were among the founders of Castleton. Hence, they were treated like royalty. Trent had been smitten with Caroline immediately.

She'd given a speech about the dairy: how long it had been running, and how Castleton was still an agricultural town. She talked about the growth possibilities for small businesses of homemade products that could be sold at the Farmers' Market. Her speech had impressed Trent.

Trent had interviewed her after her speech, and that was it. He was in love. Caroline was out of his league, but he still had hopes. He took a deep breath. *Time to put on my reporter's hat and bury my feelings towards Caroline*, he thought. Remembering how critical Caroline had been of some of his stories, calling him a gossipmonger and not a reporter, strengthened his resolve to get to the bottom of the listeria mystery no matter who got hurt. Caroline included.

Recently, Trent had seen Caroline having coffee with King-Young. At first, he had been jealous, but then he realized their relationship was a business one. After all, Caroline worked in public relations, so she was likely trying to get work to publicize King-Young's development.

Trent decided to probe her relationship with King-Young. *Maybe she was helping King-Young purchase her father's land?* The sale would certainly benefit Caroline. She'd get cash and a job promoting the development, enabling her to start her own firm. Everyone knew Caroline was ambitious. Trent hoped Caroline didn't have anything to do with what was happening, as he knew she adored her father, but he also knew the need for cold, hard cash was quite a motivator.

Trent swallowed hard and faced Caroline. *Ready to start my investigation.*

Caroline pushed her hair behind her ears and simply stared back at the reporter. She thought, *Two can play this game. I've got to find out what he knows and what he plans to write.*

Caroline did not trust Trent. Many of his stories and been one-sided and filled with rumors rather than facts. He wrote for juicy headlines, not objective reporting. Her mistrust had only grown over the time she had known him. Too many times she had seen him leave people twisting in the air due to his innuendos and side comments. While Caroline was not opposed to shading the truth, she didn't feel Trent, as a reporter, had the right to do so.

Caroline believed Trent was after her father. Well, she planned on stopping him dead in his tracks. She would control the narrative. She had a lot to gain, but also a lot to lose if the story didn't go her way. And, she had secrets she wanted to stay hidden.

"It's too bad about George, don't you think?" Trent opened. He was trying to win Caroline over. Trent knew his time with her was limited, but even so, he figured he'd start off with soft questions. He pushed his tape recorder towards her.

Caroline knew she had to be careful, so she took her time answering. "Of course, I think it's horrible and very sad. Who wouldn't? But I'm not sure what killed George, and so I don't want to spread any rumors or hurt anyone. We need to wait for the facts." Caroline carefully emphasized her last point. "Listeria as the cause of death hasn't been confirmed yet. It's just a rumor." Both, however, knew that was not true. George's death due to complications of listeria had been confirmed.

Caroline's tense tone told Trent she was worried. That made him think she was almost certain the listeria was from her father's dairy. *I just need to get her to admit it*, he thought.

Suddenly he thought of another approach. He'd play the George card! That should get a rise out of her and a good quote. Trent remembered that a few years back, Caroline's family had had a dispute with George over land boundaries. If he remembered correctly, John's cows had kept wandering onto George's land, and George had taken John to court. The final solution had John building an expensive fence to keep his cows confined. Not a good outcome for a farmer who was short on money. Trent made a mental note to look up the details, as he was sure Caroline wouldn't share them with him. *Wouldn't hurt to ask her though*, he thought.

"Didn't George and your father have a dispute over land a few years back?" Trent tried to look innocent, but knew he failed. He'd been called a weasel too many times in his life to think he could pull off an innocent look. "I seem to remember it ended with an expensive fence."

"If you know the answer, then why ask the question? I don't have time to waste, Trent. What exactly do you want? I don't like where this is going. You seem to imply my father and George had a troubled relationship. They didn't. They resolved their dispute, and things were good with them." She was trying to remain civil and end the interview, but she also had to plant seeds of doubt about the listeria and the dairy. Caroline reminded Trent how clean the dairy was and how unlikely it was as the source of listeria. "You know listeria can be manufactured in a lab." Trent looked surprised. *Got him*, she thought. *That will send him off on another tangent.* "Besides, it's highly unlikely the dairy caused the listeria outbreak."

"Well, it's interesting you jump from my question about past land disputes and fences right to listeria. You said it's unlikely the listeria is from your father's dairy. Are you implying the listeria might be from your father's dairy after all?" Trent tried to move in closer to Caroline. He had read somewhere that invading a person's space gave the invader an edge.

"Of course it's not impossible the listeria is from Dad's dairy, but I believe that's not the case." Caroline backed away from Trent. She hoped he didn't quote her, but she knew he probably would. She'd have to tell her father about this conversation. He would not be happy, but it was unavoidable, and better it was Caroline who talked to Trent than her father. He could barely keep his temper under control these days, and that would not help the situation.

"It doesn't sound like you are so positive it's NOT from your father's dairy," Trent said, moving a step closer once again to Caroline. He really wanted to get in her face and unsettle her. "After all, you and your brother would profit if your father had to sell the dairy. And your brother works in a lab, doesn't he? For once, you'd be cash rich, not just land rich."

"Look Trent, everyone can use money, especially now in this economy, but neither my brother nor I would want to see the dairy sold out from under my father." Caroline took a deep breath. "And my brother would never manufacture listeria to force the sale of the dairy."

"Really? Are you sure?" Trent stepped back and watched Caroline. Several emotions washed over her face. Trent was now convinced Caroline did want her father to sell the dairy. Plus, there were the rumors that her brother's funding for research was being cut, and John Jr. lived an expensive lifestyle in Cambridge. Also, there seemed to be no love lost between father and son. *Could they be working as a team to force the sale?*

Trent decided to probe more about her relationship with King-Young. Somehow it was all connected. Trent was sure of that. John Jr. was a player, too, but Trent believed that Caroline was the leader.

"How well do you know King-Young?" Trent hoped the change of subject would throw Caroline off, and it worked.

"What do you mean?" asked Caroline. She looked briefly like a deer caught in the headlights, then regained her composure and determination quickly. "I don't know him well."

Trent thought her answer seemed fake. "Come on, Caroline, you work in public relations, and King-Young needs all the help he can get in that arena. Are you working for him?"

"How could I possibly do that? Don't you think that would be a conflict of interest?" she parried back.

Trent noticed she avoided giving him a direct answer. Well, he'd have to find out who her firm's clients were, regardless. "That was a simple yes or no question," replied Trent.

This time Caroline glared at him. "My firm's client list is private, Trent. It's none of your business." She paused. She decided to appeal to Trent's better side. "I know that means nothing to you, but I'd think you would want the fair, unbiased story."

"I write the truth," retorted Trent.

"No, Trent, we all know you write your version of the truth. That's why no one in town will talk to you, and why no one likes you."

Caroline turned and walked quickly away, toward her car. Her father had always told her to leave once you'd made your argument. So it was time for her to leave.

"You'll be sorry," Trent called out.

"I already am," Caroline muttered as she started her car. She peeled out of the hospital parking lot and headed toward the dairy. She was not looking forward to the discussion she now had to have with her father. It would be murder. "Bad choice of words," Caroline muttered.

Trent snapped off his tape recorder as he watched her go. Time to begin to put together his story. He knew he'd include "listeria outbreak and sudden death" in his headline.

As he continued to stand in front of the lobby door, he went back over his conversation with Caroline in his head. She had been quite evasive, and in the end, as Ronnie would say, Trent thought the lady had protested a little too much.

Still, he just wasn't sure what Caroline's game was, or even if she and King-Young were a team or just two individuals with a common goal. But he intended to find out. If it killed him, he was going to nail this story.

He briefly thought of going into the hospital and talking to the nurses about George, but decided not to do so. They'd probably just refuse to talk to him anyway, so he knew he wouldn't learn anything significant. *Time to analyze what I already do know.*

George had died from complications of listeria. The listeria had turned invasive, proving fatal. Trent realized in most cases you look to the spouse, but Georgia didn't have the means or know how to produce listeria. No, Georgia would have staged an "accident," such as George falling down the stairs. This death, whether it was an accident or deliberate, was the result of the careful planning of the listeria outbreak. The careful planning convinced Trent that there was probably a team involved. It was too complex a scheme for just one person to execute.

He put his tape recorder back in his pocket and went over to his bike. It was time to go home and write down what he knew. Then he'd attend George's funeral and see what he could stir up there. *After all, didn't the murderer always show up at the funeral?* Trent intended to find out if that old mystery adage were true.

But as Trent got on his bike and pedaled away, he decided he might want to be more careful than usual and protect himself as he worked on this story. He would put everything on a flash drive and then figure out the safest place to hide it.

George had died, accident or not. And Trent had no intention of dying until he'd won his Pulitzer. Ah, he needed to start writing his acceptance speech.

The thought of grilling suspects and watching people at George's funeral put a smile back on the reporter's face. Castleton was proving to be a gold mine after all. Trent was sure he'd get a book contract after he won the Pulitzer. He could visualize himself on talk shows. Yes, this story was going to make his career. He just had to write it.

Chapter 14

It was hard to believe that less than a week had passed since George had died. So far, Trent had refrained from publicly saying the listeria had come from John's dairy, but rumors were running wild through Castleton. Besides, everyone knew it was only a matter of time before he let loose. The funeral would prove a gold mine of "information" for the reporter, and Rita and Ronnie were interested to see what he would do with it.

Rita and Ronnie sat in their car in the church parking lot. Their main goal today was to observe. After all, according to most mystery writers, the killer always appears at the funeral of the victim. As they watched people file into the church, Ronnie occasionally glanced at her sister. She could tell Rita was mentally taking notes. *Well, I have a better memory. After all, I could learn any script in a day.* Ronnie scanned the crowd. And it was quite a crowd. "I didn't realize George was so popular," remarked Ronnie.

Rita answered, "He was popular, but I'm sure the circumstances surrounding his death are what's drawing everyone here. Everyone loves a mystery."

Most were old friends and had known George for years, while others, as is the case in small towns, were there strictly out of curiosity. Still others were the funeral mavens. They were a select group of older women who went to everyone's funeral within ten miles of Castleton. Attending funerals proved the women were still alive and kicking, and there was the added benefit of going to the deceased's home for the free food afterwards. They wore their standard black funeral dress, and depending on the season, added a black coat and gloves. Hats were optional. Ronnie thought the women were like a murder of crows, appropriate for George's funeral.

Rita hoped she and Ronnie never reached that point in life. Thinking of Ronnie racing from funeral to funeral made Rita smile. Unlike the funeral clique, Ronnie would not fade into the background. Today, she was wearing a Castleberry Knit suit with a bright pink blouse. When Rita had remarked on the inappropriate color of her blouse, Ronnie had chuckled and said it was in honor of Georgia, who adored the color. Rita had decided to let it go.

"Look, it's Wally," Ronnie nudged Rita's arm and pointed, just as "Wally the Weeper" marched down the sidewalk and mounted the church steps. Wally was a local character who attended most funerals in town. He always sat in the back pew, and he cried uncontrollably and loudly during the service, regardless of whether he had had any acquaintance with the deceased or his family. And he was always the last to arrive.

"Well, time for our entrance," Ronnie said.

Rita almost corrected Ronnie, saying, "You mean your entrance?" but caught herself; instead, said, "Well, it's a nice turn-out for George."

"It is, but half the people are here because the cause of his death is a mystery, and they want to see how Georgia is acting and what is going on with her neighbor. Besides, there wasn't a wake where people could see how he looked."

"Ronnie, that's in poor taste, but it is curious Georgia didn't have a wake and quickly had him cremated," Rita commented. "You don't look any different if you die from listeria. It's not like carbon monoxide where you turn rosy, or a poison where your tongue turns purple."

"Thanks for the science lesson," Ronnie commented. "Cremation removed the chance to run more tests or do an autopsy." They stood just outside, waiting for Georgia's arrival.

Ronnie still had trouble believing George was dead. After high school, Ronnie had never seen him again until she moved back. She knew he had married Georgia, and that was about it. While Ronnie truly detested Georgia in high school, she remembered George fondly. She remembered how he used to carry her books in junior high. Poor George, he never was part of the in-crowd, but most people liked him. He was a nice kid, and he grew up to be a nice man. *It was too bad he'd had to settle for Georgia.* But Ronnie remembered George believed once you made your bed, you should lie in it. So, she was sure he put up with Georgia and made the best of it.

After their interaction at the Cultural Council meeting, Ronnie had looked forward to the possibility of working with

George on the arts center and creating green spaces. Though Georgia would have undoubtedly put a stop to their working together. *Oh well, not meant to be*, thought Ronnie.

"George would probably have liked all this attention. He hardly got any married to Georgia," Ronnie said to Rita, but really more to herself. *Who would want to hurt kind, quiet George?* A part of Ronnie hoped it was Georgia, but deep down, she didn't think Georgia had anything to do with George's death. If someone had murdered George, it was well planned out, and quite frankly, Georgia did not have the brains for that. Besides, given he had died due to listeria, most likely his death was collateral damage of introducing the listeria itself. *How sad to die randomly and for no real reason.* Just as Ronnie was about to chastise herself for her nasty thoughts about Georgia, the widow appeared. "Speak of the devil, the queen has arrived."

A black limousine pulled up to the front of the church, and Georgia got out, dressed to the nines, as their mother would say. As she entered the church, she leaned on her neighbor, Trevor, who had his arm around her. "So nice she brought her knight in shining armor," Ronnie's voice dripped with sarcasm. Rita realized it would be a long day keeping Ronnie in check.

"Be nice, Ronnie. It's a funeral for George, not a trial for Georgia," replied Rita, though secretly she agreed with her sister. "Come on, let's join the ranks." The two made their way into the church. They settled into the last row, across the aisle from Wally. It was the perfect place to observe the crowd. Though neither sister was sure what they would learn.

However, as they waited for the funeral service to start, Ronnie wished she had a pillow for her back, because try as she might, she couldn't get comfortable in the hard pew.

"For goodness sakes, Ronnie, settle down. We're in church," scolded Rita.

"That's the problem," Ronnie muttered. And she reminded herself to make sure Rita knew she wanted to be cremated and no funeral. She wanted a big party. No sad sendoff for Ronnie. *Rita would probably want a tasteful tea after her service.* Ronnie would have to ask her what she wanted. *Best to be prepared.*

The constant murmuring of the crowd brought Ronnie back to the task at hand. All around them, the sisters heard various snippets of conversation about George's death. "Odd he died." "I heard he was murdered." "Georgia got a pile of money." "Poor guy is probably happier dead." "They say it was listeria." "I'm giving up milk." Most people were speaking quietly, but the sisters did hear "listeria" repeated frequently.

"It is official that George died of listeria," Ronnie whispered. "An accidental death?"

"I think so. While Georgia might have motive to kill him, I don't think she did. And not with listeria. Georgia knows nothing about science." Rita paused and looked intently at her sister. "So, I think George's death is most likely accidental."

"I agree. So that brings us back to the listeria. Was it naturally formed, or was it developed and then planted? And if it was planted, why? That's a pretty risky scheme to force the sale of the dairy. And was there an intended victim and George accidentally got the contaminated bottle intended for someone else? You can't convince me the intended victim was George. No one gains anything from his death, except for Georgia, and we've already concluded she didn't murder him." Ronnie waited for Rita's response. But before Rita could reply, the service started. Luckily, it was a short service. Ronnie stood and tried to work out the kinks in her sore back.

Rita put her hand on her sister's arm and held her back. "Wait. I'd like to be at the end of the line. We can hear what people say to Georgia."

"And you want to see her reactions. Good idea," Ronnie smiled. She knew her sister. Rita was on the case. *Watch out; Watson is on duty.*

Finally, Rita signaled to Ronnie to join the line, and they approached Georgia. Ronnie couldn't help but think how odd it was that Georgia waited outside to greet people, creating a receiving line. It was a funeral, not a wedding. *Maybe just the widow's bad taste.*

When they finally reached her, each, in turn, hugged the widow, Rita probably more sincerely than Ronnie. But now into the role of a grieved mourner, Ronnie decided to offer condolences. She knew what it was like to lose someone you loved.

"I'm so sorry for your loss, Georgia. Even though I was gone for many years, when I returned to Castleton, George greeted me as if I had never been away. He welcomed me back like an old friend. I'll always remember he did that," Ronnie said. Her tone must have worked because Georgia had a look of shock on her face. She was not quite sure how to reply.

Ronnie's condolences sounded sincere, but it was Ronnie. Georgia finally decided that nodding her head and then ignoring Ronnie was the best response.

However, Ronnie was not quite done with her performance. Georgia stood frozen in place while Ronnie hugged her tightly. Finally, she managed a "Thank you" through gritted teeth. Ronnie then calmly stepped back, and moved past her, making way for Rita.

Rita, too, embraced Georgia. "It was a lovely memorial service, Georgia. It was so nice to have people speak about George. I'm sure he would have felt honored. He'll be missed. Remember we're here if you need us."

"Thank you, Rita. I know I can count on **you**." Georgia replied as she glared at Ronnie. But Ronnie simply nodded and smiled, pretending she hadn't heard Georgia's insult. Georgia turned back to Rita. "It's been so difficult. And as you know, George's death was suspicious."

"Well, I knew it was unexpected, but didn't realize it was actually suspicious." Rita waited a few moments and then continued, "We heard it was listeria poisoning. How very sad." Rita patted Georgia's hand.

She noticed Georgia had already removed her wedding band and switched her diamond to her right hand. Rita shot her sister a look and discreetly lifted Georgia's hand as if she were holding it. Ronnie looked at Georgia's hands and then quickly looked away. Rita didn't have to be a mind reader to know what her sister was thinking. Rita also thought it was rather hasty for Georgia to announce already that she was single. And Trevor had not left Georgia's side. It was as if the two were glued together. *That will fuel the gossip mill*, Rita thought. But since more people had gathered behind Rita, including the minister, she decided it was time for them to leave.

"I understand people are coming to your house this afternoon. We'll see you there." Rita said to the new widow.

As they were walking to their car, they heard another mention of listeria. It was one of Georgia's neighbors saying how awful listeria had killed George. He said he was going to stop buying his milk at John's dairy. After all, the listeria was deadly. Rita wanted to correct him and tell him rarely was it fatal, but now was not the time for a science lesson.

The sisters looked at each other and got into their car. The rumors were taking hold. And once Trent published his story, John's dairy would be finished.

"By the way, I heard what Georgia said." Ronnie took a deep breath and looked as if she were ready to start a diatribe about Georgia's catty remarks. Rita started to head her off, but before she could do so, Ronnie shocked her when she calmly said, "Even though I had a retort ready, I restrained myself. I respected George, and it was no place for a fight."

Rita smiled at Ronnie. Her sister continued to surprise her. "Well, Ronnie, I'm pleased you could restrain yourself." Rita reached over and patted her sister's hand. "But I'm more interested in the listeria comments we were hearing. I understand the shock of George's death has people nervous, but doesn't it seem to you as if people are over-reacting? Some of them are convinced they might be next, as if there is some sort of devious plot to kill off the senior citizens of Castleton. And even worse, they are already condemning John's dairy. There is something very peculiar about this whole listeria thing. The timing is just too perfect for certain people in town. I'm seriously beginning to believe it was introduced on purpose. Though it will be hard to identify the perpetrators and find evidence. You?"

"I agree," Ronnie replied. The sisters continued their ride in silence. "But I think the list of suspects for planting the listeria is pretty straightforward."

Rita nodded. "Let's just swing by the house, and I'll let Dewey out before we head over to Georgia's. That way we're not the first to arrive, and it will give you some time to relax and prepare yourself for this next episode," she suggested. Ronnie did look a little peaked, and Rita thought freshening up would do her sister some good.

"Next scene you mean!" Ronnie shot back. Rita noticed she had a slight smirk on her face. Ronnie continued, "I could use a splash of cold water on my face. Besides, I should take my pills." Ronnie looked thoughtful, but Rita knew she had to be thinking about more than her medicine. "You know, between the listeria hysteria and the factions in this town, there could be quite a performance at Georgia's! I had almost forgotten about the divisions in our lovely little hamlet. But seeing people sit in groups at the church reminded me how divided the town can be. How convenient to have an aisle down the middle! The pro-development people were on one side, and those against it were on the other." Ronnie chuckled.

Rita appreciated her sister's jokes. But underneath the humor was a kernel of truth. The town was divided. Not only about how it should grow and what kind of town it should become, but about this whole listeria mess, and what it meant. *It means trouble is what it means.*

Soon they were home. As they got out of the car, Rita said, "I'll just let Dewey outside to do her business, and then grab the banana bread, and we'll be off. That should give you time to take your pills and freshen up." Rita didn't wait for a reply, but instead, hurried down the walk.

Ronnie went immediately to her room, grabbed her pills, took them, and then went to the bathroom to splash some cold water on her face. She looked at herself in the mirror. *A little more make-up wouldn't hurt, either* she thought. She put on more lipstick and fluffed her hair. *Much better.* And then she was out the door and back in the car. She'd just sit there and wait for Rita. Ronnie closed her eyes and thought about everything that was happening. She'd take the time to review her list of suspects. But as she began to review the list, another thought struck her. What were the suspects guilty of: murder, accidental death, or nothing at all? She wondered, too, if George's death was the first in a line of evil events happening in their town. *Good thing we're not in Maine or I'd say we were in the midst of a Stephen King novel,* she thought. Of course, thinking of Maine and mysteries also reminded Ronnie of *Murder, She Wrote*, which brought back, for the umpteenth time, her irritation at Angela Lansbury's getting the part that should have gone to her. *And just because she was younger than me.* It still irritated her.

But as her mind started following this thread, she remembered the important thing right now was what was happening in Castleton. *"Focus, Ronnie, focus,"* she said out loud, and switched back to the mystery at hand.

Based on the comments she and Rita overheard at the church, many people were wondering not only about how and why George died, but if the danger was over. Ronnie supposed until the inspectors isolated the source of the listeria, which could take weeks, John could keep selling his milk until it was proved his dairy was the source. So, all bets were off in terms of what would happen next. And if listeria proved to be "still out there," she wondered if they were just waiting for the other shoe to drop. *Would there be a next victim? And if so, who?* Clearly, she and Rita had to get busy and solve this mystery, or things might easily spiral out of control.

Rita joined her in the car. Ronnie took the bread from her sister. It smelled delicious. "Honestly, I don't know how you got up so early to make this heavenly bread," Ronnie said, sounding genuinely amazed. "Of course, if we were in New York City, you'd have had your choice of numerous bakeries, and you could have avoided the extra work. I do miss the city sometimes."

"Yes, and in New York, we'd probably know so few of our neighbors that we wouldn't even be in this situation of having attended the memorial service of an old friend and now heading to his widow's house," Rita replied.

"Well, at least we'll have some banana bread to eat while we start our investigation," Ronnie added as they arrived at Georgia's house and parked the car at the curb.

"Onward!" Rita proclaimed.

Ronnie stopped, put her hand on Rita's arm, and said, "Wait. We're here to investigate, so let's prepare. It seemed very odd that so many people at the service were talking about listeria. Usually people don't do that: they talk about the person who has died. They don't focus on the circumstances, or cause, of death, do they? Or is it a strange Castleton rite I know nothing about? I know Castleton is a sweet, rural town, but the focus on how and why George died seems odd."

Rita turned to face her sister. "No, it has nothing to do with Castleton. I thought the same thing. And some people, and certain professions, ordinarily would be the last ones to engage in such talk. Even Ted Johnson, the pharmacist, and Dr. Johnson seemed preoccupied with the listeria, not George. Since George was a townie, I thought people would talk about George."

"I know what you mean," Ronnie added. "Also, Wendell. You'd think the Chief of Police would just express his sympathy and not talk about anything else related to the death unless he were actively investigating a case. But I saw him questioning Georgia and several of her neighbors. Makes me wonder if he suspects some sort of foul play. We won't know anything about the source of the listeria until the State finishes its inspection and tests of John's milk as well as other possible sources. So, while we wait, let's hope there was only one bottle of contaminated milk in circulation. Though I doubt that's true. And if there are other bottles out there, it clearly means George was not the target. He was a random victim."

Rita thought for a moment before she answered. "Well, let's not get ahead of ourselves, but I do think there is something rotten in our fair town. Whether it is an unexplained, sudden listeria outbreak or something more nefarious, I don't know. It certainly makes you wonder, though, doesn't it?" She exhaled a long, slow breath.

Ronnie nodded in agreement and rang the bell. "Time to get to work."

Chapter 15

As Ronnie and Rita waited for someone to answer the door, they shared more thoughts. "The more I think about it, I keep coming back to believing the listeria outbreak was planned and is part of a larger scheme. The timing benefits many people. And as for George, as we've said, I can't seem to get it out of my head that George was a random victim. And if that's the case, it's going to be really hard to find concrete evidence to link someone to planting the listeria." Rita said as she shook her head. "I realize you haven't been back long, but is there anyone you can think of who would want George dead?"

"No, I can't, and that includes Georgia. I'm sure she loves the role of forlorn widow better than beleaguered wife, but as we've said before, I doubt she would murder George." Ronnie frowned and shrugged her shoulders. "We've got to narrow down our suspect list. There are too many red herrings. A fish I never cared for, by the way."

Rita smiled at her sister. She loved Ronnie for trying to joke in the midst of mayhem. "You're on the right path. George probably wasn't meant to die, but the listeria seems to have been introduced on purpose. And it could very well force John to sell the dairy. That may be the motive behind it all." The women stood on the stoop in silence, so lost in their thoughts they didn't even hear Trent creep up behind them or pull out his recorder to tape their conversation.

"That's a neat theory, ladies," Trent said. What the sisters had said matched what Trent had been thinking, and it was nice to have his theory confirmed.

Both Ronnie and Rita jumped. Ronnie, of course, placed her hand over her heart and then raised the back of her hand to her brow. *Still a drama queen*, thought Rita. However, Trent's actions, as usual, angered her. Trent used the gossip he gained to hurt people as far as Rita was concerned, and she could not tolerate that.

"Trent, you nearly gave me a heart attack," Rita replied icily. Even as a child, Rita had disliked surprises, and she still did. And the last person she'd want eavesdropping on her and Ronnie's speculations about George's death would be Trent. He'd publish their theory before they had time to investigate it.

"You are the sneaky one, aren't you, Trent?" Ronnie glared at him. *Totally understandable that people don't trust you, Scoop,* Ronnie thought. Trent simply grinned. Ronnie frowned. Sometimes she had the occasional premonition. Maybe it came from her years of predicting the critics' reviews. And most of the time, her feelings were right. Even Rita, who based her thinking on facts, was impressed with Ronnie's skills.

Right now, Ronnie had a very bad feeling about Trent. She realized she had first had the feeling in her room when she was composing her list of suspects, but now it had returned with a vengeance. It felt to her as if a black cloud hung over him. Ronnie thought he was inadvertently putting himself in danger. And as much as she disliked him, she didn't want to see anything bad happen to him. But what could she do?

"I'm sorry, ladies. I'm so accustomed to listening to others talking, I sometimes forget to announce myself." He smirked at the ladies, bowed, and rang the bell again.

As if Trent had the magic touch, the door flew open, and there stood Lana, dressed in a pretty peach-colored dress. The dress made her look like innocence personified. However, it was cut low, as most of her clothes were, and the jersey fabric hugged her curves. It made Ronnie think Lana was not as innocent as she acted. Ronnie moved her up on her list of suspects who might have introduced the listeria.

"Please come in. Georgia is upstairs, changing. I told her I'd let people in for her." Lana stepped aside so the three could enter.

Rita smiled at Lana. "Thank you, Lana, it's nice of you to step in and try to help. We brought a banana bread to share." Rita handed Lana the bread.

"It's the least I can do," Lana said, and hurried off to the kitchen with Rita's bread.

Ronnie and Rita exchanged a look. Ronnie pulled Rita away from Trent and muttered under her breath, "Why is

Georgia upstairs changing? She needs a new outfit like I need a hole in the head. She should be wearing a simple black dress and maybe pearls. Obviously, Georgia is going to be playing the role of the merry widow. I mean 'marry' not 'merry.' Ladies, lock up your husbands!" She managed to sound disgusted and humorous at the same time.

Lana reappeared with the bread on a platter and placed it on a table overflowing with casseroles, breads, cheeses, and dips. Ronnie stared at Lana. Though she wasn't showing, her face was much fuller and she looked like she had gained weight. Ronnie was positive Lana was pregnant. The only question was: who was the father? As if in answer to her question, Ronnie noticed John quickly leave his wife's side and move towards the table. Since his plate was full, it was not food he was after. LaMerle did not look pleased. Ronnie raised her eyebrow and tapped Rita on the shoulder. "John is the father."

"Later, Ronnie. One suspect at a time. We're here for Georgia." Rita said it loud enough so that Trent would hear her. She hoped her remark would make him focus on Georgia and not follow them around, listening to every word they uttered. Rita stared at Trent, giving him her famous teacher's look. And just like all the students who didn't complete their homework or misbehaved in Rita's class, Trent couldn't hold her gaze, and he slunk off to the living room.

"I thought he'd never leave," whispered Ronnie. "Let's circulate. Take mental notes. We'll discuss what we observe at home in private."

"Roger, Miss Marple." Rita walked quickly away before Ronnie could light into her for the Miss Marple crack. Rita knew Ronnie considered herself more like Myrna Loy from the *Thin Man* series, certainly not Miss Marple. Chuckling, Rita went to the dining room table and got a cup of tea, then faded into the crowd. It was time to be as observant as possible.

John and Lana were chattering by the food table. They were in a corner, and the first thing Rita noticed was that they seemed a little too cozy. Lana kept instinctively picking lint from his jacket and then smoothing the fabric. It was the kind of thing only a wife or lover would do. It seemed to confirm what both sisters suspected. Rita wondered how serious the relationship was and what John would do once he found out Lana was pregnant.

Meanwhile, LaMerle ignored the two lovebirds, which seemed quite strange and out of character, since Rita had a strong sense that LaMerle was a fighter and would want to put Lana in her place. She noticed, however, LaMerle's eyes kept going to King-Young. *As Ronnie would say, I smell conspiracy.* Rita sipped her tea and moved on to the living room. The scene looked like it had been staged as a drawing room scene from a PBS English mystery set.

Georgia was holding court. Regally, or trying to appear regal, Georgia sat in what Ronnie would undoubtedly call the Pope's chair. It was a high-back chair from the early 1900s with claw feet and elaborate arms that made it resemble a throne. Though the chintz pattern of bright pink roses made it look absurd. Rita shuddered to think how Ronnie would describe the scene. Bad Tennessee Williams or New Orleans cathouse immediately came to mind. Poor Georgia. Her taste in decorating was completely lacking. But Georgia's lack of taste was not Rita's focus. She needed to see how Georgia was managing her sudden widowhood. And more important, if she was hiding something.

As Rita watched Georgia, it seemed as if she had changed personalities. Today, Georgia was acting like a flirty teen instead of the somber, often irritated matron of old. Georgia had changed into a smart black wool dress that was cut a little low for someone her age, not to mention a grieving widow. Her lips were painted a bright cherry red, and she had even put rouge on her cheeks. Then there was the jewelry. There was too much, and it was too sparkly. The gold and stones glistened. *Whose attention was she trying to attract?* Rita knew Ronnie was going to have a field day when they got home.

And she was cooing at several of the widowed men from the neighborhood. Given her actions, one could easily suspect Georgia of having given George the listeria. Rita shook her head and filed away her observations. She and Ronnie would analyze it all once they got home.

Mrs. Osgood, who had been Georgia's neighbor for over 40 years, sidled up to Rita and muttered, "Disgusting, isn't it?"

Rita said nothing, hoping silence would keep the woman talking. It had always worked with her students, and even Ronnie usually fell for the trap. She wanted to see what Mrs. Osgood had to say. It didn't take long for Mrs. Osgood to fall into the trap. Rita began to take mental notes.

"It's certainly NOT proper for a widow to be showing off her assets to every available man," Mrs. Osgood clucked. Rita thought she looked like a cobra staring at a mongoose. "Quite unseemly, I would say, wouldn't you?" But then, Georgia always has been kind of a tramp, hasn't she? After all, she trapped poor George into marriage and then basically has flirted with every man who crossed her path ever since."

Rita vaguely remembered rumors that dear, proper Mrs. Osgood had a secret crush on George. He was sweet and always did things for his neighbors, so Rita thought the rumors were probably true.

"Maybe it's the only black dress she has. After all, George did die rather suddenly," said Rita, hoping she had deftly sidestepped the issue.

"Oh, please, Rita. You know as well as I do that black is her second favorite color. She would have worn pink if she thought no one would say anything. I can tell you that dress is a recent purchase, and it was not bought with George's memory in mind. And all the jewelry? There to draw the eye, certainly," Mrs. Osgood commented disgustedly.

Rita's focus began to drift away, but Mrs. Osgood was not done. "Besides, how sure are we that George's death was so sudden? She could have been poisoning him with arsenic for years. She does have a garden, and she uses it." Mrs. Osgood moved in closer and said in a stage whisper, "You know, Georgia has always had a thing for her neighbor, Trevor." Rita snapped back to attention. Mrs. Osgood continued, "He's the one staring down her dress and sucking his ice cubes. And now that they are both single, I wonder what will happen." Mrs. Osgood was visibly shaking. "I'd better get something to eat before I give in to the urge to slap Georgia silly." And giving one last zinger about the lack of respect Georgia was showing Mrs. Osgood's George, she wiped her eyes with her white, lace handkerchief and marched into the kitchen.

Rita had a hard time picturing Georgia having an actual affair, but she was the type that believed she needed a man. It was clear Mrs. Osgood vehemently disliked Georgia. *Perhaps she had more than a crush on "my" George? I wonder if Georgia knew. Then again, did George?*

That idea added names to her list of suspects. Now if this were a Miss Marple novel and Mrs. Osgood was the killer, then the listeria would have been meant for Georgia, and George would have been killed accidentally. Rita thought for a moment about it as she took another sip of tea, but brushed away those flights of fancy. No, that was stretching it. She crossed Mrs. Osgood off her list. She was still convinced George was simply an accidental victim. No matter what love triangle existed, if one did, killing George was not the solution. She wondered what Ronnie was observing.

Ronnie swirled her ice cubes. The scotch was not a good one, but Ronnie was not sipping it for its taste. It was simply a good prop. In truth, Ronnie was not supposed to drink much alcohol due to the medications she took. So she was careful about when and how much liquor she consumed. But holding the drink allowed her to fit in with the crowd and to observe without appearing to be snooping.

While Lana and John were having a tête-à-tête in one corner, Ronnie saw LaMerle go to King-Young in the opposite corner. There were no intimate moments with LaMerle and King-Young, but the two did seem deep into their conversation. *Even more reason for me to move over there and eavesdrop*, thought Ronnie, and so she did.

"How much is the land worth?" LaMerle pointedly queried King-Young. Ronnie had the feeling this was not the first time LaMerle had asked this question. From her stance, LaMerle was determined to get a solid and precise number, but it was also obvious King-Young had no intention of giving a straight answer, no matter how hard LaMerle pressed him. He tried to move away, but LaMerle blocked him.

"After all I've done for you, you owe me, and I want that answer. Now." LaMerle's raised voice caused others to glance over at the two. King-Young shot a look at John and Lana, but

John was totally focused on Lana and didn't notice them, so King-Young relaxed.

"Look, I can't say exactly, but I will say it's worth well more than a million," whispered King-Young. Ronnie almost spit out her drink. She would never have guessed John's land was that valuable. "But it's not worth anything if John won't sell."

"Don't worry. He will," hissed LaMerle. "He'll have no choice."

"Well, I hope so, but he flat out told me–publicly even-- he'd die before he'd sell to me." King-Young again looked across the room at John. "Though it looks like he might need the money," King-Young chuckled, obviously referring to Lana. LaMerle ignored his barb.

"Don't worry, I will make sure he sells the land. And as for that hussy, if we were down South, she'd be strung up by midnight. Too bad we're not." LaMerle replied angrily. "But trust me, she will not see a penny of my money."

"Sugar, I believe it's John's money," chuckled King-Young. At that, LaMerle simply laughed. "We shall see," she replied cryptically.

"Well, you know the terms of our deal, LaMerle," King-Young said too smoothly. Ronnie frowned. It was his tone and mannerisms. Something seemed very familiar about that man. Automatically, Ronnie began scrolling through the men in her past. Still, no one popped to mind. She'd have to ask Rita if King-Young seemed familiar. Ronnie looked away, then back at him. *Who does he remind me of?*

Ronnie found that when she wanted something to pop into her mind, she often thought of something else. So, she returned to her list of suspects. Trent popped into her head. *Would he manufacture his story?* Ronnie thought he might, but she'd have to give it more thought. *And speaking of Trent, where is he?* she thought as she glanced around the room, but she didn't see him. LaMerle's comment about her and King-Young's deal made Ronnie focus.

"Listen, you'll get your land, and I shall get MY money." And with that, LaMerle flounced away, announcing to no one in particular, "I need a drink." The daggers she threw at John just seemed to bounce off him as he remained in deep conversation with Lana. But from the disturbed look on Lana's face, Ronnie did not think that conversation was going her way, either. John seemed more angry than happy.

King-Young watched LaMerle get a drink, observed Lana and John, then shook his head and slithered his way toward Caroline. *Now why would King-Young want to chat up Caroline?* Ronnie knew she was not in favor of John selling the land. *Or was she? There were rumors that both kids could use the cash from the sale of the land, but Caroline had appeared to be supporting John in not selling. Was that all an act?* Ronnie would have to ask Rita if Caroline had done any acting in high school. Though public relations did require people to put on acts.

But just as she was about to over to spy on Caroline and King-Young, she was stopped dead in her tracks. Trent, who had been scribbling away in his notebook, halted all conversation with a prophetic announcement. "Make sure you all read my next story. As Shakespeare said, 'There's something rotten in the village of Castleton'." And with a flourish, he slammed his notebook shut, and dashed across the room and out the door.

The room went silent, and no dared look at anyone else.

Chapter 16

Ronnie wanted to escape the shocked faces and mounting silence among Georgia's visitors, so she found Rita, and the two stepped onto the porch and watched Trent pedal off. Ronnie was thinking Trent looked like Elvira Gooch in the *Wizard of Oz*, perhaps not even as attractive, but he did look evil. Rita simply thought he was foolish and too full of himself. Both were afraid of the havoc he would create once his story was published. As possible headlines flashed through Ronnie's head, she wondered if a house would fall on him.

Rita shook her head sadly and said, "I hope he doesn't do anything foolish. That was quite the exit, but I think he opened a hornet's nest and doesn't realize how badly he could get stung. I think his story will be full of innuendo and assumptions based on rumors and hearsay."

Surprisingly, Ronnie totally agreed with her sister and had nothing more to add about Trent. "I agree. Let's go home. I'm tired, so I want to share what I heard while it's still fresh in my mind. I did note some interesting things, and I think we're on the right path. But Watson, it's going to take a lot of legwork and connecting the dots to prove anything."

Rita nodded. She was, however, more concerned that Ronnie looked so tired than she was about the mystery. She hoped all the excitement would not cause problems for her sister. So far, the Big C, as they referred to it, had remained in remission, but Rita knew how harmful stress is.

Ronnie smiled at her sister. "Lose the worried look, Rita. Your big sis is fine, just tired. Don't worry. I promise to take a nap."

The two went back into the house to say their goodbyes. Their mother had firmly instilled manners in them, and they could not possibly leave without thanking Georgia and saying goodbye, no matter how much they wanted to escape quickly.

"Let's go to Georgia first to say goodbye," Rita suggested.

And get that over with as quickly as possible, Ronnie thought. Ronnie glanced at Georgia, who was still holding court and showed no signs of abdicating. She looked as if she did not want to be interrupted. "You always were the polite one, but I think she's pre-occupied, and we could sneak out. Mother would not disown us. Besides, we'll send her a lovely note. I think Trevor has Georgia covered, literally."

Rita hesitated, and then nodded and took her sister's arm. The two quietly slipped out of the house.

Once home, Ronnie asked for some tea. Rita immediately put the kettle on and took out a tin of tea biscuits. If Ronnie is asking for tea, she must really be tired. Rita crossed her fingers. "Let her just be tired, please," Rita thought, sending a silent prayer to whomever is in charge of such things. So far, her silent prayers had been answered.

Sipping their tea while munching their biscuits, the sisters organized their thoughts. *Ronnie isn't even complaining about the biscuits, so she must have a lot on her mind*, thought Rita. Ronnie put down her teacup. Suddenly, she looked energized; even her eyes were sparkling. The change made Rita's heart sing. *Nothing like a good mystery to perk up Ronnie. A good cup of hot tea doesn't hurt either.* Clearly Rita knew she should let her sister go first as they shared what they had observed. True to form, which was Ronnie's plan, too.

"I'll go first. Here's what I noticed," said Ronnie. "First, we had to have been right about Lana. She is pregnant, and John is clearly the father. The two talked as if no one else was around, and as the saying goes, had eyes only for each other. I must admit John did seem to be a little angry with Lana, and she looked hurt, so I'm not sure he is thrilled with the pregnancy, which makes a lot of sense. I doubt he wants to be a new father at his age."

Rita nodded in agreement. John is a little long in the tooth for new fatherhood.

Ronnie continued, "I did notice LaMerle was aware of their behavior, as was King-Young, so that adds some spice to the pot, wouldn't you say?" Ronnie laughed as she sipped her tea, enjoying her narrative.

Rita could see that their sleuthing was reviving her sister, so she jumped in with her own report. "Well, Caroline noticed them, too. She didn't do anything or say anything, but I think her total silence speaks volumes. After all, Caroline has been the apple of her father's eye all her life, whereas John Jr. and John have never gotten along. John Jr. adored his mother, and once she died, he moved away and seldom returns home."

"Caroline has never liked sharing her father since her mother died. She's never cottoned to LaMerle, though I must admit I can't blame her there, but Lana is much more of a threat, especially if she is pregnant," Ronnie added.

Rita frowned. She liked Caroline, but she was practical enough to know that liking someone didn't prevent the person from doing something evil. She picked up the narrative, "And we mustn't forget the rumors about how both Caroline and John Jr. could use cash. I happen to know that John has given both kids shares in the dairy. It was a tax break for him, but could prove a windfall for the kids. So, if Lana is pregnant, she is a threat to the whole family."

Ronnie quickly jumped back in, "Oh, trust me, Lana is pregnant. She drank only juice, avoiding not only alcohol but also caffeine in the tea and coffee. And when she wasn't intimately picking lint off John's jacket, she was rubbing her stomach. And LaMerle noticed. Believe me, she noticed. If I were Lana, I would not want to be in a dark alley with LaMerle. Or Caroline for that matter, as she has no desire to become a big sister at this point in her life. And I'm beginning to think we can even add John to our list, too. It makes me wonder if Lana is due for a special bottle of milk."

"Well, our list of suspects and motives is certainly growing, but I'm still even more convinced that George was an accidental victim." Rita explained. "And according to Mrs. Osgood, Georgia is not going to be the grieving widow for long. I think it's Trevor who will be warming her bed. But I still don't think Georgia planted the listeria and murdered George. And neither did Trevor. Neither has the gumption nor brains to think through that complex a murder. I also don't think either of them would let George die. I think Georgia just didn't realize how sick George was."

"As much as I'd like to see Georgia starring in a prison movie, I agree." Ronnie laughed, "I swear, Castleton's like a geriatric *Peyton Place.*"

Rita was thrilled to hear her sister laugh. However, she couldn't help but think it was too bad that death was the cause of her joy. "I'm not so sure we should write off George's death just yet. I think our churchgoing, devout Mrs. Osgood had a thing for George, so who knows? Maybe Georgia was the intended victim?" Ronnie raised her eyebrows and looked directly at Rita.

Rita disagreed. "No, that's the plot of a cozy murder mystery, not real life. Georgia, Mrs. Osgood, George, and Trevor may fall into the star- crossed lover category, but none is a murderer. Let's deal with reality and not investigate as if we're in an English movie."

Ronnie sighed in agreement at that last statement. *Reality it is.*

Rita grabbed a pen and paper. "Let's write it all down. Seeing it in black and white will help." Rita wrote as the two once more reviewed what they had seen.

"So, I heard LaMerle say she was positive John would sell the land, and she was determined she would get her share." Ronnie paused, then blurted out, "Can you believe King-Young said John's land is worth over a million dollars?"

Rita thought about it for a moment, then replied, "That sounds like a lot, but land is precious, and Castleton is ripe for development. So, I guess no, I'm not too surprised." Then she added, almost as an afterthought, "And of course, that gives LaMerle, John's kids, and even Lana a million reasons to force John to sell the land."

Ronnie looked intently at her sister and asked, "You're thinking what I'm thinking?"

Rita nodded. "Yes, as we have said, the listeria is a way to force John to sell."

Both sisters sat in silence for a moment. "It may have started as a scare tactic, but now, it's murder," said Ronnie quietly.

"Yes, it is," Rita replied. "And I don't think it's the last one, either."

"Neither do I. And what's worse is that now Trent is going to publish his story."

The sisters contemplated the possible outcomes, none of which were good. They even composed a list of possible future victims. Trent was at the top, followed by Lana. Both wondered if they should add their own names to the list of possible future victims. Trent was at the top, followed by Lana. Both wondered if they should add their own names to the list as well. They decided not to do so. At least not yet. After all, investigators rarely died in their favorite mysteries. And Angela Lansbury had done twelve seasons of *Murder She Wrote*, plus several TV movies, much to Ronnie's chagrin.

Meanwhile, as Rita and Ronnie were reviewing all that they had observed, Trent was madly writing his Pulitzer-winning story in his head as he pedaled home. He was convinced George was murdered. And whether intentional or accidental didn't matter. Murder was murder. And murder is a front-page story!

Trent had convinced himself the listeria was not natural. It had been deliberately planted in John's milk to force him to sell the dairy. Trent's key suspects were LaMerle, who wanted the money from the sale so she could get out of Castleton; King-Young, who needed the land to develop; and John himself, who was obviously in love with Lana.

Trent's front tire hit a bump in the road, and it almost toppled him over. But it didn't shake him up enough to distract him from working out his theories. "I probably should add John's kids to the list, too, although I hate to think of Caroline in that role," he said out loud. Trent was surprised to realize his feelings for Caroline were still there, and still rather strong. He continued talking out loud to himself, "Set aside any feelings for Caroline. She may be a murderer, and that would make a good story. Besides, if she is the killer, there's no point in pining over her." He kept writing his story in his head as he pedaled toward home.

He began listing possible motives. Greed was often the motive for murder. And each suspect was motivated by greed. Jealousy was another motive that his suspects had covered in spades. Trent realized he also felt there was something off about King-Young, too. Granted, he fit the stereotype of the greedy developer, but there was more to it--something distinctly "fishy" about him. It suddenly occurred to Trent that King-Young reminded him of those characters in novels who had escaped from somewhere, came back for revenge, and had something to hide.

The fact that Trent had noticed Ronnie kept staring at King-Young, which Trent knew wasn't because of the developer's looks, proved to him that other people also thought there was something peculiar about him. Clearly, he gave people pause. "Plus, don't forget, the man seemed familiar to both Ronnie and Rita. And if he is familiar to them, where do they recognize him from? And how will I find this out?" *Better look into his past*, thought Trent.

Trent slowed his pedaling for a moment as he reviewed the scene at Georgia's one more time in his head. *Yes, I will add Caroline and Lana to the list of suspects.* Lana hadn't looked very happy with John, and she'd be in a better position if John were forced to sell. She'd be the mistress of a man with cash, which was much better than a man with a ruined dairy. And everyone knew Caroline needed money, so he moved her up his suspect list. He smiled. The only people he was certain had nothing to do with the listeria were Rita and Ronnie.

Trent sped up again. He had to get home to write up his notes. This story was going to be his ticket out of Castleton. Good that he already had his Pulitzer speech ready. He had written it when he was ten and had decided to be a reporter. He was sure he'd get to give that speech after his story about what was happening now in Castleton was published.

Trent arrived home, parked his bike, and raced upstairs to his apartment. He hated that the only place he could afford was right above where he worked. When he got his big break, he was going to make sure he lived far away from the *New York Times* offices, star reporter or not. As he put his key in the lock to unlock his door, the door simply swung open. *Odd*, he thought, *I know I locked it before I left*. However, in his excitement, he dismissed the open door and assumed he must have left it unlocked.

Immediately, he powered up his laptop and pulled out his notebook and tape recorder. Even though he had taken notes, he'd also let his recorder run the whole time he was at Georgia's. Several times, he had left his recorder hidden under a napkin so he could secretly record conversations. Trent knew it was unethical, but it was the best way to get a great story. Besides, he wouldn't name names, so no one would be able to deny anything he wrote, and he wouldn't be liable for anything.

At Georgia's, Trent had picked up some great bits of information. He had confirmed his suspicion that John and Lana were having an affair. Not only that, but she was pregnant, and John was not thrilled. He had overheard Lana tell John she was going to have the baby, so he had better get on board. She even hinted that selling the dairy would not be the worst thing to happen. Trent typed BOB for "baby on board." Until his stories were published, he always used cryptic shorthand. Given how important this story was, it was critical that he keep his notes under wraps until the story was published. Suddenly he flashed to the opened door. *Yes, I'd better be careful*, he thought. But the excitement of a prize-winning story propelled him on, and he was absorbed in his writing, forgetting to check to see if anything was missing from his apartment, or even checking to see if anyone was still in the apartment.

Next, he typed "two to tango." There definitely was more than meets the eye with Georgia. He wouldn't be surprised if she had used the bad milk to kill her husband. The question was: how had she found out about the listeria? She and LaMerle weren't close. Wait! Trent remembered that Georgia was a friend to both Caroline and King-Young, so maybe there was a connection there? Trent typed "bad milk/bad blood."

Then there was King-Young. He needed John's land; otherwise, his huge development deal was worthless. After all, he had already bought several parcels of land surrounding the dairy and had lured investors into his scheme. He thought he had been tricky by using dummy corporations, but Trent had fairly easily discovered that information. He jotted down "land of milk and honey." Trent wondered if there was a Ponzi scheme brewing. Castleton was the perfect place to launch one.

He'd have to investigate King-Young's other, previous developments more closely.

Suddenly Trent smirked. A huge light bulb had gone off in his head, and he grinned like the Cheshire cat. He had just figured out the Georgia/George/ dairy connection! They owned a parcel of land near the dairy. King-Young had probably approached them and offered them some sort of deal. Yes! The story was quickly coming together. He typed in "black widow." Trent was quite proud of himself--no one would ever figure out his shorthand. And then there were John's kids. He wrote "King Lear" in his notes.

Trent stopped his jottings to take a short break. He had just decided to treat himself to a beer when his phone rang, startling him. He picked up his phone, and a disembodied voice said, "Publish and you die."

Trent froze at first, then growled into the phone, "What the hell?" He stared at it for a moment, and then screamed, "Who is this? Are you threatening me? I AM going to publish. You can't stop me." Trent paused. His hand holding the phone shook, but the caller remained silent.

Trent parried, "I'm not afraid of you" just as the line went dead. He punched the phone off so hard he almost knocked it from his hand. *Did I hear that right?* he wondered. Nevertheless, still shaking, he went to the kitchen, and instead of a cold beer, he poured a shot of whiskey and gulped it down.

How real was the threat? He tried to reassure himself, thinking, *After all, this is Castleton, not some big, evil city.* But he also realized there was nothing to stop anyone from carrying out the threat. If he was right and the listeria had been planted on purpose, then there was a very good reason to kill him--and stop his story.

He poured himself another shot, pondering his next steps. As much as he loved secrets, he needed somewhere safe to store his information. It was his only bargaining chip. And if he couldn't publish his story, he could at least use his information to get cash to leave Castleton.

Besides, he could protect himself if he could tell the caller someone else also had his notes, so if anything happened to him, the story would still be published. Reporters always used that trick in the movies. It often didn't work, but he still thought it was his best move. But where could he stash his notes? And with whom?

He smiled. He'd tell Castleton's own Miss Marples: Rita and Ronnie. He knew his story would be safe with them.

He copied his notes onto a flash drive and deleted the notes from his computer. He slipped the flash drive into his pocket, put on his jacket, and carefully locked his door. He tested the door again before leaving. Yes, it was locked.

Hopping on his bike, Trent pedaled to Rita's. He left his bike in their front yard so it was visible. If someone was watching him, he wanted whoever had threatened him to know he was not the only one who had his information.

As he sprinted to Rita's door, he realized he could be putting them in danger, but it would protect him, and he was much more concerned about his own safety than theirs. Besides, no one would hurt those two. Everyone loved Rita and, well, Ronnie was her sister.

Trent rang the bell. He glanced over his shoulder, but didn't see anyone. Good! Safe! Standing on the porch waiting for the door to open, he once again wondered if maybe he shouldn't give the sisters his flash drive, after all. But before he could change his mind, the door swung open.

Rita looked surprised to see him, since she and Ronnie had just been discussing him, but she quickly tried to hide her feelings. "Trent. This is a surprise. Ronnie, Trent is here." Rita yelled, hoping Ronnie got the hint to hide their notes. "Come in, Trent."

Ronnie joined her sister and squeezed Rita's shoulder, signaling the notes were hidden. "Yes, come in, Trent. Are you alright?"

"No. Someone threatened to kill me."

Chapter 17

Running on instinct, Ronnie reached out, grabbed Trent, and yanked him inside. Then she quickly scanned the porch and yard. Trent half expected her to whisper, "All clear!" to Rita, who hovered nearby. *Does she suspect someone followed me?* Trent wondered.

Rita, too, checked outside. As Ronnie finally slammed the door shut, Trent breathed a sigh of relief.

"All's clear for the moment," Trent exhaled in almost one breath. "But I'm not sure for how long."

The sisters believed there was no time to waste. "Come on," Rita commanded. The three marched down the hall toward the back of the house, like an odd pull toy jerking along in a line. They settled in the family room.

Rita and Ronnie sat on opposite ends of the couch, and gestured Trent toward the overstuffed wing chair facing them. He practically collapsed onto the welcoming seat. The chair had been their father's favorite, and Trent looked woefully out of place in it, but now was not the time to think about the past. Trent was clearly scared, and he immediately started babbling.

"Someone threatened me. They said, 'Publish and you die.' I'm not kidding. Those were the exact words: 'Publish and you die.' It almost makes me not want to publish my story," Trent blurted out. He felt like a character in a suspense film. Innocent, but with killers after him.

Ronnie asked if he recognized the voice even though she was sure she knew the answer--he didn't.

"No, I couldn't recognize the voice, so I have no idea who it was.'" He swallowed hard as he felt the color coming back to his face, and his heart starting to slow toward normal again.

"Tell us precisely what happened." Rita said. And 'precise' was just what Rita, the scientist, meant. Only by knowing complete, unembellished facts could they form correct hypotheses. This was not the time for drama or innuendo.

Ronnie, however, had other ideas. She remembered her training at the Actor's Studio in New York, and it was about to come in handy. She looked straight at Trent and said calmly, "Take your time. Paint each picture carefully in your head. Give us all the details." Ronnie had used this kind of activity in acting exercises. It helped actors focus and recall details. Using one's senses to recall details and experiences often created clearer and more meaningful pictures. Ronnie also smiled at Trent, urging him on.

Trent tried to follow her instructions and began his tale again, this time taking his time. "Well, as you know, I went right home from Georgia's house, planning to write up my story. But when I got home, I found my apartment door unlocked. That seemed odd, since I'm careful about security, especially when I'm working on a big story. Don't want someone coming in and stealing my ideas, you know."

Relaxing a little, he fidgeted in the chair as he glanced at the sisters' faces, so they gently began to ask him questions to keep him on track.

"Did you notice anything out of place in your apartment?" Rita asked.

"No, strangely, nothing seemed out of the ordinary, so I got right to work. Anyway, Georgia's party..."

"Reception, Trent," Ronnie interrupted. Rita wanted to shush her sister, but didn't want an interruption to break Trent's concentration and hinder the exercise. No time now to argue over word choice.

"Right, reception." Trent continued, "Well, as you must have noticed, there was a lot going on at Georgia's house. Nobody, least of all the merry widow, seemed very upset about George's death, and people were connecting right, left, and center for many kinds of reasons. I listened carefully and took notes."

"And if you ask me, the only person who seemed at all upset about George's death was Mrs. Osgood. She appeared to be genuinely distraught. I even saw her cry, although I wondered why. Did she and George have something going on, or was she just disgusted at Georgia's behavior and lack of emotion? I'm not sure, but everybody seemed to have something other than George's death on their minds." Trent sat back in the chair.

"Please go on," Rita urged him.

Trent sat up straight and resumed his report. "Well, I tried to watch who was connecting, and how. I'm investigating the dairy and connections to King-Young's development project. And that seemed to be what everyone was concerned about rather than George. John is adamant he will not sell, but King-Young is equally sure John will. There's no love lost between those two, let me tell you. I think the listeria, the dairy, and George's death are all connected." Trent paused for a moment.

Ronnie bit her tongue. She knew she and Rita had told Trent to take his time, but he was playing it out as if he were on a television show being interviewed.

Trent continued, "At first, I thought maybe the listeria was just an accident, and John had been careless. After all, listeria often develops through mistakes in cleanliness. But the more I dug into listeria, the more suspicious it all seemed." He sat back again and waited for acknowledgment.

Rita and Ronnie nodded vaguely, murmuring encouragement, so Trent continued his narrative.

"The question is, 'Why George?' I couldn't see any reason for George to be killed. So that made me think the key was the listeria, and not George. If that were true, then it had to be something to do with the dairy."

Rita and Ronnie nodded. They had drawn the same conclusions.

Suddenly Trent looked directly at Rita and asked, "Did you know listeria can be manufactured?"

Rita tried to keep the surprise off her face. She had researched it and learned the same thing, but was shocked that Trent had discovered it also. "I believe that is true," she said as noncommittally as she could.

Trent simply smiled, full of himself, and then continued with his tale. "At Georgia's, I overheard King-Young and LaMerle arguing about the value of the land. Did you know the land is worth at least a million dollars? That's a powerful reason to force John to sell."

Again, Rita and Ronnie nodded, but said nothing.

Trent plunged ahead. "Their talk was pretty loud, and it seemed like LaMerle was trying to strike a deal with King-Young."

Ronnie and Rita were glad to have this point confirmed. Trent's story was lining up with many of their own ideas.

"We're dealing with murder." Trent sat back, expecting the sisters to agree with him. However, they didn't.

"Why does LaMerle wanting John to sell the farm make you think that George was murdered?" Rita inquired.

Ronnie added, "That seems like a pretty big leap, even for you! No one gains by George dying. His death was most likely accidental."

"I'm not so sure. I did some digging and here's what I learned. It turns out George owned a large parcel of land right by the dairy. Well, George at first had no intention of selling to King-Young, but King-Young kept upping the ante. I think he was winning George over and even if he didn't, with George out of the picture, Georgia could and would sell. Then she'd have money to live life as a rich, merry widow," Trent added and cocked an eyebrow. "Besides, a death from listeria is much more serious than just some people getting sick. That could be from a lot of things, but a death is confirmation of the listeria and will force John to sell. Ergo," Trent said in a dramatic conclusion worthy of a closing statement to a jury, "George's death might not have been so accidental." He opened both of his hands in a triumphant "ta-da" gesture and waited for the sisters to acknowledge his brilliance.

"Actually, you paint an interesting picture of the situation, Trent." Rita hadn't thought of these specific reasons why someone would want George dead. Although she was still convinced George's death was an accident, she had to admit Trent's argument was convincing. She wondered what Ronnie thought. *If it was intentional, then was Georgia working with whomever planted the listeria?*

And there's more," Trent added. "One other very important point, ladies. Did you notice John and Lana? They appeared very close, and every time LaMerle noticed them together, she seemed to get louder and angrier with King-

Young. She wants the sale to go through as soon as possible. She wants a divorce and the money before John can marry Lana."

Proud of his conclusions, Trent didn't notice the smile that passed between the sisters. It was obvious to Rita and Ronnie that Trent hadn't noticed Lana was pregnant.

Trent continued. "So, with George's death, a lot of people benefit, and there are plenty of motives to want him dead. Hence, George's death was murder. Maybe even premeditated murder." Even though he was talking about murder, Trent could hardly keep the glee out of his voice. Clearly, this story would be his big break.

"OK. Some of that makes sense, but why threaten you?" Ronnie asked.

"Obviously, I've rattled the murderer's cage. If I write my story, the murderer will be unmasked. That's why I've been threatened." Trent sat up straight and puffed out his chest. "But I will write my story. It is my finest piece of investigative reporting yet, and nothing will stop me," Trent said, his voice gathering strength with each word until it was nearly booming.

Ronnie was almost inclined to cheer, "Amen." But instead, she said, "Let's not get ahead of ourselves. And you need to be careful, Trent."

Rita chimed in, "Trent, you mustn't write a story before you have all the facts. That could be very dangerous to other people and, more important, dangerous to you," Rita warned, emphasizing the last word. "Please proceed with caution, not only for the sake of innocent people, but also for your own safety. You don't want to destroy, or worse, end, someone's life. And don't forget if your story were proven false, you'd lose all creditability as a reporter. You don't want that."

"Also once accused, a person might never shake the suspicion. Remember, people in small towns have long memories. You could become the target of revenge and be ostracized. And I'm afraid you could be gravely hurt in the process, too." Her tone reinforced the seriousness of the situation.

Trent shrugged. The glory and accompanying power of writing an award-winning story was too great a prize. He reached into his pocket and brought out his flash drive. "Do you know what this is, ladies?"

Ronnie almost snapped back a retort about his condescending tone, but before she could do so, Rita reached over and patted her sister's knee.

"Of course, we do, Trent. What do you have on that flash drive?" Although Rita was pretty sure what was going to happen next. The problem would then become what should they do with the flash drive if he did give it to them. "My notes. I haven't completed my investigation, but I want to be sure that what I have so far is safe. I'd like to leave this with you. Please keep it in a safe place, and if anything should happen to me, turn it in to the police. I'm not sure they would understand all my shorthand, but you could explain about my conclusions if it came to that. Will you do that for me?"

"Of course," Rita replied, taking the drive from his outstretched hand. She wanted him to give her the material for a couple of reasons. Maybe it would work as insurance for him, but it might also provide information for her and Ronnie. After all, he just asked them to keep it safe. He hadn't asked them not to look at it. "DO be careful, Trent, and don't get carried away inventing things that make this worse. And please take my cell phone number, so you can call us if you need anything. Let me get a slip of paper."

She started to rise, but before she could stand, Trent whipped a card from his pocket and thrust it toward her. "Here, just write it on my card," he said. Rita took it and noticed Trent's title, Reporter, was in raised typeface. Rita carefully wrote her name and number on the card and returned it to him. He placed the card back in his pocket and said, "I'll let you know when I learn more."

"Or call if you feel you are in more danger," Ronnie added, letting the emphasis linger on "danger."

"Thank you, I will," Trent replied.

"May we offer you some tea?" Rita inquired. Ronnie grimaced. She just wanted Trent to go so they could review his notes and compare them to their own. She really wished that Rita didn't always have to be so polite.

"No, thank you. I really must get going. I've got a lot to follow up on," Trent said.

"And miles to go before you sleep, and miles to go before you sleep," Ronnie added quietly.

Trent either didn't catch Ronnie's reference or chose to ignore it. He stood, offered his hand to both women, and strode back down the hall toward the front door. Once on the porch again, he turned around and said, "For such a sleepy looking town, there sure is a lot going on in Castleton, don't you think?"

"That there is."

"Thank you, ladies. I feel better now that I know you will pass this to the authorities if necessary," Trent said, practically leaping down the porch steps and dashing for his bicycle. Having accomplished his mission, he felt secure. Now it was time to win that Pulitzer.

"I hope he realizes the danger he's in," Rita said.

"We can only hope, but I think his need to publish the story trumps any common sense," replied Ronnie.

The two women watched Trent ride off. Shaking their heads at Trent's impetuousness, neither noticed the car that followed him.

"You do realize that keeping this flash drive also puts us in danger? If someone has been keeping an eye on Trent, he or she will know we have it."

"I know." Ronnie shrugged. "This feels like a bad murder mystery I made in England."

Rita agreed with her sister. She just hoped the ending was not additional deaths.

Chapter 18

After Trent left, Rita suggested they go back out to the porch. Not only was it a beautiful day, but also they had done some of their best thinking there, especially recently. Back outside, they dropped into their rockers while Dewey flopped at their feet.

They had a lot to discuss, so they began to share some points and their feelings about what Trent had told them. But after a few minutes, each time Rita started to speak, Dewey interrupted by nudging their legs with her nose. The sisters looked down at the dog. "I think she's trying to tell us something," Rita said quietly.

"She's been so good today. I think you should listen to her." Ronnie smiled at the dog and then at her sister.

Rita smiled, too. Ronnie rarely said good things about her dog, so Rita immediately made a show of taking her sister's advice. "What do you want, sweet thing?"

"I doubt Fluffy will answer you," Ronnie replied.

So much for Ronnie and Dewey establishing rapport, thought Rita.

"I think she wants to go for a walk," Ronnie said a little too sweetly.

Rita bit her tongue, stifling a sharp reply. There was no point in starting a fight. Ronnie was just being Ronnie. So instead, she reached for her sweater and Dewey's leash.

"Well, you and Rain Drop have a good walk."

Rita nodded, but she couldn't help but wonder what Ronnie had up her sleeve.

"Maybe when you come back, we can have something a little stronger than our usual tea? After all, it's cocktail hour somewhere in the world," Ronnie chuckled. "I'll be here when you and Cotton Ball return, but I can't promise I'll have waited."

Rita laughed and clipped on Dewey's leash. "Let's go, Dew Drop! Maybe a walk will give us a bit of a break from all the excitement." Rita turned toward Ronnie and said, "I'll try to organize my thoughts, and we can talk when I'm back." Rita and Dewey stepped down off the porch and across the lawn.

"Keep your ear to the ground, along with Dewey's nose," Ronnie said to their backs as she watched the pair amble toward the town green. "But don't be too long."

Ronnie closed the front door, and immediately went to Rita's computer and copied the files from Trent's flash drive onto it. Better to have another record of Trent's notes. Then she retreated to the back parlor and sank into the chair Trent had last occupied. She closed her eyes and mulled over what had happened earlier.

She couldn't help but wonder if Trent would take their advice and be cautious, or if he would get himself in trouble with his stories and accusations.

With Trent's files safely saved on their computer, Ronnie decided to start organizing her latest thoughts. She wanted to assemble them in some sort of order. That should help them when they were trying to make sense of it all and draw some specific conclusions about the recent events. She let out a deep breath, hoping that Trent would take their advice, but she doubted he would. He wanted the glory of the story too much. "Honestly, Trent, why can't you just use common sense? No one is going to steal the story from you."

When Ronnie realized she was talking out loud to a person who wasn't there, she chuckled, "Oh brother, maybe I'd better wait until Rita's back before I have a drink." She closed her eyes and rested her head on the back of the chair.

Having dozed off, Ronnie was startled by knocking at the front door. She jumped up and hurried down the hall, wondering if Rita forgot her key, and hoping that nobody else was stopping by.

The Chief of Police stood on the porch, peering through the window as she opened the door. "Oh, Wendell! Good afternoon!" She glanced nervously around, looking for any clue as to why he was there. The cruiser was parked in the driveway, but its lights were off. "Are you here to deliver a ticket because Rita let Dewey off her leash?" She laughed, hoping it might disguise her nervousness. *God, I'm behaving like some stupid ingénue. Pull yourself together!*

"Hi, Ronnie. No, Rita and Dewey are fine, but I am here on official business." He stepped into the hallway and removed his cap. Ronnie could tell by his tone it was serious.

Ronnie reached over to close the door when Rita and Dewey suddenly appeared around the corner of the porch and quickly mounted the steps. Both looked as if they had enjoyed their walk, and Ronnie hoped whatever the Chief's business was, it would not change their mood.

"Hail, hail, the gang's all here!" Rita cheerfully announced, as she unleashed her dog. She looked from her sister to the Chief. "Wendell, I hope this is a social call."

"I'm afraid it's not," Ronnie replied. Rita immediately became somber. "Ladies, may we sit down?" The Chief's expression matched the seriousness of his tone.

"Wendell, let's sit in here," Rita suggested and led the trio into the front room. All three sat and looked at each other for a few moments. The sisters waited for the Chief to speak first.

"There's been an accident, ladies. And I'm afraid it was a bad one." Wendell paused, trying to break the news gently. Then he continued, "I'm sorry to tell you this, but it seems that Trent Fowler was in the accident."

"Oh NO!" Ronnie and Rita exclaimed, almost in unison, their faces registering shock, but also something else Wendell could not quite put his finger on. "Will he be alright?" Rita quietly asked for both of them.

Wendell shook his head, and then said gently, "I'm afraid not. Trent died."

"Wait. You said it 'seems that Trent was in an accident.' Are you not sure?" Rita asked.

"My men are reconstructing the scene right now, so I don't know yet just what happened. Maybe he fell off his bike and hit his head on the road. Or maybe he swerved to avoid a deer and was thrown. We did find skid marks, so it seems as if the most likely scenario is that a car hit him. We're thinking he was in the road and a car came around the bend fast and hit him. The car swerved, but once it hit Trent, the driver didn't stop. So, it appears to be a hit and run. At least, that's the working theory."

"Where did it happen?" Rita asked.

"It was out there on the big turn in Miller's Road. A dangerous spot when you come around the corner too fast. And with no lights, it's a dark spot. So most likely the car didn't even see Trent until it was too late. The driver probably panicked and just kept going. Who knows? Maybe the driver thought he or she had hit an animal."

"I doubt the driver thought they hit a deer." Ronnie said quietly, just loud enough for Rita, but not Wendell, to hear.

"He was a very experienced, careful rider, so I doubt he would be thrown by hitting a bump," Rita said carefully. "And he had reflectors on his bike." She raised an eyebrow and Ronnie nodded. The sisters continued to stare at each other, with occasional glances at Wendell.

Wendell shook his head slowly. "Well, he wasn't careful enough, apparently. And I know it's not totally dark yet, but he should have had some reflective clothing on. At twilight, he would have blended into the scenery. I'm guessing the car didn't see him." Wendell was clearly flustered. The sisters just weren't sure why he was upset. If he truly believed it was a simple hit and run, then he should be focusing on trying to find the driver. "Well, I just wanted to let you know." Wendell twirled his hat in his hands and prepared to leave. He stood up and then walked toward the door. It was clear he wasn't planning to share any more information.

Rita considered what she knew about Trent's biking and the bike itself. He had both reflectors and lights on his bike. And she believed he was careful enough that he would have turned the light on at this hour, since it's the hardest time of day to pick things out. To her, the accident did not sound at all like an accident. She was sure it was deliberate. *What should we tell Wendell?* she wondered.

"Any leads on the driver or the car?" Ronnie asked. She hoped there was a simple solution, and she and Rita were just jumping to conclusions.

Wendell replied, "No. We don't know who the driver was. If that is what happened, then it was an accidental hit and run." Wendell paused. "That seems to be the most likely scenario."

"Trent biked that road every day for as long as he's been here in Castleton. No, it was not an accidental hit and run," Ronnie stated strongly, and Ronnie agreed.

Wendell's dismay was written all over his face. "I was afraid that was what you two would conclude," Wendell sighed. His worst nightmare was coming true. He couldn't help but wonder if this was another murder-- first George, and now Trent?

Rita asked, "You said there were skid marks? Are you saying you think somebody tried to stop? But then left the scene?"

"Well, that's one scenario. There were skid marks both in front and behind the bike. So, it looks like maybe the driver sped off." The Chief paused for a moment. "The ME says it looks like he died instantly. Of course, we'll know more after he does his examination of the body."

Almost before the last syllable was out of Wendell's mouth, Ronnie blurted out, "Well, Chief, Trent knew *something* might happen to him."

"Ronnie's right, Wendell. Trent came here earlier, and he was frightened. An anonymous caller had threatened his life. So, frankly, he may well have been murdered," Rita added.

"Murder?" Wendell gasped, but then managed to get himself under control rather quickly. "Let's not get ahead of ourselves, ladies. But tell me what you're thinking." Wendell took the sisters seriously. Both were intelligent, and both knew the townspeople and the town's happenings very well. Still, Wendell hoped it was an accidental hit and run. He could deal with that. But murder? No.

"Trent was working on a story about George's death and the listeria. He believed George's death was no accident. He thought George might have been killed as part of a larger plan," Rita explained.

Wendell's mouth fell open. "Ladies, this is Castleton, not a big city. There's no reason to believe there was anything suspicious about George's death. It was just an accident. We do have to find the source of the listeria, but George was NOT murdered."

"Maybe, maybe not," Rita replied. "But I do believe Trent's death is, at best, highly suspicious. He took the anonymous call seriously. It was a real threat. The caller told him if he published his story, he would die." Rita paused. "And he died."

"And then there are his notes," Ronnie added.

"Notes? What are you talking about?" Wendell looked confused.

"Trent brought us his notes. He asked us to give them to you if anything happened to him," Rita explained, and then stepped briskly out of the room to get Trent's flash drive.

"What?" Wendell asked, obviously confused.

Rita strode back into the room and thrust Trent's flash drive into the Chief's hand. "Here." Wendell stared at the drive. Rita continued, "We have no idea what's on it. Trent implied it might be rather cryptic, so if you have any questions, let us know. We might be able to help you decipher them. I believe Trent used a reporter's shorthand."

"Rita is good at solving those kinds of puzzles," Ronnie said proudly. Rita shushed her.

The Chief stared intently at the drive and turned it over in his hand. "Hmmm, I wonder what is on here. I'll have to get it over to the station, and we'll look at it on the computer, see what it says. But until more evidence turns up, we're classifying it an accidental hit and run."

"Then why were there skid marks in front of AND behind the bike?" Rita asked. The sisters exchanged glances. The Chief shook his head and decided to leave before he had a full-blown conspiracy on his hands.

"We're not going to borrow trouble. I'm pretty sure we'll learn it was just an accident. Just like George." Wendell tried to sound as authoritative and convincing as possible. "Please don't make more of this than it is. Let us do our job." *The last thing I need is to have these two playing detective. And if it were murder, they'd be putting themselves in danger.*

His words hung in the air for a few moments, and then Rita said, "Well, this is very sad. We appreciate hearing about it from you, Wendell, but I do have one more question. What led you to us?"

"Well, in Trent's coat pocket we found one of his cards. It had your name and a phone number on it. I didn't think you ladies were particularly close to Trent, so I found that odd, and I wanted to ask you about it."

"Yes, I wrote down my cell phone number for him since he didn't have it," Rita explained sadly. The three stood quietly for a moment.

The Chief finally turned toward the door. He added, "I also didn't want you to just hear about the accident around town."

"That's very considerate of you, Wendell. We appreciate your coming by," Rita said, as she offered her hand and ushered him out the door onto the porch.

All business again, Wendell said, "I'm sure we'll find out about arrangements soon enough after his family is notified. I think they are in New York somewhere?" The sisters nodded. Rita tried to remember if Trent had been close to his family, but she couldn't recall.

The Chief turned to go, then added, "Let's hope this is the last funeral any of us has to think about for a long time. Now take care of yourselves, ladies. We don't want anybody else having an accident or getting hurt." He smiled at the sisters, tipped his hat, stepped down the porch stairs, walked down the path, and got into his cruiser. All very officially.

Ronnie and Rita watched him back out of the driveway. Then they shut the porch door and turned toward each other.

"Accident, my foot!" Ronnie spat out. "It was murder. I wonder if we know who did it."

"If we don't, we will," Rita replied, then added, "I hope you copied the flash drive onto my computer."

"First thing I did after you and Gum Drop left for your walk," Ronnie replied. And she chuckled at how well her sister knew her.

The game was afoot, and Castleton's Sherlock and Watson were on it.

Chapter 19

The next morning, Wendell's visit and Trent's murder were still in the forefront of Ronnie's mind. She woke up slowly, letting the sunlight coming through the window warm her as she lay in bed, thinking about what they had learned. Rita was downstairs, bustling around in the kitchen. Ronnie had to admit her sister's morning rituals comforted her. Mornings were still not a good time for her, since it took too long to move about with ease.

She sighed, "Suck it up, girl. The aches and pains just mean you're alive, and that's better than being dead." Visions of poor Trent lying on the road filled her head.

Ronnie shook her head, hoping to clear her mind of those thoughts, but of course they wouldn't simply disappear. *Did he really have to die?* Only his killer could answer that question, and Ronnie was determined to find his killer. Obviously, the killer had thought Trent knew too much, but he hadn't seemed to know more than Ronnie and Rita did. The killer had made a preemptive strike, which means Trent must have known something very damaging, so he had to be eliminated quickly.

Ronnie believed the listeria outbreak had been carefully planned, so Trent must have really spooked the killer. The plan must also be on a schedule. Because Ronnie believed that she and Rita knew as much as Trent, or almost as much, she hoped they weren't in danger too. But she put that thought out of her head. After all, she still believed, as she always had, that there's no use worrying about spilt milk. *Or is there?* she wondered.

Both Rita and Ronnie thought that George's death had simply been an accident—a death that wasn't meant to happen. But unlike poor George, Trent's death, though currently classified as a hit and run accident, clearly wasn't. It had been planned. *Time to get to work, Sherlock.*

She threw back the covers just as Rita called up that breakfast was ready. Ronnie wistfully hoped it was steak and eggs, or eggs benedict with a spicy Bloody Mary, but knew in her heart it was probably a bran muffin, juice, and some sort of healthy cereal. After her next check-up, good news or not, she was certainly going to indulge in a day of good, but unhealthy, eating. She was sure Rita would try to talk her out of it, but that would make it even more fun for her.

"I'm coming. I'm sure the muffin and cereal can wait a second," Ronnie called out as she pulled on her silk robe. She loved the feel of the smooth cloth against her skin. And the lovely aquamarine color made Ronnie feel pretty, or as pretty as an aging diva with reconstructed breasts, could feel. *Yes, Rita may serve God-awful breakfasts, but her gift of the robe was perfect. I'm very lucky,* thought Ronnie.

"How did you sleep?" Rita asked as she poured her sister some juice. "It's tomato juice with some spices." Ronnie raised an eyebrow, quizzical and hopeful.

"No, don't get your hopes up. There's no vodka in it," Rita laughed. "But I thought it might be a fun treat. Besides, after last night, we need to be alert and ready to think."

"Well, this will help the old thinking cap, thanks." Ronnie broke up the blueberry muffin and put a piece in her mouth. *At least it isn't bran.*

"We do have a lot to think about now that we know what happened to Trent."

But even as she said the words, Ronnie still had a hard time accepting that someone had purposely run down Trent. An accidental death like George's was one thing, but cold-blooded murder was another thing entirely.

Oh dear, thought Ronnie, *what if George's death wasn't accidental after all?* Trent had made a convincing argument about how Georgia might have staged his death. Ronnie shook her head and quickly put that thought out of her mind. *No, I still don't think Georgia is a murderer.* Instead, she focused on trying to figure out who wanted Trent dead. The problem with that line of thinking was that there was a long list of people who might want that very outcome. Over the years, he'd made enemies, and with this latest story, enemies had taken action.

"Who'd have thought we'd be investigating murders here in sleepy Castleton?" Ronnie asked rhetorically.

Rita raised an eyebrow. "It's murder, not murders. Trent's death is murder, but George's death is not."

"Look, I agree George's was probably an accidental death, but the point is, he died. The listeria killed him, which in my book, makes two murders. George may be a collateral death, but dead is dead. And though we're convinced Georgia is innocent of murder, we need to keep her as a suspect in the listeria outbreak."

"You're right," Rita said thoughtfully.

Ronnie continued. "And I don't know about you, but I feel quite certain that what Trent was writing was true. So, we need to review those lists of suspects we've been compiling."

"I agree that Trent was on the right track," Rita said, "I think that John and his dairy and the plans for development are at the heart of the matter. But who is behind the listeria outbreak? I think it must be a team working together."

"I agree," Ronnie added with conviction.

Rita got the milk from the refrigerator and frowned. "Oh dear, we're nearly out of milk. Eat your muffin and drink your juice. I'll run to the dairy for some more milk, and we can have our cereal when I get back and figure out who and how to investigate."

"Make sure the milk is safe!" Ronnie called to Rita's back as she left.

"Not funny," Rita yelled back. "No, but true," muttered Ronnie.

She didn't really think she and Rita were in any danger, but she hadn't thought Trent was either, even with his announcement about his next story. Then came the threat on his life and his death. And the hard cold fact was someone killed him. *So much for my intuition giving me insight.* She wondered if she should be more like Rita and rely on the facts. "Well, regardless," she said, trying to convince herself, "we need to firm up our suspects." Dewey barked in agreement. "Glad someone agrees with me. Still, keep your opinions to yourself, Fur Ball, until I'm done organizing my own."

Ronnie took some paper from the cabinet drawer and began writing. Under the heading Suspects, she wrote the list: John, King-Young, Caroline, John Jr., LaMerle, Lana, and

Georgia. Then she sat back and examined the names. It occurred to her that two days ago, she would have put Trent on the list as well. She had wondered if Trent had been creating the story. She sat back in her chair, continuing to stare at the list. It made sense.

Clearly each had had a motive for using, and possibly spreading, the listeria, though for some, the motive was somewhat tenuous. Ronnie decided they had to focus on who gained the most from the listeria outbreak and who had the means and knowledge to plant the listeria. Once they figured that out, she believed it would lead them to Trent's killer.

Ronnie noticed that all her suspects were people she didn't like very much. So, to her, that meant any of them could easily have done it. Facts were nice, but in the end, Ronnie believed motive was all about feelings. And all of the people on her list had plenty of motives.

Reading the names out loud, Ronnie thought once again about who would benefit most from the spread of listeria and John subsequently having to sell the dairy. She also thought about Trent's early demise. Somehow the word "demise" seemed less threatening and horrible than "murder." Though as Ronnie took another sip of her Virgin Mary and tapped her pencil, lines from plays dealing with death, families, and murder ricocheted in her head. For some reason, she kept coming back to *King Lear,* which made her laugh at herself. Because, after all, John was much too young to be Lear, and he had only one daughter, but like Cordelia in *King Lear*, Caroline was his favorite. *But would he sell the dairy for her?* John's family would definitely benefit from the sale of the dairy. Even John. Ronnie moved them to the top of her list.

Then Ronnie thought more about King-Young. In many ways, he had the most to gain from the sale of the dairy. He'd be able to build his development, gain investors, and make a pile of money. And that seemed to be his goal for being in Castleton.

She reread the list one more time. Was she missing anyone? Ronnie decided to dismiss George's death. It would distract them and not add anything to their investigation. No matter how convincing Trent's argument was. Besides, Ronnie thought Trent was going to write about it only to add to his story, not because it was true.

As she took another sip of her Virgin Mary, Ronnie knew Rita was mentally compiling her own list of suspects. *Thank God, it's a short drive to the dairy, so her list will be short, too.* And, of course, Rita would have a perfectly rational reason for each person on her list. Ronnie sighed and picked up her pencil again. She'd better develop some reasons for her suspects, too. She knew that her not liking or trusting the people on her list was not going to make Rita support her theories. Ronnie began writing again. *Lord, I really could use some vodka.*

Ronnie began putting the suspects into teams. Yes, thinking about who would work together for a common goal made sense. And the common goal was money. Greed was quite the motivator and fit all of the people on Ronnie's list. Nobody, including Rita, could argue with that.

Ronnie frowned, looked at the kitchen clock, and muttered, "Rita, get yourself home, girl! We need to figure out our next steps." Dewey barked in agreement. However, Ronnie chose to ignore Dewey and instead, polished off her Virgin Mary. She had no choice but to wait.

Chapter 20

While Rita was driving to the dairy, Lana screeched into the dairy parking lot and jumped out of the car. She was seething. However, she knew she'd gain nothing by confronting LaMerle her current state. So she leaned back against the car and took several deep breaths while she tried to organize her thoughts. She desperately wanted to tell LaMerle that she was pregnant with John's child and they were going to get married. However, she wondered if that were even true now. Things had been tense between her and John at George's reception, and it seemed as if things were going downhill. John had been acting more and more distant, and they definitely were not getting closer as Lana had expected. Moreover, marriage seemed to have turned into a taboo subject.

John's initial reaction to her pregnancy had not been what Lana dreamed it would be. He had come to her house. She expected them to enjoy the cookies she had baked especially for him and then celebrate the good news. She had poured John his favorite scotch while she had a ginger ale. She had expected him to raise his glass in a toast to their future and new family, but John had remained silent when she told him.

There was no joyous celebration. John had set his partially eaten cookie back down on the table next to the untouched glass of scotch and just sat there, frozen. Then he got up abruptly and left, muttering he had a lot to think about, and he had to be alone. Lana had called after him to wait, but he had just driven off, racing recklessly down the road. Luckily, there was no one to witness his exit.

Coming back into her cabin, Lana had sunk into a chair and sat there staring off into space. She had never failed with men like this before, and she had to devise a new plan for dealing with this unexpected situation. The only way she could think of to try to salvage things was to confront LaMerle. She would use her pregnancy as a weapon.

As it was, Lana was pretty sure Rita and Ronnie had guessed her condition, but she also felt confident they wouldn't spread any stories about her around town, although that was of little consolation. The local gossip mills had been grinding away ever since she had first moved to Castleton. According to the rumors, Lana had been sleeping with every man she talked to. Granted, she had used men in the past, but this time, with John, it was real. *At least it is for me,* she thought.

So here she was at the dairy, about to confront her nemesis, LaMerle. She was pretty sure only LaMerle would be there at this hour, so that would be a blessing.

And as for the townspeople, they could speculate all they wanted because Lana had a plan, and she was determined to see it through. No one, especially LaMerle, was going to stop her. Lana marched into the dairy store. It was time to set her plan in motion. *You will marry me, John.*

The bell jangled loudly as Lana yanked open the door. LaMerle glanced up from her magazine and frowned when she saw Lana. *Lord, what does the princess want now?* LaMerle thought.

For some time, ever since she had learned of John's infatuation with Lana, LaMerle had been dreading this inevitable encounter, but knew she would have the upper hand. After all, John was her husband, and she planned that he would remain her husband until the dairy was sold. LaMerle placed her hand on the counter, prominently displaying her best weapon: her wedding band.

"There's no need to tear the door off the hinges, dear," said LaMerle. She gave Lana one of her beauty queen smiles and then glanced back down at her magazine. LaMerle was going to let Lana dig her own grave. Now that's a pleasant thought, LaMerle mused as she casually flipped another page. This might be fun.

"I need to speak with you," Lana stated forcefully. She was determined she would triumph. LaMerle might be his wife, but she was carrying his child.

LaMerle looked up and said in a sickeningly sweet voice, "About what, dear?"

"You know what is going on between John and me?" Lana pretended she was asking a question. She was positive LaMerle knew she and John were involved. However, LaMerle chose to play the innocent.

Let her suffer, LaMerle thought, *I'm not giving her an inch.* "No, what is going on between you and MY husband?"

"You know we've been seeing each other. I know you do! And what's more, we're in love." Lana spit the words out. There, it was now out in the open. No turning back, even if she wanted to, which she didn't. "I plan to marry John." Lana smiled. She felt stronger just saying the words aloud. Instinctively, she rubbed her stomach.

The movement did not go unnoticed by LaMerle. Nevertheless, she chose to ignore it. Instead, LaMerle's voice could have cut ice. "That's nice, dear, but has John asked you to marry him?" LaMerle inquired. Her words dripped with sarcasm and a touch of pity. LaMerle moved her hand slightly on the counter to keep the sun reflecting off her wedding band.

Lana just stood there, looking confused. LaMerle had hit her mark. Lana, unable to form words, simply stared at LaMerle. Frankly, LaMerle's question had shocked her, and she wasn't sure how to answer. True, John hadn't asked her yet, but it was just a matter of time. After all, John was an honorable man, and she could trust him to do the right thing. That had been her plan. Besides, he had said he loved her, and Lana believed he'd meant it. But then he had raced away from her when she told him she was pregnant. *I will win him over no matter what it takes.* Lana stood up straight and threw her shoulders back. She would not show LaMerle she had any doubts about what would happen next. *I could kill her,* thought Lana.

LaMerle stared back at Lana. She'd seen the flicker of doubt cross Lana's face before she'd been able to hide it. If LaMerle had not been so angry with both John and Lana, she might almost have felt pity for her. But she didn't. LaMerle recognized a fellow grifter when she saw one, and Lana was one.

LaMerle was quite certain that John had not asked Lana to marry him. And she knew that he probably never would. LaMerle had had to work hard to win John. And he had been a free man when they started their relationship. The odds on Lana succeeding were slim at best.

Lana did not know John as well as she thought she did. LaMerle knew that John, while playing the kind farmer, was cutthroat when it came to his life and success.

LaMerle had learned the hard way that under his simple farmer image, John had a cunning, dark side. Once LaMerle and John's marriage had gone downhill, there had been several close calls for LaMerle. "Accidents" that might have been fatal. LaMerle had finally warned John that she had a letter with her lawyer stating that if she died of an accident, it was to be investigated as possible murder. She'd had no more accidents.

John may have been tempted by Lana, and might even love her, but LaMerle knew John would not divorce her. He couldn't afford it. A divorce would force him to sell the dairy. And John knew LaMerle would take him to the cleaners. He may have wanted to get rid of her, but the only way that would happen is if LaMerle died. And LaMerle was absolutely certain she would not be the one to die.

Besides, the only thing John really loved was the dairy and being a farmer. So, if Lana forced his hand, he'd have to sell, and that would doom their relationship. LaMerle wanted John to sell, too, but her hand was far stronger than Lana's. In fact, LaMerle believed she could use Lana against him and get what she wanted: freedom and money. She smiled as she rolled this idea around in her mind. And she began to form another plan. And she was certain that with either plan, she would win.

Another thing LaMerle knew about John that others didn't, or had forgotten, was that John had majored in science as well as agriculture in college. This meant John would know how to introduce the listeria if he wanted to, or he could be working with someone to do so. It would be easy for him to cause the outbreak. Besides, John had also loved acting, and he was good at it.

And now, with all this drama about King-Young trying to buy John's land and John claiming he'd die before selling, LaMerle wondered what his real plan was. She'd heard the threats John had made to both King-Young and Trent. And LaMerle had a feeling that Lana now fell into the same category as Trent: a nuisance to be dealt with. And Trent was dead. So where did that leave Lana? Besides Lana's child would be a threat to his precious Caroline, and John would not want to lose Caroline. Though LaMerle suspected Caroline might take care of Lana herself, Daddy's girl that she was.

What many didn't realize was that John's temper and volatility were the main reasons LaMerle wanted to move back home. And she definitely needed to escape the war of the Camdens. John was secretly at war with the children he had now, so the last thing he wanted was a new marriage and another child. The only baby he wanted was his dairy. *Yes, Lana was a good weapon*, LaMerle thought as she rolled these thoughts around in her head.

"I know John hasn't proposed to you," LaMerle said to Lana. "You see, the only thing John truly loves is this dairy. He would do anything to keep it. If I were you, I'd be very careful what you say or do. John is not the sweet, docile man you think he is." *Leave now*, LaMerle thought.

However, Lana was not done. And clearly she was not giving up. "I know he loves the dairy, but he also loves me. You don't love him, and you never have. Everyone knows you want to move back home. This is your chance." Then Lana lobbed her last statement at LaMerle, "Let John go, and I'll make sure you have enough money to move back down south to be with your family." Lana still believed she had the winning hand, and so she smiled.

LaMerle smiled, too, and slapped the counter. "Why child, how kind of you! You truly are a noble woman looking out for my best interests."

In the blink of an eye, Lana went from looking satisfied to looking confused. She hadn't expected LaMerle to react so calmly. She must have something up her sleeve, Lana thought.

Sure enough, LaMerle looked at Lana and addressed her as if she were a naughty child about to be taught a lesson. She spoke slowly and clearly.

"Lana, listen to me--very carefully. There's a little problem with your grand scheme. John has no intention of divorcing me. He knows full well I would not hesitate to take him to the cleaners. And given that he cheated on me, and the proof is the child you are carrying, he knows a court would award me whatever I wanted. And what I would want is to see him destroyed." LaMerle paused, cocked her eyebrow, and stared at Lana, shaking her head. "And don't think for one single minute that I would hesitate to ruin your life, too."

Lana shoulders sagged at first, but then she suddenly stood straight, her fear turning to anger. "How did you know I'm pregnant?" Lana demanded.

She wasn't showing, and the only person she had told was John. Had John told LaMerle? Lana suddenly felt as if the whole world she had created in her mind was slipping away. She was used to being the one in control when it came to relationships. She had always won whatever it was she wanted, whether it was a promotion or money. Remembering that, she believed that even if she were on her own, she could still win. She would make John pay whether he married her or not.

What John and LaMerle didn't know was that Lana was much stronger and smarter than she acted. Her innocence was an act she used to hide a very cunning mind. *Yes, LaMerle, we're two peas in a pod. And I plan on being the winner.*

"Oh, please. The whole town knows you're expecting. You walk differently, and I've seen the way those snoops, Rita and Ronnie, have been eyeing you. As soon as I saw them checking you out, I knew," LaMerle snorted. "And just maybe MY husband told me the mistake he had made. So there's a little wrench in your plans."

"This is not over," Lana threatened.

"Oh, you can bet it's not. In fact, the best is yet to come." LaMerle declared. "Oh, Caroline, could you bring Lana a bottle of milk. It's on the house."

Lana suddenly froze. Caroline had heard everything. *Well, one more enemy to defeat*, thought Lana. *I can do this.*

"Here you go, Lana." Caroline smiled and handed the bottle of milk with a red sticker to Lana. "It's a special one just for you."

LaMerle's eyes lingered for only a moment on the bottle.

Lana took the bottle, mustered her dignity, and went to her car. Once inside, she sat for a few moments in frustration and anger. Then she growled to herself, "Special, indeed; yes, that's me!" Then she silently added, "I hate you both!" and

"You two will pay for this" under her breath. Then she smiled. She gunned the car out of the dairy parking lot.

Driving home, lost in thought, and determined to settle the score with both LaMerle and Caroline, Lana didn't notice Rita on the other side of the road. She started to drift to Rita's side, causing Rita to honk. Lana pulled back to her side and ignored Rita.

Suddenly she smiled once again. LaMerle and Caroline's days were numbered. Lana knew what she had to do.

Chapter 21

Pulling into the parking lot, Rita sat for a moment while she methodically reviewed what Trent had shared. The scientist in her loved to analyze things and find the logical, proven answer, so her goal was to learn how much of what Trent had shared with her and Ronnie was true, and how much was supposition. And she wanted to be certain she was prepared with any questions she might want to ask of whomever was staffing the dairy store at this time. She was sure it would be either LaMerle or Caroline, or perhaps even both of them.

The first step was to find out the identity of the members of the listeria team. Rita was sure King-Young was involved and the team leader, but who else was working with him? Her theory, and most likely Ronnie's too, was that someone at the dairy was working with King-Young. She just had to find evidence to prove who it was, because at this point, everyone had the means, opportunity, and knowledge to create a listeria outbreak and force the sale of the dairy.

Rita needed to ferret out who was working with King-Young. Most likely it was someone who had a relationship with him. Rita hated to admit it, but the prime candidate was Caroline, since King-Young approached her to do public relations for his development and Caroline had agreed to work with him.

Since she would need to be prepared to check alibis, Rita carefully reviewed the timeline of events. Either LaMerle or Caroline would have sold George the contaminated milk. So, is it possible that George was a target after all? She wondered. His death had made the listeria outbreak serious and scary. It made people afraid to buy milk and that, in turn, almost guaranteed the dairy would be ruined and John would have to sell. Rita still believed that was the ultimate goal. And if Rita and Ronnie could prove the listeria was planted, then George's death would be classified as murder. And if Trent was on his way to exposing that fact, then there was a solid reason to murder him. And plenty of suspects.

Getting a clearer picture, Rita remained in her car and kept thinking. Trent had claimed that Georgia knew about the listeria outbreak before George bought his milk. If so, Georgia could be an accessory to murder, but Rita was sure Georgia had not killed Trent. There was no damage to her car, and she had been shocked when she heard about his death. And as Ronnie would confirm, Georgia was not such a good actress that she could carry off such a surprised reaction to that deadly news. For this reason, Rita dismissed both Georgia (and Mrs. Osgood) from her list of suspects. She was sure Ronnie had done the same or had at least reluctantly moved them to the very bottom of her list. Still, it was important to find out who sold George his milk.

Rita narrowed her list of prime suspects to John, Caroline, John, Jr., LaMerle, and King-Young, She believed Ronnie most likely had the same list, although she might have kept Georgia on it out of spite.

"Time for questions. Let's go, Watson," she said aloud to embolden herself for the interviews she was about to perform. It was time to impress Ronnie and to get answers to some of the sisters' burning questions. Rita gathered her composure and entered the dairy store.

The bell over the door tinkled softly as Rita pulled open the door, but nobody was there. Rita stepped inside and was about to call out "Hello" when she heard voices coming from the open barn door. Two women were having a tense conversation. Rita crept over to listen.

It was LaMerle and Caroline. Rita recognized their voices. The two must have gone into the barn so no one entering the store would hear them. Rita smiled. Too bad. They didn't realize how clearly their voices carried into the store.

"So, what do we do about Lana? She could ruin our plans." LaMerle looked truly concerned.

"Oh, don't worry. I took care of her. She won't be a problem," Caroline said smugly.

"I don't want to know what you did," hissed LaMerle.

Caroline laughed. "Your hands are already dirty, LaMerle. Don't think you can weasel out of anything." The two became silent.

Since it was obvious to Rita that their conversation was over, she quietly and quickly made her way back to the door and opened and shut it once again. Then she called out, "Hello?" *Ronnie's not the only actress in the family*, she thought with satisfaction. She hoped they would assume she had just arrived.

Rita made her way to the coolers containing the milk. She noticed some bottles had red stickers on them, which she thought was odd. *What did the red stickers mean?* She wondered. Then she had an idea. She chose two without stickers and one with a sticker and placed them in her basket. *Let's see what happens when I buy the three bottles*, she thought. Carefully balancing the glass bottles, she walked back to the counter.

LaMerle and Caroline appeared behind the counter and greeted her. Rita smiled and then said, "Oh dear, I forgot the empties in the car. I'll get them." She went back to her car, which gave her a few minutes to think about how to question the two women about Lana. She went back in with her basket of empties. "Silly me, with all that's happening, I'm surprised I didn't forget my head."

Both women smiled. "No problem, Rita," remarked Caroline.

"Ah, glad we're on a first name basis now, Caroline." Rita glanced at the bottles in her basket. The bottle with the red dot had been replaced. Rita filed away her observation and paid for her milk. *Which one of them had replaced it? Caroline or LaMerle?* She wondered.

"By the way, was Lana just here?" Rita asked. "She practically ran me off the road as I was driving here." Rita refrained from putting her hand over her heart as that was too Ronnie for her.

Caroline took a breath, smiled, and then replied, "She was. And yes, she did seem upset when she was here. You talked to her the most, LaMerle. Any idea why she was upset?"

"I'm not sure. She asked how John was, which was odd, and then said she was feeling queasy, so she took the milk that Caroline got for her and left."

"Oh, maybe she was just sick then. Although after what happened with George, she was probably scared about purchasing milk. A lot of people are." Rita watched for reactions, but both women remained stone-faced and just stared at her. Given there was no interaction or conspiratorial glances between the two, rightly so or not, Rita concluded they were not working together.

"Any more questions, Rita?" Caroline asked as she pushed Rita's basket of milk bottles toward her, signaling the conversation was over. As she reached to pick up her basket, Rita glanced down at the magazine lying open on the counter. There Rita saw several expensive pieces of jewelry circled, and thought it looked like someone was getting ready to spend a lot of money. The pieces looked like LaMerle's taste.

"My goodness, someone's buying some beautiful, expensive jewelry," Rita commented. Again, neither replied, but LaMerle did turn red. *Gotcha*, thought Rita.

She picked up her basket, said a "sweet" goodbye, and went out to her car. She gingerly placed the milk basket on the passenger's side floor and drove home carefully.

She and Ronnie had a great deal to discuss. She made a mental note that Lana's car had several scratches on her side door and fender. She'd have to ask Wendell if any paint chips had been found at the scene of Trent's murder. Probably not, but it was worth asking.

She also added Lana to her list of prime suspects.

Chapter 22

Rita could hardly wait to discuss with Ronnie all the ideas racing through her head. In fact, she was so preoccupied she forgot to look before pulling out of the dairy parking lot. A local truck honked at her. She scolded herself, "Pay attention, Rita! Now is not the time for an accident." Still, she drove home faster than she usually did.

She knew Ronnie would be waiting impatiently. Plus, she also didn't want Ronnie to have time to spin too many stories. Rita knew her sister could easily turn what was happening into a movie script and completely ignore the facts and reality. Rita might be Watson, but she was determined to deal with the facts and find the evidence to prove their theories correct.

The truck horn made her think of Trent. She was positive he had been murdered. Wendell was still looking at it as an accidental hit and run. Well, the Chief could treat it however he wanted, but Rita and Ronnie would investigate it as a murder. *We need to check with Wendell and find out about the crime scene and what was found there*, she reminded herself.

Rita began connecting people, listeria, murder, and accidents in her mind. Now Lana had become one more piece of the crazy quilt of thoughts she was stitching together. She just wasn't sure yet what Lana's game was and how she fit into the entire mystery. She acted innocent, but Rita thought she was more conniving than she appeared, although she couldn't put her finger on just why she felt that way. Rita wanted Ronnie's input. Her sister was good at reading people and would know if Rita's instincts about Lana were on target. Instincts? *I've been spending too much time with Ronnie*, Rita thought. Still, the two were good at collaborating and solving puzzles.

As she drove home, Rita thought more about LaMerle and Caroline. They had seemed to reach a truce in their relationship. Nevertheless, she didn't believe that the two would work together. Besides, given what she'd overheard, it didn't sound as if they were working as a team. Plus, she wasn't convinced yet that Caroline wanted her father to sell the dairy, although she was positive LaMerle did. Rita also wondered about the red dot on some of the milk bottles. She wondered if it was a marker the bottle was contaminated. And if so, were those who got the contaminated milk targeted or random? Why was her red dot bottle switched?

Rita pulled into her driveway and hurried across the yard toward the house, as if on autopilot. She was so anxious to share her thoughts with Ronnie that she almost forgot to take the milk. She remembered it mid-way to the porch steps, turned around, and rushed back to get it, telling herself to focus. She grabbed the milk and raced into the house. She wanted to know what Ronnie thought about the red dot and why the bottle had been switched.

"Ronnie," Rita called out. Ronnie came out to the porch and held the door open for her.

"Why are you so riled up? There wasn't another murder, was there?"

"What? No, but I do have some interesting pieces of information we need to discuss." The two quickly went to the kitchen. Rita put the milk on the kitchen table.

"Why aren't you putting the milk away?" asked Ronnie, who looked genuinely puzzled.

"Do you notice anything different about the milk?" Rita asked. Ronnie looked over the bottles, but couldn't see anything different than usual.

"No, they all look the same. What am I missing?" Ronnie looked and sounded as if she were becoming even more confused.

"Well, when I took the bottles of milk from the cooler, one of them had a red dot on its cap. I had forgotten my basket in the car and went out to get it. When I came back in to pay for the milk, the bottle with the red dot had been exchanged." Rita explained.

"So, you think the contaminated bottles that had the listeria in them were marked with a red dot?" Rita nodded.

"Wait. That means that George may have been targeted."

"It does, although I still think he was just meant to get ill, but not die. People might have known George was not in great health since Georgia complained about it a lot, but as George was a private person, they would not have known the details of how his immune system was compromised. Thus, except for Georgia, they wouldn't have known the listeria would be deadly for him. Do you still think Georgia is innocent?"

Ronnie took a deep breath before replying. "Look, I don't like Georgia, and my guess is she didn't treat George very well during their marriage, but I don't think she would have wanted him dead. She may have wished it, but I still can't picture her being part of the listeria team. She's a loose cannon and not the brightest, so she'd be more of a liability to the team than an asset."

Rita concurred. "I agree. I even think we can remove her from our list."

"But why would someone target George? I can't picture him doing anything that would warrant someone killing him," Ronnie said. The sisters thought about George and why someone might want to target him with listeria.

Rita offered a reason first. "What about this? George is popular and everyone in town knows him from when he owned his business. Georgia has a big mouth. So, if George became ill from listeria, then the whole town would know. Agencies would be called in to investigate, and most likely John would be forced to close the dairy and sell the land."

"That makes sense. Okay, so that places King-Young front and center, just as we thought. And it has to be someone at the dairy who is in league with him." Ronnie waited to see if Rita would list the same suspects that were on her list.

"Go get your list of suspects and let's review," Rita commanded. For once, Ronnie followed her sister's orders without a complaint.

While Ronnie was gone, Rita got bowls of cereal ready for them. She poured milk into the bowls and put the bottles in the fridge. When Ronnie returned with her list and a pad and pen, she stared at her bowl of cereal and then picked it up and sniffed it.

Rita laughed. "The milk is fine. No red dot on any of the bottles."

Ronnie was not so sure. *To eat or not to eat, that is the question*, thought Ronnie. Still, Rita sniffed her bowl, too.

Rita noticed her sister staring at her, "Early and provident fear is the mother of safety."

"I'll eat to that!" Ronnie raised her spoon in salute. Rita was glad to see Ronnie smile.

"Let's eat," Rita replied. "As Shakespeare said, 'Delays have dangerous ends'," and both sisters swallowed their first spoonful. The milk tasted fine. Both sisters looked relieved. Ronnie was about to comment on how paranoid they had become, but instead simply sighed in relief.

As the sisters quietly ate, they reviewed Ronnie's list and organized their thoughts.

But before they could begin any discussion, the phone shattered their reverie. "Good Lord, what now?" Ronnie blurted, cereal flying out of her mouth. Rita quickly handed Ronnie a napkin.

"Who could be it?" Rita asked as she walked over to pick up the phone. "Oh, hello, Lana." She cocked an eyebrow, frowned, and looked toward Ronnie. Then she looked away and listened intently. "Ummm, I'm sorry to hear that. Certainly, we'll be right over." She quickly hung up and began moving.

"My God, did something happen to Lana? Has listeria struck again?" Ronnie cried. Then she quickly pushed her cereal away.

"Not sure, but Lana needs us to drive her to the hospital. She doesn't think she can drive herself." Rita grabbed her keys and purse. "Let's go. I think we'd better call an ambulance to get her. You can ride with Lana to the hospital and I'll follow."

"Good plan," Ronnie said. "I'll call the ambulance on our way to Lana's."

The sisters rushed out to the car and headed to Lana's. As soon as she slammed her door, Ronnie called for the ambulance and then asked, "Did Lana say anything else?"

"Not really. All she said was she made herself a hot chocolate with whipped cream. She used the milk from the dairy that Caroline gave her, and now she is feeling ill," Rita answered.

Ronnie noted the concern in her sister's voice. "I bet it's listeria. I wonder why she called us instead of John. He would have been the logical choice. Does she not trust him?"

"I wonder the same thing. The fact that Caroline gave her the milk may have spooked her. Plus, LaMerle may have said something to make Lana rethink her relationship with John. I don't know why she called us, but I do know the poor girl sounded desperate," Rita explained. "She said she's in great pain and feels so faint she thinks she might pass out." After thinking about it for a moment, she added, "I wonder if there's something she's not telling us."

"I'm sure there is. But more important: isn't listeria dangerous for pregnant women?" Ronnie asked. She sounded fearful.

"It is," Rita replied grimly.

The sisters quickly arrived at Lana's cottage. The ambulance arrived seconds after them. But before they could even knock, Lana opened the door. Pale as a ghost, she stood there holding her stomach, looking frail and in pain. The EMTs put her in the ambulance and Ronnie got in with Lana.

In the ambulance, Lana moaned a few times. "Please hurry." Ronnie tried to comfort her as the EMTs attended to her. One of the EMTs called ahead to the hospital.

Lana's moans grew louder and more frequent. Although it seemed to take forever, the ambulance and Rita made it to the hospital in record time. No more than fifteen minutes had passed from since Lana's phone call, but it was clear her condition was getting steadily worse.

"We're here, Lana, hold on." Ronnie urged. Suddenly everything switched to double-time. Attendants flew out the door, moved Lana from the ambulance, and rushed her inside. Ronnie followed, while Rita parked the car and then joined her sister inside.

"She was bleeding on the way here," Ronnie whispered to Rita. "She pleaded with the EMTs to save her baby. There was little they could do, though," Ronnie added.

"Well, all we can hope is that the baby survives," Rita said. Her face conveyed the sorrow of the situation.

"Maybe," Ronnie said, and then added, almost ashamed of her own honesty, "But more important, was this planned? It seems the listeria is now being used as a weapon."

Rita muttered, "You're right." She turned toward a couch in the lobby and said, "Let's sit. I don't know what more we can do right now other than wait." The sisters sat down on the worn leather couch and waited.

Both sisters replayed the last time they'd come to the hospital. That time, the outcome was known; George was dead from invasive listeria. Both sisters assumed Lana also was suffering from listeria poisoning. They sat quietly and waited for confirmation of their supposition.

They didn't have to wait long. In just a few minutes, a nurse came into the lobby and looked around the room. She noticed Rita and Ronnie rise and move toward her. Neither Rita nor Ronnie recognized the nurse, but they assumed she was looking for them, since there was nobody else in the waiting area.

"Do you have information about Lana?" Rita pleaded.

"Are you the ones who called the ambulance and followed it to the hospital? She got here just in time. Even so, the news is not good. I'm sorry to say that Lana has lost her baby. Have you notified her husband she's here? Is he on his way?" The nurse looked intently at the sisters.

Rita realized the nurse must not be from Castleton or she would presumably know the circumstances. So she explained, "I'm afraid this is a somewhat ticklish situation. Lana is single, and we're not sure of the circumstances surrounding her pregnancy. Could we talk to Lana?"

"We're admitting her, so you'll have to wait until she's ready to talk to you. There have been some complications besides the pregnancy." The nurse looked at the sisters, trying to remain calm as she delivered more dire news.

"What kind of complications?" Rita asked.

"She appears to be suffering from some kind of poisoning."

"Poison?" Ronnie and Rita asked simultaneously. But before the nurse could continue, Ronnie silently mouthed "listeria" to Rita, who nodded in agreement.

"Is there any more you can tell us?" Rita probed and then waited. Ronnie smiled and looked with empathy at the nurse. She looked so empathetic she easily won over the nurse.

"Well," the nurse paused and then continued. "She told us she had a hot chocolate with milk so we're testing her for exposure to listeria. She's showing all the symptoms--fever, muscle aches, some nausea, plus a headache and stiff neck. And her balance seems to be off. She's struggling just trying to sit up in bed. This kind of bacterial contamination is very serious when it strikes pregnant women," the nurse explained. "Almost invariably, it causes a miscarriage, as was probably the case here. Plus, it seems there was another case of listeria poisoning recently."

"It was our friend who died from it," Rita informed the nurse.

"I'm sorry to hear that, but I need to get back to Lana." The nurse headed back toward the door to the exam rooms, then turned and said, "Lana is lucky to have friends like you. If you hadn't gotten her here when you did, things might have been worse. She might have lost her own life, too." The nurse punched the swinging door and disappeared down the corridor.

Ronnie and Rita stared at the closing door and then at each other. Each let out a deep sigh. It was only 10:30 in the morning, but the day had already worn them out.

"So, is this attempted murder? Or accidental, like George?" Rita asked.

"We need to talk to Lana and find out if her milk had a red dot," Ronnie quickly added.

Later, after the nurse told them she was ready to see them, they asked Lana about the cap on her milk bottle. Lana told them she thought the cap had a red dot, but she wasn't sure.

"I think in rushing Lana here, we may have left her door unlocked. Let's see if we can find the cap," Rita suggested. Ronnie nodded in agreement, and the sisters went to their car.

As they drove to Lana's, Ronnie turned to Rita and said, "You know what it means if we find a cap with a red dot?"

Rita glumly replied, "Yes, it means Caroline is involved in some way. There's no avoiding it."

Chapter 23

Rita and Ronnie had barely made it out of the hospital parking lot when Rita's cell phone rang. She gave Ronnie a "What now?" look as she reached for her phone. "Yes, hello?" Rita snapped.

Ronnie's right eyebrow shot up in surprise. She knew her sister rarely answered her cell phone while driving, plus she had hardly ever heard Rita snap at anyone the way she just did.

"Oh, hello, Wendell. How are you?" Rita whispered "Police" to Ronnie.

Obviously! How many other Wendells are there, for heaven's sake? Good timing, though, thought Ronnie. She began giving Rita hand signals to put the phone on speaker. She was dying to know what Wendell was saying. With her hand signals, she felt as if she were auditioning for the Miracle Worker.

Rita listened carefully to the Chief, ignoring Ronnie. "Yes, we can certainly do that. We're just leaving the hospital right now, so we could be there in about ten minutes." She paused, clarifying the situation for Wendell, "No, it's Lana." She paused again and then continued, "She called and asked us to bring her to the hospital. Yes, she's ill, very ill, in fact. They've admitted her and are running tests. Yes, we can discuss Lana when we get there, alright?"

Rita closed her phone and handed it to Ronnie. "It seems Wendell has looked at Trent's flash drive and doesn't understand what it means. We'll have to interpret Trent's shorthand for him. It's a good thing Trent confided in us before he was killed."

"But we've already told him about Trent and his views on what's been happening in our messy little hamlet. And that we believe Trent's death is NOT an accident. Well murder, really. How much more of a picture do we need to paint?" Ronnie said, clearly exasperated by Wendell's lack of faith in their theories. "And now we can add Lana into the mix."

Rita replied slowly, as she was thinking things through, "Well, Wendell needs our help. I'm sure once we tell him all we've learned, he'll take us seriously. We can now paint a clear picture of the listeria outbreak, George and Trent's deaths, and what has happened to Lana. I'm sure we can convince him of the steps he must take in order stop what is going on."

Ronnie thought about Wendell before replying. He was slow, cautious, and methodical, but he also listened and was willing to explore other viewpoints than his own. "Okay, I think you're right. But we need to make as convincing a case as we can for Wendell."

In a few minutes Rita turned into the Police Station parking lot, killed the engine, and got out of the car. "This should be interesting, Miss Marple," commented Ronnie, but Rita was too distracted to notice or reply. She's organizing thoughts to figure out what she'll say, thought Ronnie.

Rita grabbed Ronnie's sleeve. "I think we should let Wendell do most of the talking. Let's see what he is thinking. Then once he's finished, we can lay out our information and theories, carefully dovetailing it with his. That way, he'll be receptive to what we say."

"I agree," Ronnie replied. "We should work on this together. Plus, we might be in danger, so having Wendell on our side is a good thing," Ronnie replied.

For someone who always presented a confident front, Ronnie was showing some fear in her eyes and even her voice. Probably nobody else would notice it, but Rita did, and it gave her more to think about as the two made their way inside to meet with Wendell. She wanted to know if there was a specific person that frightened Ronnie. And if so, Rita had an idea who it might be.

Ronnie felt odd walking into the police station with her sister beside her. In the past, it would have been Rita walking into the station to try to get Ronnie home before any charges were filed. Ronnie smiled as she recalled several close calls. When they were young, old Chief Hughes had been very accommodating, never actually booking Ronnie for her little misdeeds.

Wendell, who had been just a little younger than the two sisters, never really participated in any of their teenage shenanigans, but he did always comment on how lucky they were that Chief Hughes was understanding. Ronnie wondered if Wendell would be the same. Luckily, they had escaped punishment from the police, but not from their parents. Castleton being a small town, their parents always found out about their misdeeds, and in the end, both girls ended up being punished--Ronnie for the deed and Rita for abetting her.

These memories of childhood pranks also caused Ronnie to think about how the popular crowd she'd been part of had made fun of, and in some cases bullied, other kids. Granted, it hadn't been as rampant and dangerous as it was today, with social media that sometimes led to suicide, but it had probably damaged the victims. She regretted taking part in the bullying and wished she could apologize, but she had no idea where those kids were, and it was too late anyway. She comforted herself with the thought it had been more teasing than bullying.

Suddenly she wondered if the listeria outbreak could be some kind of revenge. She decided it was a good point to discuss with Rita, which she planned to do after they were done at the Police station.

Inside, to their embarrassment, the desk sergeant loudly announced the sisters were there to meet with the Chief. Both sisters bristled a little. It sounded more as if they were suspects about to be interrogated than the reality of their having voluntarily come to share information that might help Wendell with his investigation. The sisters decided to just laugh it off. After all, there were more important things to worry about right now. They sat on the hard wooden chairs. Just as they had as teenagers, they held hands as they waited for the Chief to join them in the office.

Wendell, looking every inch the Chief of Police, guided the sisters back to his office. His demeanor was impressive, and he had a nice, straight back. The sisters admired how he looked in his uniform. Yes, he was a good-looking man, and a kind man, too.

Rita coughed to get Ronnie's attention. It was time to focus on the investigation. Still, Ronnie planned on using her charm, as she routinely did with everybody, to convince Wendell to follow their suppositions and theories.

"Sit down, ladies. Can I get you some coffee or tea?" Wendell clearly was trying his best to be courteous, but Rita wondered if he was simply stalling, since the task facing them all was not pleasant. Wendell was a fair man, and it would take solid evidence and concrete, plausible ideas for the sisters to make him believe both what Trent had uncovered, and what they had discovered. And he certainly did not want to believe that murder had happened in his village.

"No, thanks. Let's get started." Rita tried not to sound too brisk or cold. But someone had targeted Lana, and the loss of her baby had seriously unnerved her. She also realized that as she and Ronnie continued to explore events and examine new clues, they were putting themselves in danger and possibly even becoming targets. They needed to convince Wendell of the seriousness of what was happening and that most likely there was a team at work. No one individual could pull off this mayhem. And there was not a moment to waste. If Lana had been targeted, which both sisters believed was the case, then who was next? There was clearly a deadly game being played in their beloved village, and they had to stop it.

"I agree with Rita, Wendell. How would you like to proceed?" Ronnie hoped she sounded a little more encouraging than her sister. "Would you like to ask us questions, and hopefully we can provide answers?" Ronnie knew that by answering his questions, they could subtly lead him in the direction they felt he should go to solve the mystery. They would also be creating a path for them to help him in the investigation.

Wendell let out a huge sigh. He was not happy. He'd never had to deal with a murder before, and although he truly hated to admit it, it looked like murders were happening. He still had some trouble believing that was the case, but the evidence was pointing in that direction. As a careful and thorough investigator, he always followed the trail of evidence, even if he didn't like where it was leading him. Wendell got out his pen and paper and prepared to take notes.

He cleared his throat and started in his most commanding voice, "Yes. Well, as I mentioned on the phone, we've looked at Trent's notes on his flash drive, and I'm puzzled. A lot of what he had there looked like gibberish, but I bet he probably used some reporter's shorthand. But since he visited you and gave the material to you, I thought you might clue me in about the notes."

"Did you have specific questions, Wendell?" Rita asked.

"Well, sure. For instance, he has 'two to tango' and 'baby on board,' but he also has 'bad milk/bad blood' and 'land of milk and honey.' Now those first comments seem to suggest there was some affair going on and it resulted in a baby, but there haven't been any births recently. Is he talking about long ago? And what could the 'bad milk/bad blood' be? I assume he's talking about George dying from listeria. But 'land of milk and honey' seems very nice, even positive. So, it doesn't seem to fit. Do you know what this means? I'd sure appreciate your help."

"Well, something rotten is going on here in Castleton," Ronnie began slowly, using her stage voice. Rita knew if she let Ronnie tell the story, they'd be there for hours, what with her quotations and dramatic interpretation of events. So naturally, Rita interrupted.

"Here's what's going on, Wendell." She could feel Ronnie glaring at her for stealing her spotlight, but Rita continued anyway. "We know George died of listeria. At first, we all assumed it was an accident, and most likely the listeria came from bad milk from John's dairy. That's the bad milk."

"Okay, but that has yet to be proven," commented Wendell. "We're still waiting for the state to confirm, but I agree, it does seem likely. Georgia confirmed George had bought milk there before he died."

"Right, and we agree." Ronnie intervened, sitting up straighter. There was no way she was going to let Rita win all the points. "Which begs the question-- was the listeria a natural outbreak, or was it planted?"

Wendell nodded and wrote on his pad. So far, he was not protesting about anything.

Rita gave Ronnie a silencing glare and resumed. "We think it was planted, and Trent agreed. So the spread of listeria has to do with King-Young and the development of John's dairy farm. The family is battling over whether to sell the land to King-Young. That's the bad blood. We all believe there's a lot going on in that family right now, so anyone in the family is really a suspect for working with King-Young and planting the listeria."

Ronnie noticed Rita hadn't excluded Caroline, which was good because it appeared more and more as if Caroline was involved. *But who else is part of the team,* Ronnie wondered? Ronnie decided to give Rita the stage and jump in only if Wendell objected to what Rita proposed.

Wendell looked thoughtful as Rita continued, "And we all know that King-Young has convinced the Planning Board that the development will be a boon for the town. Why, he's even agreed to the idea of an arts center to draw in tourists. He's pushed all the right buttons and gotten the majority of the town behind him. People have sold him land and invested in the development, thinking they will make a nice profit. That's the land of milk and honey."

Rita paused to let Wendell absorb the information, and Ronnie jumped right in. "Well, the arts center is a good idea, but it shows how King-Young thinks nothing of manipulating people. The local artists want green spaces and would have opposed the development. However, an arts center benefits them, so it mutes their opposition and wins them over." Rita nodded in agreement.

Wendell looked back and forth between the sisters and continued to take notes. He had to admit there was logic in what they were saying, but there was a lack of solid evidence. The planting of the listeria, if true, would be hard to prove. He'd have to break one of the team.

Rita believed they were winning Wendell over, so she kept going. "I must admit I don't think King-Young will build the arts center, but that's neither here nor there. George had been against the development and was refusing to sell King-Young a parcel of land he wanted. We know Georgia both wanted to sell the land and invest in the development."

"Wait, are you saying George was deliberately murdered?" Wendell asked, his eyes becoming wider. "I find that hard to believe."

"Wendell, you know as well as I do that people have been killed for very little money. The development represents large sums of money to people struggling or just getting by. Greed is quite the motivator," Ronnie replied. "And whether George's death was intentional, it certainly benefits a lot of people."

"Who?" Wendell asked.

"Georgia, for one," Ronnie blurted out. "But we don't think she would kill him. We think his death was collateral damage, but he may have been a target to be sickened by the listeria. George was popular and a leading citizen of Castleton. Everyone would have been talking about his getting ill. Many would have blamed John and therefore would have stopped buying his milk. That would have accomplished the goal of forcing John to sell the dairy to King-Young. So, he and the Camden family are the ones who benefit the most from George's death."

Rita spoke quietly. "The listeria is reminiscent of the Tylenol scare that happened years ago. Remember?" Wendell nodded. "People died from tampered Tylenol, but their deaths were 'accidental' or collateral damage. It didn't matter who died, just that the company that made Tylenol would suffer and have to pay out a fortune in compensation to the victims, some of whom were the ones who planted the tainted Tylenol. Here in Castleton, it really didn't matter if George died, and it could have been anyone. But George presented an opportunity, and with him being stricken, as we said, the fear of listeria would drive John to sell and maybe even compensate the victims."

Rita let those thoughts hang in the air for a moment before sharing more of their theory. It seemed as if they were winning over Wendell, which was good.

Wendell followed their thinking. He had to admit their theory was solid and made sense, but he couldn't easily figure out how to prove it and expose the person or people who were working with King-Young. Maybe I should focus just on King-

Young, he thought. He was at the heart of this, so there should be clear evidence of his wrongdoing. Good idea.

There were many reasons it would be good if the perpetrator turned out to be King-Young. First, he was from out of town, which would certainly be a relief and much better than having to investigate a neighbor. Though Wendell had to admit that for an outsider, the man seemed to know a little too much about the history of Castleton and how to play its politics. It was almost as if he knew the key players. A second reason Wendell liked having King-Young be a suspect was that the man was a developer, and nobody actually likes developers.

Somehow, though, Wendell wondered if that was too easy a solution. It almost seemed like a set-up. It reminded him of the old movies he'd seen with Ronnie years ago, such as Elmer Gantry and the Music Man. In those movies, a con man came to a small town and bamboozled the town folks. But in this case, while there wasn't any concrete evidence supporting that theory, even if it was correct. However, its resemblance to old movie plots was no help in solving things. Wendell groaned. So far, there was no concrete evidence he could take to court. Rita cleared her throat, bringing Wendell out of his reverie. He quickly refocused and encouraged her to continue.

"So, we suspect King-Young is the key player. The problem is figuring out who he is working with, since all the suspects have strong motives to see his plans succeed. He needs a person in the dairy helping him. But which one?" Rita asked. "There's no way King-Young is working solo."

"I agree," Ronnie said. She then decided to test her sister about Caroline. "Remember, though, that Caroline wants her father to be happy, and he claims he doesn't want to sell. Maybe she isn't a suspect?"

"No, we should look at her, too," Rita stated firmly. Ronnie was surprised, but happy to hear her sister say that. Ronnie's money was on her being King-Young's accomplice.

Wendell cut off the sisters. "OK. So, if George's death was accidental, that eliminates Georgia," he said. "Besides," he continued, "I can't picture her planning George's murder. So we set aside George's death and focus on King-Young and his team, whoever they are."

Rita and Ronnie nodded in agreement. It was only in the movies or in a cozy mystery set in the Cotswolds where Georgia would turn out to be the murderer.

"And then there's Lana." Rita stated calmly.

"What about Lana? I know she's in the hospital," Wendell queried.

Rita looked sadly at Ronnie. She nodded and lifted a brow as a signal that Ronnie could now take over the narration. This part was much more Ronnie than Rita: facts colored with lots of speculation.

"Lana was pregnant. She and John are the "two to tango." However, she lost the baby. And now she is very ill herself, most likely from listeria poisoning. She showed all the same symptoms as George. We're convinced the baby was John's, by the way." Ronnie added almost as an aside, then waited for that bombshell about the baby's lineage to sink in. When she saw Wendell's face turn red and heard him sputter, she continued.

"That gives LaMerle motive, so you can move her to the top of your list of suspects. She definitely did not want to lose John or have to share the sale of the land with Lana or her child. However, was she the only one working with King-Young?"

As poor Wendell was furiously scribbling away, Ronnie added, "And you need to keep John's children high on your list, too. They wouldn't want to share their inheritance with a half-sibling. The motive once again is greed. So, Lana was definitely targeted."

"Who was there when she bought the milk?" asked Wendell.

"Both LaMerle and Caroline," Rita answered. "Plus, when I went to buy milk after Lana had, one of my bottles had a red dot on it. I had forgotten my empties, so I went back to the car to retrieve them. When I came back, the bottle with the red dot had been changed out to an unmarked bottle. That makes me think someone tracked the contaminated bottles in order to target people."

"I'm sure people at the dairy will deny that, as they would say the listeria was not planted, but a natural occurrence.

So, we'd have to find a bottle with the red dot," Wendell pointed out.

Rita and Ronnie both smiled slightly. They were happy Wendell was thinking carefully about all these things and making connections between them. They both felt that was the best way for him to develop a plan to reveal the murderer. So far, Wendell tended to agree with what the sisters were hypothesizing. It made sense to him. He hated to think murder was happening in his town, but he could see now that was a real possibility that could be based on evidence, and not just speculation. Which was why he wanted to hear what they thought about Trent's death.

"Let's go back to Trent. And what he told the two of you." Wendell directed. He knew the two thought Trent was murdered, but he wanted to hear the reasons why they were convinced it was not an accidental hit and run.

Rita picked up the tale. "Trent came to see us the night he was killed. He explained his theories to us, and you now know we concur. At Georgia's, he foolishly announced he knew who was behind the listeria plot, and therefore who had killed George. He was going to publish it. Basically, the silly young man signed his own death warrant."

"That's right," Ronnie jumped back in. "Trent believed the listeria scare centered on forcing John to sell the dairy. His prime suspects were King-Young, LaMerle, John's children, and even John himself. Trent also thought it might have been Lana, trying to free John from LaMerle and the obligations of the dairy. However, given that Lana is fighting for her life in the hospital as we speak, I think we can rule her out."

"Maybe; maybe not," said Wendell. From his official police training, if not experience, he knew people who decided to kill would go to great lengths to cover their tracks, including appearing to be a victim. Consequently, Wendell decided to investigate Lana as well as the others. "Well, you ladies have certainly given me a lot to investigate." Then he stood up, signaling the end of the meeting.

"A word of caution, though, ladies?" The sisters looked at him, even though they both knew what he was about to say. "No meddling. Please keep your noses out of this investigation.

I may not have a lot of experience with murder investigations, but neither do the two of you. And given Trent's death, someone is clearly playing a deadly game. So please leave it to the police."

They nodded to Wendell and slowly walked out.

"We have to ignore his warning," said Ronnie as they settled into their car.

"Of course we do," Rita agreed. And the first thing we have to do is find the milk cap with the red dot. Let's go to Lana's now."

"And break in?" Ronnie asked, amazed that Rita would propose such an action.

"I left the doors open. We're just checking on the house." A slight smile crossed Rita's face, and the two set off for Lana's.

Once there, the sisters cautiously entered Lana's house, went to the kitchen, and began searching for the tainted milk with the red dot bottle cap. It was not in the refrigerator nor was it in the garbage. It had disappeared.

"Well, Watson, so much for that theory. No proof whatsoever," remarked Ronnie.

"Yes, Sherlock, but I think someone was here before us," Rita replied. "But how did they know to come retrieve the bottle?"

"They must have heard the ambulance and figured it was Lana. I wonder if they realize how deadly listeria is?" Ronnie asked.

"Let's go home and make our plan. We have to find evidence."

Chapter 24

The sisters drove home in silence. They were disappointed that their search of Lana's house had turned up nothing, but it had confirmed Rita's belief that there was a plan behind the distribution of the listeria-tainted milk, and both were now sure that Lana had been a victim.

"Well, it has to be either LaMerle or Caroline who sold Lana the tainted milk. I don't think it was an accident. And that makes me think that George's death wasn't an accident either," Ronnie said emphatically.

"We have to figure out if both LaMerle and Caroline are in cahoots with King-Young, or if just one of them is. Though, personally I can't see the two of them working together on anything. However, I can see them abetting each other and not giving the other away." Rita hated to admit it, but she was now thinking it was Caroline, and not LaMerle, who was deep in league with King-Young. *Oh, child, what have you gotten yourself into?* Rita wondered.

"Let's hope things don't keep escalating," Ronnie commented. She shivered thinking they might be in danger, but she knew they couldn't stop until the mystery was solved.

Still, Ronnie kept thinking about Trent's murder. It seemed unlikely he had figured out who the listeria team was. He had figured out the connection between the dairy and the development plan, and he understood the role of the listeria, but not yet who, other than King-Young, were the key players distributing the listeria. Trent's death would be the focus of any realistic investigation. That would consume the police force's time. However, if Wendell continued thinking it was an accidental hit and run, then the development plans would continue. This meant if King-Young were running a Ponzi scheme, he'd have time to complete it and then disappear.

Trent's announcement at Georgia's reception for George had been foolhardy and sealed his fate. Ronnie believed he had done it to draw the culprit or culprits out into the open, not because he knew who the murderer was. But it had backfired. Still, panicking and killing Trent was a mistake.

The sisters had been able to convince Wendell that Trent's death was murder, and now he would investigate it accordingly. Hopefully, as Wendell and the sisters pressed ahead investigating a murder, it would break up the listeria team. Ronnie felt sure that a premeditated murder had not been part of the original plan. But now was the time to unmask the team and pit them against each other as they tried to avoid being charged with murder and spending life in prison.

One thing unnerved Rita even more than the possible danger she and Ronnie were in, and that was that someone had moved with a cold-bloodedness that was frightening. Rita thought that threats or payoffs would have stopped the initial listeria investigation. Trent, despite his desire to win a Pulitzer and become a star reporter, might have settled for a payout to tailor his story to be about a listeria breakout that had happened naturally. He'd still have a newsworthy story and the money to get out of Castleton. Plus, once out of Castleton, he could confidently sell a follow-up story to a national paper, where it would be safe to publish it. However, the killer had decided the simplest solution was to murder Trent. Someone who could easily make that decision terrified Rita. And if she and Ronnie kept investigating (and they would), as with Trent, it would make them targets and put their lives in danger.

Rita kept coming back to King-Young. He had motive and means. And she believed he had the cold, calculating personality to plan and execute Trent's murder. But did his partner? As much as Rita believed Caroline was involved, she didn't think she would resort to murder. While Caroline might be greedier than she had realized, Rita didn't think she had the personality to participate in murder. *Please let that be true,* thought Rita.

So, if murder hadn't been part of Caroline's plan, then maybe they could use Trent's murder to break her. Rita was sure Caroline did not want to spend the rest of her life in jail. And if she turned on King-Young, she might work out some sort of deal. They would just have to eliminate the other suspects and find evidence to force Caroline to confess. She was sure she and Ronnie could devise a plan to do that.

But what to do about King-Young? Rita thought that getting Caroline to confess was one thing, but it wouldn't necessarily stop King-Young. Then she suddenly remembered a remark King-Young had made about John and the dairy. He had remarked that John was losing money, just like his father had running the dairy. *How had he known that? It was not a fact an outsider would know.* Rita decided they needed to find out more about the developer and his history. *What if he wasn't the outsider he claimed to be? But if that were the case, who was he? Could revenge as well as greed have been a motive?*

Returning from the Police station, the sisters walked into the house in silence. Once in the kitchen, Rita automatically began to make tea. She didn't even bother to ask if Ronnie wanted any. The whistling kettle brought them out of their thoughts.

As Rita poured the hot water into their teacups, Ronnie spoke. "So how do we solve this mess?"

Rita handed Ronnie her tea. Both held their cups for a few moments, letting them warm their hands. Rita also put out some scones. "Ah, that's what I admire about you, Ronnie. You jump in with both feet, assuming victory, and damn the consequences."

Ronnie smiled at her sister. It was true. Ronnie did not hold back. Once she'd made up her mind to do something, she simply went ahead and did it. The way she thought, solving a murder would be no different than anything else. All they had to do was develop a plan and follow it through to conclusion. They would solve the murder. Ronnie was positive that between the two of them, they could outsmart the murderer, or murderers.

"You're right, I do. But seriously, what's our first move? Do we interrogate King-Young? And how do we do it? It's not like we're best friends with him."

"No, we certainly are not," replied Rita.

"Given what's happening, we have to move fast. So come on, Watson, what do we do? We can't just call him up and say, 'King, dear, how about lunch? We'd love to chat with you about Trent, his murder, and ask if you killed him.'"

Rita almost choked on her tea. Ronnie was blunt, but Rita felt she made a good point. "Well, let's think about this," Rita said. "I was on the Planning Board, so that gives me a logical interest in what's happening in town. And I could say I was writing an article on the future of Castleton. You know, something along the lines of the death of small towns."

Rita sometimes wrote a column for the local newspaper. At first, she did it because she wanted one column in the paper not to be riddled with typos and grammatical errors, but over time, she had come to enjoy writing about Castleton and its people and what was happening in her hometown.

"I don't think I'd use the word 'death.' We don't want to tip our hand," Ronnie replied. She dropped the sarcasm and continued, "But that's a good angle to say we want to talk to him about the town's future since he seems to have taken such a large role in it. I can say I want to know more about the arts center and would love to volunteer to help plan it."

Ronnie reached for a scone and then broke it into small pieces. She nibbled on a piece. *Either Rita's scones are improving in taste, or my taste buds are dulling from my medication*, she thought.

Rita still didn't look totally convinced that plan would work, so Ronnie continued. "I'll convince him he needs my vast knowledge about the arts and dangle the prospect of investing in the development."

Rita nodded. The plan was green lighted.

"Alright, so how do we meet with him? Do we make it seem like chance and 'pretend' to bump into him, or are we direct and just call him and schedule some time?" Rita asked. She knew Ronnie would typically prefer a more dramatic scenario, such as the fake unexpected encounter, but Rita thought this was serious enough for the more practical approach.

Still, she knew the sisters had to cooperate, so she waited for Ronnie's input.

"Believe it or not, I'm for the direct approach. Setting up a fake, casual meeting will take too much time and effort on our part and would give him the opportunity to avoid talking about what we want. No, let's schedule a meeting. Plus, we can shade it so we will paint the development in a good light in anything you'd write, and right now, I think he'd love getting support from prominent locals."

"Excellent point, Watson." Rita waited for the outburst. She didn't have to wait long.

Bits of scone flew out of Ronnie's mouth as she sputtered, "Watson! How dare you call me Watson? I am the lead in this little story. I am Holmes."

Ronnie slammed down her teacup to emphasize her point. Rita hoped it didn't crack. She would have a hard time replacing it, as they were their mother's, and the pattern was no longer in vogue.

"Calm down, Sherlock, you can still be the star. Though I think I should be the one to call King-Young to set up the appointment. He'll probably want to meet in his office, which will be fine. I'll try for the appointment as soon as possible. I can say I have a deadline, and you are meeting some old friends, who might be willing to invest in an arts center or at least make an appearance at a benefit for it. The idea of money should make him move fast."

"Sounds like a good plan, Watson. While we are waiting for the meeting, who do you know at the local bank?" Ronnie inquired.

"Why?" Rita asked.

"We need to know about King-Young's finances. His deals sound like a Ponzi racket to me. So, the more we know, the better questions we can ask."

"That makes sense. Would the bank President do? I'm pretty good friends with his wife, as we exchange gardening tips. Plus, I had his kids in school, and one of them needed, oh shall we say, a little extra guidance to keep his nose clean. Kid turned out fine in the end. I think he's a CPA. Anyway, the parents are grateful."

"Excellent," Ronnie replied. "I can also open some sort of account and ask for investment advice, while you subtly ask about King-Young's finances. We need to know how solid they are. Real estate is a tricky business, and it's ripe with con artists.

That might have been something Trent found out, and it would give King-Young an additional motive to want to get rid of him."

Ronnie continued, "Also, we might want to find out how stable John and the dairy are. I'm sure LaMerle or Caroline would know, and they would have passed that information onto King-Young. With that information and the listeria, it would be easy to force John to sell."

"Good points. Something else we should investigate about King- Young is his past deals. People usually repeat what worked before, and if he had a Ponzi scheme that worked before, I'm willing to bet he'd try it again. And I hate to say it, but many in Castleton would be ripe for that type of scheme and could be easily duped."

"That's true. Castleton is not noted for having many, or any, Warren Buffets," Ronnie chuckled. "I'll start delving into King-Young's past. There must be some important hidden gems there."

"Sounds good. I'll make the appointment at the bank for tomorrow. It will be better to meet King-Young armed with more information. It might also give us a framework for our questions."

Rita smiled. Ronnie grinned, "Watson, we have a plan. " *And it's a good plan*, she thought.

Chapter 25

Ronnie went upstairs to take her medicine while Rita called the bank. "Time for Act One, Ronnie," yelled Rita. "We've got the appointment at the bank right now. I'll call King-Young after we talk with my friend, Jerry, the President."

"On a first name basis are we, Watson?" Ronnie joked as she came down the stairs. "I grabbed some checks from my old bank so I can open an account. And we're off."

Once at the bank, they were ushered right into Jerry's office. Ah, the beauty of a small town, thought Ronnie. This would never happen in the city.

"Jerry, thanks so much for taking the time to see us. I know how busy you are," Rita started out as the two shook hands. Jerry smiled and motioned for them to sit. "I know this is a special favor to us, and I really do appreciate it." Ronnie nodded her agreement. Jerry beamed.

"My pleasure, Rita. And you'll be happy to know Tim is now head accountant and doing wonderfully, as are the roses you gave my wife. You really helped us out with Tim."

Ronnie coughed, signaling Rita to get the conversation on track. A trip down memory lane was not part of the plan.

Rita picked up her cue. "I'm so glad to hear all is well with you and your family," Rita smiled broadly. "You know my sister, Ronnie?" Rita introduced the two. This is going better than I hoped, Rita thought.

"Of course. How are you, Ronnie?" Jerry focused on Ronnie, and then cast his eyes back and forth between the sisters. Jerry was no fool, and he knew this was no standard visit just to open a new account. He thought perhaps Ronnie had a sizeable amount of money and wanted investment help. Jerry focused again on Ronnie. "Now, what can we do for you?"

Ah, the royal "we." We've got him. The curtain has risen. On with the show, Ronnie thought.

"Well, I've come into some money. It's a settlement of my late husband's estate. There were some issues as he was a French citizen, but thankfully now it's all straightened out." Ronnie wrung her hands, reached into her purse, and pulled out her checkbook and a small, embroidered handkerchief. Rita noticed it had Ronnie's husband's initial on it, as well as their family crest—the one he had bought with Ronnie's money.

Rita smiled faintly at how well prepared Ronnie was for her role. And she tried not to laugh as the phrase "All the world's a stage" ran through her head. She wished Ronnie had kept the story simple, but she had hooked Jerry, so no matter.

"I'm certainly glad to hear it all worked out in your favor," replied Jerry. He was lapping it up. He looked as if he wanted to leap across the desk and kiss Ronnie's hand. And of course, Ronnie was now on a roll. Rita sat back and let her sister play out the scene.

"It did, but I tell you, my next husband is going to be an American." Rita wondered whom Ronnie had in mind for husband number five. It was five, wasn't it? Or maybe it was only four? She was pretty sure it wasn't six. Rita cleared her throat, hoping it would signal Ronnie to get to the point so Rita could ask questions about King-Young.

"I'm sure you'll have no trouble finding one, Ronnie. Now what kind of account did you want to open?" Jerry asked, hoping to find out how much money Ronnie would deposit in the bank.

However, Ronnie was not quite done with her act. "Ah, you flatter me, Jerry. The only person who has seemed interested in me is Kevin King-Young, and neither Rita nor I know much about him. And having been taken advantage of in the past, I'm reluctant to let my heart wander. Though he did recommend you and your bank." Ronnie fluttered her eyes slightly at Jerry, and then waited.

Rita couldn't believe the purple prose coming out of her sister's mouth, but she had to admit, Ronnie had deftly introduced the topic of King-Young. It was time for Rita to enter the discussion. "You know him, don't you, Jerry?" she inquired.

"Well, he does bank here, but I can't say I know him personally." Jerry was trying to be discrete, but Rita knew for a fact the man loved to gossip. Not a great trait for someone in his position, but then it was a small town. Ronnie would weasel the information out of him.

Ronnie fluttered her eyes again and inquired, "Oh, so you are warning me off him?" while Rita wondered if her sister could simper any more.

"No, but I would hold onto your money and be wary of him. He'll want you to invest in his development project. He claims his other projects were all incredible successes, but he doesn't seem to have the capital to back that up. Though I must admit for an outsider, he does seem to know the ins and outs of Castleton. He must have done a lot of research before he came here. Still, I'd wait before I invested if I were you."

Well, there's a red flag, Rita thought. *Jerry clearly thinks he's shady.*

"Well, I'll take your advice. I'll steer clear of investing any of my fortune with him. Thank you so much, Jerry," replied Ronnie, sounding completely sincere. "It's so good to have solid advice from one who knows about these things."

Rita moved in to get her own solid answers. "Are you saying he's not particularly solvent?" she asked. The sisters smiled at Jerry, who couldn't resist gossiping.

"You didn't hear it from me, but the man is on shaky ground. He needs to purchase John's dairy, or he's bought a lot of land for nothing, and in this market, that's not a good thing."

Bingo, thought Rita. "Yes, the whole development does seem to hinge on John selling the dairy. Personally, I think it would be a shame to see it sold. I do love the open land." Rita stared at Jerry.

"I agree, but on the other hand, John would make a nice profit, and why should he remain land rich but cash poor? He and his children could have a much better life if he sold the land. And as you know, you don't make money running a dairy. John's father never did either," Jerry replied, thinking green dollars win out over green grass every time.

"And don't forget LaMerle," Ronnie interjected.

"Yes, we all know where LaMerle stands on it," replied Jerry. He paused, wondering if he had said too much. Back to business. "Now about the account, Ronnie?"

"You know, Jerry, why don't you give some pamphlets? I do want to put my money in your bank, but silly me, I'm just not sure what kind of account. I'll look them over and then we can talk again?" Ronnie gave Jerry her most dazzling smile. "I will need more than one account."

"Of course." Jerry hid his disappointment, but he pulled out the appropriate pamphlets and handed them to Ronnie. "Make an appointment when you are ready."

Ronnie knew from his tone she had better put a sizable sum in the account when she opened it. Luckily, she did have money she could transfer. Yes, Jerry would be happy in the end, and he had confirmed their suspicions, so the money will have paid for good information.

Ronnie and Rita both smiled as they shook hands good-bye and headed toward the door. Jerry watched them walk away, admiring their graceful exit.

Ronnie turned and waved, and Jerry waved back, and then closed his office door. Ronnie hoped he wasn't calling King-Young, but if that were the case, they'd deal with it. Besides, if Jerry did call him right away, maybe that would make King-Young eager to meet with them.

As the two drove home, they discussed what they had learned. If nothing else, they now knew King-Young was desperate for John's dairy. He'd lose money without it. Money he apparently couldn't afford to lose. So, he certainly had a motive to make sure John had to sell the dairy. They both now agreed that King-Young was the prime suspect.

The thought that King-Young might not be the outsider he appeared to be kept niggling at both sisters, but they soon dismissed that thought, as it was time for the next interview. Besides, both believed they were on the right track.

"Time for the next call, Watson."

"I'm on it, Sherlock."

Ronnie was glad to see her sister had their roles right. Now if they could just figure out everyone else's role.

Chapter 26

Rita took a deep breath, picked up the phone, and dialed King-Young's number. She didn't have her sister's flair for the dramatic, so calling a stranger under false pretenses was not an easy task, but she was determined not to let Sherlock down. A young woman answered the phone. Rita immediately assumed her most stern teacher's tone.

"Hello. This is Rita Tisdale from the Castleton News. I was hoping to meet with Mr. King-Young to do an article on him and the development he is planning in town. We at the Castleton News are concerned only one side of the story is being told, and we'd love to share his side of the story with our readers. After all, the town should hear both sides, don't you think, dear?" Rita winked at Ronnie as the young woman agreed.

"Nice act," mouthed Ronnie.

"Why yes, an appointment in an hour is fine. I can make it. Thank you so much." Ronnie frantically motioned at Rita and shoved a pad across the table where she had written "ME TOO!" Rita nodded. "Oh, and if it's alright, I'll bring my sister, Ronnie. She's a former movie and Broadway actress and is very interested in the arts center. She would love to help Mr. King-Young plan it. And Mr. King-Young has said he was interested in meeting my sister." Rita paused dramatically. "And she has many friends, who would donate to the center."

Ronnie beamed and gave her sister the thumbs up. "We'll see you in an hour. We look forward to it. Bye-bye." Rita let out a deep breath. She hadn't realized she'd been holding it until she hung up the phone. "I never realized acting was so stressful."

"Tell me about it," laughed Ronnie. "You did great, though I must admit I thought that bye-bye was a little out of character. But otherwise, a solid, respectable job, Watson. Now I'm going to go upstairs to change. I need to look the part of a diva. And I know you are dying to ask, so I'll save you the trouble. Yes, someone did mention to me that King-Young was interested in meeting me." Fluffing her hair, Ronnie exited.

Rita guessed the person Ronnie was referring to was most likely Georgia being snide. She was also quite sure King-Young was only interested in Ronnie's money. Rumors had spread around Castleton that she had a fortune. It wasn't true, but Ronnie was financially comfortable. No need for me to burst her bubble, Rita thought. One good thing about the crime wave hitting Castleton--it certainly was giving Ronnie a new lease on life. Rita hadn't seen her sister so energized in quite some time. Although she felt it was too bad it took murder to raise her

While her sister got into costume, Rita wrote down some questions for King-Young. She could start by asking him about the development in general. He could confirm how many houses and other buildings he planned. Then she could ask about the impact on the town as a whole; how it would affect the school system, and the police and fire departments. Next, she could ease into any tax revenues the development would generate for the town, plus ask about local jobs. She vaguely remembered a plan for a series of shops within the development. In fact, she had heard some business owners had already signed leases and put down. The questions provided plenty of opportunities to discuss the dairy and the need for John's land.

And if those questions didn't provide the opening she and Ronnie needed to confirm their assumptions, then they would fall back on Plan B.

Plan B was to discuss the idea of having open spaces as part of the development. They could then weave the sale of John's land into use as part of the open spaces discussion. The main point was to establish how confident King-Young was about purchasing John's land. Then, they could mention the listeria and discuss how that would force John to sell the land. That made sense and seemed a natural flow for the upcoming conversation.

Plus, knowing his finances and how he planned to raise more money would also help them decide if the development was a Ponzi-type scheme. If it were true about the sale of leases before anything was even built, then it would be fairly easy to stop the development in some way and just abscond with all the investors' money. *I believe it is a Ponzi scheme*, thought Rita.

And that would give King-Young a stronger motive to have killed Trent.

Next, Ronnie could talk to him about the arts center. That would let them talk about LaMerle, who considered herself an artist, and Caroline who do PR for it. Ronnie would have to lie about LaMerle's talent, but she could pull that off. They could then use his reactions to LaMerle and Caroline to figure which was working with him as part of the listeria team. That covers all our bases, Rita thought.

Soon a heavy scent of *J'Adore* filled the kitchen. Rita looked up from her notes. Well, Ronnie certainly looked (and smelled) the part of a diva. She had changed from comfortable slacks and a cashmere sweater with pearls to a bright red flowing caftan. Around her neck was a stunning choker of dazzling ruby-colored stones, and a huge ring glistened on her finger. Rita was pretty sure the stones were not real, but with Ronnie, one never really knew. Ronnie looked like walking dollar signs. King-Young would be impressed.

"Looking good, Sherlock. With all your blinding bling, you should be able to pry all the information we need out of King-Young."

"All the better to knock his house down," Ronnie said as she polished the ring against her caftan sleeve. "Let's roll, Watson. I'm ready for my close-up."

Rita chuckled at the reference to Sunset Boulevard. But unlike Gloria Swanson's faded movie star, Ronnie playing detective had gotten larger than life, not smaller.

Chapter 27

Driving to King-Young's office, both sisters prepared for their roles: Rita the intrepid, curious reporter, and Ronnie, the aging diva with money to invest. Upon arriving, Rita parked the car, and the two sat, looked at each other, and took a few deep breaths.

"Ready, Sherlock?" asked Rita.

"Most definitely, Watson," Ronnie replied. And they walked confidently into the developer's suite of offices. *Shabby and makeshift*, thought Ronnie as she looked around.

The furniture was Ikea variety, and his young receptionist looked like an intern. Ronnie wondered if she was and therefore was "free" help. Ronnie guessed King-Young would immediately downplay the office and tell them it was just a "satellite" while he worked on the development deal. Rita glanced at her sister. She raised an eyebrow and nodded. Both were now convinced the development deal was a scam and King-Young really needed John's land to pull it off. Pieces of the puzzle were falling into place nicely.

The receptionist announced their arrival. "The ladies who called are here for your appointment. I'm off to class." She pointed to King-Young's office door and left. *Definitely an intern and free help,* Ronnie mused.

King-Young rose as soon as the two women entered his office. His office was sparse, and everything looked like it was rented. Set up for a quick getaway. However, his suit was Armani, and his loafers appeared to be hand-made Italian leather. His hair was perfect too. Both sisters wondered if it was a wig. Clearly, any money in the development paid for his high life.

"So now, what can I do for you lovely ladies?" King-Young inquired in his unctuous voice. With a sweep of his hand, he gestured them toward the chairs across from him.

Ronnie recognized a fellow thespian. King-Young's patter was tone perfect and well-rehearsed. He'd clearly honed his act. This is going to be very interesting, Ronnie thought. A master class in acting. However, Ronnie was confident she was a better actor. She glanced at Rita as they sat. Rita smiled, cueing Ronnie she could take the lead to put King-Young at ease. Then they'd go in for the kill.

Ronnie faced King-Young and played the opening gambit. "I'd love to discuss the arts center first. It would be a great lead for Rita's article."

Rita nodded and took out her tape recorder. "You don't mind if we tape this, do you? That way I can get your quotes perfect."

King-Young nodded and answered, "That's fine," giving a huge smile. *Those teeth are definitely caps*, Ronnie noted.

"Well, I think the arts center would be a definite drawing card, so I am willing to support it and work with you to see it become a reality. The people coming to the arts center would infuse money into the local businesses and really generate new interest in, and income for, the town." King-Young spread his arms wide as he spoke.

He's good, noted Ronnie. *Very good.*

"Well, I couldn't agree with you more. And as a former actress, both on the Broadway stage and in television and movies, I must say the idea of an arts center is quite dear to my heart. I think we'd make a good team and would appreciate your help in making the arts center a reality. Would you be willing to be co-chairman of the fundraising committee?"

"I'd be more than happy to do so," King-Young proclaimed. *Oh, this is going well*, he thought. *Now if I can only reel her into investing.*

"That's wonderful. Now Rita, why don't you ask your questions." Ronnie sat back. She knew Rita was ready. *Time to squeeze information out of the star player.*

"Mr. King-Young," began Rita.

"Call me King. Everyone does."

Ronnie almost laughed out loud as she thought, *Talk about living out your name. He thinks he's the king of Castleton.*

"Of course, King. Why did you choose Castleton to build your development?" She planned on lobbing easy questions, so he let his guard down as the interview progressed. Then she'd nail him.

The question proved effective, because King-Young droned on. "Castleton is the perfect town to develop. There are pockets of money, so people can afford custom-designed homes, and there is land available, so the lots can be large enough to be private. You're near cities, so people can easily commute, and many people want to experience the quality of life that a small, rural town offers, but at the same time have all the amenities of city living. My development will answer those needs." King-Young paused and smiled widely at the women.

Rita looked up and smiled back. *He's learned his lines well, and delivers them with authority that almost sounds sincere,* Rita thought, but both sisters knew not to trust him. However, they nodded and smiled, keeping the game going.

Encouraged, King-Young continued, "Of course, my development will be more than the McMansions everyone fears. It will become part of the fabric of community life here." Rita nodded as if in approval and moved the tape recorder closer to him on his desk. Like a pro, King-Young spoke directly into it.

Rita looked up and asked her next question. "So, will there be job opportunities for some of the local people?"

"Of course. My developments have a history of improving the economic conditions of the towns in which they are built, and my word is my bond. Believe me, things will be much improved when I'm done. Castleton will be set up for growth."

Rita pretended to be in awe and believe every word. However, her research on his other developments painted the opposite of the rosy picture he was now painting. In the articles Rita had found, people had complained about the shoddy workmanship, and some had taken him to court to try to get back the money they had invested. In fact, if Rita remembered correctly, he had never even finished the last project. He had secretly left town, leaving behind a "ghost" development, filled with ruined green spaces, partially finished buildings, and muddy, incomplete roads. He'd basically absconded with the money.

It surprised her that his past failures had not been brought up at the meetings. But even if they had been, Rita was sure he had a story ready to overcome any hesitation on the town's part.

And given his presentation skills and ability to talk in perfect sound bites, people would fall for it. Rita was glad she and Ronnie had not invested in the development.

"Can you tell me some other towns where you have developed similar communities?"

King-Young hesitated. Rita and Ronnie waited. The spin was about to begin.

Still, Rita smiled brightly as she sat waiting for his reply, thanking the Internet, where you could find all sorts of key information. Even if the stories she had found were slanted against King-Young, he was not the successful, big shot real estate maven was pretending to be. His answer also would show how he could manipulate a situation.

"I'll send you information about my past accomplishments. That's easier than me listing all my successes. I don't want to appear to be bragging. Besides, the focus should be on what is happening here in Castleton. That's what the people will be interested in," he replied smoothly.

"That's true." Rita continued with her questions. "The rumors are that you need to buy John Camden's land in order to complete the development, given its large scope. Is that true?"

"It would be better if I can acquire his land, but if I can't, I can always scale back the development or make other changes," King-Young replied calmly.

"Well, most likely that won't be a problem with the listeria outbreak," Ronnie chimed in. "It looks like John will be forced to sell."

King-Young shuffled papers on his desk, stalling for time. "That is a dire situation, but it hasn't been proven yet that the listeria outbreak came from his dairy. However, if that proves true and John has to sell, he'll get more than a fair price from me."

"And you have the money to buy the land?" Rita asked sweetly.

"Once the land becomes available, there are many in Castleton who want to invest in the development, so money is not a problem." He smiled at the sisters. "I think that covers everything." King -Young rose from his chair to escort them out of his office.

"If you buy John's land, you'd also have Caroline do your PR work, wouldn't you?" Rita inquired. Her gentle tone masked her real purpose.

"Caroline is already working with me, so yes, I assume she would continue," King -Young replied blandly. Rita's heart sank. She was now convinced Caroline was his partner.

As they were leaving, Ronnie stopped in front of a painting hanging on his wall. She saw the signature was LaMerle's. "You're collecting local artists?" Ronnie asked. Then she had a sudden brainstorm on how to check his alibi the night Trent was murdered.

"Yes, I do. That painting is by LaMerle Camden. She's a talented artist," King replied to the unasked question. "I try to support local artists, and that's why I support the arts center."

Rita was about to comment about LaMerle wanting to sell the dairy, but before she could, Ronnie turned around and faced King-Young, cutting Rita off.

"Well, you should check out Linda Conway. She's a talented artist and is gaining recognition. She'd be a good investment. I own a few of her pieces." Ronnie turned away, and then turned back. "In fact, she had a showing a week ago. It was the same night poor Trent Fowler was killed. He was going to cover the show."

"Trent killed? I thought Trent's death was a hit and run accident," King-Young sputtered. However, as Ronnie stared at him, his look quickly changed from one of panic to concern.

"No, the Chief of Police is classifying it as a homicide," Rita said. "He'll be questioning people as to their whereabouts that night."

"You weren't at the opening. Where were you?" Ronnie asked nonchalantly.

King-Young took his time replying. "No, I was out of town at a real estate convention. You know how those are. They are like our version of the Oscars." King-Young chuckled and gave Ronnie a huge grin and a wink.

"Yes, parties where the wine flows, and the next day no one remember who was even there," replied Ronnie, chuckling along.

"Oh, people will remember me as I gave a speech," King-Young said coolly. "Well, I believe we are done now." He gestured for them to leave. Ronnie noticed a thin veneer of sweat on his upper lip. *He's worried about his alibi*, Ronnie concluded.

"Yes, I have everything I need. Thank you so much," Rita replied. The sisters exited.

On their way to the car, Ronnie commented. "You left your recorder there."

Grinning, Rita said, "I know. I want to see if he makes a phone call. We'll wait and go back and get it in ten minutes."

While the sisters waited, King-Young made two phone calls. The first was to the editor of the local paper where he found out that there was no story planned, but the editor said if Rita submitted it, they'd publish it. King-Young hung up and then made another call.

"The Snoop sisters were just here. They may be a problem. I think they have figured out the listeria plan and that we're partners. Keep away from them. I'll decide how to eliminate the problem." Then he slammed the phone down.

After waiting ten minutes, Rita raced back to King-Young's office and without hesitating, entered his office. King-Young looked up, confused. "What do you want?"

Rita didn't answer, but walked directly to his desk and pocketed her recorder. "Oh, I forgot my recorder." Then without a word, she left.

"Those two are now a serious problem," King-Young muttered.

Chapter 28

Rita and Ronnie sat at their kitchen table and listened to the recording. When they heard he'd called the editor, they had a moment of panic, but it passed as they listened to the second call. Rita quietly sipped her tea before commenting.

"He confirmed we were right about the listeria outbreak," Rita said. "We need to be very careful, as I don't think King-Young will hesitate to try to stop us from investigating further."

"Unfortunately, I think you're right. I also don't think we are the only ones now in danger. I think Lana is too. Someone has the red cap identifying the tainted milk, and whoever has it knows its purpose. That puts Lana in danger. I think we'd better warn her. It might be best if she leaves town for a while." Ronnie sat back. "So, what are our next steps?"

"First, let's visit Lana. Then we can share the tape with Wendell. I think it gives him enough evidence to question King-Young and the people at the dairy. King-Young practically admitted the listeria outbreak was planned, so Wendell can investigate that. Hopefully, it will protect us and Lana." Rita waited to see if Ronnie agreed.

"Makes sense. I think we should also meet with Georgia, LaMerle, and Caroline. We need to figure out who King-Young was talking to about the listeria."

"Okay. Let's set up meetings with the three women." Rita looked at her sister. "Do we meet them together, or divide and conquer?"

Ronnie thought about it and then responded. She had a plan. "I think divide and conquer is best. I'll take Georgia." Rita started to protest, but Ronnie held up her hand. "Look, I know we don't have a great relationship, but I also think I can force her to be honest with me. You're better at working Caroline, and we should double-team LaMerle. Then we can report what we learn to Wendell to help him with his investigation."

"Sounds good, Sherlock. So how do we set up the meetings?"

"Well, I think surprising Georgia by showing up at her door will work best. If you could bake a banana bread, that will be my excuse. Then I'll give her the third degree on where she was when Trent was killed and also quiz her about the listeria. We have to find out their whereabouts at that time since there was no art opening." Ronnie smiled at her sister.

"That was a good move, but you're lucky he just believed there was an opening." Rita had had to turn away when Ronnie pitched the art opening. "I had to turn away to hide my astonishment at that bold lie."

"It worked, and that's what matters. I knew he has no real interest in local artists, so I wasn't worried. He bought LaMerle's painting so she'd be on his side with the sale. He really is good at reading and manipulating people."

"He is, and that's why we need to be careful." Rita went to the phone. "I'll schedule lunch with LaMerle and then coffee the same day with Caroline. I don't want to give them a chance to share notes."

"Good plan, Watson. Make the calls and then we'll visit Lana first."

Rita called LaMerle and scheduled lunch for the next day. Then she called Caroline and scheduled coffee at her house. She turned to Ronnie and said, "You can meet with Georgia when Caroline comes here." Ronnie nodded. She thought it best if she simply went to Georgia with no warning, so she didn't call her.

"Time to go see Lana."

The two sisters went out to the car and drove to the hospital, but Lana had been discharged. So they drove immediately to her secluded cottage.

Chapter 29

Rita and Ronnie pulled into Lana's driveway, parked, then went to her door and knocked. The sisters became nervous when she didn't answer the door. Ronnie knocked again, loudly.

"Yes, coming," Lana finally answered. She yanked open the door.

"Oh, hello. I was upstairs and didn't hear you knocking." She looked flustered.

"Did we catch you at a bad time? We just wanted to check on you," Rita said, starting to move inside. Ronnie crowded behind her.

"No, it's fine. Come in." Lana stepped aside so the sisters could enter. Both noticed immediately that Lana had a suitcase by the stairs.

"Are you going away" Ronnie asked, looking concerned. *She's either scared and is fleeing or escaping. Which is it?* Ronnie wondered.

"Yes, given all that's happened, I want to get away. My lease is monthly, and so I'm thinking I may just move, but I definitely need to get away." Lana went to the couch and sat down. "Would you like tea or coffee?" she asked, sounding like a perfect hostess. But both Rita and Ronnie could see she was far from being a hostess who was happy that friends had come over.

Rita and Ronnie sat on the couch. "No, we're fine," Rita assured her. "As I said, we just wanted to check on you and see how you are."

Ronnie cut in. "We also have a few questions for you."

Looking surprised by Ronnie's statement and tone, Lana sat up straighter on the couch. "What do you want to know?" she asked.

"We're so sorry about your loss," Rita said with sympathy. "Thank you. It was a shock as well as painful. I can hardly believe I was sold a bottle of milk that had listeria," she replied in a soft voice. Nevertheless, Ronnie picked up a harsh undertone in her voice. *She thinks it was deliberate. LaMerle or Caroline.*

"I'm sure it wasn't intentional," Rita said. Lana remained silent, so Rita asked, "Did you notice anything odd about your bottle of milk? Did it have a dot on the cap?"

Lana shook her head. "No, not that I remember, but I became ill quickly after drinking it, so if it did have a marking on the cap, I probably wouldn't have noticed." Lana clasped her hands together and looked away.

"We are so sorry, and can understand why you want to leave," Rita said.

Ronnie leaned in and patted Lana's hands. "I think it's a good idea for you to get away. Where will you go?"

"I'm not sure. I'll just drive up the coast and then stop when I'm tired." Lana replied.

"Please call us if you want to talk. You have our number," Rita said kindly.

"Thank you, but I think I just need to be alone. Don't worry about me. I'm a survivor," Lana stated firmly, then stood up.

Rita and Ronnie took their cue. They hugged Lana and left.

She stood in the doorway and watched them drive away. Once they were out of sight, she walked down to her mailbox and opened it. Her envelope containing the bottle cap with the red dot was gone. In its place was an envelope with money and a note. Lana read the note.

"Here's your payment. Keep to the agreement and leave town now." Lana counted the money and smiled. The cap with the red dot was gone, but she had photographed it as she had thought it was odd. It was an insurance policy for her. However, even with this evidence, she was taking no chances. She got her suitcase, put it in her trunk, and backed out of her driveway. *Goodbye, Castleton.*

With the money, she had time to set up her next score. She'd find another John, except this time he'd be single and rich. Love would not be part of the plan.

As she drove away, she noticed Rita and Ronnie on their way to the police station. She was sure the sisters would give

Wendell an earful. Lana debated on stopping and sharing the photo of the red bottle cap, but decided not to. Better to escape while she could. Maybe she'd anonymously email the photo later. Maybe.

As she checked her rearview mirror one last time, she saw a black SUV pull behind Rita. She shrugged and kept going. *Goodbye, Castleton.*

Chapter 30

Driving to the police station, the sisters discussed what had transpired with Lana. "So, Watson, what did we learn?" Ronnie asked.

Rita reviewed their conversation in her memory before replying.

"She seemed distant and bitter. Of course, that could be due to her loss."

"I'm sure that's part of it, but I also noticed a harsh tone in her voice. She clearly thinks she was targeted by either Caroline, LaMerle, or both." Ronnie said. Rita nodded in agreement.

"What I found really interesting is that I didn't say the cap had a red dot, I just said "dot." But when she replied, she said it had a red dot. So, whoever gave her the milk knew it was bad. But why did she lie?" Rita sounded genuinely puzzled.

"Good question. Do you think whoever sold her the milk went back to Lana's for the cap and bottle?" Ronnie asked, although she wasn't sure that was what happened. Another thought occurred to her. "What if Lana noticed the cap before she drank the milk and kept it? She could use it for extortion." Ronnie thought that was a real possibility, and she liked her idea.

"She'd have to have hidden it before she drank the milk. You think she's that cunning?" Rita wasn't sure. But her sister was a good judge of character, so her idea was credible.

"I do. I think there's a lot we don't know about Lana, and I find it interesting she'd planned on escaping town before we even warned her."

"Let's say you're right. Who did she blackmail? Caroline or LaMerle?" Rita hoped it wasn't Caroline, but the more they learned, the more things pointed to Caroline.

"I know you don't want to hear it, but I think it's Caroline. If you think about it, Lana being pregnant could work to LaMerle's advantage. Once the dairy was sold, she'd have John over a barrel, and Lana would probably be on LaMerle's side to make sure John sold the dairy. She'd want John to have money." Ronnie was pleased with her line of inquiry.

Rita was silent, taking in everything Ronnie had said. "Well, that will be our focus tomorrow when we meet with Caroline and LaMerle. You can still meet with Georgia to confirm we should eliminate her, but I think we're right about her. She's innocent," Rita replied.

Good we're on the same page, thought Ronnie.

"On to Wendell and the Police station," Rita said, patting the tape recorder.

"Onward, Watson." Ronnie couldn't wait to see Wendell's reaction to the recording. They guessed some of his reaction, but not all of it.

As they were driving to the Police Station to see Wendell and share their recording of King-Young, a large, black SUV appeared behind them. It was speeding, so Rita pulled over to the side of the road to let it pass. However, the SUV sped up and pulled directly behind Rita's car.

"What's happening?" Ronnie screamed as the car moved closer.

"Brace yourself. That SUV is going to ram us," Rita cried.

She had just finished warning Ronnie, when the SUV rammed her car, crunching metal. Rita's car flew off the road and down an embankment. She tried to brake, but couldn't. There was nothing she could do.

A tree loomed directly in front of them. Rita and Ronnie leaned back and prayed as the car careened into the tree. The crushed engine died, and smoke filled the air. The windshield cracked and shattered. The air bags exploded, knocking them unconscious. A figure appeared at Rita's door, opened it, and searched for the tape recorder. Finding it, the figure closed Rita's door and vanished.

Eventually Rita began to come to. She opened her eyes and moaned.

But the figure had disappeared.

Chapter 31

As Rita slowly became more aware of the situation, she deflated the air bag and began to assess the situation. Except for bruising from the bag, she was fine. She asked Ronnie, "Are you alright?"

Ronnie groaned. "I think so. Help me pop the air bag." Once the bag popped, Rita checked Ronnie. She had a bloody nose and was bruised, but otherwise was okay.

"We're very lucky. Now let's get out of the car. And we need to call for help," Rita said. They crawled out of the car. Ronnie tried to smile, but it hurt too much.

"Let's take the tape recorder with us," Ronnie suggested. They searched the car, front, back, and even checked under the seats, but they couldn't find it.

"Whoever drove us off the road must have taken it," Rita said, her voice weaker and less forceful than normal.

Ronnie observed that Rita was pale and appeared shaken. She looked like Ronnie herself felt--scared and angry. But they were safe, and that's what mattered most. However, they were also missing a crucial piece of evidence.

"I don't suppose you backed up the recording?" Ronnie asked.

"No, but I remember it word for word. Hopefully, Wendell will believe us."

Rita called Wendell to report the accident, and Ronnie could tell from her side of the conversation that he was concerned. *He'll believe us*, Ronnie thought. *Why else would we have been run off the road? It had to be King-Young. He was the only one who knew we had him on tape.* Things were definitely heating up.

Rita rubbed her shoulder, but it was too painful to move. She and Ronnie just stood there, frozen, waiting for Wendell. *We're like statues*, thought Ronnie.

Of course, Wendell would be furious they'd investigated on their own. With the tape, they would have quickly won him over. Now, however, he'd simply have to believe and trust them as to what had been recorded.

Both hoped that would be the case.

Rita kept saying, "That's right" into the phone. Finally, she hung up.

"Well, what does the Chief have to say? Is he on his way to rescue us?" Ronnie wished she had time to clean up and fix her face and hair, but knew it was a lost cause.

"Yes, he is, and he's quite concerned. He'll take down the accident details and file a formal accident report," Rita said and pocketed her phone.

"Accident, my foot. We both know it was attempted murder," Ronnie sputtered.

Rita replied, "You're right. If not out and out attempted murder, it was surely an attempt to scare us off our investigation and retrieve the tape recorder."

"Sorry, but I'm not giving up, Watson."

"Oh, neither am I, Sherlock."

Rita looked down at the car. It had stopped steaming, but clearly was totaled. "On the bright side, with no car, we can sit home and solve the mystery."

Ronnie smiled and gave a thumbs up sign.

"That's the spirit." Rita tried to sound encouraging. "Though we should still keep our meetings. We can take a taxi to them if necessary."

"I can walk to Georgia's, so that's not a problem," Ronnie reassured her sister. "Though we could use the accident as a carrot for our meetings. Caroline, LaMerle, and Georgia will want to know what happened."

"True. We'll deal with them tomorrow. Remember, tomorrow is another day.

"Don't steal my lines." Both tried to smile, but couldn't.

Ronnie looked up and down the road. "Who do you think ran us off the road? My money is on King-Young."

"I'd say that's a safe bet," Rita replied. Then she asked, "Did you get a good look at the car?"

"Large, black SUV with tinted windows." Ronnie paused and then added smugly, "I didn't get the plate number, but it was a rental." She waited for Rita's reaction.

"How do you know?" Ronnie was no car aficionado, so Rita hoped there was a logical reason why she had reached that conclusion and not just because her gut told her it was a rental car.

"The license plate had a rental sticker on it. It was Hertz. Maybe Wendell can trace the car." Ronnie paused and then continued, "But King-Young is smart, so I'm sure he would have used a fake license and credit card." Since Rita nodded, Ronnie continued her train of thought.

"Which then raises the question, why would he have a fake license and credit card? That screams that the development deal was a Ponzi scheme from the very beginning. It also raises the question, who is King-Young, really?"

Both sisters were quiet as they thought about it. After a moment, Rita said, "There's another way of looking at it. What if that is his false identity? You've always said there was something off about him. And remember that slip of the tongue when he referred to us in the past? How did he know we've always been curious? And we all thought he seemed familiar— as if we knew him."

"You're right!" Ronnie replied. "Plus, remember how we couldn't find anything on him more than five years back? That's odd, especially for a developer who thrives on social media. He claims to have been in the business for over 30 years, so where are those missing 25 years?

I think that points to King-Young being a new identity. But why would he need a new identity here in Castleton? Something doesn't add up."

They were about to continue their speculation on King-Young's identity and his past when Wendell arrived. The flashing lights gave both sisters a headache. Once again, they realized how lucky they had been to escape with just a few scratches.

Turning off the flashers, Wendell got out of the car, raced over and grabbed Ronnie in a bear hug. She groaned in pain as Rita gave her a crooked smile through her sore lips.

"I'm fine, Wendell. You can let go," Ronnie urged impatiently.

"Of course, sorry. Hope I didn't hurt you." Trying to cover his embarrassment, he turned toward Rita. "Are you okay, too, Rita?"

Feeling better now that Wendell was there, Rita controlled her urge to laugh. It was just like back in high school with a local boy falling for Ronnie. *I knew Wendell had always liked Ronnie. Guess he still does,* Rita thought. *Too bad she doesn't feel the same way.*

Rita was succinct and business-like. "I'm fine, Wendell, thanks. Here's what happened."

Wendell got out an accident report form and filled it out as Rita described in detail how they were run off the road. She took her time, making sure Wendell understood the gravity of the situation. She also hoped he realized it was not an accident.

"Ronnie is sure it was a rental," Rita concluded.

"It was. And we know it was King-Young driving," added Ronnie, who was not about to be left out of the story even if she was not necessarily recounting facts.

"Are you sure? Did you see him?" Wendell asked. Somehow, he had doubts either sister had seen the driver. The accident had been fast, and the driver had left the scene. It echoed Trent's murder. This time, luckily, Rita and Ronnie had survived, but it was still attempted murder. *There's a killer on the loose, and I have to catch him,* Wendell thought.

Ronnie hesitated. *Better not lie.* "Look, we'd been to interview him, and we recorded the interview. In the recording, he talked to his partner about the listeria," Ronnie blurted out.

"Wait. What? You interviewed him? And there's a recording?" Wendell stared at the sisters and shook his head.

Rita jumped in. "Wendell, please calm down. Yes, we, well I, went to talk with him for an article for the local paper. Ronnie came along to discuss the arts center."

Wendell's stare was turning into a glare. He was not happy. "And?"

"I interviewed him about his proposed development. I asked about his finances, which are shaky, according to Jerry at the bank." Wendell groaned, but Rita pressed on. "For him to succeed, he needs John's land. He didn't admit anything about the listeria outbreak to us, but he agreed it would benefit him."

Wendell cut in. "I thought you said he admitted to working with someone at the dairy to cause the listeria outbreak."

"Look, we left behind the tape recorder. It was running and taped two phone calls he made after we left. The first was to the editor of the paper where he learned there was no story." Ronnie looked at Rita, who signaled her sister to keep going. "The second call was to his accomplice, and he said we were onto the listeria outbreak being planned; he also implied we knew who was behind it. Thus, we are now a problem for King-Young and whomever he is working with to force John to sell his land." Ronnie took a breath and waited to see Wendell's reaction.

"Where's the tape recorder?" he asked.

Wendell believes us, the sisters thought. They felt truly relieved. "It's missing. Whoever ran us off the road must have taken it. That's why we believe it was King-Young. He's the only one who knew we had it."

"What about the person he called after you left?" Wendell was buying into their theory, but he wanted more facts before he took any action.

"Well, he talked to the person after we left and before Rita reclaimed the recorder, but he never used any names," Ronnie stated emphatically.

"Okay. Still, this gives me enough to pull him in for questioning," Wendell said mostly to himself. He slowly added, "I wonder where the rental car is. I doubt he returned it to the rental agency, although we can start the search there. I'm sure he is using a fake identity. When we were investigating Trent's murder, we found no relevant information about him, nor any record of him renting a car." Wendell continued rolling ideas around in his mind.

"So, you agree it is King-Young?" Rita asked.

"I agree it most likely is King-Young. As I said, I can pull him in for questioning, but I'll have to prove it's him," Wendell replied, emphasizing "prove." Then he added, "I'll get my deputy checking out all the local Hertz rental agencies with his picture. And I'll have them check if any damaged rentals were returned."

"We think he probably rented it under a false identity. And if he did, he may just leave it at the airport, probably in long-term parking, especially if the car is damaged. That's what I would do," Ronnie reported.

"Yes, you have so much experience with these things," Wendell commented wryly. Though he did actually agree with her. He thought this whole scheme was sounding like one of Ronnie's movies, but he did agree with her theory. It was logical, and it made sense.

Wendell was surprised Ronnie was being the logical sister, but maybe Rita had put forth the theory and Ronnie was claiming it for her own. Ronnie had done that in the past. And since Wendell knew how competitive the sisters had always been, he wasn't going anywhere near that hornet's nest.

"Come on, let me drive you home," Wendell said.

"Thank you, but just let me call Bill at the garage. The car has to be towed," Rita said as she pulled out her phone. But just as she was about to dial, she saw Bill's truck arriving. "That was fast. The joys of a small town."

"I took the liberty of calling him," Wendell confessed. "Unfortunately, you know how Bill loves to gossip, so let's hope he didn't stop for coffee, or this will be all over town." The three looked up to see Bill smiling and waving a take-out coffee cup. "There goes any chance of keeping this story to ourselves," Wendell sighed and shook his head.

"Lord, look at that mess. Someone drove you off the road, huh, Rita? I know you wouldn't cause an accident like this. Now, you, Ronnie, maybe," Bill added, chuckling.

Ronnie sputtered and yelled, "I'm a good driver, too, Bill Hayes. You should have seen me driving in Rome and around the Arc de Triomphe in Paris."

Bill laughed and went down the embankment to inspect the car, shaking his head as he got to it. "Wow, this is bad. You two are lucky you made it out alive."

Rita saw a flicker of pain cross her sister's face. "Wendell, time to get us home. Ronnie needs her medicine, and I need a good soak."

Wendell nodded, and the three walked to his cruiser.

"I'll tow it in, Rita. Talk to you tomorrow. Hate to say it, but I think it's totaled," Bill yelled. He waved as they all got in the cruiser and drove off.

As they drove home, Ronnie softly spoke. "Wendell, we'll work with you. Once we have a plan, we'll tell you. How's that?"

"Since I'm sure that's all I'm going to get, I'll take it." Wendell let out a sigh as he pulled into the sisters' driveway. "Here you are. Lock your doors, please."

"We will," they said in chorus. Then they went onto the porch, opened the front door, and waved goodbye to Wendell. He waved back and drove off.

"Safe at last," Rita said as she locked the door.

"Yes, we're safe. But I don't think we were meant to die, but just be scared off the case," Ronnie said and sat down. "Not that a little accident is going to stop us." Ronnie was trying to sound determined, but Rita noticed her voice was shaky. She longed for some tea and as if reading her mind, Rita immediately began making it.

Good, she read my mind again, Rita thought, then gently suggested, "Why don't you go take your medicine, put on some comfortable clothes, and then come back down? The tea will be waiting for you."

"Sounds like a good idea. I will. Thank you," Ronnie said, and then went slowly up to her room.

Rita shook the teakettle angrily before placing it on the stove. She was furious at what had happened. *I could just kill King-Young*, she thought.

In a few minutes Ronnie wandered back into the kitchen and picked up the warm cup of tea. "This is nice. I'm beginning to like these tea rituals."

"Me, too." Rita chimed in. Then she shared a thought with Ronnie. "Why don't I call Caroline, tell her about the accident, and ask her to come here for coffee? We can use the accident to our advantage."

"We?" Ronnie raised an eyebrow. "I thought you wanted to talk to Caroline alone."

"I did, but given what's happened, I think it's better if we both interrogate her."

"OK. I can be bad cop, and you can be good cop," Ronnie joked.

"No, I'll be Watson and you're Sherlock," Rita replied, laughing lightly.

Then she called the dairy. She recognized Caroline's voice, so she said, "Hello, Caroline. It's Rita." In no mood to pussyfoot, she decided to play hardball. "We need to talk. We were just run off the road and could have been killed. It's time to put an end to this mess. We know you're involved. You talk, and we'll listen. We'll do our best to help you." Rita paused and listened to Caroline's reaction. "Yes, that sounds fine. We'll see you tomorrow."

"That was blunt," Ronnie said.

"There's no time to play games. She needs to own up to what she has done. Rita proclaimed solemnly. She had the same rule when she was teaching-- make a mistake, but own it.

"We'll force her to confess, and then we can plan how to end this." Ronnie sipped her tea. "Let's hope she doesn't bring us any milk." She laughed. "I think the end is in sight."

Rita sipped her tea. She couldn't see the ending. Things were too complicated, and given what was likely to come, she hoped they would all get out of it alive.

Chapter 32

King-Young picked up his cell phone and pressed one of his speed dial numbers. He wasn't sure if Caroline would ignore his call or answer it, but he hoped she would answer. The two of them had issues to clear up. As the phone kept ringing, King-Young formulated the message he would leave if she didn't answer.

Then he heard Caroline answer timidly, "Hello?"

Good, she didn't avoid my call. Still, King-Young waited a few seconds before responding. It was important he controlled this discussion. Caroline sounded panicky, and he needed to calm her down and keep her focused. There was too much at stake.

"Caroline, it's me."

"I know. What do you want?" Caroline hissed into the phone.

King-Young used a gentle tone. "Are you alone?" There was no point in continuing the conversation if anyone could hear her side of it.

"Yes, I'm alone. My father is out haying, and I have no idea where the lovely LaMerle is." Caroline had tried to resist digging at LaMerle, but she couldn't. She would never accept LaMerle, even if she were on their side.

King-Young debated telling her about Rita and Ronnie and their little accident. He had hoped Ronnie would have been driving, as she was known to be a poor driver. But he had just wanted to scare them silent, not kill them, so, mission accomplished.

Caroline couldn't stand the silence. She wanted to end this call and her involvement with King-Young. "We agreed not to talk." She chewed her lip, and she felt like things were closing in on her.

Rita had told her about their accident, and she knew King-Young was behind it. Hurting Rita and Ronnie was going too far. He was out of control. Caroline wondered if, and how, she could stop him. *Who knows what he will do next and who will he go after?*

What had seemed a simple plan had turned into a dangerous nightmare. People were supposed to get sick, not die. And the rumors and listeria would force the sale of the dairy. It had sounded so easy. Nothing would be traced back to Caroline or King-Young, but it had gotten totally out of hand. King-Young had promised nothing bad would happen and nothing would blow back on them. But he had pushed things to the extreme, and now she was in too deep. *Get it over with*, she thought.

"Patience, my dear. Let me talk," King-Young began.

Caroline cut him off immediately. "I'm not your dear." *Careful, don't get him angry. He's dangerous.* "Sorry. Why are you calling?" She attempted to modulate her voice, but desperately wanted the call over and King-Young out of her life. She no longer trusted anything he said.

"This little plan of ours is not complete yet." King-Young paused. He could hear Caroline take a deep breath. Now was the time to press her. "We still have a few loose ends to tie up."

"What loose ends?" Caroline asked the question, but didn't want to hear the answer. She was terrified of what the answer might be. She knew she had to stop him, but how?

She knew very well that one of the loose ends was her father. The whole plan had been to force John to sell the dairy. The sale of the dairy was what had drawn King-Young and Caroline together. Both would benefit from the sale. However, the once simple plan had mushroomed into murder--something Caroline had never imagined and certainly had not agreed to.

At this point, Caroline wouldn't be surprised if she also were a loose end he had to tie up. She wouldn't put anything past him. She was positive he had killed Trent, though she had no proof. Her biggest fear, however, was that her father was on the developer's hit list. Caroline needed the money from the sale, but not at the cost of anyone's life. George's death was an accident, but Trent's was murder, which meant that King-Young was a killer.

"You know exactly what loose ends I'm talking about, so don't play dumb with me. We must force your father to sell the dairy. If he doesn't sell me the land, we've done all this work for nothing. And I'd hate to see you go to prison for murder."

"I didn't commit any murder," Caroline hissed. *Granted, George had died from the listeria, but that was NOT my fault. How could I have known the listeria would kill him? He was only supposed to get sick. No, it was clearly an accident. No jury would ever convict me of murder. Still, King-Young could turn against me and say I planted the listeria. But he had no concrete evidence. It would be just his word against mine. And most people would believe me. Besides, he killed Trent, and that could be proven.*

Caroline knew she just needed to get ahead of him and get her story out there first. She'd use Rita to her advantage, as Rita would believe anything she said. She repeated to King-Young that she didn't murder anyone, more strongly this time. She felt if she kept saying it, it was true.

"You go right ahead and keep trying to convince yourself that George's death was an accident. That his death was one of those unfortunate events that happen all the time. But I'm not so sure a jury of your peers would agree." The developer's laughter pierced her heart.

"It WAS an accident." Caroline was not going to back down. She would not let him railroad her. He was the killer; she was not. "Besides, it was all your idea. You got the listeria. All I did was inject a few bottles with it."

King-Young remained silent, but Caroline kept going. She wanted to strike while she could. "This whole plan has your fingerprints all over it. No one would believe a word you say. Everyone thinks you're the bad guy. Not me." Caroline let out a deep breath. *There, now he'll back down.*

But he didn't. "Honey, you can play the innocent all you want. But you remember the red dot? That was all you, not me," King-Young replied softly. "It's your fingerprints all over that move. And that proves you targeted George. And he died." King-Young let that truth settle over her for a moment. He heard her draw in her breath before she spoke.

"No one knows about the red dots. Those bottles are all gone." *Calm down, Caroline. He's just trying to scare you.* Caroline had paid Lana off and retrieved the bottle cap with the red dot from her. And she had destroyed the others, so she knew she was safe.

"I know about Lana." King-Young said quietly, but in a tone that was very threatening. He again waited for his statement sink in, and then he resumed. "Are you sure she won't talk? And LaMerle saw the bottle you took back from Rita as well as the one you gave Lana. Think you can trust your stepmother to not throw you under the bus? You can't be that naive. You know she'd save herself first."

"So, calm down and listen to me. All you have to do now is what you have needed to do all along: convince your father to sell. I'll give him a deposit, and he can sign the deed over to me. Once he does, I'll give him the rest of the money for the sale. Then we'll be done, and we can go our separate ways. Doesn't that sound good?" He knew he had hooked her. She wanted it over.

"Fine. I'll work on my father." Caroline was sure her father would not sign over the deed, but she'd figure out a way to work around it. The family trust was the holder of the deed, and she, John Jr., and LaMerle were part of the trust, so she had some leverage there. She had to manipulate Rita, and also get Rita and Ronnie on her side. It wouldn't be easy, but she'd done enough PR campaigns to know how to win people over.

I can do this. You're dead, King-Young, she thought.

Chapter 33

King-Young hung up with Caroline, satisfied he was in control. However, he thought it would be good to push John's buttons. He knew John had a temper, and he could use the threat of exposing Caroline and having her end up in prison to ensure John fell into line when Caroline approached him. Besides, he liked the idea of cornering John and riling him up.

Hopping into his Escalade, he raced to the dairy. First, he'd check out the fields as Caroline had said her father was out haying. *Hmmm, perhaps a haying accident?* But King-Young dismissed that idea. There had been too many accidents, and as tempting as it was, he thought it was too risky at this point in the game. Besides, John really had no choice but to sell his land.

As the smell of cow manure wafted through the car's windows, the developer quickly closed them. He laughed. Getting rid of the dairy would truly benefit the town.

Slowing to the posted speed limit, he knew no one ever went this slowly but he also didn't want to be on the Chief's radar. The last thing he needed was to have Wendell run a check on his license. He didn't need the police or anyone else checking into his past. He'd carefully covered his tracks so far. The rental car was at the airport, wiped clean. And he'd used cash as well as a fake identity plus a disguise when he rented it, so no one could trace it back to him. Besides, he'd be long gone before the snoop sisters, or anyone else for that matter, figured out who he really was.

Georgia would soon deliver her final payment. He smiled at the thought of how it would sweeten the pot even more. And he had also turned over the deeds people had used as collateral--traded them at the bank for cash. Plus, he had plenty of other cash from other investors. All in all, plenty to fund his disappearance and a new life.

Finally, he spotted a green John Deere tractor coming into view in the fields on the right. King-Young slowed to verify it was John, haying. It was. The sun was hot, and John looked like he could use a distraction. King-Young laughed. *Here we go. One distraction coming up.*

King-Young eased his SUV onto the shoulder and stopped. He sat and watched John haying for a moment, then cut the engine and got out and started across the field. He picked his way cautiously to John, trying to avoid any piles of cow chips. He did not want his prize boots getting spoiled. Even though he was careful, he did slip one time. "Shit," he muttered. Then he laughed. *It is exactly that.* As King-Young moved closer to the tractor through the uncut hay, John continued driving it across the field in rows--first one way, then the other.

"Hey, John," King-Young yelled. He pushed his sunglasses up on top of his head and waved his arm in the air to get John's attention. The tractor made such as racket, he was sure John wouldn't hear him, but his wave worked.

John saw him, stopped, and turned off the tractor, waiting for him to arrive. John hoped his hat hid his face so King-Young could not see his scowl. When the developer was almost at the tractor, John noticed he had a slight limp. *Odd,* John thought, *never noticed him limping before.*

As King-Young got closer, John felt himself becoming more and more agitated. *The man is nothing but a thieving bully,* John thought. And he should know, because he had had a lifetime of experience with bullies. He recalled a group of older kids who made fun of John being the "farmer boy." From calling him "stinky" to making fun of his work boots, they never let up. It had stopped once John became a star athlete in high school and suddenly was popular with them except for Kevin, who had never let up referring to him as "milk boy." John knew he thought of him the same way, so the two were enemies from the get-go.

Taking deep breaths to try to calm himself, John waited for the verbal assault to begin. The thought of starting up the tractor, letting it slip out of gear, and running over King-Young was tempting, and people would think it was accident. John felt his hand reaching for the keys. Luckily, King-Young stopped beside the tractor, and the murderous moment passed.

King-Young flashed John a menacing smile. The sun seemed to gleam off his pearly white teeth as he surveyed the field. In a sotto-sweet voice, he said "Well now, here you are out working in your fields, sweating away, when you could be sitting on a patio with your lovely wife down south, nice and cool, sipping a mint julep, and planning where you'd like to go out for dinner. With one very smart decision, John, you could be living that scene." He swept his arm around, pointing out the fields. "And the time for that decision is now. Sell."

"I've made my decision, and you know what it is. It hasn't changed, and it won't change, no matter what you do to try to force me to sell. You are NOT getting my land." John glared at the developer. "So, if that's all you wanted, then turn yourself around in your fancy tooled boots and hightail it back to your flashy city car. I wouldn't want you to get dirty, or worse, in my fields." John turned on the tractor and revved the engine.

But the harsh words did not move King-Young. "Don't be a fool, John. It's time for you to sell. I know it, you know it, and your family knows it." King-Young paused again. He truly loved dramatic effects. "Speaking of family, I was just talking with your lovely daughter," he said as if he'd caught Caroline doing something she shouldn't. He continued, "She's mighty smart, John. She knows you're holding a winning hand. Listen to her."

"I'm not a gambling man, and I make my OWN decisions." John clenched his fists, unclenched them, and continued in a calmer voice, "You keep away from my family. And stay out of my fields and affairs."

"Affairs. Now that is a good choice of words," King-Young smirked. It had always been so easy to set John off, and he loved it every time he did. Still, he was not foolhardy, so he took a step back from the tractor, and out of its path, before adding, "You should ask your wife and daughter about affairs." The two men stared at each other, and then King-Young turned to go, but not without firing one last shot at John. "This land will be mine."

"Well, right now it's mine, so get off it now." John stood up on the tractor, bracing his legs against the seat. "Before there's an accident with this tractor."

King-Young stopped and turned back to face John, and then glared at him. "Was that a threat? You'd better be careful, John. You're in no position to threaten me." He shook his head. *He's a bigger fool than I thought. Always was.*

John yelled, "I said 'Get off my land.' That's not a threat. That's an order."

King-Young threw back his head and laughed. Then he shot another arrow at John. It was aimed for the heart. And he intended it to be a kill shot.

"I'm not the one you need to worry about, John. Ask your daughter what she's been up to lately. Your lovely little Caroline is in trouble. Big trouble. And she's in danger. It's about time you realized it." King-Young began walking away.

"Hold it right there. What are you talking about? Are you threatening Caroline?"

King-Young turned back, stood his ground, and replied, "I'm not threatening Caroline. I don't need to. She's dug her own grave." He pointed his finger at John, then said, "I know what she's done. Her little game isn't over, either. Ask her about the listeria outbreak." He figured that should push John over the edge.

John tried his best to sound strong. "I don't know what you're talking about, but Caroline would never hurt me." John said the words, but somehow, he wasn't sure if they rang true. He knew Caroline needed money. She clearly wanted to start her own business. Did Caroline have anything to do with the listeria? Or worse, with King-Young? *Oh, Caroline, what have you done?* But he couldn't let King-Young see his fear and misery. So, he sat tall and repeated, "Caroline would never hurt me." But both men knew the words rang false.

"Just sell the land and this will all be over."

"Get out of my sight before I do something I regret." *There has to be a way out of this nightmare.* John put the tractor in gear. He noticed King-Young walked faster towards the gate and out of the field. *He's scared, but what do I do? I've got to solve this problem once and for all, no matter what it takes.*

King-Young finally reached the Escalade, proud that he had not limped. He yanked open the car door and got in. He rubbed his leg to ease the stiffness, and he could feel his foot swelling. Odd how the stupid foot still bothered him after all these years.

However, not one to be introspective, King-Young started his car and pumped the gas. He caught a glimpse of himself in the visor mirror. He looked smug and satisfied. No one would ever connect the masterful King-Young with that hurt, crippled boy from long ago. Then he noticed his hair. Damn! He reached up and adjusted the wig. *Probably happened when I put my sunglasses up there.*

He pulled out onto the road, and his smugness returned full force as he charged along. The war was raging, and there was no chance of a peaceful settlement. It was a fight to the finish, and King-Young was determined to win. Feeling very satisfied, he thought *Victory is mine!* as he raced along.

Chapter 34

John started haying again, but couldn't concentrate. A strangled laugh escaped his constricted throat. Once again, he shut down the tractor. He yanked his cell phone from his overall pocket and, fuming, punched in his daughter's number.

When Caroline finally answered, John tried to remain calm. He said tersely, "Caroline, I just had a visit from King-Young. He made some serious accusations against you. What's going on?" Caroline remained silent, but John refused to let her off the hook. This was too serious. He demanded, "What's this about you knowing all about the listeria? Tell me what's going on. And tell me the truth. NOW!" John waited for Caroline's reply.

"I'm not sure what you mean, Daddy," Caroline answered cautiously. She hoped to quiet her father's fears and maintain some calm between them.

"Don't play coy with me, Caroline. What did King-Young mean about you being involved in planting listeria? Explain yourself, girl. He seems to think he can send you to prison."

Caroline decided to lie. It was the only solution for now. After all, her father had always believed her in the past, and she was confident she could fool him. "Daddy, I'm not sure what he's talking about. But you don't need to worry. Everything will be fine. I'll take care of everything." Then she resorted to the oldest father/daughter trick in the book. She cried. Loudly.

Hearing his daughter sobbing made John back off a little. She'd always had him wrapped around her little finger. He answered, "I hope that everything really is fine, but we need to talk. I hope our only problem is that thief trying to get my land. Still, he made some pretty serious accusations against you."

"Oh, Daddy, you know King-Young. He's an expert at deceit and lies."

John interrupted. "Caroline, his threats were serious."

"He threatened you? What did he threaten? He's dangerous, Dad." Caroline's voice suddenly sounded very calm as she struggled to suppress the fear rising in it.

"Not me, but you. He said he knew what you did, and if he turned you in, you'd go to prison. He said the only way to save you was for me to sell." John continued, "He said if I don't sell, he'll turn you in, and I'll end up dead: the victim of an accident." John waited. That was stretching the truth, but John was desperate to know what role Caroline was playing. *Confess, baby girl.* "What did King-Young mean about you being involved with the listeria outbreak? Explain to me. Now."

Caroline knew they were not idle threats. She spoke slowly into the phone, "Daddy, I'm so sorry. I'll fix this. I promise. I'm so sorry," and then hung up, sitting there stunned and staring at her phone. *How did things get so out of control?* She had been asking that question over and over in her head for a while now.

John also stared at his phone for a few minutes after it went dead. He snapped it shut and put it back in his pocket, crying, "Oh, my little girl, what HAVE you done?" But more important, he wondered if Caroline could really fix the mess. He also wondered what King-Young would be willing to do to get his land. He prayed there was a solution, but felt he and Caroline were cornered, and King-Young was holding all the trump cards.

While John was pondering all of this, Caroline reviewed her initial meetings with King-Young. He had fooled and seduced her from the very beginning, holding out the promise of money.

Initially, it had all seemed so simple. He had approached her at the dairy and asked her to go for drinks. Flattered by his attention, she had agreed. She had known he wanted to buy the dairy from her father, and she thought it would be better for her father if she knew what his plans were. Plus, always on the lookout for clients so she could start her own PR firm, she figured King-Young would be a good connection for her future.

Then like a magician, he had convinced her to join him in getting her father to sell the dairy. It was clear to Caroline now that King-Young had researched her, and he knew her vulnerabilities and her weaknesses. He had quickly painted a rosy picture of how Caroline and her family would profit from the sale of the dairy. *And admit it, Caroline, you were greedy.*

So she had agreed to work with King-Young to force the sale. She knew enough science and with her brother's help, it was easy to create the listeria culture, and then make sure it was transferred to a few bottles of milk. She had assumed she somehow would be able to pin the listeria outbreak on LaMerle or it could be a "natural" happening. A couple of people would get sick, and the listeria scare would force the sale of the dairy. Simple and harmless.

Caroline had marked the tainted bottles with a red dot and sold the first one to George. He was a prominent member of the community, and Georgia was a renowned gossip, so the tale of listeria would spread quickly. Then they'd sell a few more tainted bottles. The state agency would come in, test the milk, and find the listeria. The dairy would have to close, and thus John would be forced to sell.

But George had died. Caroline had wanted to abandon the plan, but it was too late. King-Young had her trapped and there was no stopping him. Caroline shuddered. Still, there had to be a way out.

She began to formulate a solution. She would use Rita and Ronnie to help her put the blame solely on King-Young and LaMerle. And in the process, she would make herself an innocent dupe, who had been coerced by King-Young to participate in his plan.

She realized the meeting with Rita tomorrow was crucial, so she rehearsed her story again and again in her head. Caroline didn't like having to play the victim, but if it saved her skin, she would do so. Besides, the thought of throwing her stepmother under the bus gave Caroline a certain sense of satisfaction. After all, LaMerle had made her father's life miserable, and Caroline would weave a story so that she became King-Young's accomplice. LaMerle would pay for her past actions. Everyone in town knew LaMerle wanted John to sell the dairy so she could move back down south. So it would be easy to set up LaMerle as the scapegoat.

It was time to start putting the solution in place. Caroline picked up the phone and called Rita. She wanted to make sure they were still meeting tomorrow.

After only a couple of rings, Rita picked up. "Hello?" Her voice sounded weak.

"Hi, Rita. It's Caroline. I just want to make sure we are still meeting tomorrow. I'm concerned with what happened to you and Ronnie." Caroline paused while Rita confirmed the meeting. "I'm so glad, because I have a lot to share with the two of you."

"Yes, well Ronnie and I were just talking about you," Rita answered.

Caroline remained silent on the other end while Rita told her they believed there was a lot she needed to explain.

Caroline played the sympathy card immediately in her reply. "You're right. I do. And I need your help," she pleaded. "I think I'm in danger, and so is my father. We can use your support."

"We're here for you. We'll see you tomorrow." Rita hung up.

Caroline breathed a sigh of relief and said, "Rita will help me. I know she will."

Chapter 35

The next morning, Rita and Ronnie sat in the living room, waiting for Caroline to arrive. Rita had baked some oatmeal raisin cookies, which she knew were Caroline's favorite.

Many days Caroline had come over after school and the two had sat and talked, eating cookies while Rita sipped her tea and Caroline drank milk. Rita tried to counsel Caroline after her mother had died and John remarried. In the end, Caroline had looked at Rita as a second mother. Rita realized that might end today, and it made her sad.

Seeing her sister deep in thought, Ronnie also felt sad. She knew it would be painful for Rita, but they had to force Caroline to come clean and confess to the listeria outbreak plan. They needed her help solving the mysteries so they could trap King-Young. She wondered if Caroline would work with Wendell and the two of them. She wasn't sure, but she trusted Rita to try to resolve things.

"How did Caroline sound when you talked yesterday?" Ronnie was trying to gauge both Rita's and Caroline's feelings.

Rita took her time replying. "She sounded scared. I'm sure she knows she's made a horrible mistake working with King-Young, but I'm not sure if we'll be able to force a confession out of her."

"You always did have a soft spot for her." Ronnie took a deep breath, and continued, speaking quietly and gently. "You're not Oprah. You can't solve all her problems as much as I know you want to help her. Very bad things were done, and people must pay for their crimes." Then she paused.

"I'm aware of that," Rita said sharply. "Let's see what Caroline has to say, and then we'll lead her to confess. And I hope she'll agree to help Wendell and us trap King-Young. He's the real villain."

Ronnie urged, "We have to set Caroline on the right path. She will have to live with her actions for the rest of her life, and that might be punishment enough. Wendell is a fair man, and if Caroline assists him in arresting King-Young, he'd do all he could to get her a fair deal."

"You're right. King-Young is the leader and orchestrated the whole plan." Ronnie reached over and took her sister's hand. "I think we can win Caroline over to our side."

Rita nodded in appreciation and replied, "Thank you, Ronnie."

Just then, the doorbell rang. Caroline had arrived. *Showtime,* thought the sisters.

Rita ushered Caroline into the living room and told her, "I made your favorite cookies," then asked her what she would like to drink. Ronnie almost blurted out, "No milk," but instead, hid it with a cough.

"Tea would be good," Caroline replied meekly. In her head, she began playing out her story. She needed to convince Rita and Ronnie that she had also been a victim. After all, King-Young had manipulated her. What had happened to George was not her fault.

She would plead that she had had no idea how dangerous listeria was to George, who had a compromised immune system. Plus, she would plead ignorance about George's health. And that was partially true, as she knew he was not that well, but didn't know details. *Yes, this could work,* she thought.

Caroline felt herself gaining in strength. She'd win over the sisters.

She'd stick close to the truth, but use some white lies and omissions to bolster her story and diminish her role. From her years in Rita's class, she knew very well that Rita had always been able to detect when a student was lying, embellishing a story, or giving an excuse. However, she also knew her former teacher had a soft spot for her, and she planned to use that to her advantage. As for Ronnie, she simply had to hope she could win her over, too. She wasn't sure she could, but she would give it her best shot.

However, while Rita prepared the tea and then brought it out, Ronnie had remained silent. *Not a good sign,* Caroline thought. She and Rita drank their tea black, while Ronnie added lemon to hers. Caroline noticed Rita served the tea with sugar, but no milk. It made her wonder how much the two sisters knew and what was supposition on their part. Well, no matter what, Caroline knew if she hoped to get out of this mess at all, she needed Rita's support and help.

The three sipped their tea. Caroline and Ronnie each had a cookie.

The sisters anxiously waited for Caroline to share her story.

While they waited, Rita thought about how well and how long she had known Caroline. She wondered if her knowledge was just memories of a favorite student who was no longer the person she had been. She hoped not. She knew in her heart that Caroline was a truly decent young woman, but greed had caused her to make some very foolish and dangerous decisions. Rita also believed that King-Young had manipulated Caroline. Rita was willing to give Caroline the benefit of the doubt, but she knew Ronnie would not. As the silence lengthened, Rita stepped in.

"What do you want to tell us, dear?" Rita asked gently.

"I don't know where to start," Caroline began, then fell silent and looked intently at Rita and Ronnie.

To get the conversation flowing, Rita said, "Why don't you let me start? I think it will help you." Caroline looked grateful for the suggestion, and she nodded at Rita.

As Caroline waited for her to begin, she remembered a long-ago biology lesson Rita had taught about bacteria. It had led to a discussion of listeria and how it formed. Caroline still had her notes from that ill-fated lesson. In fact, she had consulted them to help her formulate the listeria plan. She wondered if Rita remembered that lesson, too. She hoped Rita didn't.

"Caroline, you need to know that Ronnie and I have discovered several pieces of important information. Information that worries us a great deal." Rita paused a moment to let the remark sink in, then plunged ahead. "During some discussions with Wendell, and also due to some things Ronnie and I have observed, you are under suspicion for the listeria distribution."

Both sisters waited for Caroline's reaction. *Would she tell the truth or deny it?*

"Oh no," Caroline whispered. The shock in her voice and on her face were evident as she added, "I had no idea this had gone as far as Wendell." She gulped. "I've been such a fool. It was never supposed to be like this." Caroline's mind went into spin overdrive. It was going to be harder to downplay her role than she had anticipated. Still, she could minimize her role by sharing that LaMerle had participated in the plan. It would be her word against LaMerle's, and people would believe her over LaMerle, so that would work in her favor.

"Well, I'm sure it wasn't, but unfortunately, this is how it is. You are playing a dangerous game. A game with lives at stake. And Kevin King-Young is a nasty piece of work. He will stop at nothing to achieve his goals. He won't think twice about eliminating people in his way."

Caroline knew that what Rita was saying was all true. So, she felt sure that Rita and Ronnie had pinned Trent's death on King-Young and also gone to Wendell with their theory. She was sure it had been credible enough to convince Wendell that Trent's death was murder and also that King-Young was the probable killer. Wendell was now most likely using his team to gather evidence to arrest King-Young. Though he had been careful, Caroline was sure that some trace evidence would be found, and if that happened, he would try to implicate her.

She thought she had carefully hidden her involvement with the developer. Everybody in town believed he was after her whole family, and Caroline was her father's best ally working against what the developer was trying to do. Clearly, she had misjudged Rita and Ronnie's deductive powers. *I never should have partnered with King-Young. Greed has trapped me,* she despaired. There would be no money now, just prison waiting for her. Her only hope was to somehow work a deal. And she needed Rita to do that.

Ronnie, however, remained a problem. Caroline glanced at Ronnie, who had a poker face and sat there in silence. Caroline realized the more data she got from Rita, the better she could spin her story. "How did you connect me with King-Young?" she asked.

"Well, for one thing, there are several pictures of the two of you together," Ronnie stated. Ronnie, playing the role of bad cop, waited for Caroline's reaction.

"Pictures? What are you talking about?" She was completely dumbfounded. *Who could have taken pictures of them? It must have been Trent.*

Caroline panicked, but then her PR training kicked in. People hated the developer, not her. She'd pull out the victim card. Still, she had to be careful how she played it. So far, she figured that while the sisters knew she had been involved in the planting of the listeria, they pegged King-Young as the mastermind.

This allowed Caroline to minimize her role. King-Young calling the shots and making key decisions worked in Caroline's favor. She would admit to planting the listeria, but then downplay her role in everything that happened after that. And she would also add LaMerle into the mix.

"As you know, Ronnie and I have had some discussions with Wendell. He has the flash drive that belonged to Trent. It turns out that drive contains not only Trent's notes about his investigation into the whole dairy sale debacle, but also pictures of you and King-Young alone, engaged in what look like very serious conversations. So, tell us about your involvement."

Caroline started slowly, "It is true I worked with King-Young to get the listeria out there. He promised me it would be harmless. You know--just create bad publicity for the dairy. People would get sick, so customers would stop buying milk, and then Dad would be forced to sell." Caroline paused. Rita and Ronnie sat stone- faced. *Time to weave in my motivation,* she thought.

"Yes, I wanted the money to open my own firm, but Dad needs to get out of the business. His health is not great, and he needs to either figure out what to do with LaMerle or have the cash to get rid of her. I wanted my father happy, too. The sale of the dairy solves everyone's problems. Plus, even though Dad claims to love farming, he is getting tired of it, and then there is a possible future with Lana to think about, too."

Rita and Ronnie remained silent. Though Rita looked as if she believed her, Caroline knew Ronnie was still not on her side. After a brief pause, she continued in what she hoped was a convincing voice, determined to clear her name as best she could.

"No one was supposed to get hurt. NO one." Caroline took a deep breath and waited to see if the sisters were buying her story. *The pathetic thing is, that part of it is true*, she thought.

Caroline sounded like an inexperienced 10-year-old, not the educated young woman she was. "It seemed like such a simple, innocent plan," she muttered.

"Clearly, it was not." Ronnie harrumphed. She was losing more respect for Caroline by the minute. *Did she honestly think she could finesse her way out of this? She's still trying to save her own skin.* Ronnie had spun enough creative PR stories herself to know a fake one when she heard it. And Caroline was weaving a good one.

Rita shot Ronnie a look, but kept pushing, "Caroline, this is serious. Someone is systematically murdering people in town."

Caroline began to tremble as Rita's words slowly sank in. She had not thought of what was happening as murder. Or she had convinced herself it wasn't, but Rita was right.

"George died because of the listeria. While that death may have been accidental, Trent was murdered. Ronnie and I were deliberately driven off the road. What may have started out as a simple plan has turned into calculated, premeditated murders. And I believe we haven't seen the last murder, either. King-Young is tying up loose ends, and who knows who is on his list. It could even be you, Caroline, or your father."

The remark about her father in danger was like a sucker punch. She realized Rita was absolutely right.

Rita pressed on. "Right now, Wendell is putting the pieces together to try to end this and prevent any future killings." She fixed her gaze directly on Caroline. "We need your help."

When Rita paused, Ronnie jumped in, in full attack mode, "What are you going to do?"

Caroline looked from Rita to Ronnie, then slowly turned her attention back to Rita, focusing just on her. She tried to stall so she could think. "I can't tell you how sorry I am that King-Young went after you. I had no idea he would do that. Thank God you're all right. You ARE, aren't you?" She sounded and looked sincere.

Rita nodded. "We're fine, dear."

She's winning back Rita, Ronnie thought. And she had to hand it to her. *If she's acting, she's missed her calling.* But Ronnie believed she couldn't be that good in fact, so that meant she was sincere. Ronnie began to think Caroline might be more innocent than she had at first thought. *Rita may be right about her. And if she helps us, she may be able to dig herself out of this mess. After all, Wendell does have a soft heart, just like Rita.*

"We're probably on King-Young's list of loose ends, but Wendell is keeping an eye on us. We're fine for now. But I'm very worried about where this is leading, Caroline. It's not over yet." Rita took Caroline's hands in her own. "King-Young appears to be getting more and more desperate, and that's not good. It's time to tell Wendell all the details before someone else dies. Who knows who might be next? It's time to confess."

Caroline nodded. *Rita is right. And that's also my ticket out. It was time to play my cards, shaping my confession to protect me and place the blame totally on King-Young.*

Chapter 36

Caroline swallowed hard and began talking. "Things are out of hand, and I now know King-Young is deadly. Our lives are in danger. He's threatened my father, and he's threatened me, too. I'm positive he means it. He must be stopped. Now." Her voice cracked as she pleaded, "I need your help. I'm not sure what to do and how to stop that man."

Ronnie believed Caroline was finally being honest with them. It was clear the poor girl was terrified. So, Rita was right; murder had not been part of Caroline's plan. And probably no other death was, either. Nevertheless, Ronnie was about to make an acid comment that it was convenient for Caroline now to be placing all the blame squarely on King-Young.

But Rita jumped in. "I want to believe you," she said, reaching out and placing her hand reassuringly on Caroline's arm. "But you did take a long time to decide to stop King-Young."

"I know. And I'm sorry I was such a fool. I never believed he would resort to murder. You have to believe me, Mrs. Tisdale, I mean Rita." She paused, composed herself, and stated strongly, this time with even more conviction, "We have to stop him. And I need you. I can't do it alone."

Rita couldn't ignore Caroline's plea, and she knew Ronnie could not either. "I'll do anything to stop him. Anything." Caroline got up and began to pace the room. The pacing did not calm her, but neither sister stopped her.

"I'm worried," Rita said, "and I'm not sure we can stop him, but Wendell can."

"I'll give Wendell any details he needs so he can understand what the plan was. I don't care what happens to me, but I can't let King-Young hurt my father." *Or let my father do something stupid*, she thought. She knew her father's temper, and he was close to exploding.

"Alright, let's make a plan. Then we can bring it to Wendell," Ronnie suggested.

Caroline swallowed hard and agreed. "Fine. And then Wendell can bring in King-Young for questioning," Caroline said, looking once again back and forth between the sisters. She sank back onto the couch in relief. *This nightmare will soon be over.* Having the sisters' help lifted a huge burden from her shoulders. She could almost see the light at the end of the tunnel.

"Ronnie," Rita said sharply. "Let's get a pen and some paper and make some notes." She grabbed her sister's arm and steered her down the hall. "Wait here, Caroline; we'll be right back," Rita called over her shoulder as she and Ronnie scurried toward the kitchen.

In the kitchen, Rita quickly pulled the door shut behind them. They needed to plan first, without Caroline. Rita still doesn't totally trust her, thought Ronnie. And that's a good thing.

Almost in a whisper, Rita said, "Caroline seemed surprised we've been worried about her, and that we knew of her involvement with King-Young." Ronnie nodded in agreement. "She also seemed genuinely shocked when I mentioned Trent's notes, and especially his pictures."

"Yes, but oh for God's sake, how naïve!" Ronnie spat out. "She's lived in Castleton long enough to realize how small towns work. Nothing goes unnoticed in a small town. Even I know that. And everyone knows what a dogged reporter Trent was. He pursued his stories like a lawyer chasing an ambulance." Ronnie was on a roll.

Rita had to get her back on track. "You're right. But Caroline is young, and she's always been naïve. Plus, she's been living in the city and has forgotten how small towns work. And I think she had some idea that her plan was so simple, no one would get hurt, and she and King-Young would achieve their goals. She treated the plan like one of her PR campaigns. Smoke and mirrors. She just didn't realize who she was dealing with and how deadly it could turn."

Ronnie sighed. Sometimes she hated Rita's logic, but this time, her sister was right. "Fine. Surely we can use Caroline to trap King-Young, but how?"

Rita answered, "We'll get Wendell over here to hear Caroline's whole story and get him involved in the plan. He'll know what we need to do to get the evidence against King-Young."

Ronnie agreed, "Yes, we need to get Wendell over here right away."

"Good. Now let's get back in there before Caroline loses her nerve or worse, changes her mind," Rita suggested. She put her hand on Ronnie's shoulder and steered her toward the living room, where they rejoined Caroline.

Rita said, "Caroline, we need to call Wendell and have him come over. Then he'll be able to pick up King-Young, and at the very least, bring him in for questioning. Most likely he'll get a search warrant, too. It all depends on how much information you give him," Rita hoped her tone stressed the importance of Caroline's providing detailed, complete information.

"I'll tell him whatever he needs to know. I promise." Caroline sounded sincerely relieved for the first time in quite a while.

"Good. If you're honest, then I think the end is in sight," Rita replied as she picked up the phone and dialed Wendell. It was not a good conversation, but Wendell agreed to come over.

Chapter 37

Wendell hung up the phone in his office. "Damn those two," he muttered. He had asked them not to play detectives, but of course, they had mounted their own investigation.

Now they had Caroline at their house, and he needed to get over there immediately. He'd planned to go pick up King-Young for questioning, but now he had to question Caroline. *Delays implementing my plan,* thought Wendell.

Still, he knew he couldn't just leave the sisters alone with Caroline.

Wendell and his men had been onto the fact that the team behind the listeria was most likely Caroline and King-Young. The Chief had decided to focus on King-Young, as he felt that the out-of-towner was the ringleader.

However, he now believed King-Young wasn't an outsider. The man knew too much about Castleton and had too much inside information.

As for Caroline, Wendell had known her since she was a little girl, and although he didn't want to believe how involved she was, he knew that greed could be a powerful motivator. Still, she was not a cold-blooded killer. She was not a suspect in Trent's murder or in the attack on Rita and Ronnie. In fact, Wendell knew Caroline adored Rita and considered her a second mother.

Wendell frowned at the phone. Rita's call, saying they had Caroline at their house, caused his stomach to churn. *What scheme had those fool women concocted now? And how have they involved Caroline at this point?* "Lord, save me from amateur detectives," he muttered. Grabbing his jacket, he set off for Rita's house. *Please let this not be a fool's errand.*

But given that everything that the sisters had hypothesized so far had proven correct, Wendell believed that Caroline would give him the missing pieces to complete the puzzle.

"You leaving for the day?" asked the dispatcher, Charlene, as Wendell marched by her desk. She threw back her blonde hair and shamelessly batted her turquoise-lidded eyes. *Spare me*, thought Wendell. He knew Charlene liked him, but he was only interested in Ronnie.

Wendell replied curtly, "No, I'm off to see Rita and Ronnie. And then I plan to go to King-Young's place. I'll be back by the end of the day. If anyone asks, you have no idea where I am."

Charlene nodded. Wendell hoped for once Charlene could keep quiet. Better for no one to know about Rita and Ronnie's involvement and the fact that he was questioning Caroline.

On his way to Rita and Ronnie's, Wendell reviewed the facts. Trent had been killed in a deliberate hit and run. So far, his team had not turned up any evidence linking King-Young to the murder. His Escalade was clean, and he appeared to have a semi-solid alibi for the night of the murder. Still, Wendell's gut told him King-Young was responsible for both Trent's murder and running Rita and Ronnie off the road. Trent had died from blunt force trauma after being driven off the road and landing on a pile of rocks, not from having been hit by a car, so that explained why King-Young's car could be clean. Or maybe he had "borrowed" a car from someone at the conference. And Ronnie's claim of seeing a rental sticker on the car that had run them off the road was most likely correct.

But even if a rental, it was the same kind of car as the developer's, so that gave Wendell a solid reason to pull him in for questioning. Plus, he was sure that Caroline would provide more information, maybe even enough to arrest him. To cover all of his bases, Wendell armed his men with a photo of King-Young he had printed off Trent's flash drive, and he had his men checking car rental agencies.

However, he was still on somewhat shaky ground trying to pin Trent's murder on King-Young. It would be hard to break his alibi for the time of Trent's murder, as he'd given a speech that night in front of a large crowd. So, there were plenty of witnesses who would say he had been there. But Wendell knew King-Young could have slipped out and had time to run down Trent and return to the conference. Few would have noticed him missing.

Plus, liquor had flowed freely, and no one had been able to confirm that the developer had been there the whole time. Wendell had even had his detective painstakingly interview everyone at the event who knew him, as well as ask if they noticed anything odd about their cars.

And they had uncovered one promising clue. One woman had said that the driver's seat position seemed wrong when she got in her car the next day, but she had simply dismissed it. However, after thinking more about it, she also recalled the driver's side had dirt on the floor mats, which was not there previously. And the woman also admitted she had left her purse with her car keys on the back of her chair during the dinner and speeches, so King-Young could have had access to her keys and "borrowed" her car. She didn't remember if she had spoken with King-Young at her table, but others at her table remembered him stopping by when she had been in the restroom, so he had had the opportunity to lift her car keys. Wendell believed it was a slim, but certainly possible, explanation.

The police were currently processing her car to see if any trace evidence turned up. Wendell was willing to bet something would surface.

At least he hoped it did. So Wendell could also use that theory to bring him in. And with Caroline's testimony about the developer being the mastermind, then that provided the motivation for King-Young to eliminate Trent. *Yes, that all fit.* It was enough for Wendell to have gotten a search warrant for King-Young's place.

Even before Trent had been killed, Wendell had begun investigating the developer. Rita and Ronnie's conviction that there was something off about him had aroused Wendell's suspicions. And they had been right. To say the man was shady was an understatement. King-Young's other real estate developments had never actually been completed. On more than one occasion, he had procured money from gullible investors, purchased land locally (to which he held the title, using the investors' money, and then, for a variety of reasons, never built the developments.

Instead, he sold the land and then disappeared. Most of the prior investors had never pressed charges, because they didn't want to admit, or have their friends and neighbors learn, they'd been fooled so easily. It was fraud. Another thing Wendell could investigate and charge him with. Wendell hated the thought of his neighbors being fleeced.

Wendell was surprised King-Young hadn't been taken to court, but he had stayed just this side of the law and slipped away before he could suffer any consequences. *Even more reason I'm going to nail that bastard*, Wendell thought. *Plus, I'd look like a hero to Ronnie.*

Wendell smiled, but quickly dismissed that thought. Granted, he had had a blazing crush on Ronnie since he was twelve, but she was still out of his league. However, he believed she was warming to him. Wendell sat up straighter in his seat. Winning Ronnie's heart was a long shot, but he was going to try.

Finally, Wendell arrived at Rita's. *Time to focus.* His beefy finger pressed Rita's doorbell with more force than necessary. And he kept pressing it until Rita whipped open the door.

"You can stop ringing the bell, Wendell." Rita looked the Chief over. He looked exasperated. Rita was sure he was angry that she and Ronnie had interfered with his investigation, but she also knew Wendell still had a crush on Ronnie, and that might help her, Ronnie, and even Caroline. "Come in. We're having tea."

"Drinking tea and solving murders, no doubt," Wendell muttered sarcastically as he followed Rita through the front hall and toward the living room. He could hear Ronnie making soothing noises as Caroline talked softly. *That woman could tame a cobra if she set her mind to it*, he thought. He wasn't sure if that was a compliment or an insult, or if he should simply be scared of her.

"I could make you a cup if you'd like. Tea helps us think and calms us." Rita looked back over her shoulder and smiled, "While we're solving murders." Wendell groaned, started to reply, and then thought better of it. "Ronnie and Caroline,

Wendell is here," Rita announced as she and the Chief entered the living room.

Both women immediately went silent and looked over at him. Caroline looked scared, whereas Ronnie looked triumphant.

Wendell shook his head. "Well, ladies, why don't you tell me what you know and what plan you three have hatched?"

"Plan, what makes you think we have a plan, Wendell?" Ronnie asked in her stage voice. Rita rolled her eyes.

"Because I know the two of you, and I don't think I was invited here for tea and crumpets. You sounded pretty serious on the phone, Rita."

Ronnie was about to make some glib remark about how she didn't know Wendell liked crumpets, but the look on Rita's face stopped her. It was time for business. "Rita, why don't you explain?" said Ronnie, passing the gauntlet to her sister.

Rita began. "I'm sure you know Caroline has been working with King-Young?" Wendell nodded, and so Rita continued. "She obtained the listeria and tainted the milk from John's dairy. She's going to tell you the whole story." Rita nodded at Caroline.

"I never meant to hurt anyone," Caroline blurted out.

Wendell held up his hand. "I don't think you should talk, Caroline. Wait until you have a lawyer present."

Ronnie cocked her head toward the Chief. She had forgotten what a good, decent man Wendell is. He didn't want Caroline to incriminate herself. He wanted to focus on the real culprit, King-Young. *And rightly so*, thought Ronnie.

"Rita, please continue" Wendell ordered, trying to establish some sense of control over the situation. He knew Rita would give him clear information to work with and he wasn't sure how Caroline would skew the story. He liked Caroline, but he also knew anyone in her situation would bend the truth to make them look as good as possible.

"The plan was simple, really. The tainted milk would make some people sick, and then the Board of Health would shut down the dairy. John, under pressure from LaMerle and Caroline, would be forced to sell the dairy to the developer, who would then build his development." Rita felt satisfied. Everything was now out in the open.

Wendell looked at Caroline, and she nodded slowly and then looked down at the pillow in her lap. It was clear she was ashamed. The Chief felt a little sorry for her. Still, he knew at some point he'd have to find out how involved she was in everything. He frowned. It would be hard to disprove or prove whatever story she told. Inevitably, it would be her word against the words of the other suspects.

Ronnie picked up the narrative. "However, there began to be several unforeseen problems. First, George drank the tainted milk--and died." Ronnie gazed at Caroline. "George's death was a completely unexpected accident.

But it proved too big a story for Trent to ignore it, so he began digging. He discovered the listeria had been deliberately planted and was not just random bad luck for John. Someone-- or some people--were trying to force John to sell. You must remember Trent's grand announcement at Georgia's house right after George's funeral."

Leave it to Ronnie to pick up the dramatic parts, Wendell thought. "Half of Castleton heard his remarks," Wendell replied.

Ronnie glared at Wendell. Interrupting her flow of the story was irritating. Nevertheless, she continued. "Now where was I? Oh yes, so, basically Trent sealed his fate with that announcement. He alerted those behind the scheme that he would not rest until he had exposed them.
Really, the poor boy didn't know he had signed his own death warrant."

Ronnie paused for a moment, then continued, "There was no way King-Young was going to allow Trent to expose him. Plus, it would allow others from his past schemes to track him down as all that happened in Castleton became public. At the very least, it would leave him open to more lawsuits and possible jail time for fraud." Rita shook her head in disgust, knowing that Ronnie was absolutely right.

Wendell said, "I agree that King-Young killed Trent and also that he had way too much to lose if he became front-page news. And you're right about him having run previous development scams. Although those were strictly financial scams. He would set up bogus companies, woo investors, obtain loans from local banks, and then escape with the cash. He's a con artist, pure and simple."

"Why didn't the Zoning Board know that?" Rita sputtered.

"Oh, that I get." Ronnie said knowingly. "It's no different than trying to sell a movie. He razzled and dazzled them, like the lawyer Billy Flynn in *Chicago* or the con man, Professor Hill, in *The Music Man*. People see the chance to make easy money and they want to believe, so they do. Face it, many in Castleton were ripe for the pickings."

Rita shook her head in disgust, knowing Ronnie was absolutely right. "You hit the nail on the head, Ronnie."

Wendell let the silence settle over them all. He wanted the women to stop investigating, so he shared more information about how devious and dangerous King-Young was. "The strange thing is that in towns with those other proposed developments, people I spoke with described his physical appearance differently than here. His height and hair color didn't match what he looks like now. Plus, he seems to have changed his voice, too. We're still looking into that. It is often true that multiple witnesses of the same scene give very different descriptions of people and cars, but it is something to consider.

His change in appearance may have something to do with his reason for running his scam here in Castleton. Besides, as you two and others have pointed out, there is something vaguely familiar about him. And if it's true, and he has prior knowledge of Castleton, he may have had a stronger motive for what has happened. Perhaps revenge."

Ronnie suddenly piped up, "This all makes sense now. King-Young is playing a role, so naturally he's in costume, too. If you think about his interactions, they are definitely staged in the way he talks and what he says.

That's what's off about him. Knowing this also makes your idea of revenge more likely. He does act as if he is getting even with people in Castleton. So, here's a mystery we have to solve: who is King-Young? That may give us his motivation."

Caroline suddenly felt a little less foolish. Clearly, she was not the only one who had been taken in. Ronnie was implying that King-Young had fooled the whole town. She realized she could use that idea. It made her more the victim than the accomplice. Now she just had to wait to tell her story with that spin.

Wendell had to hand it to the sisters. They had thought this through, and they worked well as a team. But he wanted to cut them off before they did anything else. For instance, he could see them trying to use Caroline to get King-Young to confess.

Still, Wendell did not want them playing detectives. *After all, this was not an episode of Killing She Talks, or whatever it was called,* he thought. And Ronnie was not Angela Lansbury. For one thing, Ronnie was younger and much more dramatic. *Focus, Wendell!*

He decided to share his next steps in order to halt their investigation.

Hopefully, that would keep the amateur sleuths from trying to solve this. Wendell hoped they would see he was on top of things. *It's worth a try anyway*, he thought.

"I've got enough circumstantial evidence and testimonies to pull in King-Young for questioning. We also have a search warrant for his place, so hopefully we'll find what we need to arrest him before he manages to orchestrate his disappearance."

"Well, you'd better hurry to pick him up, as I'm sure the rumor drums are beating, and he's aware that you're after him," Ronnie said as she stood to usher him out.

However, before he left, he gave one last warning for the sisters to stay out of the investigation. "Now that you know what is happening, I'm ordering you to cease and desist your investigation. You three stay here and keep yourselves safe— and out of the way of the official police business." And with that, he tapped two fingers against his cap, almost saluting Ronnie, and raced out the door.

Wendell jumped into his cruiser and headed toward the outskirts of town, where King-Young rented an apartment in a condo complex. He said a silent prayer that he could catch King-Young there before he had a chance to escape.

Ronnie was right; King-Young was most likely aware that Wendell was after him. And given what the police had learned from his past schemes, he would undoubtedly have a carefully crafted exit plan. He'd be ready to disappear as soon as he felt them closing in. *Well, that time is now*, Wendell said, almost out loud.

Wendell was obsessed with getting his man. None of the other departments in the area s where King-Young had run his Ponzi schemes had been able to catch him, and Wendell had no intention of adding his name to that list of failures.

Wendell pressed the accelerator hard as his eyes searched for any sign of King-Young's car. He could almost see his photo on the front page of the local paper, cuffing King-Young's hands behind his back as he held the criminal against his cruiser. Everyone, including Ronnie, would be impressed with him.

But as he got further out of town, he worried more and more that the suspect had vanished. He knew Charlene had a tendency to gossip, as did several of his men, so the odds were high that he was already executing his escape plan. The Chief pounded the steering wheel in frustration as he tore down the road, his speedometer quickly climbing.

As he drove, he cradled the radio mic in his hand and barked the order, "Charlene, tell the boys to get over to King-Young's place. I'm on my way there now to pick him up and bring him in for questioning about the listeria and Trent Fowler's death. Tell them to keep their cruiser out of sight. I don't want anything to spook him before I arrive. I've got the search warrant with me, so we'll be able to search his place." *Please, let him be there*, Wendell prayed.

Opening the dispatch microphone, Charlene loudly relayed the Chief's orders. Once she had finished her critical task, she sat back hard in her chair. Hopefully, everything would work out. For once, she had not spilled the beans about Wendell's plans. She'd only hinted at it when she was at the local diner on her coffee break. She smiled at the thought that she might even be mentioned in the paper once King-Young was arrested. After all, her dispatch work had been critical.

Wendell hit the street where King-Young lived, and he slowed down.

The street looked normal. "Good," he said in a stage whisper as he pulled into the parking lot. *The boys have done a good job staying out of sight*, he thought as he scanned the lot for any sign of them--or anything else out of the ordinary. He saw and heard nothing.

And it bothered him that King-Young's car was not in the parking lot. *Where is he?*

Chapter 38

Georgia slowed down as she drove by Rita's house. She watched Wendell jump in his cruiser and drive off. *Something's up,* she thought, as Wendell raced past her on his way out of town. She noted he was driving toward the complex where King-Young lived. Clearly, he was in a rush to get there. *Why?*

Georgia also noted Caroline's car in Rita's driveway and wondered what Caroline was doing there. She was sure the sisters were grilling her.

Georgia smiled as she drove. *Sorry, Wendell, but you won't find King-Young at home.* She was on her way to meet him at the Castleton Inn. *I'll have to tell him about Wendell,* she thought. She couldn't wait to meet with him. Everything was working out for her just as she wanted.

The development was going to make her rich. She couldn't wait to get out of Castleton. King-Young had talked her into investing $20,000 in his development, promising her a huge return. It had sounded too good to be true, and George, if he were here, would have told her it was. But George was dead, and now she was making her own decisions. Once King-Young had told her about the other investors, Georgia couldn't give him the money fast enough. One of the investors was her next-door neighbor, Trevor. And Trevor had reassured her they'd both be rich before long. Now Georgia and Trevor had big plans for what they were going to do with their share of the profits. Georgia couldn't wait.

King-Young was in the lobby of the inn, waiting for her. Before her eyes had adjusted, he called out her name. Georgia jumped, startled out of her daydream. *Put your business hat on, old girl,* thought Georgia.

As they moved into the dining room, he said, "My goodness, Georgia, you are skittish today. What's up?" King-Young asked coolly.

"Well, it's not every day I hand over $20,000 to someone!" Georgia stammered.

"Don't worry. It will be one of your very best investments. Ever," King-Young replied authoritatively. Gently, he pried the envelope from her hands. "Is this for me?"

"You know it is. And before you ask, yes, it's all cash, just like you told me." Georgia stood there, feeling proud. She was going to be rich. *And I can spend it however I want.* George's death was proving very good for Georgia. *Goodbye, Castleton.*

She could barely wait until the hostess had seated them at their table, and although actually it was none of her business, she couldn't resist asking King-Young a question. *Besides, I'm one of the investors now, so I have a right to know,* she reasoned.

"Did Caroline invest in your development, too? I know Trevor did, but I wonder who else is joining us in this venture." She was hardly able to contain her excitement.

Startled at the mention of Caroline, King-Young nodded. "Uh, yes, Caroline is heavily invested. Why do you suddenly ask about her?"

"I just saw her car at Rita and Ronnie's. I bet they are questioning her about the development. I also saw Wendell driving away from Rita's. He looked like he was headed toward your place, and boy, did he seem to be in a hurry!"

King-Young abruptly stood up. "What's the matter?" Georgia asked.

For just a moment, King-Young's face appeared to register concern, but it was so fleeting Georgia wondered if she had imagined it. King-Young turned back to Georgia, smiled at her, and oozed confidence.

Georgia didn't fully trust his confidence, but dollar signs danced in her head, and she stopped wondering if there was something fishy about the development.

Given the list of smart businessmen, including Trevor, who had invested, Georgia had no intention of letting her investment be refused, but she'd show her old nemesis who the savvy, smart investor is. She couldn't wait to rub her success in Ronnie's face.

King-Young put the envelope in his pocket and patted it. "Nothing. Everything is fine. I'm sorry, but we can't have lunch after all. I have to take care of some urgent business, including recording your investment and share of the development." King-Young turned to go and then stopped and asked, "Did you tell Wendell or anyone else that you were meeting me here?"

Georgia was taken aback by King-Young's sudden change of mood. "No, why on earth would I tell him? I had no reason to talk to him or anyone else about our meeting."

King-Young looked relieved. "Good," he replied. He turned toward the door.

Georgia called out. "You'll send me the documents, right? I need the deed, too,"

King-Young simply waved his hand and kept going.

Georgia decided she might as well call Trevor to come meet her for lunch. *We could have some champagne to celebrate our investments. And we're at the inn, so who knows what might happen?*

Inside his car, King-Young began to sweat. He worried about what Rita and Ronnie were discussing with Caroline. He was sure they were trying to get Caroline to confess her part in the listeria outbreak. And knowing Caroline, she'd be claiming it was all his idea and he was the main culprit. It was true, of course, but there was nothing he could do about Caroline now. *It's time to depart good old Castleton while I can.*

He smiled broadly. He'd never been caught before, and he plans to keep that perfect record unsullied. Planning had always been at the heart of his schemes. Ever since he was little, he had made lists and checked things off. And he had always stayed ahead of the game.

This scheme was no different. Knowing Georgia's cash was the last "investment" he had to collect, King-Young had already closed out his bank account and cleaned out his apartment. He was pretty sure he had not left anything behind that would reveal his plan. Though he did leave one thing behind for Wendell, Rita, and Ronnie. It would shake them up and be the icing on this cake.

It had taken years to plan, but it was so worth it. *As they say, revenge is a delicious dish, and I've served it successfully.* He chuckled softly. Feeling renewed confidence, he headed his car out of town.

Once Castleton was behind him in the rear-view mirror, he pulled over and glanced around. No one. He quickly pulled off his wig, then opened the window and tossed it out. Next, off came the shoulder pads. He went from broad and athletic looking to slim and delicate. Then he pulled off his boots and put on loafers. He no longer needed the extra inches the boots added. Finally, out came the contacts. Once again, his eyes were dull brown, not brilliant blue. Those he shoved in glove compartment. *I did like the blue eyes.*

Slowly, he pulled back onto the road. No sense getting a ticket, though he already had a new license in his wallet. He rolled down the window, let the air hit him, and then laughed again, this time louder. *I made it. I never really liked this stupid town. And it was sweet getting revenge on all who made my life so miserable for so many years. Yes, I will enjoy spending their money.* The thought that half of Castleton would be waking up to realize they had been fleeced sent shivers of joy through him. *Yes, being a con artist is definitely the life for me.*

King-Young wished he could have been a fly on the wall when Wendell, Ronnie, and Rita discovered his high school yearbook in the panel in the closet, but he'd had to escape while he could. He knew Ronnie and Rita would figure out his identity. But he was sure Ronnie would secretly applaud his acting. He patted the envelope in his pocket again and whistled as he drove away. *Ah, life in the fast lane is very good.* King-Young began to plan his next con.

Chapter 39

Wendell sprang from his cruiser and charged up the walk to the suspect's apartment. He raised his arm, signaling his men to come out of hiding and join him. Then they waited, hands positioned nervously on their guns as they watched the Chief step to King-Young's front door.

Wendell banged on the door. "Police. Open up." The words echoed through the quiet parking lot. Nothing. Wendell let out a quick breath and commanded, "King, open up. NOW!"

Unsure of how long to wait before taking more action, he banged harder on the door. "Last warning, King!" Wendell yelled. The officers at the perimeter of the building looked nervously back and forth at each other and surveyed the lot, but still saw and heard nothing. Their hands shook, but they kept their guns pointed towards King-Young's door.

The Chief made a decision. *Time to go in.* Suddenly calm, He put his left hand on the doorknob, looked back at his men, and nodded. The knob turned in his hand. The apartment was unlocked! Wendell swung the door wide open. He pulled out his gun and stepped inside. Then he motioned his squad to join him, and the two officers quickly followed him into the apartment.

They did a careful sweep of the place. The two officers yelled, "Clear." The apartment was empty; King-Young was not there. The men returned to the living room. Wendell's worst nightmare had come true. His suspect had disappeared; his vanishing act was complete.

It seemed clear to Wendell that someone had either tipped him off, or he had heard rumors of his imminent arrest. "Damn it all," Wendell nearly shouted, then worked to get his disappointment under control. "Where is he?" Wendell wondered out loud.

The Chief looked around at the vacant apartment. He was not sure just what his next move should be, but since he had had the foresight to get the search warrant, he decided he and his officers would search the apartment. Hopefully, they would discover clues as to King-Young's involvement in the development Ponzi scheme, and maybe even where he might be now.

However, as they carefully searched, the men found no evidence of his having been there. Everywhere they looked, empty shelves, nearly barren rooms, and bare closets revealed no sign of life, and no clues. No papers or magazines, no clothes in the closet, no stray shoes on the floor. It was as if no one had ever been there. Only the scent of bleach lingered in the air. And that was the clue Wendell did not want to find.

The suspect had wiped the place clean, removing any trace of his having been there. No chance of fingerprints. Like Houdini, he had pulled off the perfect escape. Still, the men kept searching, but the more they searched, the more their hope dimmed.

King-Young had bragged about his computer savvy, but nowhere were there any electronics. Useless, unplugged surge protectors snaked across the floor. He had carefully removed all computers, eliminating all hope of finding any evidence about his plans.

The bed was mussed up, looking as if something had been thrown on it – *suitcases being packed*? However, that clue was useless. Wendell and his men went through drawers, cabinets, and swept the bathroom, but found nothing.

The three officers stood together, shaking their heads in disbelief. *He must have been scouring the place for days in order to leave it this clean*, Wendell surmised. That meant this plan had been a long time in the making. The Chief wondered if the previous schemes King-Young had run were practice for the one played out in Castleton. If so, that reinforced the revenge theory.

"Let's search the bedroom one more time," he ordered. But just as they were about to repeat their search, they heard a car pull into King-Young's parking space. Wendell prayed it was the suspect, planning to do one final sweep of his apartment before leaving town. Wendell put his index finger to his lips and silently mouthed, "Shhhhh" to the officers. He drew his gun again and quietly stepped to the door. Yanking it open, he found himself staring down the barrel of his gun at Rita and Ronnie.

"Oh, for Pete's sake! What are you two doing here?" he barked, sounding more embarrassed than angry, as he looked at the women in exasperation.

"That's not a very pleasant greeting, Chief!" Ronnie drawled, while Rita stood there silently for a moment. She was as startled at the Chief's outburst as he was to see them.

Once Wendell had put the gun away, Rita replied, "We borrowed Caroline's car and came over to detain King-Young if necessary. You know, to keep him here until you arrived. But obviously he was one step ahead of us all." Ronnie was about to add her two cents, but Rita silenced her with a look.

"You should know, we've found nothing so far," he agonized. "But no use crying over spilt milk. We're about to search the bedroom one more time. Maybe we'll get lucky. You two wait at that built-in breakfast nook in the kitchen. And stay there. You don't want to contaminate the scene," Wendell said as he and his men went into the bedroom.

Ronnie and Rita walked to the kitchen and sat down. Ronnie felt bad for Wendell, who looked totally frustrated. She wanted to tell him that he should have moved in on King-Young once he had Trent's flash drive, but worrying that it would make him feel worse prevented her from doing so.

Besides, in the end, his dogged determination had solved the mystery. And Ronnie was confident Wendell would find King-Young. She smiled as they waited for the officers to complete their search. The two waited patiently, fingers crossed that Wendell would find something.

In the bedroom, the Chief pushed open the partially closed closet door and peered inside. He was about to close the door, when he noticed a panel that seemed loose. He moved in closer and pulled the panel open. A book fell out.

"Well, I'll be damned." Wendell raced into the kitchen with his find. His men followed him. "Look at this," Wendell exclaimed. It was a Castleton High School yearbook! It was the same year as Ronnie and John's class. "Why would he have this?" Wendell asked.

Opening the book, they saw the initials K.R. written inside. Wendell, Ronnie, and Rita stared at the initials. Then they looked at each other and nodded simultaneously.

"Who's K.R, Chief?", the officers asked.

Ronnie jumped right in with "Kevin Roijeunne," stealing a bit of Wendell's thunder, but too excited to hold back. Rita shook her head in disbelief and said, "Wendell, why don't you tell them?"

"Well, there was this kid in our school, Kevin Roijeunne," Wendell began.

"Roijeunne is French for King-Young," interjected Ronnie. Rita glared at her sister and mouthed, "Let Wendell talk." Ronnie nodded and stopped talking.

"Right. It is." Wendell resumed. "As I was saying, he went to our school. He was in Ronnie and John's class. Poor kid never fit in with any group. He was always an outsider. His parents were French Canadian. They were a poor family. His father was the janitor at the high school, and we all sort of made fun of him. Like pantsing him and imitating his nasal voice. Not our finest moment. He really hated John, didn't he?" Ronnie and Rita nodded their confirmation.

Rita remembered Kevin was jealous of John being a star athlete and therefore suddenly becoming a member of the popular crowd that Kevin wanted to join. The two never got along, though John tried to be nice to him. Kevin, however, never let up on calling John names and spreading rumors about him.

Rita had never understood Kevin's animosity toward them, but it seemed to grow over time. *High school feelings rarely went away*, she mused. Georgia and Ronnie were a prime example of how people reverted to their high school roles.

"I remember Kevin saying he'd get even with all of us, but I never thought he'd seek this kind of revenge," Wendell stated quietly.

"So this is all about revenge? Seems really extreme for just some high school antics," said one of the officers.

"Well, there's more to his story," Wendell explained. "John got really fed up with Kevin spreading rumors, so we set him up to take the fall for some school vandalism. We broke some windows and painted graffiti, and we put the blame on Kevin. We all said he did it. The police charged him with vandalism, and the school put him on probation. He lost his college scholarship." Wendell paused.

Rita and Ronnie looked away. *Definitely not our finest moment*, they thought, agreeing with what Wendell said earlier.

. "I remember him saying he'd get even with us," Wendell said. "Still, I can't believe he waited this long to get revenge on us."

"Now, so much makes sense about how King-Young, AKA Kevin, knew so much about Castleton and how to manipulate the people here. He knew who was greedy and who would fall for his scheme. He had all the background information." Ronnie said. The Chief agreed.

"Why didn't any of you recognize him?" Ralph asked.

Ronnie quickly explained, "He had altered his appearance. I'm sure he wore a wig, probably used colored contact lenses, and remember he always wore boots, which made him seem taller. He'd been scrawny in high school, but by now had somehow filled out. Plus, he had changed his voice, making it deeper and more authoritative. I don't remember him being that good an actor in high school, but he had years to practice his act as an adult. I must admit he gave quite the performance once he came back to town. Fooled us all."

Rita grimaced, and then asked, "Didn't he have a club foot?" Wendell and Ronnie nodded, as Rita continued. "He must have had surgery to fix it, and then he must have worked out so that he didn't physically resemble the Kevin we all knew in school. The only thing that didn't change was how much he hated John and the rest of us who tormented him."

Ronnie nodded. "And after graduation he disappeared. We never got a chance to make amends. His motive behind his scheme clearly was revenge," Ronnie concluded. "Well, and greed, too."

"Enough with the reminiscences." Wendell turned to his men. "Take the yearbook and scan his photo. Then use the computer program we have to age it. We can use the aged photo to put out a BOLO on him. Hopefully, someone will spot him."

Wendell next ordered the men to gather and bag the scant evidence they had found. One of the men found a bar of soap that had been overlooked. Wendell wasn't sure if fingerprints or DNA could be retrieved from it, but they carefully bagged it just in case.

So far, all the evidence against King-Young and Trent's murder was circumstantial, but they could arrest him for fraud. They were still processing the woman's car from the real estate conference King-Young had attended on the night Trent was killed. Wendell hoped something would turn up from that.

Killers often left DNA behind no matter how careful they were. Plus, he knew they would find the rental car he used to run Ronnie and Rita off the road. Then they could add attempted murder to the charges.

"You boys head back to the station, process the evidence that we found, and get to work on the photo. Once the new image is ready, we'll immediately release the BOLO with the photo.

"Let's set up a hotline, too. I'm sure tips will come in once his photo is out there. He's upped his game to murder, and that makes him much more dangerous than your average con man. He must be stopped," Wendell commanded. His tone startled Ronnie and Rita, but they knew how determined he was to put King-Young behind bars. Then in a bit calmer voice, he said, "I'll be along shortly. I'm just going to follow Rita and Ronnie back. We can issue an APB, too."

Rita and Ronnie were glad for Wendell's protection. Both were feeling vulnerable.

"OK, Chief," the officers replied as they walked out the door and toward the parking lot. Both men were pumped. At last, they were doing real police work and not simply locating cows that had escaped their pastures. They were resolved to capture King-Young.

Wendell escorted Rita and Ronnie to Caroline's car and saw them safely home. He would talk with the DA and come back later for Caroline, who had come out to Rita's porch when she saw them drive up with the cruiser following closely behind.

Wendell called out the cruiser window, "Caroline, I'll be in touch after I talk with the DA. In the meantime, you probably shouldn't talk with anybody about what happened. And stick around until we've seen the DA together. Don't head back to the city before I give you the go-ahead." Caroline nodded.

Drained, Wendell called into the station to check on things and make sure the BOLO had gone out. It had, and there was good news. King-Young's rental car had been found at the airport. Paint on the rental matched Rita's car. And even better, in the woman's car from the real estate event, the officers found hair from a wig, plus fingerprints that did not match those of the owner. Hopefully, they would be a match for King-Young.

We're coming for you, thought Wendell.

Chapter 40

Two weeks later, Rita and Ronnie sat on the porch, slowly rocking back and forth, sipping their tea. Well, Rita sipped hers, while Ronnie gulped hers down as if it were medicine. Ronnie still had an aversion to tea, but no longer missed her coffee. And, she had to admit that although she didn't care for the tea, drinking it did provide her a quiet time to talk with Rita, and she enjoyed that very much.

"You need a spoonful of sugar with your tea?" Rita asked, smiling at her sister.

"Well, it would help it go down." Ronnie laughed. "And I appreciate your effort, Mary Poppins."

"Sorry it's not a café au lait, and we're not in Paris," Rita replied.

"C'est la vie," Ronnie said in her best French accent. It is what it is.

A gentle breeze blew across the porch. Even though King-Young had not yet surfaced, things had settled down in Castleton. Life seemed to be returning to normal. Neighbors walked by and waved. The sisters waved back, although Ronnie had sly comments about most of those who passed by. However, Rita, wanting to enjoy the peaceful morning, simply ignored her sister. "Let's just enjoy the peace and quiet," she told Ronnie.

Wendell drove by and tooted. A huge grin broke out on Ronnie's face, and she waved.

She looks like she's sixteen again, Rita thought.

Rita smiled and continued rocking. Ronnie's cancer appeared to be in remission, and she seemed stronger every day. Plus, Wendell had finally mustered up the courage to ask Ronnie out, and she had accepted. As Ronnie had watched Wendell work the case and saw his patience and kindness to those who were victims of King-Young's con game, she had realized what a good man he was. Their budding relationship also had buoyed her spirits. So, all was good in Castleton.

"You know, for a few weeks there, I almost wondered if things would ever be quiet again," Ronnie said.

"I know exactly what you mean," Rita agreed.

"Of course, we shouldn't complain. You've got to admit it was very exciting. How often do we get to help solve a murder?" She looked over at Rita and winked.

"True," said Rita, nodding. Though she believed they could each do without that kind of excitement.

Wendell had promised he would stop by later that afternoon to update them on Caroline and the search for King-Young.

Each became lost in her thoughts as they continued to rock. There was plenty to think about, given what had happened. The series of events, from the listeria outbreak to George's death and Trent's murder, had riled up the entire town. It would take time to recover.

The most frustrating thing for many people in town, not just Wendell, was that the main villain, King-Young (neither sister could refer to him by his real name--their former classmate, Kevin Roijeunne) had never been caught.

Wendell had acted as swiftly as he could, issuing an APB and a BOLO, alerting all the surrounding police departments and even those throughout the state, but King-Young had once again disappeared. And who knew what he looked like now?

Nevertheless, it bothered the three of them to know that somewhere out there, King-Young was laughing at those left behind in Castleton.

The only bright spot in the scheme was that after Rita and Ronnie had told Wendell about the con man's finances, he'd had a talk with the bank president, Jerry. He had asked Jerry to mark the bills on any large cash withdrawals that were paid to King-Young. Jerry had marked the bills Georgia had withdrawn, so hopefully those could be traced and they would help catch King-Young.

"I wonder what has happened to Lana." Ronnie suddenly said.

Rita stared at her sister. "What made you think of Lana?" Ronnie pointed at a young couple pushing a carriage on the sidewalk across the street.

"Oh," Rita said thoughtfully, then continued, "I wonder, too. I think after losing the baby and John, she just wanted to leave Castleton behind."

Though the way she had left seemed rather suspicious to both Rita and Ronnie. She would have needed money to leave, and Ronnie was convinced Lana had blackmailed LaMerle or Caroline, or both, but since neither would admit it, they would never know.

Ronnie wondered if Rita would be willing to talk about Trent. Now and then she did, and other times, the subject was taboo. She decided to plunge ahead.

"It's a shame Trent had to die, but he was foolish and not only provoked King-Young, but appeared to be getting far too close to learning, and then revealing, all the details of the scheme. Poor Trent; he was so desperate for a huge story that he lost his sense of reason. The Castleton Ledger would never have been enough for him, and he'd eventually have had to admit it and move on. Besides, he had stepped on so many toes during the time he was here." Ronnie knew Rita still felt guilty they had failed to protect Trent.

Rita agreed with Ronnie's assessment of Trent. "You're right. In the end, Trent seemed to enjoy digging up the dirt, so unfortunately, he sealed his own fate.

"Well, journalism is a dirty business today anyway. It's almost as if it's gone back to the muckraking days of Hearst and his infamous yellow papers. Stories are bought and sold. Fake news makes headlines."

Ronnie was glad she had been in the entertainment industry before the advent of social media. She often wondered what rumors about her life would be out there today, regardless of whether they were true.

"Speaking of stories being bought and sold, I'm sure people are wondering if you're going to try to sell the story of Trent's murder." Rita looked slyly at her sister. She'd heard Ronnie talking with friends in New York and California, and she knew Ronnie probably would not stop until she'd made some splashy headlines of her own.

"I may have mentioned the story to a few friends. We'll see." Ronnie waved her hand in the air as she spoke. "I'm more excited about the possibility of turning one of the vacant school buildings into an art center than I am in selling the story. After all, the center would benefit the entire town, and I'm sure we could include a theatre. And we could produce plays in which I would have the lead role. Lots of wonderful mystery plays. Ronnie's eyes twinkled.

Rita chuckled at her sister's last comment. *Always the star.* Then she breathed a sigh of relief. Rita hoped the story came to nothing. The last thing they needed in Castleton was the chaos of the town being turned into a movie set with a bunch of actors all over the place. However, Rita did fully support the arts center, and if it had a theater, all the better. She could picture Ronnie taking it over, starring in productions, and even directing. And at least any murder would be on the stage.

"Thank goodness Wendell helped Caroline, as he said he would," Rita remarked, changing the subject. "No one could prove she created the listeria and contaminated the milk. And Wendell's testimony of lack of evidence prevented the DA from pressing serious charges against her.

"Yes, Caroline was lucky indeed. Wendell was very good to her, even testifying that there was no proof that she targeted people with the contaminated milk. You saw the red dots on bottles, but the police did not turn up any of those in their investigation, so they could not use them as evidence. And when LaMerle backed up Caroline that they never existed, there was little the DA could do. Odd, how the two protected each other, but it worked out for both of them."

Actually, Ronnie was exasperated Caroline had gotten off so lightly, but given that Rita still cared a great deal for Caroline, she knew better than to argue with her sister about it.

The sisters looked up from their conversation as a familiar blue Buick pulled up in front of the house and jerked to a stop. It was Georgia.

"Be nice," Rita admonished her sister, who smirked back at her remark and tone. "I mean it," Rita stressed.

"All right, Holmes," Ronnie said softly.

"And let's retire the Watson and Holmes stuff," Rita winked at her sister.

"Don't worry. I don't plan on murdering her. Well, not today," Ronnie replied in an overly sweet voice. Both sisters laughed.

Georgia stomped up onto the porch and glared at Rita and Ronnie as they kept rocking. "What are you two laughing about? If you ask me, there's not much to laugh about in Castleton right now," Georgia said acidly.

"Why Georgia, I don't believe we DID ask you," Ronnie started.

Rita shot her a loaded glance; Ronnie understood the look and could practically hear the words behind it. *Don't egg her on. The last time Georgia stopped by early in the morning all hell broke loose.*

For once, Ronnie behaved, and just rocked quietly in her chair, biting her tongue. *Maybe Georgia will leave sooner if I remain silent.* Ronnie wondered if her tongue would bleed.

Rita looked at her sister out of the corner of her eye and replied, "Just a silly joke between us, Georgia." Trying to regain her composure, Rita cleared her throat. Then, attempting to steer the subject in a different direction, she softly asked Georgia, "How are you doing now that things have settled down a bit?"

"Settled down? Ha, I've lost $20,000 dollars! Someone I thought I knew robbed me. I mean, I thought King-Young was my friend!" Georgia wailed, her self-pity loud enough for the entire town to hear. "Plus, don't forget this was all after the tragedy of losing my husband."

"Yes, you have suffered," Rita said, hoping Georgia would calm down. "I don't know how you manage to cope."

Exasperated, Ronnie could be silent no longer, but she knew how to play it. "Georgia, you weren't actually robbed. Let's face it, you thought you were investing in King-Young's enterprise, and you willingly gave him your money." Ronnie spoke semi-sweetly, but put distinct emphasis on "gave."

"It was another Ponzi scheme, much like Bernie Madoff's. He showed you projected profits, and like many others in town, you fell for it, too."

Rita cut Ronnie off. No sense in making Georgia look foolish. "Ronnie is right. He conned half the town, including businessmen who should have known better." *Thank goodness we didn't invest*, thought Rita.

Ronnie also decided to throw Georgia a bone. "Don't forget Jerry marked your bills, and when they get traced back to King- Young, you will be the hero."

Rita almost fell out of her chair in surprise. *Ronnie never ceases to amaze me.* Who knew she'd cast Georgia, her archenemy, as the hero? *It seems miracles really can happen.*

The bone Ronnie threw Georgia worked, as Georgia quickly changed her tune. "I always suspected King-Young was a con man," she said as a last ditch effort to convince them she had been "taken in" only as part of the plan to expose and capture King-Young.

Ronnie chose to let Georgia have her moment of glory. "Of course, you did, dear," Ronnie muttered under her breath. She chose to let Georgia have her moment of glory.

After a moment or two, Rita spoke up, trying to get Georgia to leave. "Well, let's all look on the bright side. Customers have returned to the dairy to support John, Caroline has been punished, John and LaMerle appear to have reconciled, and you and the other investors are suing King-Young's companies. Hopefully, you'll get some money back."

Rita knew King-Young's investors would probably never see a penny back, as she was sure King-Young had emptied the coffers of his companies, and the lawsuits would be fruitless. However, she refused to take away people's hope that they would recover their money.

"Well, the reason I really stopped by is I wanted to tell you that I am taking a little trip with Trevor. He and I are going away to recover! We're going to Bermuda. It's calm and peaceful there. No con men."

Ronnie looked at Rita and smiled smugly. *Here's the real reason Georgia came over. She must have heard I am seeing Wendell, and just like in high school, wants to make me jealous that she is seeing Trevor.*

Rita expected Ronnie to rise to the bait, but she didn't.

Instead, Ronnie replied sweetly, "See, you're not alone." Then after a brief pause, added, "I hope you have a lovely trip." She withheld her next line: *And may you disappear into the*

Bermuda Triangle. But she also thought *Time to let high school rivalries die.*

Rita winked at Ronnie in approval. "Yes, I'm sure it will be wonderful. I went there on my honeymoon." Rita smiled.

"We're not getting married." Georgia preened. "Not yet anyway. Though Trevor is very interested in making a life with me."

Rita put her hand firmly on her sister's arm, holding it on the arm of the chair. "I'm sure he is."

Ronnie didn't take that bait either, but simply smiled at Georgia, much to Rita's relief. *Maybe we can grow up*, Rita mused.

Finally satisfied she had accomplished what she came for, Georgia waltzed off to her car and then grandly waved goodbye.

"What a total drama queen!" Ronnie exclaimed as she and Rita watched Georgia's car disappear down the street.

Rita managed not to laugh at the irony of Ronnie calling Georgia a drama queen. *Talk about the pot calling the kettle black,* Rita thought.

"Ronnie, you do have to admit it's very sad that King-Young fooled the whole town. So many of our friends and neighbors were taken in by his promises of quick money. Everyone started to make plans for big changes before they realized they'd been had. I'm not sure Castleton will ever be the same. The town has lost its innocence."

Ronnie was not sure how innocent a town Castleton had been before, but it seemed churlish to argue the point.

"Well, at least King-Young is gone, never to return, except hopefully in handcuffs," sighed Rita.

"I'm not so sure about that, Watson. I mean darling sister," Ronnie replied. "Let's focus on the arts center. It's the only good thing that has come from all of this. I think we have a good shot at establishing it with a small theater. And what could go wrong there?" Ronnie asked rhetorically. Both sisters refused to acknowledge all the dramas that had happened on Ronnie's film sets and her theater productions.

The sisters resumed rocking, observing life on the stage of Castleton. Yes, things were quiet and peaceful. Nothing would go wrong now. Would it?

About the Authors

Joan Hoyt has been a professional writer for many years, specializing in computer manuals and other technical documentation. She has also taught literature and writing courses at the college level in several universities in New England and the Midwest. She is an avid Red Sox fan who loves small town New England life, the setting for much of her writing. Joan lives in Massachusetts with her husband, two dogs, and three cats.

Gare Thompson is a seasoned author of K-12 educational books, media content, and scripts, and is a former teacher and educational publishing executive. He is also a playwright whose plays have been produced off-Broadway. Gare has also written best-selling children's books. He lives in Massachusetts with his family.

Made in United States
North Haven, CT
20 September 2023

41796784R10147